FELONY AND FEALTY

LELA MYERS

CONTENTS

CHAPTER 1
HOMESICKNESS

In her rain-drenched cloak, Lily plodded along on horseback down the muddy path, shoulders rounded against the chill. It was raining in Evesbury—usual for the early spring—and it took a week for her to patrol the small territory in Albrin. The wet sounds of the horse's hooves suctioning and pulling free of the mud filled the air as she pushed on.

As a Hawk, it was Lily's job to keep the peace in her territory. She regularly patrolled for signs of criminal activity or dangerous animals. In her two years in the position, she'd never caught anyone on that patrol route, but she knew if she let her guard down, someone would take advantage of it.

The broadleaf forest that separated her little cabin from the castle was finally becoming visible through the light mist coating the ground. She looked forward to lighting a fire and drying her clothes while finally enjoying a warm meal.

Despite her hunched posture, her eyes scanned the trail warily. Years of training had instilled her with a quiet vigilance, and that had saved her life on more than one occasion. Being caught off guard wasn't an option.

Surrounded by a shroud of misty drizzle, she urged her horse beneath the scant shelter of the forest canopy, the leaves offering little respite from the permeating moisture. Lightning flashed, followed shortly by thunder.

Rista stiffened, and Lily laid a calming hand on the horse's neck. Rista did well with loud noises, thanks to her training by the Hawks, but a week of constant thunder could get on anyone's nerves.

Rista took a small step sideways, and Lily squeezed the horse gently, growing more vigilant. More determined, Rista whinnied again. And with a start, Lily realized the little horse was not complaining about the thunder but offering a warning.

Lily focused, straining her ears to discern what had made her horse so agitated.

A sound emerged above the plodding of hooves and the pouring of rain. A repetitive noise, almost like words—over and over again.

As she came to a stop, she was eventually able to make it out: a group, chanting nearby.

She edged the small horse off the main path and further into the tree line. Then, with one smooth motion, she readied an arrow on her bow. It rested across her lap as she used her knees to guide Rista around the trunks to pursue the disturbance.

"Kill the thief! Kill the thief!"

The words became clearer as Lily neared the source. The amount of noise they were making would drown out any Rista produced. She would likely get close enough to see what was happening without anyone noticing her. Not that she needed to rely on that. Her skills in reconnaissance and speckled green cloak—one of many tools available to a Hawk—allowed her to blend into the foliage.

The sound seemed to be coming from the direction of the castle and surrounding village.

Lily brought Rista a few yards short of the forest's edge.

A steep hill crested before Lily as lightning spiderwebbed across the darkened skies, momentarily backlighting the silhouette of Evesbury Castle, illuminating its perched position atop the rugged peak. On a clear day, it would be just visible through the last of the forest's foliage.

"Kill the thief!"

Lily's eyes scanned the hillside for the source of the chanting and fell on a group of people.

No, not a group, she realized. They carried torches, pitchforks, and all other manners of weaponized farming equipment. It was a mob, and they were descending the slope away from the castle.

Lily leaned under a branch to consider the castle. It looked to be intact. Then again, even a small army of threadbare peasants wielding pitchforks was unlikely to breach the imposing battlements of the fortified castle. The small mob that had appeared was hardly a threat.

The job appeared straightforward. Stop the mob, find the organizers, and turn them in to the local lord to deal with. And only then turn her focus to the thief they were hunting.

Lightning flashed again as the mob drew closer.

Her steely gaze flicked back to inspect her sparse arsenal—only twenty-five arrows remaining in the quiver jostling at her hip. While a full extra quiver lay bundled in her pack, accessing it during combat would cost precious time and mobility.

Not that she wanted to kill them all...

No, hopefully, a single warning shot would be enough to stop them. Thanks to the efforts of Hawks over centuries, she had a strong enough reputation that she could typically defuse situations without casualties—if those involved had any sense. If not, blustering into the crowd would result in bloodshed.

And Lily planned to emerge without losing a drop.

She narrowed her eyes as the mob drew closer.

At the front, the apparent leader hefted a torch high.

Shooting it out of his hand was an option. The fire would draw attention, but the soaking rain would keep it from spreading anywhere destructive.

Lily raised her bow, drawing back the arrow. Her thumb touched the corner of her lip as she reached full draw. Then she let out a breath, and the string slipped from her fingers.

The arrow arched through the sky, on an easy path toward the man's torch.

Flames spluttered from the torch as it was ripped out of his hand. His yelp of shock propelled the mob from their trace, the wall of men disbanding to prevent their cloaks from catching.

Heavy boots trampled discarded lanterns. A few hands desperately patted against wool cloaks, and wild eyes seemed to look for stray embers on the wind.

For a moment, they were no longer her adversaries. They were scared. Just like the farmers Lily had saved from bandits on the way to market. Just like the families begging her to find their missing child. They were *people* with lives and dreams.

Lily emerged from the trees, another arrow already notched and ready. "Put the weapons down and no one gets hurt." Her voice came out steadily, cutting through the chaos of the now uncertain mob.

Eyes turned to her, and whispers sprung up as the crowd jostled with each other. Suddenly, no one wanted to be in front.

"I wouldn't do that if I were you," a deep male voice warned from behind her.

A jolt of dread buried itself deep in Lily's stomach as her head whipped around to the sound of the voice, keeping her bow pointed vaguely at the mob.

It took a moment for her eyes to adjust to the darkness behind her. But lightning flashed again, glinting off a matching bow trained on her. A hooded figure stood beside a mature oak tree. His cloak was the same pattern as her own, which grabbed onto the dread in her stomach and twisted it.

She'd ridden right past him and hadn't even noticed.

The figure shrugged off his hood. She recognized the face it revealed and the smirk that rested upon it. It was the same smirk that he'd given her each time she passed an assessment. The same cocky tilt to the head that had lured her in, made her want his approval. She'd thought she'd won it after her appointment as a Hawk. They'd gotten along well the last time they spoke, but with an arrow aimed at her spine, that didn't matter much.

"You're lucky, really," the man drawled, "that you met us here instead of that cabin. There are so few entrances to barricade, and once a fire caught... Well, that would be quite a bit more ... painful ... than being shot, don't you think?"

"What are you doing here?" Lily hissed. "This is my fief."

"Then why are you aiming at your farmers?" Randson Sharpe took two steps toward her when a branch crunched underfoot.

Lily's head whipped back around to see the mob had been inching toward her.

They froze, and Randson cleared his throat to regain Lily's attention. His cold eyes glared unmoving into her as he recited, "I, Randson Sharpe, in my authority as a Hawk for the Kingdom of Albrin—"

"Stop it." Lily's chest tightened at the series of words she, too, had memorized.

"Come now, Lily," he tutted. "The formalities are important. At least save your protest until you hear the charge."

Lily bristled with anger. She knew fleeing before the charges were read was seen as an admission of guilt.

"With the powers vested in me by His Majesty King Aldrich of Albrin, I do hereby authorize the arrest of Lily..." He tilted his head with a smile. "I don't believe I've ever heard your last name."

"I don't have one," Lily spat out. Randson was aware of that. Every Hawk was aware of it. She had been an orphan and had never known her last name.

"No matter," Randson said far too casually. "I authorize the arrest of Lily for the felony crime of attempted thievery against the crown."

The world became a dull buzz, broken only by her heartbeat growing louder with each passing second. Becoming a Hawk was supposed to be the end of it. All of it. She didn't know how he had discovered the truth, but that didn't matter now.

Her luck had run out.

So, Lily made a decision. She yanked Rista to the side and ducked, hoping the sudden movement would prompt a hasty shot from Randson.

In an instant, his arrow whistled through the space her chest had just occupied.

Lily turned in the saddle to shoot back.

She pressed Rista into a gallop before she could see if the arrow connected. The horse burst toward the angry mob, causing a cacophony of shouts as they dove out of the way. A torch was flung in front of—no, *at*—Lily, and Rista reared up. Catching herself just in time, Lily clutched at the horn of her saddle to avoid sliding off, the arrow meant for her head hissing past close enough for her to feel its fletching graze her hair.

Perfect aim if she hadn't unexpectedly been forced to change direction.

The mob regained their wits, closing in. Fire raged around her. Pitchforks threatened the air. Lightning struck a nearby tree, followed by deafening thunder. Every direction held danger, and the world was closing in on her, caging her.

The castle was visible for a split second as another lightning strike permeated the air. A black bolt, surrounded by a blur of fire and anger.

Heartbeat pounding against her chest, Lily steeled herself as she accepted there was only one option left to take. Only one escape route open to her.

Rista backed up, pushing townsmen out of the way, and on Lily's urging, the little horse charged, leaping over the flames.

For a blistering instant, her vision washed out in a scarlet blaze, the roaring flames consuming her senses. Smoke stung Lily's nostrils and brought tears to her eyes.

Then Rista's feet connected with the ground at a gallop as Lily ducked low and held on. Her trained instincts told her to move, and she jerked Rista sideways.

An arrow tore past, a path of pain bursting through her upper arm as she cried out.

She pushed Rista faster. Swerved into the trees to add cover. Hoped to find sanctuary in their obstruction to his perfect aim. If she gave Randson a clear shot, there was no chance he'd miss again.

Lucky for her, she had no intention of giving him that opening.

Lily galloped the horse long enough to lose any immediate pursuit before slowing into a canter.

Her gaze flicked to the brighter patch of gray that signified the impending dawn. She didn't know where she was going, and she didn't have much of a choice. If Randson had been sent to kill her, it meant the king knew about her past.

And that made her one of the most wanted criminals in Albrin.

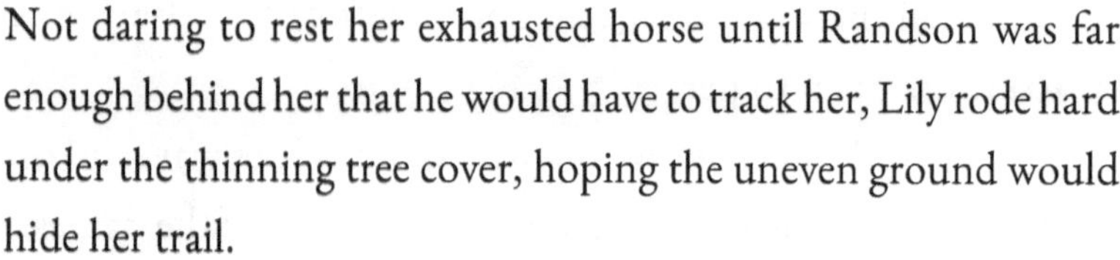

Not daring to rest her exhausted horse until Randson was far enough behind her that he would have to track her, Lily rode hard under the thinning tree cover, hoping the uneven ground would hide her trail.

She stopped eventually at a stream and tossed some cirin leaves in her mouth to deal with the pain in her arm, gulping down water to chase away the bitterness. Rista drank gratefully too, and Lily examined the small horse for any signs of injury in the encounter.

Mercifully, the worst of the damage was a few singed hairs on her tail. Rista wouldn't be in any pain.

Lily gave the horse a few pats on her neck. "Thank you."

Rista nosed Lily in the chest, and she laughed.

Unfastening the map case from her saddle, Lily retrieved the parchment from within its rain-proof confines and spread the crinkly document atop a dry, moss-flecked boulder to examine her options. She crouched as she considered her next move. Randson would acquire whatever resources he needed to find her; the felony charge made sure of that. Resources that Lily had come to rely on. Recalling her days of hardship—of having nothing—she realized she would need to use her old survival skills. Tap into the strategies she and her brother had used to survive on the streets.

The problem was, she and her brother had been thieves, and Hawks were trained to *catch* thieves. Thus, she faced an enemy who knew what her past self would do—and what her present self was taught. To level the playing field with ground neither of them knew meant only one thing. Leaving the country.

She jabbed a stick into the ground and stared cross-eyed at the map, hoping something new would stand out to her.

Evesbury sat on the east coast of the country, but it only had a small trading port. Randson was smart. He would've sent notice to the port guards to apprehend her if she went there. Given the likely reward for her capture, they'd be happy to comply. That was probably how he'd mustered the villagers, too.

She could go north to where her mentor and brother were stationed. But then they'd have to use a northern port, and the last place Lily wanted to end up was Kalturind, a harsh country across the northern sea. Besides, if she'd been implicated, Nick wouldn't have escaped his connection to her and their shared history. It was likely another Hawk or two had been sent to apprehend him. She could only hope he'd escaped and avoided those who'd turned against her.

The west held only a vast, uncrossable ocean.

The south, however, was the nearest point to the continent. From there, if she outran the orders to close the port, she could stow away on a fishing boat—or perhaps a private merchant's ship.

The small port town of Fallhafen would be the best choice. It wasn't marked as a port on standard Hawk maps, because it solely operated fishing boats and ferries to the mainland. There was a chance it would be overlooked. If not, it was one of the last places Randson would look for her.

She rolled up her map and placed it back in the case.

A few minutes later, they were moving again. They adopted a ground-eating trot to take them the remainder of the distance to the port. Time was her best ally, and so she no longer bothered covering their tracks as they dashed across the countryside.

The scene flashed in her mind, pieces of imagery. Villagers she knew shouting, brandishing pitchforks. Torches thrown to block her path. The man who was supposed to be one of her strongest allies shooting at her. Randson.

He'd caught her so off guard, she'd panicked.

Even with him there, she should have been able to handle it. Was her retreat just proving him right? She *was* running like a common criminal. Surely, in the years since she'd stolen, she'd proven she could help people. And maybe the work she had done as a Hawk had rewritten some of the transgressions of her past.

As the miles passed, chains of guilt pulled her back.

Her throbbing arm had taken the worst of the damage. In that way, she was lucky. Randson had the legal justification to kill her, and she'd fled. Given the amount of functionality she had, the arrow had simply skimmed the skin. The lethal broad-head would certainly leave a scar, but Lily already carried plenty of them.

Daylight receded, and she kept riding south. The transition to night made her feel like she could outrun the sadness. The loneliness.

Nick and Jarek were stationed in the north. Together, they were a powerhouse, but the king knew that. If he even suspected Jarek had helped them, he'd overwhelm the two Hawks with numbers. Either they were dead, or on the run like her.

She, on the other hand, was nothing but a target. There was no doubting they were hunting her.

The Hawks were a bit of an old boy's club. In fact, Lily was the first to break the trend. She thought the king appointing her to Evesbury meant acceptance, but apparently not. Apparently, her years of service to the Kingdom of Albrin meant nothing. She'd be executed for the one mistake of her past. She could only hope Nick had been spared; demotion to cleaning latrines was punishment enough.

When midnight approached, their pace slowed—more for the horse's sake than her own.

She was tempted to follow a Hawk's standard sleeping protocols but realized Randson would expect that.

Instead of searching for a grove of trees to conceal herself, she sought out a farmhouse with a horse in the pasture and left Rista standing there. The loyal horse wouldn't wander off at night.

Lily huddled her slight frame against a crooked fence post to minimize her silhouette. From a distance, she would be invisible, melting into the shadows, and Rista would look like she was in the pasture.

In a twist of fate, she was fortunate she'd been traveling prior to the attack. It meant she could shed her damp cloak in favor of wrapping up in the dry blanket always carried in her saddle bag.

She rested her head on Rista's saddle and surrendered to the exhaustion of the day, letting it catch up to and overtake her.

CHAPTER 2

UNEXPECTED GUESTS

In the morning, Lily took stock of her supplies. She had maybe a day's worth of rations left. Logically, she knew she could hunt. She could trap. She was equipped to survive. But that all required relative security...

The hairs on the back of her neck still stood up. And that little voice in the back of her head screamed, *run*. But if Randson was in Evesbury, that meant he'd abandoned his fief. His cabin would be sitting empty. Better yet, it was located between her and Fallhafen. The detour would cost her a few hours at most.

The weather held, though the windchill still had her shivering. Still, she'd take the cold over an arrow in her back any day. Her midday meal was a few strips of hard jerky and a break to refill her canteen from a stream. Then she was riding again.

Reaching the fief of Montshire made her slow down and move Rista off the road. They continued parallel to it instead; far enough away she could dip out of sight if needed. She didn't know exactly where Randson's cabin was located, but she knew where Hawk cabins generally were in relation to the fief's castle.

Lily followed smaller and smaller trails, peering through the trees in hopes of spotting it.

Soon she entered a clearing, her eyes scanning for that familiar green cloak that could spell her demise. To her left was a modest cabin with a shingle roof. A clothesline ran between it and a small shed the horses would take shelter in when it rained.

Beside it, a horse paced in a small paddock. It was a shaggy little thing, black with white feet. The horse neighed, trotting over to the nearest fence.

Rista responded and shook her mane. Hawk horses knew each other's smells and enjoyed a bond almost as close as the Hawks themselves. Rista's friendly response indicated this was the right place. But *why* was a horse there?

The hairs on the back of Lily's neck tingled. She swung Rista back to the safety of the tree line and dismounted, trusting the little horse to conceal herself. She grabbed her cloak back from her bag, wrapped it around her, and pulled the hood up to hide her face.

Hugging the shadows, Lily stealthily circled the secluded clearing, scanning the silent cabin for any hints of occupancy. The clothesline was empty. The shutters were closed tight. No smoke came from the chimney. All signs led her to believe the cabin was empty—safe.

The horse trotted around the paddock again and stared at her. She knew she was nearly invisible to humans, but Hawk horses had a way of *knowing*.

The horse whinnied.

Lily brought her open hand in a circle, ending with a closed fist. The signal for Hawk horses to be silent.

The horse whinnied again, pawing at the ground. It shook its head and blew air from its nostrils.

Jerk.

Lily repeated the gesture, and the horse trotted in a tight circle. That's not what I meant, she thought.

The horse stopped to face her again, jerking its head back to the cabin. Still, there was no sign of life. Lily couldn't imagine a Hawk hearing the commotion and not reacting in some way.

"What is it?" she whispered.

The horse walked up next to the cabin and touched it with its nose, then turned to face Lily once again.

Leaving no trail as she reversed course through the brush, Lily returned to where Rista stood waiting. After securing the stirrups aloft and tucking the reins up on the saddle, she sent the horse trotting cautiously into the clearing.

Rista walked over to their other horse, and they greeted each other. Then Rista trotted over to the cabin door and looked at Lily, pawing the ground.

Lily might've not trusted the strange horse, but she did trust her own, so she approached the cabin from the side, ducking out of sight of the shuttered window just in case. The horses watched as she rounded the corner. She quickly made the silence motion again, and this time neither horse whinnied.

Her steps were cushioned by a carpet of grass as she ducked under another window. She reached the door and laid her hand on the handle, then hesitated. Nothing about this situation felt right. Breaking into a cabin—a Hawk cabin—felt like a betrayal of who she had become.

Instead of opening the door, she pressed her cheek to the ground in an attempt to peer under it. All she could see was darkness.

She used her hands to block out the sun's light in hopes it would help.

It didn't.

Maybe the horse was still in training, and that's why it had been left while its owner went on a dangerous mission. To rely on an unpredictable animal would be a risk unwise to take.

Lily straightened, testing the door handle. It was unlocked, which was strange. Surely, Randson hadn't left it that way.

She took a deep breath, her free hand resting on the hilt of one of her knives.

On the mental count of three, she shoved the door and launched herself forward, landing in a roll on the cabin's rug.

Twisting out of her maneuver and into a fighter's crouch, Lily faced the door just in time to duck to the side.

A flash of metal plunged downward and narrowly missed her. Its trajectory reminiscent of an axe splitting wood.

The knife protruded from the rug with a wobble as its wielder turned to her, eyes wide with fury.

They stayed there like that, frozen for an instant. Then the woman let go of the knife and backed away, hands in the air. "Lily, I'm sorry, I wasn't expecting you."

Lily blinked at her a couple of times. The woman looked different from the last time they'd seen each other a few years prior. Her black hair, which she'd once worn in a long braid, was now a short, shaggy mess. The angles of her face had strengthened as she'd matured. Her own green cloak wrapped around her shoulders, though it hung open with her arms raised.

A Hawk. She dressed like a Hawk.

"Tori." Lily asked, "What are you doing here?"

"I live here," Tori defended. She lowered her hands to hang neutrally at her sides. "I should be asking you that question!"

Lily yanked the knife from the floor, then reversed it, holding the handle out. The last time she'd seen Tori, the woman had been just a wide-eyed girl eager to be a Hawk. She hadn't been assigned a mentor yet, but if she lived there...

"Randson's your mentor?"

Tori shifted on her feet, crossing her arms over her chest. "Yes."

Lily gestured with the knife again, urging Tori to take it.

The woman did, sheathing it at her side. "He left to kill you."

"Yet I wasn't who that was intended for." Lily nodded at the gash in the rug. "Why weren't you with him?"

"I—" Tori faltered and turned her back to Lily before walking into the kitchen and grabbing a sack. "I tried to stop him." She shrugged and grabbed a half-loaf of bread, placing it in the sack. "I lost."

Lily watched Tori's every weary movement, the hunch of her shoulders, the occasional impatient swipe of an escaped hair. Though Tori's eyes stayed averted, focused on her task, her reddened knuckles gripped white with each item she collected and packed away. She thought back to Tori's words. There should be no reason for Tori to oppose the arrest. Randson had gone to kill her, not arrest her.

"Why?"

Tori looked at her like she'd asked why the sun rose and set. "The only reason they let me in was because you'd done it first. I couldn't be a Hawk without you."

"I'm sure that's not true," Lily reassured. She'd had to work harder because of her gender, yes, but she wasn't anything special. And given her status as a felon, Tori would perhaps have been an even better candidate.

"Whatever," Tori dismissed with a wave of her hand. "You're leaving, right? You came for supplies?"

"I did."

"Take me with you." Tori turned, offering the sack.

Lily accepted the bag quicker than she accepted Tori's request. She looked over the woman carefully again. Her hands were balled into fists at her sides, her back straight, but her shoulders were too high. The streaks on her face ... looked like tears.

"You thought I was Randson?"

Tori nodded once, her gaze unable to meet Lily's.

Lily considered for a moment longer. That attack would have failed on Randson, as well. But the fact that Tori was willing to take that risk meant she was afraid. *Very* afraid. The decision was made.

"Wash your face and get packed."

◆─◯─◆

It took the rest of the week to reach Fallhafen. Lily had hardly spoken as they rode. Not that Tori had tried to fill the silence. The days seemed to grow longer and longer, each hour more draining than the last. The horses moved diligently, but by the time they reached the port town, even they seemed to only be motivated by the idea of rest.

In Fallhafen, they blended in amongst the other weary travelers. Lily managed to purchase passage on the last ship of the day to the mainland. The captain set a steep price, and they wouldn't have hammocks, just space on deck. But it was worth it.

Bound for Valessa, a large country on the continent, to the southeast of Albrin, the ship offered escape. It was also the closest country to Albrin, making it the most affordable way out of the island nation. A few extra argenti bought the captain's silence. Their presence would not be documented nor spoken of once they departed.

Within the hour, the horses were loaded, and Tori and Lily were on board, waiting for the boat to move.

Lily watched the gangplank for any threats, pulled out a coin, and said to Tori, "Heads is Casseterre, tails is Valessa."

Tori raised her eyebrows. "Your plan is to flip a coin to decide where we go?"

Lily nodded. "Randson knows both of us too well. He could follow our logic to find us. He can't follow random chance."

Tori went quiet, clearly thinking. Her hand went to the feather on a cord around her neck. It was a wood carving; the marking of an apprentice as opposed to Lily's gold cast metal. She twisted it around, making it climb the cord it hung from. After a moment, she looked at Lily. "Are we ever going back?" she asked with a frown.

Lily realized she wasn't fooling anyone. This wasn't just some random stranger. Tori was training to be a Hawk. She had been hoping this moment would never come, and her gut twisted as she found herself facing it down. It had turned over in her head a million times. There was no good way to tell the truth.

"I can't go back to Albrin. I ... I'm a fugitive, Tori." She glanced quickly to the gangplank, which still connected them to land. "I don't know why you wanted to come, but if you leave these shores with me, you'll be an accomplice. You should go back."

Tori didn't move from her seat. She pulled her knees to her chest and shook her head. "I'm not going back there." Tori's eyes were fixated on the planks of the ship.

"Then you do the honors." Lily held out the coin, breaking Tori's gaze.

Tori's hand closed around the coin, but she didn't flip it. Instead, she looked at Lily and asked, "Why did he want to kill you?"

There it was again. *Kill*, not arrest. "He didn't tell you?"

Tori shook her head.

Lily sighed and looked back to the gangplank, where a woman carried a screaming bundle that must have been a small child. If Tori was really going to do this, she deserved to know the truth. And it looked like they may be each other's only company for a while. Still, she was drudging up memories from a past Lily had thought long buried. "When Nick and I were very young, we lost our parents..."

"I know that," Tori grumbled.

"We had to survive, fell in with the wrong group of people." Lily looked at Tori now, watching the understanding dawn. "If we wanted something, we had to take it. We were thirteen and hadn't been caught. But, one day, the royal family passed through our town. I was caught with picks in the lock." She looked to Tori, expecting judgment or hatred.

The woman merely watched her with a furrowed brow, so Lily continued.

"It was Jarek who caught us. Instead of turning us in, he gave us a choice. Learn to be Hawks, use our skills for good. Or try to explain ourselves to the king—"

"Why would he do that?"

Lily shrugged, leaning against the ship's railing. She'd asked Jarek herself, but in his usual gruff manner, he'd refused to explain. Jarek did things for his own reasons. Questioning them was like asking a fish why it swam or grass why it grew.

"There was no deal?" Tori asked. "Jarek didn't make you do anything?"

"Other than training? No. We never spoke of it beyond that day. At first, we were just grateful for a bed and warm meals. We weren't about to question it. And then"—Lily shrugged again—"we saw what it was all about."

"What do you mean?"

"I'd always thought a Hawk's job was to punish criminals, and to an extent that's true. But it's more than that. It's like a family. We protect people who can't protect themselves. Stand up for those who don't have the means to make their voice heard. I fell in love with that. With helping people, feeling like I was part of something bigger." Something bigger that was now turned against her. She'd worked so hard for acceptance, and in only a few years it had been snatched from her grasp.

"Must be nice," Tori said with a startling amount of venom.

Lily watched the other woman, but Tori didn't seem to notice being under scrutiny as she turned the coin over in her hand. "He hurt you, didn't he?"

Tori didn't look up. The muscles in her jaw tensed as she nodded once.

Lily wanted to ask how. Wanted to know exactly what he'd done, and for how long. When she'd entered the cabin a few days ago, Tori had been ready to kill. But she'd only known the woman for a few days, so she didn't press.

They were quiet for a few minutes. Then Tori cleared her throat. "Why?"

A deckhand shouted to a man on the dock, and the boat rocked to one side.

"Why, what?" Lilt thought she'd explained herself clearly enough. It was the first time she'd voiced that story, and she wasn't eager to repeat herself.

"Why bring me with you? I'll just be a burden." She sighed. "I should have stayed."

Lily didn't speak and continued to scan the people boarding, as much as to spot a threat as to gather her thoughts. "First off, you won't be a burden. You're in your fourth year of training. You can take care of yourself." Her voice sounded confident despite the uncertainty around them, and she added, "I'm not going to leave you somewhere he can hurt you."

Lily watched two sailors pull the gangplank off the dock. They untied a few ropes, and the boat lurched into motion.

She turned her attention back to Tori after confirming they would depart any moment. The woman's shoulders were hunched as she hugged her legs to her chest. Tired bags hung under her eyes, though at least she'd washed the streaks off her face since they'd met in the cabin. Tori hadn't even flinched at the lurching of the boat. She just turned the coin over in her hand. Again and again.

With a flick of her thumb, the coin spun in the air. Tori's arm darted out to catch it with surprising speed. She covered it with one hand and turned to Lily before revealing.

The carved face of King Aldrich of Albrin stared up at them.

"Casseterre it is then," Tori said, tucking the coin into her coin pouch.

Toward the stern, people stood, waving at a few who remained behind on the docks. Sailors darted back and forth across the deck. A few poor souls huddled near the railing and clutched their stomachs. No one seemed to pay any mind to the two women huddled at the bow of the ship.

"Get some sleep," Lily said with a soft smile. "It's been a rough week."

It hit her then. It had been a week.

Every instant of missed sleep flooded over her. Her legs shook like they were about to collapse, and her eyes burned with the desire to close. She lowered herself to the deck.

Tori looked at her, and whatever anger she may have held was absent from her gaze. "You're the one who needs the sleep, Lily."

"I won't find sleep here. I'll wake up every time a board creaks. I always do." It was an instinct that had saved her many times but had inconvenienced her many more.

"I'll keep watch ... if it'll make you feel better," Tori volunteered.

How to keep a proper watch was one of the first things apprentices learned, so their masters could get some sleep on the road. Tori was more than qualified, and Lily did not have the energy left to protest.

CHAPTER 3

MARITIME MERRIMENT

Somewhere past midnight, Lily startled awake to the gentle creak of rigging and the hushed rush of waves gliding past the bow. Squinting against the shadows, she recognized Tori, who was snoring softly beside her.

That alone brought Lily fully alert. Tori was *not* supposed to be asleep.

Lily sat up, looking around. The night was clear, and many had opted to sleep on the deck instead of in the cramped quarters below. It was peaceful, and the rocking of the ship was a calming lull. No wonder Tori had dozed off.

A figure stood at the helm in stark contrast to the dark sky.

She stood quietly, feeling more refreshed than she had in ages. The sea breeze pulled the last traces of fatigue from her as it tugged at her hair and clothes. The tight braid she always wore—a compromise to be allowed to keep her long hair—begged to be released, so her fingers pulled the strands apart. As a final step, she yanked out a few pins that were used to keep stray hairs in place, letting her messy brown hair whip freely.

The wind felt good in her hair, on her body. She'd never admit to anyone how much she loved being on boats. To anyone who knew her many stories, a boat should have been a bad omen. But Lily knew it was never what happened *on* the boat that was bad. It had always been *after*. Always at the destination.

Sailing was like flying, and as long as there wasn't a storm, she stomached it fine.

A rope squeaked in a pulley as the wind shifted, and the helmsman had to adjust. The stars blinked down at her, and she wondered if Nick was looking at the same ones. Probably not. He liked to take the first shift of a watch and sleep in the early mornings.

She chose to believe it was sea salt burning her eyes as the coast of her home sunk below the horizon. When the last glimpse of land disappeared, so did the life she'd built. Her years of training melted away, every good deed she'd done falling into the ocean with her tears. She'd be a felon, a fugitive. Forever hunted. Always looking over her shoulder to catch the flicker of a green cloak.

As she watched, the sky to the east began to lighten. The sun peeked over the horizon, turning the sky brilliant golds and pinks. Her tears dried with the creeping light.

A board creaked beside her, and she turned to see Tori stir. Lily put her hair back in the tight braid and sat. "You were supposed to keep watch," she said as the woman's eyes opened. That kind of slip deserved more of a reprimand, but, after the tension of the last few days, Lily didn't have it in her.

Tori looked down the ship vacantly. "I would kill for some coffee right now."

Lily frowned, but she left the young woman alone and went to talk to the captain.

He nodded a greeting as she walked over.

"How long until we arrive?"

The man shrugged, looking up at a wind indicator. It stood straight out from the top of the mast. "If the wind holds, we'll arrive midday tomorrow. If we have to row, it'll take longer."

The crossing to the country of Valessa was short in distance, but a rogue storm could make it perilous. Still, there were almost daily ships making the trip.

Lily thanked the man and went to turn away, but her eyes caught on something on the horizon. A speck against the different shades of blue. "Should we be concerned about that?"

The captain shielded his eyes from the sun with a weathered hand, then shrugged. "It's another ship. Most likely, they'll just pass."

Lily went back to the bow, where Tori was standing and stretching. She leaned on the rail and the woman joined her.

"Sorry I fell asleep," Tori said, her voice little more than a whisper. There was the briefest glint of fear in her eyes. Though Tori's posture seemed relaxed, she never let Lily out of her sight. She was afraid.

Lily stopped her lecture before it tumbled out. Yes, taking a watch was important, but not important enough to drive a rift between them this early in their travels. "You were exhausted too." Her head tilted toward the horizon. "Keep an eye on that ship. Could mean trouble."

"What about you?" Tori asked, all business as her eyes scanned the sea until she found the ship.

"I'll take a look around and get us some food," Lily responded, then pushed away from the railing and crossed the deck.

Lily collected their rations of bread for the trip from the quartermaster. And sure enough, when she returned to Tori's side, the boat had gotten closer, but it was still too far to distinguish the flag fluttering from the sole mast.

She heard their lookout scramble down from the crow's nest and nonchalantly moved to where she could overhear the conversation.

"It's a Kalturi, sir," the lookout said.

The captain cursed.

Kalturi pirates were sizable men who would do anything for a profit. They weren't known for their remarkable speed or aim, but the brutes were formidable beasts, nonetheless. To most people, they were little more than legends. It was rare to survive a direct encounter, but evidence of their actions always remained, always proving they were real. Mutilated bodies flung around towns. Everything of value missing. Lily had had enough dealing with them to last a lifetime.

She sauntered over, inserting herself into the conversation. "Is there any chance to outrun them?" It was unlikely but had to be asked. Kalturi ships were built for speed. It was better than facing them, though.

The captain shook his head. "Don't worry about it. It's just a harmless boat." Even without overhearing the news, Lily could have known he was lying from the way his eyes darted between the ship and her face.

She raised a skeptical eyebrow but kept her voice low—controlled. "I think a Kalturi ship coming toward us is something to worry about."

The captain's eyes flicked to the bow slung over her shoulder, and he seemed to come to a realization. He looked around to make sure no one was listening. "I have fifty aurus, but I don't think that will be enough."

Sometimes the Kalturi could be paid off. But fifty aurus were scraps to them. Especially at this time of year, when their boat was laden with gold and returning north before the storm season hit.

"What do Kalturi usually do with a ship at sea? I've only seen them raid on land."

The captain stiffened. "Kill lots of the crew, if they're feeling merciful."

Lily already knew what happened if they weren't. She'd experienced it. "Any weapons?" she asked with a frown.

The man shook his head. "Some knives, but nothing to hold off Kalturi."

Many years prior, a Hawk had given her a piece of advice: she was better off using knives on herself than an angry Kalturi. At least that way it would be clean. She'd never quite agreed with that assessment, but from his constant furtive glances at the ship, it seemed the captain might.

"I'll tell you what," she said. "If you get everyone below deck, I can possibly save your ship."

"*Possibly*?"

Lily shrugged. "They're Kalturi. I offer no guarantees."

The captain's eyes narrowed as he regarded her. Then he nodded, telling the lookout to pass on the message.

"What's your plan?" Tori asked as Lily returned to her. She had moved closer, positioning herself to overhear the conversation.

"We continue with your training." Lily grinned.

"My training?"

Leaning against the ship's mast, Lily watched the muted shape of the ship cut through the distant waves. Her hand settled to the dagger at her belt as she thought. It was a hard shot. Not impossible, but difficult. "Everyone will be below deck, so we only have ourselves and the necessary crew to worry about."

Tori nodded, and Lily watched something in her eyes shift. She was beginning to analyze the situation. Good.

"There are two things that keep that boat headed our way: the rudder and the sails. The rudder is controlled by the skipari."

Tori raised her eyebrows in question.

"The captain," Lily clarified. "The sails are held in place with ropes. If they board, it's twenty of them and two of us."

She waited for Tori to connect the dots. The woman nodded, then nodded again more confidently. "We need to keep the boat from reaching us. So, we need to take out either the sails or the rudder."

"And what do you think is the best way to do that?" Lily prompted.

Tori thought for a moment.

The sails were a giant target, but a hole in them wouldn't do much. The skipari on the other hand—

"We need to take out the skipari."

Lily nodded, content that Tori had come to the best conclusion. "If you take out the skipari, there will be no one controlling the rudder. The ship will be coming fast, so they'll turn and come to almost a stop."

"Will that be enough?"

"We have to hope so," Lily said.

"If it's not?"

Lily gestured to the crow's nest. "I'll be up there. If they get close enough to board, get up there with me, and I'll cover you." Then it would be a race to see who killed who first. Of course, Lily didn't want to demoralize Tori with that knowledge.

She watched the woman assess the distance of the Kalturi ship. Watched her figure out the angles. Gave her a chance to ask any last-minute questions.

When she was confident Tori understood the plan, Lily scrambled up the mast and crouched in the recently vacated crow's nest. The passengers and most of the crew were herded below deck by the frantic-looking captain, leaving only her, Tori, and the few crew that were necessary to keep the boat moving.

They went silent as the ship approached.

Orders carried on the wind in a language unfamiliar to the crew. Lily knew only a few words. The meaning was obvious, though. They were shouting orders to board. No doubt they expected the ship to prove an easy bonus on their way home.

Tori braced her hip against the railing as she selected an arrow and laid it on the bowstring. The Kalturi ship was close enough now to make out the crew. In a few more moments, the apprentice would be able to take proper aim.

Tori drew an arrow but looked hesitantly at the mass of armored men just visible above the bulwarks. No one person would stop the wall of metal and meat that could sink a ship in under a minute.

Now.

Tori didn't loose.

The ship grew nearer. Lily began to make out weathered, cruel faces.

"Now!" she called down.

Tori glanced at Lily, then back at the Kalturi. She lowered her shaking arm and rolled out her shoulders. Resetting the shot.

Then, Tori raised the bow again. Trained it on the skipari.

The boat was getting too close.

"Now, Tori! Now!"

At a shouted command, the men hurled hooks toward Lily's ship.

"Now!"

Tori let go of the string with a jerk.

The arrow arched across the sky, invisible for a moment.

But it was already too late. The hooks bit into the wood of the railing, fastening the two vessels together.

Tori's arrow struck the upper arm of the skipari two breaths later. A moment too late. He let out a Kalturi curse as he clutched at the shaft, letting go of the wheel.

The Kalturi vessel lurched violently sideways, pulling their small ship with it. Lily clutched the edge of the crow's nest as their ship tipped further and further to the side at the sudden change of momentum.

At least the Kalturi were as thrown off as she was.

"Cut the ropes!" Lily shouted, hoping Tori had enough sense to listen, and looked up to see she was fast approaching the yardarm of the Kalturi ship. Too fast. She was on a collision course with it.

Lily danced across the yardarm, leaping across to the other ship. In the chaos, no one noticed as she nearly missed the jump, only managing to catch herself by her fingertips.

A resounding crash sounded behind her as she struggled for a more solid grip. Wood splinters pelted her back, and she grit her teeth against the pain. Unable to face the carnage she knew must be behind, she didn't look back to see the destroyed crow's nest.

Her groaning muscles stole her attention instead as she hauled herself up and hurried to crouch in a stable position above the sails.

When she looked down, Tori was hacking at the ropes.

One snapped, but four more still connected the two vessels. And the Kalturi were quickly reeling them together. There wasn't enough time to separate completely.

Lily took out her large knife and hacked at the ropes below. The last of the fibers gave way, and a corner of the large square canvas floated downward. She sheathed her knife at her hip, and she yanked at the rope, unwinding it from each section of the canvas. The sail sunk down, draping over the Kalturi, and their war cry transformed into confused shouting.

That should buy Tori some more time, she thought. Her eyes bounced between the apprentice and her foe.

The skipari looked up from where he had regained control of the rudder. He had broken off the shaft of the arrow, leaving just the broadhead embedded in his bulging bicep.

"Bad choice, lass. Now come down from there, and we might just let you live." He was a burly-looking man with a voice to match, his chest the size of a barrel. And it took him half the effort to shout up to Lily as it did for her to shout down. He seemed about half as concerned as Lily felt, as well.

Tori ducked under the railing, seeing the opportunity Lily had granted. There were no eyes on her. As the Kalturi focused their anger on Lily, they disregarded Tori completely. It was the perfect diversion. Lily commanded their attention; Tori systematically weakened their offense—rope by rope.

Lily frantically grabbed her flint and steel, holding it to the remains of the tar-covered rope. "If you don't leave them alone,

I'll burn your ship." Her heart desperately tried to drown out all other sounds, but she projected calmness. That was the trick with this type of thing. Ice out the inferno inside until all they saw was the surface stillness.

Some said the Kalturi could smell fear. If that was true, she'd be dead ten times over, but they could see it in body language and hear it in a voice.

The skipari laughed. "Then we'll just take your ship!"

A few of the men around him chuckled, jostling with each other for a better position in the carnage they anticipated. She scanned the faces and mercifully didn't recognize any of them.

Tori cut another rope and began work on the next, but the Kalturi were now freeing themselves from the sail, and a few heads turned toward the now three severed ropes.

Lily had to buy more time. "With a full cargo hold? No, you have too many valuables to trade this ship for a passenger vessel."

It was a guess. There were a few petrified faces on board, people huddled together out of the way. Captives taken during the raids to be sold as slaves. That alone indicated a semi-successful raiding season.

Lily's gaze met with that of a young boy, no more than ten. "It's not worth it," she insisted.

A disturbing grin crept across the skipari's bearded face. "Board the ship," he ordered.

The crew had now completely freed themselves from the sail and turned to the captured vessel with greedy eyes.

Lily cursed, hooked her legs around the yardarm to stabilize herself, and pulled her bow from around her shoulders. In moments, she was sending arrow after arrow into the Kalturi. The swaying of the ship made them moving targets, and she was on a moving base. But she had trained for moments like these.

Her first arrow cut through a Kalturi's neck as he stepped onto the ship's railing in preparation to leap. He tumbled into the frothing sea between the vessels.

Her second arrow knocked into a helmeted head. It didn't pierce the thick metal, but it did rattle the brain inside it and forced them to slow down.

The fourth rope snapped, and she was forced to stabilize herself again.

The ships began to drift apart, their yardarms letting out a high-pitched shriek as they scraped against each other once again.

The skipari noticed, too. They couldn't bring the ships together with only one rope. He glared up at Lily. If looks could kill, Lily would be splattered on the deck below.

At an order in their language, the Kalturi turned from the ship. They released the last hook, and the ships started to pull away from each other.

Fifteen angry faces approached the mast Lily was perched atop. Shields were raised against her volley of arrows. She was their quarry now.

Lily looked at her ship. By some stroke of luck, their sails remained undamaged. It was picking up speed, would be able to create distance before the Kalturi restrung their sail. Possibly before Lily could jump.

Gathering her strength, willing it into her legs, she stood on the rounded material of the yardarm. The swaying of the waves alone threatened to shake her off. Still, she couldn't resist calling down to the skipari, "Tell your chief I say hi!"

Then she sprinted down the yardarm, pumping her legs. Moving quickly enough for her center of balance to remain above the wood.

She reached the end and pushed with every muscle in her legs, leaping for her ship.

One of the ropes that held the sail in place became her point of focus.

Arms stretched to capacity, her fingers brushed the material, then she closed her grip around it. Her legs swung down, but she held the rope. Even as the tar-coated cord burned her hands, she slid down to the deck below.

"Ylgir," the word hit Lily like an arrow as she regained her footing.

She turned to seek out the source.

The skipari smirked. He knew the word struck home the instant she'd reacted.

Lily schooled her features to a mask of calm as she stood beside Tori, clenching her fists to calm some of the burning. The ships drifted apart. Lily didn't dare take her eyes off the Kalturi until they faded away over the horizon.

CHAPTER 4

BORDER HOPPING IS FUN

As their ship glided into the busy harbor the next day under a blazing afternoon sun, the pungent scents of sea salt, fresh fish, and horse dung swirled together to welcome Lily's arrival in Valessa. All along the bustling docks, a hodgepodge chorus of strange tongues mingled on the breeze. Despite the smell it bore, Lily was grateful for the wind. The heat would have been unbearable otherwise. Especially since they had to wait for the horses to be unloaded, a time-consuming task that set her on edge and forced her to linger in one place longer than was ideal.

"Lily?" Tori asked while they sat on a bench. "Can we go get some food?"

Lily pursed her lips in thought. "I'd rather get away from the coast as soon as we can."

Tori accepted the explanation without a word and fetched a canteen of clean water from a public well and brought it back. She gently poured the water over the rope burns on Lily's hands.

The cooling sensation offered more relief than she would admit to her companion. But she couldn't stop her shoulders from slumping as she allowed herself to be tended to. There was nothing to do but wait, after all.

By the time the horses were unloaded, it was nearing dusk, and clouds had rolled in, casting the sky awash in pink and orange. In Fallhafen, it had been as simple as walking the horses on. In Valessa—due to the height of the docks—it was a much more complicated process requiring a crane and a team of men.

"We should find an inn," Tori suggested as they led the horses down the main street.

It wasn't entirely a bad suggestion. Remaining out on the docks only increased the likelihood of drawing attention. Lily had wound cloth around her hands to protect the burns from further friction but couldn't help fiddling with the wrappings. Thankfully, the small scab on her arm—courtesy of Randson—was barely noticeable after the week of travel.

People shoved past on all sides, only moving aside for carts. Colorful sheets were draped above the street to provide shade at midday. As the first drops of rain began to fall, they also provided shelter.

Lily ultimately shook her head. "We need to get moving."

Tori leveled a gaze at her. "The next ship doesn't come until midday tomorrow. We may as well spend the night in beds."

They *should* take a comfortable night while they had the chance. Warm food and a cup of coffee would serve them both well. Especially with the traveling that was ahead of them. There were a million reasons to avoid staying, but even Lily couldn't ignore the fact it would be their last chance for a warm meal and soft bed in a long while.

"Alright," She sighed. "Do you speak any Valessan?"

The other girl shook her head.

"Fairly large inn, then. They're more likely to speak the trade language."

They turned into the next inn, The Black Ladle—if the image engraved on the signboard meant anything. After quick negotiations, they secured a room and meals.

The warmth of a ham stew filled their stomachs, radiating out in the way only a hearty meal could. It was a welcome break to the cold rations they'd had—and would continue to have.

Lily leaned against her seat, then shot up as a splinter drove into her back. She closed her eyes and pushed back the memories the pain brought up. The ache that spread across her tired frame as the small reminder turned into waves of discomfort.

That night, Lily lay on her stomach on the bed, her shirt off to expose her back.

Tori knocked on the door.

"I'm ready."

The door creaked open and shut again as Tori walked to Lily's bedside. The gasp told Lily that Tori did not expect to see the scars there.

"What happened?"

Lily turned her head to the side so she could talk. "The Kalturi happened."

The scars on her back practically burned as Tori took them in. The story of her time in Kalturind was legend in Albrin, more myth than fact at that point. She had saved Princess Adelaide from discovery, but the cost was always left out.

The bed shifted as Tori sat beside her. There was a sharp pinch, and Lily flinched. Then another. Tori pulled out splinter after splinter.

Lily's fingers curled into the sheets against the pain. It wasn't unbearable, and it brought her back to Kalturi and the torture she'd endured. She tried to distract herself by asking, "Why try to stop Randson?"

Tori was quiet for a long moment, completely failing at distraction as she picked more splinters from Lily's back. Eventually, she confessed, "I could never have been a Hawk if you hadn't first. They would have laughed me out."

"You could've," Lily responded thinly as another stinging splinter was retrieved.

"No. Because I didn't dream of it until you rode through my town." Tori continued to pick the splinters out one by one while Lily lay there.

She'd never set out to inspire anyone to follow her. She was a thief. Nobody should look up to her. Her life wasn't one to be desired. A stroke of luck had bought her the last nine years of her life. And the truth had burned it all down.

When she was done, Tori draped the cool blankets over Lily's back and left her alone to recover.

— ⊙ —

"Are they going to let us cross the border?" Tori asked.

Any reasonably competent border patrol would question two women traveling alone, no matter what lie they conjured. And it would leave evidence of where they'd been.

It had taken them almost a week to ride to the border between Valessa and Casseterre. The distance wasn't far, but it required traversing the low-lying mountains that separated the countries. In that time, they had gained almost seven thousand feet of elevation. It had grown colder, and scrublands had turned into leafy forests.

"Do you want to sneak around?" Lily asked. She had no problem with it, but Tori didn't have the same history as her.

Tori shrugged. "May as well."

Somehow, that seemed the easiest solution. They'd gone from enforcing one country's laws to dodging another's. Her fingers tightened painfully—but unnoticeably—around the saddle, biting into her now unwrapped hands. She'd dragged Tori so low.

Lily steered Rista off the road. She knew border posts were sparse, primarily watching key merchant crossings. Securing an entire border was an exhausting use of manpower. It was the taxes they were after. Carts carrying anything with value couldn't go off-road. But sneaking two horses around wouldn't be difficult.

They both easily slipped into a trained silence. Their horses knew to pick their way quietly, too. The women ducked and leaned around branches instead of pushing them away. To break them would leave a path—a sign of their presence—and that would be unacceptable. With their hoods up, they would be nearly impossible to spot.

Lily thought back to some of the stories Jarek had told her and Nick around the fire in the evenings. Casseterrans spoke of marauders lying in wait to ambush and extort travelers. Most traveled in guarded caravans, for a marauder would either make you give up everything or kill you and take it all anyway. If Jarek was to be believed, no one was governing the forsaken country.

Lily sensed Tori's repeated glances her way. She knew what the look meant. *Are we over the border? Can we talk yet?*

Lily doubted it.

The horses continued their silent journey through the trees. They kept their heads forward, maintaining an unconcerned appearance on the off chance someone they hadn't spotted was watching, but their eyes never waned, attentively scanning their surroundings with the trained series of checks they'd been taught.

Finally, Lily turned to smile at Tori. "I'm pretty sure we're across now."

Tori smiled, her shoulders rounding slightly, and started turning her horse back toward the road, but Lily reached out to grab her reins.

Tori frowned, glaring at Lily's hand until she released the horse. "Marauders."

"We can take them," Tori commented. Her hands fidgeted with the reins, a habit Lily had been trained out of because their horses responded to little movements. It seemed Marlett had grown used to Tori instead.

Lily raised an eyebrow. "Like you took the skipari?"

Tori looked down, muttering, "It was a hard shot."

It *was* a hard shot. But Tori was a good archer. Better than good, from what Lily had heard of her assessments. She shouldn't have missed. "We're trying to stay inconspicuous. That normally involves not leaving a trail of bodies." Lily inclined her head meaningfully.

Tori looked dejected—and a little relieved.

Lily pulled her horse to a stop, feeling this conversation was too important to have while constantly ducking below branches. "Tori, have you ever killed anyone?"

Tori took a second to reply. The change in pace was bound to throw her off balance. Lily had been pushing them hard since they left Albrin. In fact, they hadn't stopped for anything that didn't involve food, sleep, or water.

"Umm." Tori looked at the ground. "No. Not exactly."

"Was the skipari the first person you shot?" Lily asked.

Tori nodded. Her hands twisted around the reins again.

"That's good," Lily said. "I'd lost track of the number of people I'd killed by the time I was your age." As soon as the words spilled out of her mouth, she realized how casual her tone was. How cold. For anyone else, that fact would be traumatic.

"I feel like I'm ... like I'm the only one who *hasn't*," Tori muttered.

That was probably true. Their job didn't allow it. She had been one of the first apprentices who'd started after the war, when the killing had slowed down.

"And you don't like that?" Lily asked, reading the girl's expression and body language.

"Yes. Well, no. I don't *want* to kill someone, but—"

"You think it makes you weak."

Tori nodded. "I..." She almost said something else, but the words seemed to desert her.

"Who told you that?" Lily asked.

"Randson..." Tori's hands stopped twisting the reins in what appeared to be defeat.

Lily breathed deeply. The sudden violence made sense. She was just now beginning to understand that the Randson she'd known hadn't really been him at all.

"Exactly," Lily eventually replied, moving Rista so she could lay a comforting hand on Tori's arm. "Not killing people doesn't make you weak, Tori. But ... I know how people talk."

Tori looked up, giving Lily a pained smile.

"Taking someone's life shouldn't be done lightly," Lily continued. "Consider yourself lucky you haven't had to face that yet."

"*Yet*," Tori repeated. "We're on the run in a foreign country."

Lily waited for the woman to continue, knowing this pause didn't mean she was done speaking. She'd had years to consider that one day this could be her life, while Tori had been on a journey of righteousness.

"I was going to be a Hawk. This path ... there's going to be a situation where I need to ... and I'm worried I won't be able to make the call."

"You will," Lily reassured, "because when your life is on the line, you fight like it. If you're truly afraid you might not make it out, all care for the other person goes out the window. And it's almost *too* easy." Lily found herself almost speaking to the trees.

Tori was quiet for a moment. Likely at Lily's change in tone. "When was the first time you killed someone?" she asked, her voice filling with compassion and curiosity.

Stories were told about Lily and Nick, but not the story of her first kill. They were often twisted into brave warriors. The truth was far more desperate than that. Uglier than whatever made it into the ears of citizens.

"I don't really know," Lily answered.

The look on Tori's face terrified her.

"Not because it didn't stick with me," she hurried to clarify. "It was in the war. An army was marching on Kalturind's capital, Narea. And I came up with a plan to … take care … of some of them. When it was over, people were dead as a direct result of my actions. But it wasn't by my hand."

Lily sorted through the events of the time. And, to her credit, Tori waited patiently. She'd gone over this before. It no longer controlled her. But the memories were still unpleasant to relive. She took a deep breath and said, "There was a skirmish in the woods."

Those few days had changed her life, and she had come out a different person. But there wasn't a single moment that changed her. It all blurred together in a way, like recalling a vivid nightmare months later.

Tori seemed to find her cloak was not draping satisfactorily and took her time adjusting it. Another subtle sign of her unfinished training.

Lily took her silence as a sign, an invitation to continue. "We were ambushed. I was up in a tree, and the skirmish was happening below me. One snuck up on Jarek, who was engaged elsewhere. He was going to stab him in the back. So, I shot him."

"Just like that? You didn't try to talk or..." Tori's protest died out, and she looked away, a diminutive blush marring her cheeks.

"Again," Lily said in a gentle tone, "in the moment, it's too easy. Panic can make the unthinkable become the only option."

CHAPTER 5
OLD HABITS

They avoided everyone and everything for a few days. Towns, roads, and anything that could bring interaction—or leave a trail—was a potential threat.

They turned south under the idea that the further they got from Albrin, the safer they would be. Of course, they had no way of knowing if they were safe. They couldn't contact anyone in Albrin to see if their pursuit endured, if it was just Randson following them, or if he had help.

If they gave him the chance, one or both of them would be dead.

No. The choice to run had become irreversible when Lily left Evesbury. She would be dodging authorities and hiding until she died. There would never be a night for as long as she lived that the threat of danger didn't keep her awake for a few moments longer.

More than once, Lily had heard Tori crying at night. She wished she had the words to comfort her. She wished she wasn't so close to crying herself. Sometimes, she even wished she'd refused to bring her along.

Tori had taken on the majority of camp work while Lily's hands healed. When they had, they split the work evenly.

Despite her guilt at taking Tori from her life, Lily was glad for the company. Besides the helping hand, having Tori there eased the loneliness into something tolerable.

"We need something other than meat," Tori said.

They were sitting around a low fire, roasting a squirrel Lily'd shot earlier that day. Surviving off hunting and hardtack since their coin ran out had been their only option. The last of their hardtack had run out a week before. They hadn't resorted to stealing yet, but their digestive systems were feeling the effects of eating exclusively meat. Lily had kept a few argenti hidden. She knew it was too easy to tell Aldrich's face from another ruler's, though.

"We do," Lily agreed. "I wish I knew which plants were edible."

"But you don't," Tori pointed out, just as she had the last three times they'd discussed the matter.

"But I don't," Lily grumbled. "We'll find a town tomorrow." She turned the squirrel over the flames. Her gut tightened, from the carnivorous diet or apprehension she didn't know.

"Do you think he's still following us?" Tori asked, poking at the ground with a stick.

Lily hesitated in her answer. "Yes. I don't think he'd let us go without a fight."

Tori sighed.

At least they'd taken to sleeping the whole night, but they never stopped moving. Not even for a day. Their path was erratic, too, sometimes taking the most difficult routes over rocky outcrops and dense forest. But the idea of a Hawk trying to kill them was enough motivation to move in the morning and not stop until the setting sun required it. It kept them in the saddle and, more importantly, off the roads.

"What day is it?" Lily asked.

"Friday. I think," Tori said.

Saturday would be the ideal day to go seek rations. Saturday was market day. It was when people from the countryside flooded town looking to sell and buy. A day they stood the best chance of slipping in unnoticed.

———◆◇◆———

Lily tracked the thin tendrils of smoke that ribboned into the sky, marking the town's location somewhere amidst the forest that obscured the settlement from view.

Beside her, as she dismounted, Tori pulled her cloak tighter against the chill, squinting toward their elusive destination. They'd agreed Lily stood a better chance of getting around any marauders on foot. Tori had said it was because Lily was a full Hawk.

Tori would wait with the horses as close as she safely could.

Lily didn't tell Tori, but part of the reason she left the woman was to protect her. From becoming like her. Or doing something the old Lily would resort to for survival.

She didn't know how she'd be able to get food with no coin. Each country had a distinct coinage. They agreed on the value of an aurus, argenti, or ramar; which were made of gold, silver, and copper, respectively. The difference was whose face graced the coin. Gold was gold, but coins from Albrin would be noticed in a small village. Using the coins increased the risk someone would follow them. When they crossed the border from Valessa, she'd simply told Tori they'd run out.

Lily smiled at Tori, despite the dread inching its way up her spine.

Tori returned the gesture, and Lily set off.

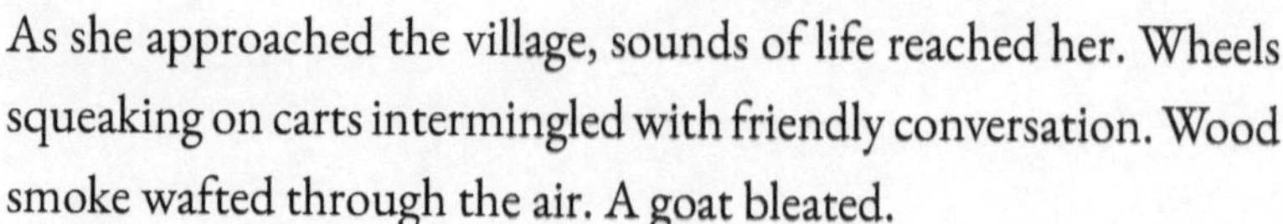

As she approached the village, sounds of life reached her. Wheels squeaking on carts intermingled with friendly conversation. Wood smoke wafted through the air. A goat bleated.

Lily moved to a crouch, creeping her way to the edge of the trees.

The town was sparse, a single main thoroughfare perhaps ten buildings long. It looked like it had a single tavern. On a night like tonight, Lily would bet it was full.

She could see stalls erected in what would be the main square. Rough-cut boards held up tattered tarps that provided shade to the merchants. People milled from stall to stall. Sometimes they browsed, other times it seemed they were just catching up with friends.

A shepherd herded his flock down a main road. It looked like he wasn't stopped, which gave Lily the reassurance she needed to step clear of the trees and onto the main road.

Nobody questioned her, though she did get a couple of looks. Strangers weren't uncommon at these marketplaces; they weren't frequent either. People would know she was there. She wouldn't pass unnoticed. That was the problem with small villages.

Wandering past worn stalls loaded with goods, Lily strained to discern the shouted prices, her stomach twisting with each transaction. They were all beyond what she could afford. She could maybe get them five apples. It would be a short-term solution, but it would clear them out. That wasn't what they needed. And it would risk leaving a trail in coins.

Lily looked to the horizon. The sun was just beginning to touch the treetops in the west. It had taken them most of the day to find the nearest town. Lily had warned Tori it might be late before she returned.

Her eyes found their way to coin purses hanging on waists.

She tore them away just as fast, only to notice how close some products rested to the edge of their stalls. The pain gnawing at her gut was all too familiar. All it would take was brushing by, perhaps a stumble, and food would simply fall into her pocket.

Nick would distract the barrel-shaped man while Lily slipped a few of the brass buttons into her boot to sell later.

But Nick wasn't there.

They weren't frightened children anymore. She couldn't argue that she didn't know it was wrong, or that she had to when there were still a few coins back with the horses.

She made her way to what accounted for an alley. The buildings were fairly spaced out, but she found a trail off the main road that didn't seem well-traveled. Her back rested against a wall, eyes still on the marketplace. As expected, anything of value was packed up well before the sun set. She assumed livestock would be herded away too. It didn't matter, that wasn't what she was after.

As darkness fell, Lily worked her way out of the alley. The stalls were still set up, but it seemed most of the people had gone to their homes—or the tavern.

And that's where she headed, too.

She was rusty, but if everyone was drunk, it would be easy to slip her hand into a pouch or two. A few coins, not enough to harm anyone, would be all she'd take. Then in the next town they could buy food with Casseterran coin.

Maybe Randson was right. It hadn't taken long at all for her to go back to her childhood solutions. Maybe if she thought more, she could come up with something else. Jarek certainly would never have considered it an option. Stealing was part of who she was, or at least she had a natural tendency toward it.

The only place she'd ever belong was on the streets with Nick, and, in all likelihood, she'd never see him again.

The tavern door opened.

Her movements stilled.

A wave of noise entered the street, punctuated by an angry shout in a language Lily didn't understand.

A shadow of a woman was thrown to the ground, and an angry man stormed out after her, holding something large in his raised hand.

The woman shouted. A plea for the man to stop in Casseterran.

Lily understood that. Even if she hadn't known the word, she knew the fear in the woman's voice. She drew and nocked an arrow, watching as the scene unfolded. They paid no notice to her.

More shouting persisted as the woman on the ground tried to scramble away.

Lily hurried along the wall, getting closer to the man. She traded her bow for a dagger, reversing her grip so she had a fist with the weight of the pommel behind it. Killing the man wasn't the intention. Injuring him would draw attention.

So, she would knock him out.

Suddenly, he swung the object at the woman.

Lily struck, her fist connecting squarely with his temple.

He crumpled, dropping what appeared to be an unlit torch.

Lily could see the woman in the light passing under the tavern door. She crawled backward, exposing long, bare limbs. Her face was shrouded in shadow, but Lily could guess at the expression of fear on it.

Lily tossed her cloak to the woman before kneeling to pull the man's hands behind his back.

The woman grabbed the cloak, wrapping herself in it as she watched curiously, no longer retreating.

"Do you speak the trade language?" Lily asked as she took the man's belt and used it to tie his hands behind his back in a practiced movement.

"Yes," the woman responded. Her voice carried an accent, but Lily could still understand what she was saying.

Lily began dragging the man toward the side of the road. "My name is Lily," she said. "Are you okay?"

The woman stood up. "Yes."

"Do you live here? Can I help you get home?" Lily asked. She grunted as she dropped the man against a wall and half tucked him behind a barrel.

"He was going to kill me." The woman shook her head.

"Well then, you better get out of here before he wakes up," Lily replied.

The woman nodded as if she hadn't noticed Lily's tone and made her way toward a back road. It looked like it led around the tavern to a stable. She stopped suddenly, looking toward Lily. "Why?"

"I couldn't stand by and watch someone die."

The woman hesitated as she turned to the road, then back to Lily. "Stay with me? Until I can go?"

Lily obliged, following the woman down the road. She was, in fact, led to a dingy stable. Only two horses occupied it, a shaggy pack mule and a slightly less shaggy riding horse. It was that horse the woman approached. She worked quickly, taking the tack from a shelf on the far wall. Digging around in some straw produced a saddle bag, which she attached to the horse easily.

"Where are you going?" Lily asked as the woman worked.

"I don't know," she admitted. "Down the road to the next town, I guess."

Lily could hear the fear in the woman's voice, but it was still too dark to make out her expressions.

The woman looked up, then started removing the cloak. "You need this back."

Lily held out a hand to stop her. "Keep it." She frowned for a moment. It would definitely pose challenges. Still, keeping this woman safe for a day or two was worth the risk. "Why don't you come with me?" Lily offered.

The woman froze. She still only half had the cloak on. "Where are you going?"

"I'm not sure either. But it's better than staying around here."

"Alright."

Lily knew Tori would be anxious. Instead of her normal careful steps, she stepped on leaves and brushed against branches. The woman moved quietly, so naturally, and Lily wanted to ensure Tori wouldn't be surprised at *their* arrival. Having her untrained horse's awkward steps helped, too.

As they got closer, she made the agreed-upon bird call, knowing it would put Tori at ease.

A bush rustled, and Tori stepped clear, pulling her cloak free from the branches. "Who's this?" Tori asked, gesturing at Lily's new companion. Her voice was hostile, but it made sense. The woman's arrival didn't match with what they had been doing so far, the way they'd avoided everyone.

"Kyraa," the woman said.

"She's just with us to the next town," Lily explained. She took Kyraa's horse and tied the reins to a tree before Tori had a chance to protest.

"Thank you," Kyraa said, loosening a strap and removing a small saddle bag. She was traveling light, but she had all the essentials. It wasn't that she was closed off to conversation. Lily knew she would answer if she was asked questions. She was just quiet, not so much as humming to herself as she took care of her horse and set up her bedroll.

Tori caught Lily's eye, jerking her head toward the woods. Then she walked in that direction.

Lily made sure Kyraa was getting settled all right before following, ducking behind a few trees until they were out of sight of the camp.

"What is this?" Tori asked. She crossed her arms, turning to face Lily.

"She was attacked," Lily replied. "I couldn't just leave her."

"What happened to having to stay hidden?" Tori pulled up the hem of her cloak, fidgeting with it.

"We are staying hidden," Lily protested. She could understand Tori's concern. She had the same concern herself. But her heart wouldn't let her make another cruel decision. "Look, this doesn't have to be long. But I promised I'd get her to the next town."

Tori sighed.

Lily knew this must be a shock after the last month. Before that, they'd seen each other maybe a handful of days over four years. The most Tori knew of Lily was from the time they'd been traveling together. Of course this would seem like an abrupt change.

"Did you at least get food?"

Lily shook her head, heart aching at the disappointed slump of Tori's shoulders. In her haste, she'd completely forgotten about food. "Tori, it's late. Can we deal with this tomorrow?"

Tori sighed again but allowed Lily to lead her back to camp.

Kyraa didn't seem bothered that they had clearly been talking about her. She was almost asleep, curled on a bedroll.

Lily offered to take the first watch, hoping Tori would accept it as a peace offering. Her companion simply nodded, climbing into her own bedroll and facing the forest.

CHAPTER 6

LEARNING TO FLY

Kyraa didn't ask where breakfast was the next morning. She didn't mention the early rise. Her presence didn't interrupt the quiet Tori and Lily usually enjoyed. Though, they *were* more on edge.

In the morning light, they could finally make out details of her face. Her lips were stained red, and the black makeup around her eyes had been smudged by sleep. In the daylight, it looked overdone, but the flickering firelight of a tavern was another matter. She had changed into a tunic and pants that looked much more comfortable for riding.

The first hour of the morning passed in a tense silence as they readied their horses and rode away from the town. As the day grew warmer, the tension started to melt, if only slightly.

"So, what happened last night?" Tori finally asked.

Kyraa pursed her lips as she thought. "I was attacked. Lily saved my life."

"Why did he attack you?" Lily asked. She thought she knew the answer. The remains of makeup and her outfit the night before left few options.

"He said my prices were ridiculous," Kyraa replied. "Which is wrong."

"Prices?" Tori asked, "Prices for what?"

Lily glanced at Kyraa, a look that communicated knowledge but also grace. Sharing wasn't necessary.

"I work as an escort," Kyraa said. There was no hesitation in her voice, and as she spoke, she raised her chin slightly, as if daring the other women to challenge her.

Lily watched a series of dots connect in Tori's mind so fast there was only one thing to say.

"Oh. Umm, why?"

Lily pinned Tori with a piercing glare. It wasn't that she wasn't curious; it was that they'd just met the woman. It wasn't their place to ask.

Kyraa herself had an amused look. Maybe she'd gotten the question a hundred times before.

Lily leaned forward. Just because she hadn't asked didn't mean she didn't want the answer.

"Why do people have jobs?" Kyraa asked.

Tori swallowed, fidgeting with the reins in her hands. "To make coin, to survive."

Kyraa nodded once before fixing her eyes on the ground ahead of her horse.

Tori looked at Lily, who shrugged. She wasn't going to push the matter, just as she hadn't pushed Tori on the details of her past with Randson. It was Kyraa's choice to make, not theirs.

They spent the day riding parallel but off the main road. That way they would be able to find a town quickly, before dinner, if Lily's plan was to work out. Tori tracked the road, riding out to view it every now and then before returning to ensure they were on the right path.

After one of those returns, Kyraa brought up, "I have had an idea."

"Good for you," Lily said, almost on reflex. She softened a bit before asking, "What is it?"

Kyraa looked at Lily curiously, clearly a little taken aback by her tone. Still, she continued, "That was not the first time something like that has happened. I have a feeling it will not be the last. You two are very capable. But you don't have coin."

"What made it obvious?" Tori asked sarcastically. They did look worse for wear, unnaturally thin. The fact that they hadn't eaten the previous night or that morning would also indicate they couldn't afford basic food.

Lily shot her a glare before prompting Kyraa to continue.

"I can spare an argenti or two. I propose we work together. You keep me safe, I keep us fed."

Lily looked at Tori. Tori frowned.

Lily turned back to Kyraa. "We'll have to discuss."

"Of course," Kyraa replied.

Lily and Tori moved a few yards away, speaking in hushed tones.

"What happened to 'no contact?'" Tori asked. "What happened to 'we have to be untraceable on the run?'" There was bitterness in her voice. And hurt.

"I don't think we'll be traceable. I'll set the routes. We can still avoid roads." Even as she said it, Lily's mind churned, trying to find the best way to make it work. Of course, there would be logistical issues. But, morally, could she refuse? Her leaving wouldn't change

Kyraa's job. The least she could do was try and keep her safe. And then she wouldn't have to steal.

"You don't think two female archers threatening people will be noticed?" Tori asked.

Lily thought it was an apt summation of the potential pitfall.

Tori took a deep breath, tapping her fingers idly on the saddle. "Look, it's not, she's not, the issue. It's the switch. We've been on the run for a month, and suddenly it's okay to take more risks?" Tori caught her own rise in tone and took a few more deep breaths, once again fidgeting with the hem of her cloak.

"We didn't run out of coin," Lily admitted.

Tori looked at her sharply. Her eyes were narrowed with suspicion, but she didn't interrupt.

Lily continued, "Our coins have Aldrich's face on it. The coin she gets doesn't. Isn't having a way to make more at least better than leaving the little we have like a trail pointing straight toward us?" Lily felt a pang of guilt at using Kyraa in that way. But at least they'd be earning their way.

Tori looked down, and Lily remembered why the woman was there. She'd never stated the worst of it, but Lily knew. The fear that had driven Tori to attack her in the cabin could only really come from one place.

"And isn't it safer for her to not be alone?" Lily implored.

Tori shifted her body, and when she looked back up at Lily, something had clouded her eyes. "Fine, but if this goes south, I reserve the right to say I told you so."

Lily smiled, leading the way back to where Kyraa was waiting patiently.

"Okay," Lily said to their new acquaintance.

Kyraa's shoulders relaxed as she breathed out what looked like relief. "Thank you."

Lily nodded once before swinging Rista to the left and taking them toward town.

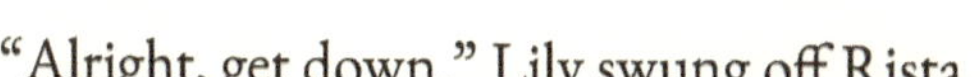

"Alright, get down." Lily swung off Rista.

They'd stopped in a low, tree-filled valley. The clouds had been growing darker throughout the day. It would rain that night, and they'd be grateful for the cover later.

Her two companions stopped, glancing at each other.

"Why are we stopping early?" Tori asked.

They'd ridden until dusk. Always. Sometimes longer. Now they still had a good two hours of daylight left.

"If there's two of you now, it's enough to do some training," Lily explained. "We'll set up camp here and have about an hour of light left."

When traveling, it really took three people to train. A mentor, an apprentice, and an extra set of eyes to prevent an ambush.

Over the days since they'd met Kyraa, Lily had been thinking of Tori. Kyraa had seemed perfectly content; Tori, on the other hand, was brimming with restless energy. When they set up camp, she couldn't seem to sit still. She volunteered for all the first watches. She was directionless and unfocused. Even with their loss of muscle mass and weight, the need to train—to do *something* other than sleep and ride—even gnawed at Lily.

Tori and Lily moved to untack the horses, reins dropped freely.

"You don't hitch your horses?" Kyraa dismounted and led her horse to a tree.

"No need," Tori explained. "They won't wander far."

Hawk horses were some of the most highly trained animals on the planet. They knew to stay close in case their riders needed to leave fast. Lily hoped that information wasn't something that Kyraa noted as anything remarkable.

"That's nice."

The first order of business was to set up camp. With three of them, it became an easy process. Kyraa was self-sufficient as far as her tent and a bedroll, and they shared tasks like setting up a fire and gathering wood.

They hadn't lit the fire yet. There was no need while the sun still poked through the branches. When it set, the air would begin to nip at them, and they'd appreciate the warmth.

"What training?" Tori asked as she sat, leaning against her saddle.

Lily was walking in a small circle, brushing her foot over the ground to nudge fallen sticks out of the way. "Just because we're here doesn't mean you're off the hook for training. You need to at least maintain your skills."

Tori raised her eyebrows. After all, until now, Lily hadn't even made her shoot her bow. "There's no point. If we're not going back—"

"You should always be ready to defend yourself." Lily glanced at Kyraa, who lounged on her bedroll and listened casually. "You too."

"That is why *you* are here, is it not?" Kyraa asked, propping herself up on her elbows.

Lily tightened her lips. "I'm not going to be in the room." No, she certainly wouldn't be doing that. "You need to be able to protect yourself long enough for me to get there."

"Later, I'm tired." Kyraa laid back down, turning her back to both women.

Lily nudged her with a foot. "You'll be tired if anything happens. You still need to be ready."

Tori was already going through some basic stretches. She had been training to be a Hawk; she was no stranger to hard work.

Lily was getting nowhere, so she was grateful when Tori walked around to Kyraa's face and offered her a hand. "Come on," she said, "It can actually be fun."

Kyraa looked at the woman, looked at the extended hand of the woman who'd argued against her presence. She ignored the offer and pushed herself to her feet. Brushing her hands off on her riding leggings, she huffed after looking over the land Lily had cleared of debris. "Okay, but you have to let me teach you two Casseterran. There are too many cities here where the trade language is unwelcome."

"Deal," Lily replied. "How are you so good at the trade language, anyway?"

Kyraa suddenly found it difficult to maintain eye contact. "My father was from Albrin. He taught my mother and I."

"What brought your father here?" Lily kept her tone neutral.

"I don't know. He went back when I was twelve, said he'd send coin for my mom and me. That didn't happen." Her tone was heavy with disgust, her discomfort palpable.

Lily decided to let the subject drop before the weight became too much. She looked at Tori, who shrugged and made her own way over to where the other two were waiting.

"Right," Lily said, setting her hands on her hips. It occurred to her then that she had never been on this side of training before. "I'm guessing Randson didn't give you much close combat training?"

Tori shook her head, as was expected.

Bows kept Hawks safe, kept them out of close encounters. The running theory was that if they used bows right, they'd never have to deal with close combat. Lily found that idea ridiculous and had ended up in numerous grapples for her life. Luckily, after the first two, Jarek had come to the same realization. As a result, she was perhaps the best Hawk when it came to close combat.

"You won't win on strength," Lily began.

Kyraa rolled her eyes, and Tori sighed.

"You likely won't win on speed, either. So, you need to be clever." Lily realized she was almost word for word repeating a lesson her mentor, Jarek, had given her and Nick. She leveled her gaze at Tori. "If you're in close quarters, a bow is useless. It *will* happen at some point."

She remembered Jarek nodding at Brennus, who had brought along a wooden practice sword to demonstrate techniques. Brennus was Adelaide's husband, but first, he had been a knight in training in the same fief Lily and Nick had completed their apprenticeship.

Lily, of course, didn't have a sword.

She glanced around and picked up a fallen branch that was the approximate length of an arming sword. A few quick slashes from one of her heavy knives brought it to one long, smooth branch that would serve her function. "Say your opponent has a sword."

Tori drew her knives, one in each hand, and took a ready stance. It was a sword defense technique Hawks were taught.

Lily was glad Tori had at least been introduced and smiled. "Good, but what if..." Lily paused, trying to find something new to show the girl. "What if you're unarmed?"

"Why would I be unarmed?" Tori asked.

Lily shrugged. "Peaceful meetings go wrong. You were searched. It happens, so it's best to be prepared."

Tori conceded the point and sheathed her knives. "So, I'm unarmed. Now what?"

Lily demonstrated a swordsman's stance, teaching Tori to avoid the blade and use momentum to her advantage.

Tori absorbed most of it. Many of the principles were the same as any other combat situation. Don't react to your opponent. Make them do something. Then respond.

Draw the action you want; control the situation.

They continued until they were in a heated spar.

Tori was a quick learner. Within a week, she'd be able to hold her own against an amateur swordsman. This particular aspect of her training had been a bit neglected, but the discipline and focus Tori had learned elsewhere was evident. It came with being a woman in their field. There weren't many among the recruits, even now. But she'd often seen them working harder and longer for less recognition.

Lily waited until Tori seemed to be fully focused, drawn into the fight with determination to win. Then she dropped, darting her leg out as her opponent moved to step within her guard.

Tori hit the ground.

She tucked her arms to avoid breaking a wrist and rolled out of it. Straight into the waiting branch being held at her neck. The apprentice held her hands up in defeat.

Lily stepped back, lowering the branch. "Sorry."

Tori smiled to let her know no harm was done, straightened, and brushed sweat from her brow. "That was clever."

"People get used to one style of fighting and aren't ready for it to switch. Never get complacent," Lily said.

Tori nodded. "But I can switch too. I could throw a knife instead of fighting with it," she suggested.

"You have to be careful, though." Lily glanced pointedly at the knives Tori carried. "If you're only carrying two and you miss, you'll find it difficult to win the fight with only one."

"That's why you carry so many."

Lily carried ten knives at all times. They were expensive, so she'd collected them slowly over the years. One in each boot, one on each thigh, one strapped to each forearm under the leather bracers that protected her arm from a bowstring, one on either side of her ribs, and the standard two at her hip. "According to Jarek, no Hawk has lost their life by losing a knife. It's just come a little too close for comfort for me."

They continued this. Again and again until Tori was able to pull off the maneuver. Lily grinned with pride, despite the sharp pain in her rib where Tori had scored a solid hit. There was something satisfying about leaving training with a bruise to show for it.

Kyraa watched with her arms crossed the entire time. "I don't see how you expect *me* to learn *that*."

"I don't," Lily admitted. "You start with the basics." She held out her hand with her palm up and open.

Kyraa stared at her, then took a hesitant step forward. She placed her hand in Lily's upturned one, watching carefully.

Lily shifted her grip up to Kyraa's wrist and squeezed, holding her in place. The hold wasn't punishing, but if Kyraa struggled, the tighter it would get.

Kyraa said something that sounded angry as she tried to pull away violently.

Lily held firm.

"I don't understand what you're saying," Lily said in an even tone.

Kyraa's brow furrowed angrily as she yanked again. "I said, 'what are you doing?'"

"Try to get out," Lily dared. Still, her tone remained even, un-bothered, even as Kyraa yanked and twisted to try to free her arm.

Kyraa dropped to the ground without warning, yanking Lily a step forward.

Lily let out a surprised gasp, but her grip held firm.

Kyraa glowered at her and stood, brushing the dirt off her butt with her free hand. "You are stronger than me. I can't."

"Are the men you see weaker than you?"

Kyraa glared defiantly for a moment before she saw the logic, and her features softened. "Then what do I do?"

Lily turned her hand until her palm faced up. "You can't move through my arm. So, you need to go where my fingers and thumb meet."

Kyraa jerked her arm skyward in an attempt to free herself. Lily was not at all surprised, and her grip only tightened.

Kyraa muttered something again.

"What was that?" Lily asked.

"You will know when you start learning Casseterran."

That was fair enough.

Kyraa slacked her arm, waiting for Lily's instruction.

Lily showed her the correct placement. How her hand had to move to the outside of Lily's wrist, and how that twist pulled Lily's grip apart. And, attempting the action, Kyraa was able to break Lily's grip and pull her arm free.

"Good," Lily said. "Now try it again." She gestured to Kyraa's hand, and she begrudgingly let Lily grab hold.

Kyraa practiced again and again. When she got the hang of one thing, Lily would switch hands, or add another variation.

An hour later, the women were drenched in sweat. Trying to not die wasn't an easy thing when your opponent was focused on killing you. Lily eventually called a stop.

Kyraa collapsed on the ground, spreading out on the cool dirt. "You do this every day?"

"Or something similar." Lily panted out a few shallow breaths. "It does get easier the more you do it." She nodded to Tori. "You get some shooting in. I'll start the coffee."

Tori sighed, but she gathered up her bow without protest and began loosing arrows at different knots in a gnarled tree.

Lily heard her mumbles beforehand, calling her shot. They never shot at the same target twice, so it was an easy way to let your mentor know what your goal was. It was a habit left over from the early years of apprenticeship, pointless now that the variation between targets was only millimeters.

Sitting on a large rock, she watched as Tori self-regulated her practice. That was a skill they learned in second-year. Lily was only there to point out the tiniest of mistakes.

That was if Tori had been making any.

Lily found Tori's shooting comparable to Jarek's in style, and Jarek was known as the best shot of all the Hawks. Of course, amongst the Hawks, they were talking about hairsbreadth distinctions. Still, it was a title Jarek carried with pride.

Maybe one day, if she ever made it back to Albrin, Tori would overtake him.

CHAPTER 7
THE NEWSBOY

Lily watched from afar as Kyraa counted out the argenti and handed the coins to the barkeep. She nodded in polite but guarded recognition toward her two friends but had chosen to stay separated across the room. The barkeep slid a drink toward Kyraa before gathering two more flagons and carrying them over to where Lily and Tori waited.

As had become usual, they'd selected a corner booth to keep an eye on the rest of the tavern. Lily was positioned so she could watch the door, her back to the wall, and Tori could see the stairs to the rooms. The tavern was well-kept, a sign of an owner who cared. Being the only one in town, they could have left it a mess and received the same amount of business.

In the last month of working together, Kyraa had demonstrated a penchant for choosing the right taverns. She'd done circuits of the country a few times and remembered her favorite spots.

Patrons filed in as the sun set. Every table filled itself, groups of old friends gathering around and conversing over food and drink. Kyraa chatted expertly, flirting and bumping into supposedly single men at the bar.

Lily and Tori stayed planted at their corner table, talking over the meal they had been slowly picking at for hours. It had gone cold long ago, but if they were eating, no one paid them much attention, so Lily took a bite of a cold carrot.

Kyraa laughed, touching a man lightly on the shoulder.

Tori raised an eyebrow. A silent signal.

Kyraa made quick eye contact with Tori and nodded as she led the man upstairs. The nod was slight, only perceptible to someone looking for it.

Tori collected her things, shoving one last bite of food into her mouth before she disappeared up the steps after them.

Lily waited patiently, finishing off her meal. When no one was looking, she slipped some of Tori's food aside to give the girl later. The arrangement with Kyraa was mutually beneficial, but it put them all on a rather tight budget. A tight budget was better than no budget at all. Their stomachs were thankful for that fact.

Still, it felt pointless. They were barely managing to scrape by. Kyraa could only make so much from a town like this in a week. They'd figured out the logistics quickly enough, and the routine was beginning to drag. It was either a long day on horseback or a long night waiting for the all-clear.

Now, the only bright spot in their day was when they traded lessons.

Lily pushed a few soggy vegetables around in the dregs of cold chicken broth. Kyraa seemed perfectly content with the situation. If anything, she was less scared. It *was* nice to have more companionship, but Tori and Kyraa were closer to each other in age and had bonded quickly.

Which left her sitting alone in a tavern, with a quarter bowl of soup, a crust of bread, and two sips of water left in her cup.

The room fell silent as a man sauntered in.

He appeared to be in his mid-forties, with a muscular build and short, cropped hair. Candlelight glinted off his worn armor. It had once been fine. Now it was battered and dirty. Still, it would sell for a good price.

Lily knew his type. They lay in wait on the roads, waiting for the defenseless to pass by so they could charge them. Occasionally, someone would challenge them. And on those occasions, one of the parties didn't get to walk away.

That had probably been where he acquired the armor. Far from a castle as they were, she doubted he had purchased it fairly. More likely, he'd won it, killing its previous owner and taking their possessions as spoils.

The man strode across the room carefully, and people moved out of his way.

The barkeep had an ale waiting.

The man grabbed it before turning to survey the room. His eyes landed on Lily, and he stalked over, sliding into the seat across from her without waiting for an invitation.

He smiled—or leered, she couldn't quite decide. One of his front teeth was missing, giving his face a lopsided appearance.

Lily had to try to keep her eyes from drifting to it. "What do you want?" she asked in rough Casseterran. Kyraa had taken the time on their journeys to teach her and Tori. Lily thought it was going well, but the man's expression indicated it might not be as well as she thought.

The man's smile narrowed. "You aren't from here," he said. Lily felt no need to reply. It was obvious in her accent where she was from. "Where is the girl you arrived with?"

They'd moved to using the roads, deciding speed and ease of travel was worth it. Their decision has been in no small part due to Kyraa's insisting and their newfound income. "Sneaking around, we're targets," Kyraa had explained. "If we pay the tolls, we're just like everyone else."

The man had likely seen them and decided they didn't have enough to be worth stopping.

"She's occupied," Lily replied. It was easy for men to tell what Kyraa did for a living. It was apparent in how she wore her hair, in the way she dressed and carried herself.

Of course, there were occasions when Kyraa didn't want her profession known. In rougher towns, she would tie her hair up in a tight bun, change into rough spun wool clothes, and remove all traces of her jewelry. It was second nature to her. She transformed into a different person when she needed to hide. Someone worrying about a family in need, not where her next meal would come from.

The man openly frowned now. "Can we go outside?"

Lily was glad the conversation around the room had resumed. Now that he'd settled somewhere, people were happy to go about their daily lives.

He must have seen the look on her face. "No, not like that." He took a deep breath, then said something that amounted to a curse, but Lily wasn't entirely sure which one. "I have family in Albrin. I know that accent."

Lily paused for a moment, considering. His words felt sincere. His eyes darting around the room seemed out of fear of being overheard.

There weren't the usual nervous glances she would have expected if the man had been a threat. What had been fear when he'd entered now seemed to be ease. Still, it was the first mention of Albrin she'd gotten since arriving in Casseterre.

Lily smiled. "Oh really? What part?" She hoped her tone carried well. It was difficult when she had to sort through the words, trying to find the right ones. Her aim was for casual interest to hide the burning curiosity.

"The North." The man took a deep swig of his ale, then wiped his mouth with the back of his hand. "Apparently, they lost track of one of their"—he waved a hand as he searched for the word—"large birds. But people. Bird people. Know anything about that?"

Lily's heart sank. It seemed he had no more information than she had. Her thoughts were cast to Jarek and Nick, who were in the northern fiefs. Lily didn't know if the king knew of their betrayals, too. If he did, Nick would be banished or killed for their shared past, and Jarek for harboring thieves.

"I don't," Lily half-lied. "I've been out of the country for quite a while. How did you hear of this?"

The man grunted and took another swig from his ale. "Buddy of mine was working up in Lidon when some Albrini man came through town. Ranting about some thief messing things up."

Lily kept her face neutral, even though her insides were screaming. She was the Hawk they were looking for. She could only hope the man was a peasant out for the reward, not a Hawk. A Hawk's authority was significantly lessened beyond Albrin's borders, but they never lost their skills.

"Can't say I know him," she clipped. She finished her drink and stood, grabbed her bow, and hurried up the stairs and into their room before anyone could follow.

Tori looked up as the door closed.

"One night," Lily said. "Then we get far away." Kyraa usually liked to stay multiple nights so word could get out. Lily liked to keep moving as much as possible. Over time, they'd settled on a two-night compromise.

"What happened?" Tori asked as her eyes darted around Lily's face, responding to the nervous energy she was doing nothing to hide.

Lily couldn't explain the way the man's words had reached her very core, prodded at the base fear that had driven their whole wild run. "I just—I have a bad feeling."

"You *always* have a bad feeling."

Tori was right, but that didn't make Lily feel any less attacked. "There's a man from Albrin in Casseterre."

Tori gave her a baleful look. "So? People move. That doesn't mean you're being followed."

"But if word has spread, someone has to have brought the news here. And that someone could be rewarded for my capture."

Tori's face began to sink. "Oh. But why does that mean we have to leave? Kyraa says she likes this town. She knows some people."

Lily shook her head. "Because if someone knows, they could lead Randson to us."

"Does the man know you're the thief?" Tori raised an eyebrow. "No—"

"Take a moment, Lily, and *really* think. I don't know Jarek well, but I'm sure he'd tell you not to overreact."

That was true. Jarek always thought things through. He always seemed calm. He was what Lily was supposed to emulate as a Hawk. She leaned against the closed door. No, there was no indication the man had any idea who they were, aside from Lily dismissing herself quickly. If this was somewhere Kyraa knew well, they could maybe expect to make a little extra. It would be a calculated risk, maybe riskier than she liked, but she wasn't the only one to consider. They could stay another night. One night couldn't do any harm.

Lily screwed the cap on the last of the three canteens and slung it over her shoulder. It rattled against the others as she stood, making her way back to camp. They were between towns, and it forced them to camp in the woods. The frost had left them all chilled, despite the small fire they'd lit.

Lily crossed the clearing, handing canteens to Tori and Kyraa where they were sitting on a log. They always seemed to be sitting together nowadays.

Kyraa took a swig from her canteen and said, "I was just telling Tori I think we should head toward Avisier."

"Avisier?" Lily asked. "Why there?" She settled herself on a small rock.

"Well"—Kyraa's voice was full and warm—"if you are going to continue insisting on camping while we travel, we should start heading south for the winter. And I've always had luck at Avisier."

A quick glance at Tori's hopeful expression told her the woman agreed. They'd likely been discussing the proposal before Lily returned.

"I see no reason not to. As long as you know the way," Lily consented. She'd never been to the south of Casseterre, but it sounded nice enough. And she didn't particularly feel like freezing all winter. She'd already done that once.

"We could probably stay there a while, too," Kyraa added too casually to not be planned.

Lily gave Kyraa a tired look. This particular argument never seemed to get dropped. "No, we have to keep moving."

"What are you running from, anyway?" Kyraa asked, the warmth in her voice replaced by frustration.

Lily shook her head. "It doesn't matter." Her tone left no room for argument, but somehow that didn't stop the discussion.

Kyraa stood and kicked dirt over the last embers of their fire, sending a cloud of dust into the morning light. "You haven't let us stay in the same place more than two nights. You make us cut across huge swaths of land with no roads. We change directions at the drop of a hat. Clearly, it matters."

"She deserves to know," Tori insisted with more conviction in her voice than Lily had heard before. As they traveled, Kyraa and Tori had grown closer. Some of Kyraa's confidence was wearing off on the younger woman. "If you don't tell her, I will."

Lily looked at Tori, trying to see her thoughts. This was the first time the apprentice had taken such a firm stance. She occasionally questioned Lily but rarely argued beyond that. Tori had been more than compliant. She could have left ages before. She could have refused to travel with Lily. She'd thought Tori would, when Kyraa joined them. If their friendship was what gave Tori this new confidence, maybe it was time to listen.

"A Hawk."

"A bird," Kyraa said bluntly.

Of course, she had no idea what they were talking about. Hawks weren't widely known outside Albrin. That also explained the man's confusion at a 'bird person' from the tavern.

Lily rubbed a hand over her forehead, collecting her thoughts. "Tori and I belong to a group called Hawks. In Albrin, we—they—protect the kingdom."

"I'm not technically a Hawk," Tori interjected.

"You're as good as." And it was true. Tori had all the training, all the skills. The only thing missing was the paperwork. "It wasn't safe for us there anymore. Another Hawk—I'm worried he's hunting us."

Kyraa gave Lily a long look. Then her face softened as she looked at Tori. "Is this 'he' the man you told me about?"

Tori nodded, shuffling her feet in the dirt.

Lily didn't miss the gentle hand Kyraa laid on the other woman's back.

"Then I don't blame you for running. But that was months ago. I'd venture you're safe now."

Lily shook her head. "I can't risk it. The second I let my guard down, he'll show up." It was a paranoid thought, Lily knew that. But so often the worst possible outcome happened. She would rather be paranoid than dead.

Kyraa huffed. "Well, we better get moving, then."

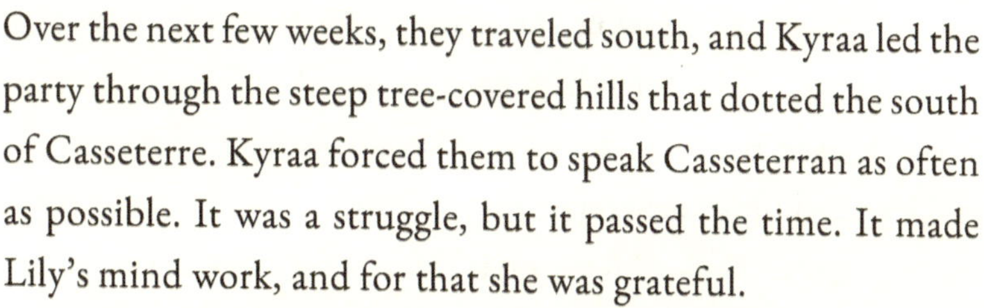

Over the next few weeks, they traveled south, and Kyraa led the party through the steep tree-covered hills that dotted the south of Casseterre. Kyraa forced them to speak Casseterran as often as possible. It was a struggle, but it passed the time. It made Lily's mind work, and for that she was grateful.

To Kyraa's credit, she took more interest in learning to defend herself. She designed situations, and Lily figured out ways to get out of them. It created a change of pace for her to take on a different role in their training sessions.

Kyraa sat on a log now, and Lily was on the ground in front of her, wrapping a strip of cloth around her foot and ankle. Kyraa hissed in pain as Lily bent the joint. "How long will this hurt for?"

"Hopefully just a few days," Lily replied. "It's better than the alternative."

"I suppose," Kyraa mused.

"I'll admit it's not something I've used a lot. How do you come up with these scenarios?"

Kyraa had described a situation where someone drove a shoulder into her hips and tried to pick her up. Lily had never seen it in actual combat, but she supposed that might be because her combatants were usually armed.

"It happened"—Kyraa's gaze fixated on Lily's hands as she wrapped the ankle—"and I didn't know what to do."

Lily fumbled with the bandages and looked up, trying to read Kyraa's expression. But the woman's face was stoic, and her eyes were averted.

"They've all happened, Lily." Lily looked up to Tori, who was leaning against a tree while she sharpened a dagger. "Everything Kyraa has asked about has happened to one of us."

Lily looked between the women, hoping one of them would break and admit it was a joke. It seemed they were closer to breaking into tears. "I'm—I'm so sorry." Her mind raced through the scenarios she'd been asked to teach them a way out of. Takedowns, ground fighting, escaping from being bent over a table. She hadn't even stopped to consider how those scenarios might happen in the first place.

"You got me out," Tori stated.

"And now it will not happen again," Kyraa added.

"Still." Lily's heart ached at the thought. She would teach the women everything she knew if it meant they didn't have to go through those events again.

Their journey continued for a few days before they reached Avisier. They smelled the city first. Wood smoke floated on the air more than a mile out from all the fires contained within the city walls.

Then they heard it.

It started with the metallic clank of hammers on metal. As they drew closer, a hum filled the air. It was the sound of horses and people and carts all blending together as city traffic.

The walled city appeared abruptly as they cleared the dense forest. Towering gray walls jutted above the surrounding fields. Square watchtowers rose on two of the five corners, crenellations casting jagged shadows over the landscape. It sat on the opposite bank of a wide, meandering river, accessible via a tall arched bridge.

The bridge looked like it offered the only entrance, as the river wound around three sides. It was bustling with horses, people on foot, and a cart piled high with cabbages.

"No. No way. You didn't say it was a city." Lily found herself backing into the tree line as she spoke. They hadn't gone into a city proper before. The most they'd risked was a large town. It was too much. The close confines had felt threatening in the early days. The number of eyes overwhelming. And the nearby authority meant a lot more rules with much stronger consequences.

"I can make much more coin in the city," Kyraa said in Casseterran. "And I know some people here."

They followed Lily back into the shelter of the trees, turning the horses to face each other. "And if you get caught? It's illegal in most cities."

Kyraa shrugged. "You can't create demand for a service and then punish the people providing it. Besides, the officers pay well."

"And if they're paid more to turn you in?" Lily asked.

Kyraa sighed. "Fine. Nobody who ranks higher than a knight. Does that make you feel better?"

"Not really."

"Well, I am going in. You're welcome to camp out here if you want. I might be a few nights." Kyraa turned her horse toward where they'd seen the bridge. She trotted in the direction of the bridge without looking back.

Tori started after her.

"Where are you going?" Lily asked.

Tori turned her head back, and Kyraa waited as she said, "I'm tired of running, Lily."

Lily found herself rooted to the spot, watching as her companions picked their way through the trees. She could leave now, head to another country, but she'd grown close to her companions. They had something good. And the idea of being on her own again...

She turned Rista toward the bridge.

CHAPTER 8

THROUGH THE GATE

Entering the city was like going back in time. Suddenly, she was a child again, dodging between horses and carts to get away from an angry merchant. The walls pressed in around her as the crowd ebbed and flowed.

On foot, they would make faster time, she thought as she edged Rista into the next rare, large opening to progress through the crowd. Not wanting to ditch the horse, she pressed forward regardless and found new gaps to guide her horse through the mass of bodies and obstructions.

Kyraa seemed to know where she was going, so the two Hawks followed wordlessly as they were led around the outer ring of the city.

Buildings were squished together, the upper floors jutting out over the street for a few more feet of precious space. Vendors hawked their goods as ladies shouted to each other from the windows above.

Kyraa ducked into an alley, forcing Tori and Lily to follow her. They dismounted, leading the horses to a crowded stable.

This routine was well practiced. Kyraa entered the tavern first as Lily and Tori split her belongings between them. They would sit down, and food would appear, having been ordered by Kyraa. Normally, they were there well before evening crowds filled the building and would take a moment to get acquainted with their rooms. It seemed there was no calm time of day in this tavern, though.

So, Lily left Tori watching their food as she and Kyraa got settled.

Kyraa had a single bag she used to spruce up the room. It carried flimsy, sheer curtains, incense, and a silk sheet. Lily knew this was the most expensive thing Kyraa owned. Her jewelry was a cheap replica she'd received when her mother passed away. Her clothes were bought cheaply and modified by hand.

Lily kept the more day-to-day necessities in her and Tori's room. Spare clothes, cooking utensils, and miscellaneous supplies sat in bags on the floor, ready to go if they had to make a hurried exit.

Kyraa did her makeup in a small handheld mirror next, darkening around her eyes and applying red to her lips. She changed into her outfit for the night, a red dress with a skirt just a little too slim to be considered proper and straps that could snap if a breeze went the wrong way.

Once she was ready, the two women returned to the dining area.

Lily had the first watch when Kyraa found her company for the night. She sat on her bed with a knife drawn. Her bow was unstrung, leaning against the wall with her quiver. The quarters were too close for her bow to be of much use. She preferred her knives anyway.

She listened, not too closely, just for Kyraa to shout for help. Over the next four hours, no shout came, so she woke Tori to switch places and fell into an uneasy sleep.

They watched the man Kyraa had been with leave in the morning while they were sipping coffee.

Kyraa trotted down a couple minutes behind him, sat across from Lily and beside Tori, and quietly ordered an omelet and coffee.

"Good morning," Lily greeted in Casseterran, which had become their normal breakfast practice.

Kyraa smiled, returning the greeting. She reached into her purse and handed Lily a handful of silver. "I'm going to stay here today. But there's no reason you two need to."

"Want us to get you anything?" Tori asked, eyeing the coins with surprise. That explained Kyraa's good mood. Maybe the city *was* worth it.

Kyraa shook her head, stabbing an egg.

Tori sent a questioning look at Lily, and she shrugged. It was Casseterran coin. Spending it in a city would draw less attention.

They left the horses stabled, venturing out on foot. Lily had been right in her initial thoughts. It was much easier to get around without horses. On foot, she didn't feel so out of place. She could dart around people and blend in, her childhood reflexes coming back to her.

Tori was another story. More than once, Lily had to yank her out of the path of a carriage or wagon.

"Be aware of your valuables," Lily warned.

Tori reflexively reached for her coin purse, but Lily grabbed her hand before she could. "If you walk around touching it, you just told all the thieves where your coin is."

Tori nodded sagely as Lily covered her actions by pretending to show Tori something as they walked.

A few well-placed questions got them directions to the main marketplace. It would be nice if they could get their hands on some fresh fruit. Tavern food rarely included fruit, or it was an extra expense. They'd bring some back for Kyraa if they lucked out and found any they could afford.

As they neared the center of the city, buildings got bigger, and streets got wider. The imposing walls of the city's castle were just visible over the rooftops.

It was clear when they reached the marketplace. Stalls were set up similarly to the stalls in smaller villages, like where she'd met Kyraa. The difference was the wares. A city like this received trade from around the country, perhaps even imported goods from elsewhere. That meant horse tack and smithed goods and jewelry instead of just food and basic farm supplies.

Lily spotted something red and tugged on Tori's arm to bring her over to the booth.

"Are those apples?" Tori asked, surprised.

"I think—"

"Do not say that," the lady running the booth hissed in Casseterran. Her eyes darted around, examining the multitude of people passing in and out of earshot. Deep worry lines and sunspots marked her skin. Her hair was pulled back in a severe bun as if she thought pulling it tight enough would make the wrinkles disappear.

"Say what?" Lily asked in Casseterran.

The lady looked her up and down. "Anything in that language. Baron D'Lavaud does not like it."

Lily realized then she'd spoken to Tori in the trade language. "So?" she asked, not bothering with Casseterran. It seemed the woman understood them either way.

"It is forbidden for anyone but nobility to use it," the lady said, now in quiet Casseterran.

Tori rolled her eyes. "That has got to be the stupidest rule I've heard to date."

The lady's eyes widened, and Lily turned around to see an armored man had fixed his eyes on them.

As she watched, he put a hand on his sword with an expression all too familiar to Lily.

So, she whipped around to Tori, hissing. "Go. Now. I'll meet you back at the tavern," she said quietly, but she was in much too great a hurry to attempt Casseterran.

Sure enough, the man started stalking toward them.

Tori backed a few steps away, her eyes wide with panic. "But—"

"Go," Lily insisted, shoving Tori away.

The man whistled, and Lily saw armored men around the square begin to work their way toward her. City guards, then.

Tori stumbled back, turned, and, with one last glance over her shoulder, slipped away into the crowd.

Lily allowed the man to grab her arm. She knew running would only increase her guilt.

"Say that again," the man hissed in Casseterran.

Lily noticed the crowd moving away. That would destroy her chance of blending in if she got out of his grasp, but perhaps it was better they were out of harm's way. A guard's head swiveled. Maybe he had seen that she wasn't alone. She only hoped Tori was wise enough to get as far as she could as fast as she could.

Lily took a moment to choose her words in the only slightly familiar language. "Sorry. I am not from here and did not realize the trade language was illegal." She and Nick had learned that when caught, their best hope was to talk their way out of trouble and hope for some sympathy. She put on her best, flustered smile, hoping the guard would pity her.

"You admit to your crime," the man stated. His glare told her all she needed to know. There was no getting out of this. At least, not with her child-like grasp of Casseterran. A flash of green caught Lily's eye, and she noticed a guard's gaze follow Tori through the crowd.

"This is such a stupid law," Lily muttered it to herself, drawing the attention of the searching man firmly to her. At least she'd managed to find the words in Casseterran.

Lily didn't see his fist in time to do anything about the blow that fell on her face.

A grunt left her lips, and her cheek burned as she glared at the man, calculating.

In an instant, she'd drawn her knife, slashing at the hand that held her.

The man let go with a curse.

Lily stood ready, a knife now in both hands. But she could see in her periphery that she was surrounded. She could kill two, maybe three, of the men before she was completely overwhelmed. Her arrest would happen either way. She didn't need murder charges against her.

So Lily sheathed her knives, holding her hands up in surrender.

Guards grabbed her arms and yanked them behind her back. She made eye contact with Tori, who looked ready to draw her bow, and shook her head.

Lily was half shoved and half dragged toward the castle. It was all she could do to keep her balance. She couldn't fight the men stripping her of her belongings, as her wrists were pinned against her back. Vice-like grips tightened on her arms with any slight attempt to wriggle away—the bruises were already forming—and she kept her eyes on the ground.

As they reached the gates of the palace, two guards peeled away. They stopped and talked to whoever manned the entrance.

Lily realized then that the gates were kept closed. In Albrin, they would be open unless something went wrong. And if the gates were always closed, it would be near impossible to escape once she passed through them.

She wrenched one arm free, ignoring the pain it caused her as she whirled, her fist connecting with the face of one guard. He released her other arm in surprise, and she lunged forward, grabbing at his wrists.

Arms wrapped around her waist, yanking her back before she could get a grip.

She threw her head back with a satisfying crack against a nose, but the grip on her waist didn't loosen. More cursing filled the air as she drove her elbow back, only to be met with the unfortunate solid metal of armor.

Lily struggled.

Hands closed on her shoulders, then someone picked her feet up.

She writhed and kicked and tried to hit, but every time one grip loosened, another replaced it. The swarm of people surrounding her became so overwhelming she lost track. Blow after blow rained down on her, more than she was dealing out. Her gut ached from the force of them, but this castle was fortified. She wouldn't be locked up without a fight and only wished she'd started fighting before letting them disarm her. At least she'd have taken a few down with her before being caged.

She added her own curse to the flurry as the gates of the castle passed above her head. And it earned her another blow to the face. Blood coated her mouth.

She spit it back out, hoping she hit someone in the chaos.

Then the sky disappeared, replaced with rough wooden planks. The world seemed to tilt as she was dragged downstairs. One of her hands slipped free, and she grabbed at a banister before the strength of four men overcame her grip.

She spat another curse. Shouted as she was dragged into darkness and thrown into a cell.

Her body hit the ground with a twisted thud, then she was up, charging toward the bars before the sound faded.

The key grated in the used lock, sealing Lily inside with a menacing click. Even as she hurled herself desperately toward the barred doors, hands outstretched to snatch at freedom, the men were already departing down the hall, keys jangling callously at their belts. Out of reach. Leaving with her last hope of freedom.

They rounded a corner, and Lily heard another door close.

She turned furiously to examine the cell.

Three of the walls were made of rough hewn stone and were rapidly closing in on her. Her spluttered breathing echoed off the stone as she whipped around toward where she'd come from. The fourth wall was replaced by a series of rusted iron bars that faced what Lily assumed was a hallway. A window too small to crawl through sat high in the back wall of the cell, also barricaded with iron.

Her hands pushed against the bars, then she peered down the hallway to see a door she presumed was locked and rammed into the barred door. Hopeful the lock hadn't caught in place.

She had to get out.

She had to get out before she was crushed.

She had to get—

"Well, that was some show."

Lily turned to see a woman sitting against very still walls. She was huddled in a back corner of the cell, wrapped in a dark cloak. Her face showed the beginnings of wrinkles. Her voice sounded older than her thin face looked.

"You may as well sit down. You won't get through those bars." Her voice rasped as she spoke. The woman shifted, indicating where Lily should sit.

Lily took a deep breath. Even though the space felt like it was crushing her, the walls were still. In fact, now that she looked, they were each long enough to lie down beside. She settled herself on the dirt floor, pulling her cloak tighter around herself as she leaned against the cold stone wall.

"Cecilia," the woman said. Her breathing sounded labored.

"Lily."

The woman shifted again with a sigh. "Why are you here?" she asked in Casseterran.

"Do you speak the trade language?" Lily asked in her strained imitation of an otherwise beautiful language.

The woman shook her head.

Lily took a deep breath, stalling for time as she thought about the words. "Is the trade language really forbidden here?"

Cecilia nodded. "Has been since D'Lavaud took power."

"Took power?" Lily asked.

Cecilia nodded again, slowly this time. "He killed Baron Rouselle in a duel. Took control of the castle." She paused for a labored breath. "And the lands around it."

Lily frowned. "I thought that rule was only on the roads."

Cecilia shook her head. "No. Rule of Conquest is everywhere."

Lily didn't understand one of the words, but she understood the idea.

Cecilia continued her explanation, "If we agreed to a fight, and you won, you would own everything I own, though that is not a lot."

Lily shook her head. "Okay, that is an even worse law than removing an entire language." What better way to encourage assassination? She'd heard of countries where there were exchanges resulting from duels, but those had to be agreed to by both parties. Sometimes territories changed hands, yes, but not without someone wagering it in a bet.

Cecilia laughed before it turned into labored breathing. "It is how this country has been for hundreds of years."

Lily laughed, then coughed as some blood found its way to her throat.

A hand rested on her back as she leaned forward in an attempt to clear it. When the coughing stopped, the hand turned her face toward Cecilia.

"You made them angry." She touched the already swelling wound under Lily's eye gingerly.

"Apparently," Lily replied. She could see on Cecilia's face the desire to help. But the cell was barren. There was nothing the other woman could do. Lily smiled despite how it sent her cheek throbbing. "It's alright, I've had worse."

"That doesn't make this matter any less."

Cecilia's conviction, the care in her voice, made Lily's heart swell.

Lily decided there and then. This woman who sounded much older than she probably was. This woman who appeared to have been in the dark for ages. This woman whose hands were thin and weak from however long she'd been locked up. This woman who cared for someone she'd just met.

Lily decided she would protect her.

CHAPTER 9

AN OLD DOG

Lily was awake. It took her a moment to realize why. Then she heard the creak of a door closing, followed by footsteps. She must have woken up when the door was opened.

Her body ached from the struggle with the guards. The bruises around her eye throbbed. She could still feel their grip on her arms, an ever-present reminder that she'd lost. With her eyes closed, she tried to orient herself. Her back was against the wall, and she was probably facing the bars. She'd grown into a habit of facing the entrance through years of training, and that's where she'd gone to sleep.

Keeping her breathing even and slow was important, not giving any sign she'd awoken. The weakness in her limbs meant fighting again would not be an option. Not yet, anyway.

Her eyelids flicked open slightly, so she was watching through her eyelashes. It was still dark, the faintest bit of moonlight flitting in through the window.

Someone was walking up to the cell. They were tall and thin, silhouetted in the dark. The figure hurried to the bars and knelt.

"Mother," he said in quiet Casseterran.

Lily heard Cecilia moving from across the cell.

The older woman met the figure at the bars and said, "Edmund, darling, how are you?"

"I am fine, Mom. I brought you something," the man replied, voice heavy with relief. There was the sound of clothes shuffling as the man—Edmund—handed his mother something. "You have a new roommate."

"Yes," Cecilia whispered before taking a long breath. "Let us hope she lasts longer than the last one."

There was a moment of quiet. Then Edmund said, "I have to go. I am sorry I can not stay longer."

"It is nice to see your face, even if only for a minute."

They exchanged goodbyes before the man left. Cecilia made her way back to where she had been sleeping and curled up.

Only when her cellmate had settled did she follow her back to sleep.

❈

Lily drifted awake to muted, thin shafts of light filtering into her cramped cell. Bleary-eyed and sluggish, she reached instinctively for her waterskin to soothe her dry throat before reality crystallized—she was weaponless, thirsty, and in pain. Everything was gone.

The air tasted stale in her mouth as she painfully swallowed, eyes trailing the bars that caged her.

"They should bring us water soon," Cecilia told her.

Lily pushed back the fog of sleep to puzzle out the words. She raised herself up, sore muscles groaning in protest. "Not a lot, I suppose?"

Cecilia smiled back. "No, but it will keep you alive until your trial," she spoke slowly, giving Lily time to translate.

Lily raised an eyebrow. "I get a trial?" She had assumed this was her punishment. Sitting in the cramped cell with nothing to do, nothing to eat, and nothing to drink for however long whoever was in charge deemed fit.

Cecilia shrugged. It looked like it took her more effort than it was worth. "Technically. It will not be much of one."

"How long have you been here?" Lily asked.

"Five years."

A door opened and both of them stopped to listen.

A servant shambled in, passing two thin slices of bread through the bars and setting cups of water just outside. Then she hurried out, never making eye contact with the prisoners.

Lily reached through the bars to pull in their cups. They were spaced wide enough that her whole shoulder could push through, just not her head. It was probably a coin-saving decision to space the bars as far apart as possible.

When she turned to hand a cup to Cecilia, the older woman was reaching into her cloak. She pulled out a large carrot and snapped it in half. Her bony hand extended, offering a piece to Lily. "My son brought me this last night."

"I don't—"

"Take it," Cecilia said. "You will get precious little besides moldy bread here."

Lily took the carrot.

Sure enough, they had far from the fresh Casseterran bread Lily knew would be coming out of the ovens that morning. Their slices were stale, crumbling in their hands instead of tearing softly.

Lily ate around a fuzzy blue patch. The water, at least, was cool and fresh. It probably came from a well in the courtyard, just as it would for the rest of the castle.

"Why are you here?" Lily asked, gesturing around them when they'd finished eating.

Cecilia sighed. "I was in the wrong place at the wrong time, I suppose."

"And you haven't had a trial?" Lily asked. She knew it was expensive to hold someone, even giving them as little food as they did, and was surprised that the coin-pinching in their meals didn't extend to the principle of keeping prisoners.

"I have." Cecilia paused. "My son was able to talk them into keeping me alive."

There was no good way to respond. Unable to think of one in the trade language, there was no way Lily would be able to translate it to Casseterran. So they lapsed into silence for a moment. Still, that left the question as to where people who were found guilty ended up.

"What happens to most people?" Lily asked.

"Some are hurt, others are killed."

"Right." Waiting it out wouldn't be an option. She pulled a pin out of her hair, moving toward the bars as she bent it, first into a straight line, then a hook at the end. It may take a few tries to get the right shape to bypass the wards, but it seemed she had plenty of time.

"What are you doing?"

"Not waiting for a trial I'm going to lose." Even if it was what she deserved. After all, she'd committed the crime in the middle of the marketplace. There were plenty of witnesses.

Lily reached through the bars, the rust scraping against her arms. She ran her fingers over the face of the lock, feeling for the keyhole.

Once she did, the pin slipped in easily.

As a child, she'd had plenty of practice. But it had been years since she'd left that life, and what had once been muscle memory felt like a dream. Admittedly, needing to wrap her arms around the bars and do it backward was a hindrance. Her elbows and wrists were held at awkward angles, and she had to sit in a half crouch that soon had her thighs and hamstrings aching.

Lily wiggled around, trying to get a feel for the wards, but all she felt was resistance. She had some movement up and down, but none to the side. Reaching around the wards to nudge the locking bolt itself was impossible. She worked at the lock for nearly an hour before her arms were too sore to continue. She tucked the pin out of sight amongst her clothes as she sat back, defeated. But ... there was time to work. There was nothing *but* time.

"Someone almost escaped, once," Cecilia said.

Lily peered at the woman who sat against the opposite wall. Standing, she would be taller than Lily, despite the sickness in her voice making her seem so small. "What happened?"

"She was killed," Cecilia said. Her eyes flicked down before returning to Lily's face. "Please, I do not want that for you."

Lily frowned. "How long does it usually take for a trial?"

"One month. Two."

That was plenty of time. Kyraa had wanted to stay in the city, after all. Tori could protect her that long. Lily would talk to the baron, and if that didn't work, she'd break out.

Soon enough, they'd be on the road. Together again.

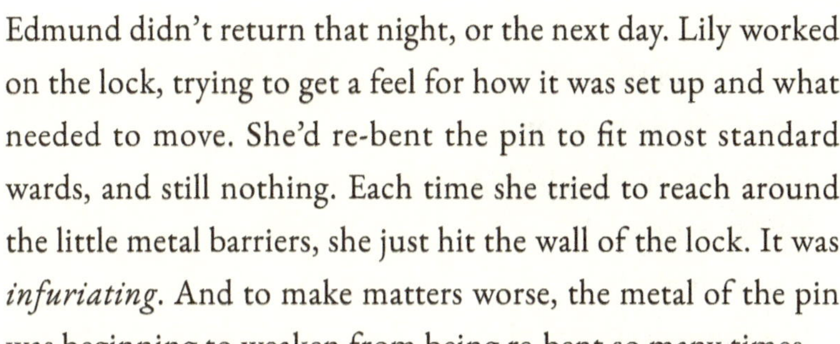

Edmund didn't return that night, or the next day. Lily worked on the lock, trying to get a feel for how it was set up and what needed to move. She'd re-bent the pin to fit most standard wards, and still nothing. Each time she tried to reach around the little metal barriers, she just hit the wall of the lock. It was *infuriating*. And to make matters worse, the metal of the pin was beginning to weaken from being re-bent so many times.

Lily sat back on her heels with a frustrated sigh, tucked the pin away, and rolled out her sore wrists.

"Have you picked a lock before?" Cecilia asked.

Lily nodded, then stood, wrapping a hand around the cold metal of the bar to balance as she pulled one knee to her chest to stretch. She felt Cecilia's gaze rake up and down her, so asked, "Why?" Lily switched legs, savoring the stretch in the small space.

"You seem nice," Cecilia continued. Or maybe the last word translated into honest. Or good. All things thieves were not.

Lily shrugged. "I had to."

When she turned to look at Cecilia, the woman was watching her with curiosity.

"You were in prison?"

"I, umm, my parents died when I was young. My brother and I, we had nothing."

Surprise flashed across Cecilia's face but was quickly replaced by understanding. She said something Lily couldn't understand, then corrected at the confusion Lily let show. "You took things from people."

"I did," Lily admitted quietly.

A long moment passed. To avoid Cecilia's gaze, Lily looked around their little cell.

"*Did*. You do not now?"

Lily shook her head. "No. Not in a long time."

"What happened?"

"I got caught."

Her thoughts returned to that fateful night. The royal family had been in the city, which meant an increased guard presence. She and Nick had been starving, waiting for them to leave so they could risk stealing something to eat. They'd thought the royals had left when they climbed through the window. The room had already been stripped, but sometimes the housekeepers missed things.

Nick kept watch while Lily had raided the room. Her attention had caught on the trunk at the foot of the oversized bed. She tried to lift the heavy lid, but it was still locked. She'd spent an hour trying to pick it. The chest was heavy, full. It wouldn't have food, but if they'd found clothes or blankets, they could've sold them in another town.

That lock had been smaller than this one. She remembered the narrow opening, much narrower than the locks she was used to working on. The warding had proved impossible there, too.

Her head shot up at the creak of a door. She backed away from the cell bars to hide her guilt, praying nobody had seen her at the lock.

A thin man appeared from around the corner. His pale face had a small smattering of freckles across the nose.

Curly black hair fell into his eyes, and he pushed it back. Blue. The lightest blue Lily had ever seen outside a baby.

Cecilia's smile told Lily that this was Edmund.

"Lily, meet my son. This is Edmund," Cecilia said. "Edmund, my new roommate, Lily."

Edmund nodded.

Lily smiled at the use of the term roommate. If it had been five years, she supposed Cecilia had begun using the terminology to make her situation seem less bleak.

"I brought some food," Edmund said. He handed over two strips of jerky, one to each of them.

Lily accepted it gratefully. She was surprised. She'd expected him to only bring food for his mother. "Thanks."

"How long do you have?" Cecilia asked.

Edmund lowered himself to the ground across the bars. "A couple minutes"—he looked at Lily—"I saw you come in. You put up quite the fight."

Lily shrugged, not really knowing the proper response.

"That will not be good for you at the trial," Edmund continued. "They mean to kill you."

"They will find that a lot harder than they anticipate," Lily replied. They would be far from the first to try.

Edmund laughed.

"What?"

"Your accent is adorable," Edmund said with a broad smile. His smile shrunk as he added, "I hope you are right."

"What's been happening?" Cecilia asked.

Edmund nodded toward Lily. "She is the talk of the castle." He turned to look at her. "Did you really say the rule was"—he tilted his head before saying the final word with a heavy Casseterran accent—"*stupid*?"

"Is it not?" Lily asked in Casseterran. It was clear that was the only language the small family was comfortable using. That meant more practice for her, at least.

"You have not been in Casseterre long," Edmund replied. "No matter how 'stupid' it is," he stumbled over a version of the trade language again. The vowels were drawn out in a way that brought a smile to Lily's face. "D'Lavaud is law. Our opinions do not matter."

"What about the king?" Lily asked.

They both laughed at that.

Though Cecilia soon started to wheeze, and Edmund grabbed her hand through the bars, suddenly brimming with concern. "Is it getting worse?"

Cecilia smiled weakly as her breath came back. "A little. The last rain did not help."

"I will see if I can get you a warmer cloak," Edmund said.

Lily watched as they talked for a few minutes about people she didn't know and places she'd never been. It was a light conversation, as Cecilia couldn't contribute much without gasping for air. Still, Lily could see how much the woman appreciated Edmund's updates on the world.

Edmund eventually left a few minutes later, saying if he stayed much longer, people would wonder where he was. Somehow, the conversation had made Lily feel lighter. It was nice to know Cecilia hadn't been completely alone. It was nice to see a spark of kindness in their situation.

"Your breathing…" Lily said, unsure how to ask the question she wanted.

"The damp gets into everything." After a pause, Cecilia added, "Even the lungs."

"It is not damp."

"Wait until it rains," Cecilia reassured her.

Lily didn't have to wait long. It rained that night. It almost didn't matter that they had four walls and a roof. The temperature plummeted a half hour before the rain started. It plunged further when the sun set.

Water poured in through their little window, pooling on the floor. They both huddled in the far corner in a sad attempt to stay dry. Then the ceiling started leaking small drips, which turned into steady streams, and there was no escaping it.

Lily could tell Cecilia was grateful for the extra body heat as the two women pressed against each other. She fell asleep curled up beside Lily when it was well past midnight. The constant cracks of thunder kept Lily wide awake, watching Cecilia shiver.

Eventually, Lily took her cloak off and laid it across the older woman. Seeing her suffering only added to the punishment of the cell.

"You didn't have to do that." Cecilia pushed herself up from the muddy ground she'd slept on, then pulled the cloak from her shoulders and held it out to Lily.

With the rising sun, Lily had moved back to working on the lock. Some silly part of her hoped the rain had loosened it, though logically she knew that wasn't true. Her motivation to get out had simply increased.

Lily turned, and the mud squeaked underfoot. She took her picks from the lock before she could forget. "You needed it more than me."

Celia smiled her thanks as she wrapped the cloak around herself once again.

The door opened and footsteps hurried in.

"They let me bring the food," Edmund said, passing a larger slice of bread through to his mom. "It is warm. And I managed to get some coffee."

Only once his mother was eating did he turn to Lily, handing her a warm slice of bread and steaming coffee. Their knuckles brushed as Lily accepted the cup with a smile.

She drank gratefully as Edmund returned to fussing over his mother. Lily was glad his attention was on his mother, or he may have noticed the slight blush rising to Lily's cheeks.

Cecilia reassured him she was fine. But her voice was weak, and she had to take more pauses to breathe than normal.

Edmund pulled the cloaks tighter around her through the bars, shooting Lily a thankful glance. He coaxed his mother into a gentle sleep and rubbed her back through the bars. That was where he stayed for a long while, longer than Lily had seen him do before.

Then his attention turned to her. "You want to escape."

"Yes."

"Get her out," Edmund's voice cracked. His eyes were glistening with barely contained tears as he looked at Lily.

It was a plea. A plea Lily couldn't ignore.

"Of course."

TEN YEARS PRIOR

Lily's head snapped up as her brother's whistle pierced the air. A lock pick clattered against the stone floor. She cursed under her breath as she snatched it up.

Nick's warning meant someone had been spotted entering the house, but it didn't mean they would come into this room. She just had to focus, crack the lock on this chest, and get out.

She stuck the pick back in the lock, wiggling it up and down to get past the ward she'd found. Still, she hit the back of the lock cylinder. A board in the hallway creaked, and she worked quicker. She twisted the pick, only to be met with resistance. She kept hitting the back of the chamber, not the bolt that kept the chest shut.

This was a more sophisticated lock than normal, but she and Nick were more desperate than normal. The royal family had been in the city, the increased security making it near impossible for them to find any marks. No one was dumb enough to rob the royals. They were supposed to be scrounging for anything that might have been left behind.

A floorboard creaked directly outside the door.

Lily froze, her breathing measured. Every instinct screamed at her to run and hide, but if this was just someone passing by, the noise would risk exposing her.

She counted in her head as she waited. Twenty, then thirty seconds. No other sound.

Her focus returned to the tools in her hands.

The doorknob jiggled.

Lily bolted upright, looking at the open window. She'd locked the door to give herself a warning if someone came. It didn't matter how much the hunger in her stomach gnawed at her; she had to leave now. Tucking the lock picks into her belt, she heard the sickening click of a lock.

She darted to the window and leapt out.

Only to make a strangled choking sound as a hand caught the back of her shirt.

The hand hauled her roughly back through the window.

"What do you think you're doing?" The breath was sour with old garlic.

Lily grabbed the hands holding her, twisting, and kicking, and thrashing. The grip didn't loosen.

An arm wrapped around her, pinning her arms to her side. "A feisty one, isn't she?"

She felt the laugh of the man holding her. Both hands had shifted now. He had her thoroughly pinned, but at least she could breathe.

"I didn't know they were a pair," the voice was calm, entirely too calm. It settled into the pit of Lily's stomach with a deep dread.

A silhouette appeared in the window. It was cloaked, with the arm of a bow peaking over one shoulder. A Hawk.

They were so screwed.

———◆○◆———

Lily paced the small chamber she'd been thrown in, rubbing her cold arms despite the fire roaring in the corner. She didn't know if Nick had been caught, but she certainly wasn't about to sell him out. There was no hope for her. She'd receive years in the dungeon, and that was if she was lucky.

If not, they might cut off a hand so she couldn't pick locks again. Or an ear, so everyone who looked at her knew she'd been caught.

There was nothing to do now but wait. She'd been moved to the highest tower of the keep. Too high for her to consider climbing out a window. Nick might have risked it, but, well, she wasn't him. The only furniture in the room was a plain table with two chairs. A table she hadn't sat at once in the hour she'd been there.

Voices sounded in the hallway, and Lily looked up from her pacing. The door opened and a cloaked figure slipped in.

He was tall, but not particularly broad-shouldered. His slightly chapped lips were set in a grim line. His face had a few days of stubble, and he looked at her with hard, unamused eyes. He closed the door behind him and stepped into the room, carrying a tray. Barely sparing her a glance, he set it on the table with a clatter, jarring after the hour of near silence Lily experienced.

"Eat." His voice was rough and gravelly as he slid into one of the chairs.

Lily shook her head. "I'm not hungry." Her voice sounded so small compared with the presence he commanded in the room.

She hoped beyond hope he didn't hear the immediate grumble of her stomach. She hoped he didn't notice the twinge of pain that flickered across her face.

He looked at her, cocking one eyebrow in a disbelieving manner. "Come now. You're as thin as a twig. You mean to tell me you were stealing for fun, not necessity?"

Lily shook her head hurriedly, only to realize her mistake. She looked at the food now. Bread, and a hearty-looking broth. Her stomach betrayed her with a rumble loud enough she was certain he heard it.

The man pushed the tray to the edge of the table. "Sit. Eat." His voice changed then, brimming with a deep authority.

Almost before she knew what she was doing, Lily had sat and picked up the bread. She was surprised at its warmth. Bread was normally cooked in the morning, but this seemed fresh.

"Do you know who I am?"

Lily shook her head as she took a tentative bite of the crust. The truth was, she had some idea. The way he moved without a sound, his cloak, the bow that he wore, still swung over his shoulder. This man was a Hawk, the king's personal law enforcement. That didn't mean she knew his name.

"But you know what I am."

Even though it wasn't a question, it brokered a response. Lily nodded, then bit her tongue to stop herself from talking. This was an interrogation. What was she doing cooperating? She set the bread back on the plate and pushed it away from her.

The man looked pointedly at the bread, then back at her. "Your brother ate everything we gave him."

Lily pressed her lips together, leaning back and crossing her arms, though her stomach protested with renewed vigor.

She expected the man to come at her with threats. Or with a million questions. Instead, he just stared at her. His gaze made her want to squirm. But she could wait him out. Surely, he had more important things to deal with than a child thief.

"Please sir, I was starving," she blurted.

His face didn't shift. He didn't even blink. "I know. That's why I brought you food. Your brother told me everything."

No. He couldn't have sold her out. Then again, they had literally caught her in the act. Had even taken the lock picks from her before putting her in the room.

"So, it's not a trick?" She kicked herself under the table. He wouldn't tell her if it was.

"It's not a trick, Lily."

No, not with him knowing her name. Only her brother could have told him that.

She slowly reached for the bread and began to chew quietly as she waited for him to tell her what would happen next.

"Your thievery is unrefined. That was a pin and tumbler lock, you have to listen to it. I shouldn't expect better though, it's hard to work well on an empty stomach. Still, there's some talent there, if you'd be willing to put in the work."

"What work?" she asked around a mouthful of bread.

The man raised his eyebrow again, and she had a feeling her words had come out more jumbled than intelligible. So she took a draft of the soup to wash it down instead and nearly melted at the flavor. It had been ages since she'd had anything so good.

"What work?" she repeated.

"I'm in need of an apprentice. Well, I suppose two now. You and your brother worked so smoothly together; I thought you were the same person. Or ... I could tell the baron."

CHAPTER 11
NEW TRICKS

Lily's head clouded with thoughts of the lock. She had sketched what she knew of the inner workings in the dirt, then swept them away before their meals were delivered. She had tried to picture the mechanics of it, tried to picture how every direction could be warded so even the sharpest bends of her pin couldn't bypass them.

She wasn't surprised she'd dreamed of the last lock she'd failed to pick....

The next day, Lily approached the lock more critically. She reached around the bars, no pins this time, and ran her fingers over the rough surface. The keyhole was narrow. Like the lock on the chest had been.

Jarek's words from that night inspired her now.

She had to listen to the lock.

Methodically, she inserted the pick once again, shallowly this time. Instead of large sweeping motions, she poked at the edges.

There, something gave.

As she levered her hand down, her pick moved up. Slowly, so slowly, she made minute adjustments. This must be the pin part of a pin and tumbler lock.

There was a slight click. Lily froze, waiting to see what happened. She twisted her pick and heard another click. When she went back to where she had been, she found the pin had fallen back into place. But at least it was progress.

For the next four days, that's all the progress she could make. She ascertained that there were multiple pins, but she couldn't figure out how many. Get one to stay up while she worked on others was evading her. She just knew that at different points, the top of the lock cylinder seemed to lift.

For four days her routine had consisted of waking up, eating the meager food she was given, and trying to pick the lock for however long her arms could stand it. The other hours she filled by speaking with Cecilia, practicing her Casseterran. Sometimes she would work out, but the food wasn't enough to support her as it was. She'd never had much extra on her bones, and now her skin pulled tight to her ribs.

The only break in the monotony was Edmund. Every few days he would stop by, bringing news of someone in the castle Lily didn't know, but Cecilia seemed thrilled to hear about it every time. He also brought food. Food that *wasn't* moldy bread. It was ever only small amounts he could smuggle, but the change in diet was appreciated by both women.

On the fifth day, Lily's pin broke.

A curse spilled from her lips. She pulled the first piece out of the lock, and defeat dragged her shoulders down. When she reached for the second piece, she met with resistance.

Great, it was stuck.

She wiggled gently, trying to free it. With the now familiar sound of a pin dropping, it popped free.

With the now familiar sound of a pin dropping...

Lily's brow furrowed in concentration. Something had been holding the pin up. It wasn't her make-shift pick, that had been angled down. But she'd been twisting when it had snapped. Maybe that was what had held the pin up.

With renewed vigor, Lily stuck the broken pick back in the bottom of the lock. She twisted. It was subtle, but the lock twisted slightly like it would with a key. Maybe, if she rotated while picking the lock, the pins would stay in their picked position.

"What is it?" Cecilia asked, clearly seeing the change in Lily's body language.

"I think I figured it out," Lily said, the excitement evident in her slightly raised voice.

Cecilia placed a hand on Lily's arm, slowly pulling her away from the lock. "Not now. You would be killed."

"It is better than sitting around and waiting for a trial." It was better than sitting around and waiting for someone else to decide what to do with her. At least, if she tried to escape, her fate would be her own.

Cecilia smiled. "Yes, but you have time. Take the best chances."

"You can come with."

"I will only slow you down."

Lily shook her head. But she knew the woman didn't have enough breath to continue debating, so she let it rest. When the time came, she wouldn't be left behind.

The damp had stayed in their cell much longer than Lily knew it would linger outside. Cecilia had weakened as a result. She couldn't move across the cell without being winded. Lily had taken to retrieving their food and drink and delivering it to the woman.

Edmund came that night. Huddled against the far wall, Lily pretended to be asleep to give him and his mother as much privacy as could be had.

"I might be able to get D'Lavaud to let you see a doctor."

"No. It is not worth it."

"It is to me," Edmund insisted. He clutched his mother's hand to his chest, over his heart. Lily could hear the pain in his voice, behind the wall of ease he put up to keep his mother unworried.

"Just help me see the sky again," Cecilia said. "I miss it." She sounded so resigned.

"I will."

Lily's heart broke.

Edmund still had hope, but Cecilia would likely not live long in or out of a jail cell. She didn't blame him for not coming to terms with that. They went quiet for a while, and Lily eventually drifted back to sleep.

<hr>

A few more days had passed, and with each one Lily made more and more progress with the lock. Her diagrams in the dirt were growing detailed—intricate—as she felt out the inner shape with her picks. It was a much more delicate job than the warded locks she'd learned on, but she was certain it was only a matter of time before she cracked it.

When Lily brought Cecilia their morning food, the woman shifted, pulling something from her cloak. "Edmund brought this last night," Cecilia said, handing Lily a small parchment.

Lily unfolded it. On it were lines and words she only understood because she was familiar with castles. It was a map. Edmund had given her a map of the castle and marked where guards stood and rotated.

She couldn't help the smile on her face. Guards had been her biggest worry. With this, she would know where they would be. On the way in, she'd been so busy fighting she wasn't even sure she knew the way out. Now she did. Of course, there were still problems. The lock hadn't been successfully picked yet. The gate would still be closed.

But this was a step. A big one.

"You have to plan," Cecilia cautioned, looking at Lily with a stern set to her jaw.

"Of course." Lily laughed. "But this helps."

"It took six guards to get you in here," Cecilia said. "On the way out, you'll run into more."

"I need weapons to beat them."

"What about the gate?"

Lily shrugged. "I'll have to find a time when it's open. I can't get it up, and these walls are too high to jump down and expect to walk it off."

A violent coughing fit overtook Cecilia, shaking her entire body.

Lily handed her the cup of water they tried to make last through the day to ease her symptoms. "We'll get you out."

"Don't worry about me. You have so much more ahead of you."

The words were like a punch in the gut. She was on the run. She didn't know if she'd ever be able to return home. Could certainly never start building a life somewhere. She'd returned to the common criminal she always had been at the first sign of conflict.

"I have nothing ahead of me."

"Do not say that!"

Lily was shocked at the tone. She'd never heard Cecilia angry, never heard such firmness in her voice. It seemed to take a lot out of her, because she had to take multiple labored breaths before continuing.

"I do not know what exactly, but you have made it through the unimaginable. You will make it through this and come out with your fire burning brighter than ever before." Cecilia's breathing sped up and became heavy as she closed her eyes, so Lily leaned her back against the wall gently, helping her to a comfortable position.

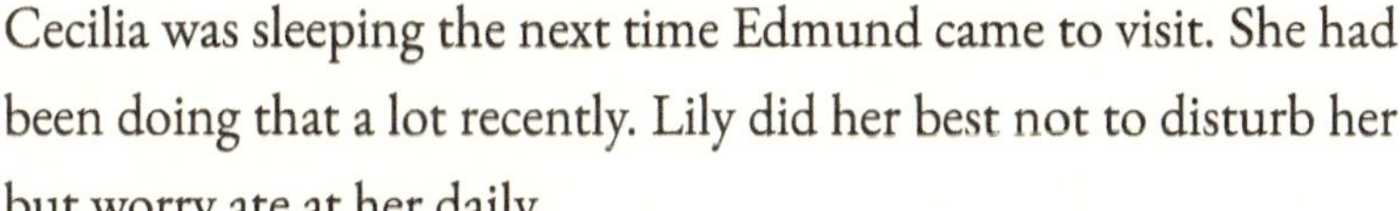

Cecilia was sleeping the next time Edmund came to visit. She had been doing that a lot recently. Lily did her best not to disturb her but worry ate at her daily.

"How is she?" Edmund asked, crouching on the other side of the bars.

"Not great," Lily replied. "But she will not admit it has gotten any worse."

Edmund smiled slightly, chuckling to himself. "No, I do not imagine she would."

"You want to get her out," Lily said.

Edmund didn't take his eyes off his mom when he nodded. "With the map, do you think...?"

Lily wished she could say yes, but she couldn't. She shook her head. "Not with the gate closed, and not unarmed."

Edmund nodded again. "You know how to fight."

"Fighting unarmed can only get me so far," Lily conceded the point. "With my bow, I might pull it off."

"How far?" Edmund asked.

Lily pulled out the map, showing him a point just outside the dungeons. On her side of that point, the guards were stationed alone or in pairs. She could leverage the element of surprise. But once she was on the main floor, there would be too many guards in the vicinity. If any raised an alarm, she'd be swarmed in an instant. "After this, there are too many of them."

Edmund was nodding to himself, deep in thought.

"Can I ask you a question?" Lily asked.

"Go ahead."

"Why have you not done this before?"

"It was never this desperate, or this likely," he responded easily. He must have seen the hesitation on Lily's face and added, "I have never been a warrior. I am better with a pen than with a sword."

"Some would say that is more noble."

"Not many," Edmund replied, "And not here. It has not gotten me very far at all."

Lily reached through the bars to rub his arm lightly. "It *is* valuable. Do not let anyone tell you otherwise."

CHAPTER 12
THE VIGIL

Edmund's body was tense as he walked toward the cell. He kept his pace normal, but each movement was stiff—and forced.

"What is it?" Lily asked. Normally they wouldn't get a visit for a few days, but this was a mere eight hours after his last.

"Tonight, at sunset, the gates will be up. I will have your weapons and meet you in the stairwell."

"Edmund," Cecilia said weakly.

Edmund nodded to his mom, but his eyes were locked on Lily's. "Get her out."

Just as suddenly as he entered, he was gone, rushing off before his absence was noticed in the castle above.

Lily turned to Cecilia, who just nodded at the lock. "Better get to work."

Their meal for the day had already come. The odds of someone catching Lily in the process were low. The odds of them trying to open the cell without unlocking it were even lower.

Lily crouched by the door, grabbing her pins and reaching around to begin to fiddle with the lock.

And she stayed there for hours.

Her arms ached, but taking a break would have undone all her progress. So, she crouched by the bars and kept moving the picks in the lock, feeling for one pin and the next. And the next.

Then, with a quiet click, the last pin snapped into place.

Lily slumped back as the door swung open slightly, a wave of relief washing over her body. She tore a small piece of fabric from the bottom of her cloak, folding it and wedging it into the frame to prevent the door from locking again. She pulled the door closed so they at least looked contained if anyone checked.

Cecilia was beaming when she turned to her. "I knew you could," she said.

Lily recounted the plan, showing the woman the route they would take on the map and where they'd meet Edmund. They had to plan their timing just right. Too soon and the gate would still be closed, they wouldn't be able to make it out. Too late and they'd run into the guards that were screening whoever came in.

As the day progressed, Lily watched the light through the window shift in the now familiar pattern. When it glowed in a long orange rectangle, creeping up the opposite wall, the time seemed right.

She reached up the side of her shirt, unclasping the knife sheath she kept there. How nobody had found it when she was arrested, she didn't know. Maybe, with all the thrashing, they'd thought it was a rib, as she wasn't exactly the picture of eating well.

"Wait," Cecilia said.

"What?"

"The guards are going to shift. Listen."

Of course the guards would shift. And of course Cecilia knew when. She'd been there long enough to know their patterns like clockwork.

Over the last weeks, Lily should have been listening, should have been trying to figure out the rhythms of the castle too. Already, that mistake had almost cost them. It was much easier to catch a guard unaware during the middle of their shift than the beginning or end.

Lily froze, straining her ears to listen. Sure enough, she heard voices as new guards replaced the old.

Eventually the voices settled down and Cecilia nodded, struggling to stand.

Lily helped the woman to her feet and pushed their cell door open. They crept around the corner, and, for the first time, Lily properly saw where she'd been kept. They were in one of many smaller cell blocks that could be accessed through this door.

Thankfully, she didn't see anyone in the cells they passed.

Set high in the door was a small window with three bars across it. Lily motioned for Cecilia to wait as she glided to the window and peeked out.

Two guards stood on either side of the door. Well, *stood* was a generous term. They more leaned against the wall, already resigned to a boring shift of guarding a mostly empty dungeon. Their ineptitude would serve her plans.

Lily ducked back down, out of sight, considering. She'd never heard Edmund dealing with keys. Perhaps the lock was broken. Perhaps the guards never checked that it was locked. Or perhaps the servant with their morning meal left it open just to avoid dealing with keys and full hands. After all, the cell was locked, wasn't it?

Lily laid her hand on the doorknob and twisted it painfully slowly.

It twisted. It didn't squeak. And it didn't feel locked. She looked back to where Cecilia was watching and readied her dagger.

The older woman nodded.

She slammed the door outwards and into a guard, causing him to slump immediately as the other grabbed his sword. Lily was ready and had already smashed the hilt of her dagger against his temple. He crumpled, sword only half out of its scabbard. They were a pathetic display of the weakness that had dragged her to her cell so many days ago.

Lily hooked her arms under his shoulders and dragged him into her cell. When she dragged the other guard, he had a loop of keys on his belt, so she snatched them and used them to lock the cell door before tossing them just out of reach.

When she returned, Cecilia was leaning against the wall where Lily had left her.

She offered her arm for the older woman to lean on as they made their way down the hall. Their progress up the steps was slow. Lily itched to keep moving as Cecilia constantly paused for breath, but she waited, helping the woman up a couple of steps at a time. She only remembered going down one staircase and was glad the climb wouldn't have to happen again.

A shadow loomed on the curved wall ahead.

Lily stopped walking and crouched, peeking around the curve of the staircase far below eye level. She was looking up at a tall man with curly black hair and a familiar face. *Edmund.*

She stood and helped Cecilia around the corner.

Edmund's face lit up at seeing his mother. He dropped the bag he'd been carrying to embrace her, and she wrapped her arms around him, holding with more strength than Lily thought she'd ever see out of the woman. Her face looked younger as she relaxed, despite her smile making her lines more apparent.

Lily dove into the bag. It was indeed filled with her confiscated possessions. She strapped her daggers into their usual positions and slung the quiver over her shoulder. She was a few arrows short, but not significantly so. As she fastened the cloak over her shoulders, it was like a wrap of security. Like she had her armor back. Like he'd given her a piece of herself back.

"We need to go." She hated to break up the reunion, but she knew they didn't have much time.

Edmund took his mother's arm, freeing Lily to proceed a few yards ahead. "Left," he whispered.

She nodded, glancing around the corner before progressing.

The hall narrowed, and Lily recognized from the map that they were within the curtain wall that surrounded the main keep. Above them was a wooden platform that would allow guards to patrol the wall. She walked with a knife ready in each hand instead of her bow. It would be useless in the winding passageways. And with limited arrows, she'd need them all if they reached the outer gates.

The passage ahead of them ended in an abrupt wall of stone, with a ladder leading to a trapdoor above their heads. The wall of a watchtower.

To their right was a small door, an easy barricade if needed, offering access to the wall. This section of the curtain wall would be isolated within itself, blocked off by the watchtowers on either end. It was standard castle design, so if one section of the wall was infiltrated, the rest would still be held.

There was no way they could get closer to the gate without going into the bailey—the open space between a castle's walls and the keep—where, if they were spotted, they would be surrounded by guards and trapped by the walls.

Or they could go up. Take this section of the wall and fight their way out. Castles were meant to keep people out, not in.

Lily took one look at Cecilia's labored walk and knew she would never make it up the ladder.

"Hug the wall," Lily instructed. "Heads down."

She let the mother and son catch up and gave Cecilia a moment to breathe. Then she opened the door to the courtyard.

The rickety clanks of the gate being raised reached her ears and brought a smile to her face. Right on time.

Holding the door open for Edmund and Cecilia, the pair hobbled through, and Lily eased the door shut behind them and emerged into the light. It was hard to not savor the sight of the sky, but a glimpse of crossbowmen atop the walls was sufficient motivation to keep moving.

They made their way toward the gate, hoping that whoever was coming in was enough distraction to get them out. Lily could always shoot back at the walls once they were outside, giving them time to get to the cover of the city if needed.

Clinging to the shadows of the stone walls, they pushed on. Lily wished they could move faster, but they were limited by Cecilia. Her eyes darted around, catching the movements of the guards as she continued to face forward. There were people in the courtyard.

It seemed the castle was as booming as the city, just with a distinct separation between them.

Her worst fear was that someone would recognize them, so they wore their hoods up. It was a cool enough day. Nobody would question it. And a few of the people crossing the courtyard wore their own hoods.

Edmund, unfortunately, didn't have a hood. He did wear a sword on his hip. At least if they got into danger, he might be able to help. Even an untrained man with a pointy sword was better than no pointy sword.

The clanking stopped as the gate fully opened, and Lily saw an ornate carriage begin to make its way through. Lily ushered Cecilia and Edmund in front of her, trying to get them to the gate before it began to close. Desperate to—

Shouting cut through the air.

A crossbow bolt tore across her field of vision, inches in front of her.

She loosed an arrow back as she ducked. Making an effort to move erratically, she darted away from the gate, shooting up at a guard that was leveling his crossbow in her direction.

The guards around the carriage drew swords, moving toward Lily. A man in intricate armor stepped out of the carriage, shouting orders as he drew his own blade.

All around her, the crowd parted, replaced by an armored wall of guards. She turned in the hopes of catching a glance of Edmund and Cecilia, but they were nowhere in the sea of faces watching her. Her hope shifted to the idea of them having slipped away in the chaos.

She loosed two shots at the nearest guards before the awful clank of the gate closing reached her with finality. There would be no escape for her.

She whirled with her bow drawn. The deadly arrow dared anyone to approach.

"Pathetic."

She trained her aim on a broad man in ornate armor who had spoken.

He stood with his head cocked to the side as if evaluating her. It made her stomach crawl.

She pushed her shoulders back to stand up straighter.

The man only laughed, turning to one of the guards around him and saying what must have been a joke in Casseterran. She had a feeling it wasn't flattering.

The man stepped forward, sword drawn.

Her bow remained trained on him.

He jerked his sword upwards, saying something.

Lily frowned as she tried to interpret the words. "I'll shoot," she warned, taking a step back.

The man bristled, repeating the same phrase in Casseterran. Something like, *challenge*? At her obvious lack of understanding, he jerked the sword again in annoyance. He said something else. *Fight*? Was he challenging her to a *fight*?

She slowly let the tension out of the bow, taking the chance to glance around her. None of the guards seemed to be advancing—or even looked concerned. Instead, they had formed a ring and were watching with mild interest.

The man in front of her nodded as she set down the bow and took out a knife. Then he barked a word in Casseterran and charged at her.

At first, she stumbled back, not wanting to risk getting tripped up in her bow. The man chuckled as this made him swing short.

She took the chance to ram her shoulder forward, catching the man off guard.

He grunted but had enough weight on her that he didn't budge. His reaction was to grab the back of her shirt with his free hand in an attempt to pull her away.

She locked his sword arm under her own. The cross guard dug into her back, but it forced him to choose. Let go of her, or the sword.

He dropped his sword and grabbed at Lily's neck and arm.

She was held at arm's length. Her wrist caught in his iron grip. Fumbling with her left hand, she grabbed the knife strapped to her thigh.

The man was talking to someone behind her in a boastful tone. Careless enough that he didn't notice the knife Lily drew until she shoved it through his chin. Ego so overflowing that a smirk still graced his putrid lips when the blade met his tongue.

His hand fell away before Lily missed a breath. Then the man's knees began to collapse as he fell.

She turned to the next attacker, but nobody approached.

Three men stood, watching her, swords out, but they didn't advance. They ignored the blood on her knife and the fire in her eyes. No crossbow bolts found their way into her exposed back. Everything, except the dying man, was still.

He let out a choking sound as he collapsed completely. Slumped on the ground, his yellow doublet soaked in blood. His sword was decorated with a gaudy lion on the hilt, now completely discarded in the dirt. His face held a dying surprise. It was angry, wrinkles above his brow looking like they had been branded in by constant scowls. One of the guards took a slow step forward, and Lily darted a step back, still in a ready stance.

He set his hand in front of the dead man's nose as if feeling for breath. Then he stood, turning to the courtyard. "Dead," he announced in Casseterran.

The three men murmured to each other.

Lily dared a glance back and finally spotted Edmund, just in time to watch him drop to a knee.

As she turned toward the three men, they were doing the same. The movement swept over the courtyard. People who had darted aside during the fight bowed their heads, resting on one knee.

"Congratulations, baroness." The man who had checked the dead body was the one to speak.

Lily looked at Edmund, who gave a pointed glance at the body on the ground. "Right of Conquest." There were tears in his eyes, and he shook without restraint.

Baroness?

Her eyes darted to the figure next to him. Cecilia was lying on her back, the fletching of a bolt sticking out of her chest. She darted over, dropping her knife as she knelt beside Cecilia.

Still breathing, staring up at the sky as her chest shook.

Lily turned to a guard. "Get her some help."

That broke the stillness.

The courtyard sprung to life.

Edmund was right back to his mother's side, ignoring everyone as he leaned over her, clutching her hand. Lily looked at the wound. The bolt wasn't centered, not into her heart. But that didn't mean it hadn't hit something important.

Edmund reached for the bolt.

Lily moved his hand away. "It's safer to leave it in," she explained.

A man came, kneeling beside them, and Lily retreated slightly so he had more room to work.

"Do you know any medicine?" he asked in Casseterran.

"A little," Lily replied nervously.

"Pressure here." He pointed at an area next to the bolt.

She put pressure on it, watching as he dug in his bag.

"Will she live?" Edmund asked, his voice choked with tears.

"Too soon to tell." He laid a cloth on the ground, organizing a few tools. Among them was a sharp surgeon's knife.

"Here?" Lily asked, surprised.

"We can not move her. How are you with blood?"

"Fine," Lily replied at the same time Edmund said, "Awful."

"You might want to step away." The doctor leveled his gaze at Edmund.

"I will not leave her." His grip tightened on his mother's hand, and he leaned forward, brushing a hair out of her face. Lily could have sworn the woman smiled, though she doubted she had much coherent thought.

"Keep applying pressure," the doctor instructed Lily as he grabbed the shaft of the crossbow bolt.

Lily pressed a little harder, knowing what was about to happen. The doctor yanked the bolt out as she expected, and blood gushed after it. He told her a new place to put her hand, and she pressed down. It helped a little, but Lily didn't blame Edmund for turning his face away.

The next few minutes were a blur as the doctor tried to stop the bleeding.

Sheets of linen were soaked trying to absorb it just so he could see what he was doing. Eventually, he stitched the wound up and told Lily she could let go.

Lily sat back, hands coated in blood. Someone brought over bowls of water, and she gladly took the opportunity to wash herself off.

Edmund grabbed a cloth and began cleaning as much blood off his mother as possible. "Now?"

The doctor shook his head. "We have to wait and see. I am sorry, Edmund."

"Keep her out here," Edmund said. "She wants to see the sky."

"Can we get some cushions and blankets?" Lily asked.

Soon, people were working around Cecilia to make sure she was comfortable. They propped her head on pillows and draped a blanket over her. Someone brought Edmund a tray of food: crackers, cheese, and some dried meats. He set it between him and Lily, barely taking his eyes off his mother but inviting Lily to share.

The sun began to set, and it grew cold, an icy veil of darkness unfurling across the courtyard. Lily was less focused than Edmund and watched as people gathered around, laying out old blankets and lighting candles as the sun disappeared.

They paid her no attention.

The candles set the space aglow as sad faces sat vigil. Every hour, the doctor would get up from where he sat with a small family to check on Cecilia. Every hour, Lily pretended not to notice the immense sadness in his eyes.

It was near midnight when Cecilia shuddered.

Then her chest stopped moving.

Edmund froze, and Lily leaned forward, sparing him the pain, and put her hand by Cecilia's nose. She felt no breath, just fearful gazes as she closed Cecilia's eyes.

Edmund broke out in sobs, clutching his mother to his chest as if she were a child. He rocked back and forth, crying into her shoulder. It was devastating, so Lily did the only thing she could think of to soothe him and rubbed his back gently.

His sobs were the only sound piercing through the courtyard. Wails of despair. Of time having run out.

Nobody moved from where they sat for a long time, not until the sobs had become a gentle cry.

Then there was singing.

Lily couldn't tell who started it. It was a woman's voice, a few rows back amongst the crowd. She started slowly, her voice high and lilting. Then a man joined in from the other side of the courtyard. He sang the same words, his lower voice filling it out. Slowly, more and more voices joined in.

Lily didn't have the mental space to translate, but the melody rose and fell. It had hard sounds in the right places and soft sounds guiding the notes into each other. It sounded *ancient*, and she could envision the ghosts of the past dancing to it sometime long ago. It rose to the heavens. So many voices Lily could've sworn the city had joined in.

Slowly, Edmund laid his mother down. He held her hand still as he looked up, his voice joining in the chorus. Lily realized the song was repeating.

Eventually, people broke off. Started singing differently. Some sang the first verse while others were on the second, creating a haunting round that echoed off the castle walls.

Lily felt a grip on her hand and looked down to see Edmund had grabbed it. It offered her the final drop of courage she needed, and she joined her voice into the song, able to follow the sounds at least loosely. Singing was never her gift, but that didn't matter. With everyone's voices together, every piece seemed to fit exactly where it needed to be.

The courtyard was a strange mosaic of families and friends in all different types of clothing, lying on the ground or on one another's chests.

Lily and Edmund were awake long after the rest of the castle had fallen asleep on their blankets, though.

He wiped his eyes, still staring down at the still form of his mother. "Can she be buried in the castle's graveyard?" Edmund asked.

"I'm not the one to ask," Lily responded quietly.

Edmund looked up at her, his eyes rimmed with red from crying. "Yes, you are. It's yours now."

"Who did I fight?" Lily narrowed her eyes.

"Baron D'Lavaud."

Lily glanced over to see his body had been removed. She wondered how much of the singing was for him, and how much was for Cecilia.

"It's Right of Conquest. He challenged you, and you won."

Which made everything he owned hers. If she could keep it. If she even wanted it. She should find Kyraa and Tori and get as far away from this place as possible. But Edmund was still watching her, waiting for her to decide the fate of his mother.

"Of course she can."

Edmund dropped his mother's hand, turning and embracing Lily. He clung to her like his life depended on it. And perhaps it did. She wrapped her arms around him, gently rubbing his back as he held on.

He was still leaning into her when the sun rose and people began to stir. A man came up and wrapped the body in a sheet while someone else brought a cart over. They lifted Cecilia gently into it, and Edmund allowed them to take her away.

Lily stood and brushed the dirt off her pants, then helped Edmund up. "Let's get you some sleep."

"Right." He began walking, then turned for Lily. "Come with? I don't want to be alone."

Lily nodded. She followed him as he made his way to a small room on the third floor.

Every movement seemed like his brain was elsewhere. Eyes vacant and steps unsure. He hesitated as he went toward a chest, then he shrugged, pulled off his shoes, and crawled into a small bed.

On seeing him pat the space beside him, Lily sat down, her legs hanging over the edge.

Edmund turned so he faced the wall. Away from her. He fell asleep quickly, as was to be expected from the long and emotional night he'd just survived.

Lily herself hadn't had a good night's sleep in months. She was *exhausted*. A castle, especially a room as warm as his, was probably the safest she'd felt since her Hawk cabin. And surely, she would wake before Edmund...

No, she couldn't possibly sleep.

Still, she felt her eyes growing heavy as she fought to stay awake.

CHAPTER 13

MOURNING

Lily bolted awake as she felt Edmund stirring. Their backs had been pressed together in an attempt to fit on the small bed, and Lily's feet were still hanging off the side. Her indecision on falling asleep with him was clear because she also remained on top of the covers.

She and Edmund sat up at the same time. There was no way to pretend she hadn't been asleep.

"I'm sorry," Lily said, not realizing Edmund likely didn't understand her trade language. She hurried to stand up, making her way toward the door. "I didn't mean to. I'll go." She glanced back to see Edmund watching her with an amused smile.

"Thank you," he said in Casseterran.

Lily's hand was on the doorknob before she stopped. "I do not know where to go."

She must have said it in Casseterran, because Edmund stood up and said, "I'll show you."

Peeking out a window as she followed him down a series of halls—and judging by the sunlight pouring in—it was mid-afternoon. She hadn't just slept a little, it seemed.

Edmund guided her up a flight of stairs, hastily running his fingers through his messy hair.

There were guards outside the room they stopped at, but with one glance at the odd pair, they stepped aside. Edmund opened the door and let them into a small room with a door on the opposite side. "This is my office," Edmund said.

Lily hadn't quite recognized the word for office, but given the room was bare except for a bench, a desk, and a chair, that had to be what he meant.

"Your office?" she asked.

"I was his personal secretary," Edmund admitted. "I guess this is whoever's office you want it to be now."

He opened the next door, leading Lily into a large, lavishly furnished suite of rooms. The walls were painted with a repeating pattern of gold roses and thorns on a blue backdrop. Plush red furniture populated the room. Alabaster statues stood in alcoves, and the walls were buried by paintings and tapestries. Everywhere she looked, excess cascaded. The floor was even blanketed in elaborate carpets that probably cost more than most people made in a decade. To her left was a door, likely leading into a smaller bed chamber.

"This is your room, unless you want to change. It is the nicest in the castle."

"It's a dead man's room."

"It is a castle," Edmund countered. "All the rooms are."

"But does he not have heirs? Does nobody care?"

In most countries, the first-born male heir inherited a position on the death of the parent. Sometimes women were involved in the hierarchy. Other times, it passed to their husbands or sons. That was how it worked—unless a ruler stripped a lesser noble of their title. Unless a war was waged or a battle won.

She had escaped prison and killed someone. Had stolen a castle. Being rewarded for it felt *wrong*.

Edmund looked down, running his hands through his hair. Probably trying to find words Lily would understand. "He had no family. People will care now. But only because they will want Avisier." He looked back up, making eye contact with Lily. "Do not let them take it." Despite speaking in an unfamiliar language, his voice held weight.

Lily turned to Edmund, confusion obvious on her face. "I have no idea what I'm doing," she confessed. "I know you're going through a lot, but..."

"Of course I will help." His gaze softened as he looked at her.

Lily turned back to the room and looked around before sweeping a bunch of pillows off the couch. She sat down, inviting Edmund beside her. "What happens next?"

He settled his arm casually across the back of the couch as he joined her. "That is your choice. Dinner? Ryia is probably cooking something good to try to impress you."

"What happens at dinner?"

"You might give a speech," Edmund suggested. Lily shook her head emphatically, so Edmund redirected, "Seating is usually based on hierarchy."

Lily knew that was common in castles. The tables would likely be arranged in such a way it would be difficult to ignore. "And who comes to this dinner?"

"With you, whoever you invite. There is a private room for you and a hall for everyone else."

Lily frowned at that. Albrin, at least, tended to have everyone eating together. "I'll eat with everyone."

Edmund began to teach her about life in the castle. Who did what, where things went. Between the language and the sheer volume, Lily couldn't track it all. She did her best to smile and nod along, catching what she could. Her face must not have hidden it well, though, because Edmund paused and gave an apologetic look.

"Please stay as my secretary," she asked when he paused. "I mean, you don't have to if you don't want to, but ... I need help. Please."

Edmund tilted his head. "I'll stay."

Lily realized she was still wearing the clothes she'd been arrested in. Yet looking around the room revealed only men's clothes that would be far too large for her. "How do I find something clean to change into?" she asked.

"I will find you something," Edmund said, standing up.

"Thank you."

Edmund asked around the castle until he found Lily a dress that would fit. Lily normally avoided dresses, but she was dying to get out of the clothes she'd been wearing for the last month. They'd formed a smelly shell around her.

So, she donned the orange and gold dress that almost swallowed her. Mentally, she thanked Jarek for forcing her to go on missions that required more elaborate dresses. At least now she didn't need to ask for help to get the gown on. She strapped knives under the bodice and the skirt, unwilling to be completely unarmed. Her bow would look too confrontational, so she left that in the room. For now.

Edmund waited respectfully in the chamber that served as her living room. He had also changed into something less wrinkled and dirty—a nice blue doublet that made his eye sparkle. Or maybe that was the lingering tears.

He smiled at her, holding the door open, and she thanked him as he offered her his arm and escorted her down to the main hall. His eyes looked weary. His body still moved as if part of his mind had permanently retreated to another place. And it *had*.

"There is a head table." Edmund leaned in so only she could hear. "Go to the center seat. Head Steward Simeon Stowell will be on your right. Captain of the Guard, Tristan Basinger, on your left."

"Where will you be?" Lily asked.

"Beside Tristan."

She breathed a sigh of relief that he would be close.

"They will all stand when we enter," Edmund warned. "And they will not sit until you do."

That was all he had time for before they were at the doors. Lily forced a mask of control over her face. That was something she *could* do. Had been *trained* to do.

The hall was crowded already, though not every seat was taken. The vaulted ceiling let in the evening light through windows cut into the walls. People bustled around long tables, catching up with each other. Lily was glad her grasp on the language wasn't terrific, or she was sure she'd overhear them discussing her.

Someone noticed her out of the corner of their eye, and the whole room stood as news of her arrival spread.

There were four wooden banquet tables, one horizontal across the hall from her and the other three at right angles to it. The three tables had piles of food in large bowls and on serving platters for people to take from. Ham and potatoes wafted to her, luring her in with their tantalizing scents.

As she grew closer, she realized the head table already had food on individual plates.

Lily was forced to make her way around the room. The layout ensured she provided those in attendance with a walk that bordered on being a spectacle.

Vaulted ceilings towered above her, echoing every footstep back.

Edmund fell into pace behind her, instead of walking next to her like he had in the halls. Lily realized this was probably her formal introduction.

She thought back to her friendship with Princess Adelaide. Over the years, she'd attended many formal events with her. She imitated the woman as best she could, pushing her shoulders back and holding her chin up. Despite every instinct saying to look around, her eyes stayed locked ahead.

The center seat was easily found. Only two seats at the head table remained open. She merely chose the centermost and sat quickly, wanting the ordeal of everyone staring at her to be done.

When the eyes didn't leave her, she snatched up her fork, taking an awkward bite of a pork chop as everyone sat down.

One of the men beside her didn't turn away. He simply said, "My lady, my name is Simeon Stowell. I was Head Steward under D'Lavaud." The introduction sounded practiced as if he'd been through many changes of leadership.

"Lily," she said. "If you would like to continue as Head Steward, I would be happy to have you." She was suddenly very happy Kyraa had insisted she learn the formal version of you, despite Lily's protests that it was useless.

The man smiled, revealing age lines that nearly disappeared when his face was neutral. "It would be my pleasure."

Lily turned to the man on her other side. "Tristan Basinger, Captain of the Guard?"

He was less practiced than Simeon had been, but Lily could see the hope on his face.

"If you'd like to stay," she said with indifference, "I have no intention of displacing people."

"My lady, your accent. Where is it from?" he asked.

Lily laughed. Of course she spoke with an accent. She was surprised that was the man's second question. "Albrin. I grew up there."

"What part?" Simeon asked. "I spent some time there."

Lily frowned. Anything too specific getting out would alert Randson to her. "I'd rather not talk about it."

Just like that, the subject was dropped. That was a perk of being in charge.

Lily hurried through the meal, keeping to small talk. People flowed through the room, some leaving early, others joining late. There were a few angry glances her way, but that was to be expected. Lily excused herself as soon as she was full—and it was socially acceptable.

At least she seemed to get on with the people running the castle. Still, with the Casseterran, the dress, the sudden pressure that came with her title, she wanted it to be over as quickly as possible.

Her room was easy enough to find, and a guard opened the first door for her as he saw her approaching. Lily noticed a bandage wrapped against his arm, a tinge of pink showing through. She recognized the wound; it was where she'd shot a crossbowman the night prior, intending to make him drop his weapon.

"Was that me?" she asked.

The man nodded once, eyes darting to the floor as his head offered a slight bow.

"I'm sorry," Lily said, then quickly disappeared into her room to avoid more conversation.

✦

Lily woke up as the sun beamed through the windows. She had a brief moment of panic at the unfamiliar location, but upon seeing no immediate threat was able to calm herself.

With the plush pillows and heavy comforter, she was lulled back to sleep for the first time in a long while.

She woke again an hour later, forcing herself off the thick mattress. The cold wood bit into her feet and she jerked them back up, searching for the carpet. Most of the floor was covered in a patchwork of expensive rugs. Lily's distaste for the ostentatiousness turned to gratefulness as the gaudy carpeting protected her bare feet from the cold bite of the floor. Clothes had been brought for her the night prior, but she hadn't bothered moving them from the coffee table in the main room. She hadn't even bothered looking at them.

Today would be a new day.

Now awake after a restful night of sleep, she picked up a pile, carried them back to her bedroom, and plopped them on the comforter. She saw among it her one set of spare clothes that had been taken. They reeked with the sourness of sweat left unwashed too long. Asking about the laundry procedure later would have to be a priority.

She hung the dresses she'd been given in the wardrobe, shoving the too-big tunics and pants aside. Soon the castle would realize she preferred tunics and pants, but for today she could deal with a dress. Having something clean was all that mattered for now and selected black, ready for Cecilia's funeral later that morning.

The dress fit her well enough. She supposed it helped that the corset allowed the bodice to adjust quite a bit. It was long for her, but that was nothing she couldn't handle.

Back in her living room sat the bag Edmund had brought her. She dug through it, pulling out a needle and thread. After roughly hemming the dress, she made her way out into the antechamber that doubled as Edmund's office.

A slip of paper was sitting on what had previously been a clear desk.

Lily picked it up to read but found it impossible. Some of the words looked like Casseterran, but they had far too many letters. The signature said Edmund. That, at least, she could tell.

She sighed, leaving the room to find the two guards outside her room. "What does this say?" she asked in Casseterran, handing one the paper.

He bowed slightly as he received it, then began reading, "Funeral is this morning. Arranged a meeting with Simeon this afternoon."

Lily thanked the man, then made her way down to where they'd eaten the night prior.

Breakfast was like Albrin. Informal. With food laid out on tables for people to take as they pleased. The mild familiarity of customs soothed her somewhat. But Lily didn't bother sitting. She slathered a piece of toast with jam and ate it as she walked the hallways.

The castle was busy, and she received more than a few confused glances. She tried to return them with smiles, but people averted their gaze as soon as Lily showed any sign of looking their way. The blatant dismissal stung, but she was used to being alone. As a Hawk, she'd often run into those who were afraid or intimidated. This would be no different, right?

Trailing her fingers along the lime wash walls, Lily wandered the maze of monotonous corridors, attempting to map the sprawling castle layout mentally. Given the luxury of her bedchamber, the rest of the castle was far more austere. The lower ceilings reflected any sound, making her soft footfalls seem deafening, while the endless passageways were almost stripped bare. Not a torch sconce or ornate tapestry in sight to lend warmth.

Eventually, she started to see more people in black. She followed the mourners to the graveyard, where a crowd gathered around the empty grave. The headstone had already been placed, though the name hadn't been carved into it yet.

Lily joined the crowd at the back, now thankful to be ignored.

It was an overcast day, as if the world was mourning along with them. Lily wished she could wrap up in her cloak to stave off the cold, but she'd left it inside. Around her, women pulled shawls tight around their shoulders, and men buttoned their coats to their chins.

A musician started strumming his lute as a few more people trickled in behind her. It was a sad melody. The notes hung in the air as if suspended by the mourning around them. Down the hill, a casket appeared. It was carried by a few people Lily had seen around the castle, though she couldn't say for certain who they were. They weren't dressed in the finest clothes, but they were wearing all black.

The coffin was simple. No ornate decorations. The light wood was oiled, at least. Edmund followed behind in a black doublet, his head bowed so she could barely see his face beneath his hat.

A man from the group stepped forward, and the funeral began.

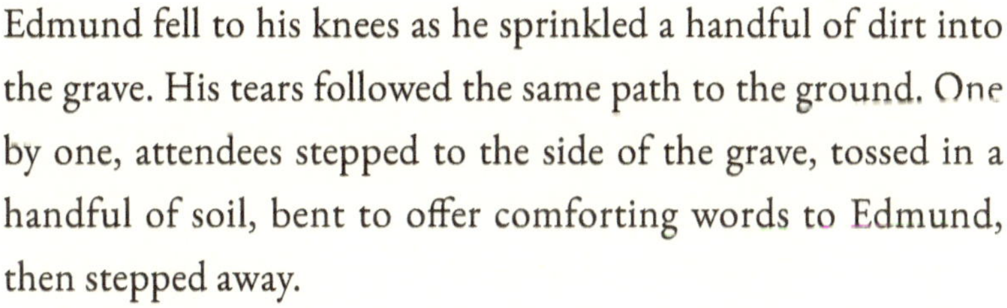

Edmund fell to his knees as he sprinkled a handful of dirt into the grave. His tears followed the same path to the ground. One by one, attendees stepped to the side of the grave, tossed in a handful of soil, bent to offer comforting words to Edmund, then stepped away.

Lily made her way under a tree, watching as the crowd dissipated.

Slightly further up the hill, surrounded by a cluster of old headstones, was a second fresh grave. The dirt was still brown as if even the grass didn't care for the person beneath. Its smooth, blank headstone stuck out like a sore thumb amongst a field of crumbling markers.

Lily hadn't been aware of a funeral, but she knew whose grave it was.

She watched the last attendee hug Edmund, then walk back down the slope to the castle proper.

Edmund remained kneeling beside the grave, and Lily stepped up beside him, scraping a handful of soil from what remained of the pile and sprinkling it in. She knelt beside Edmund with a sigh as her skirt billowed around her ankles.

His cheeks shined with tears.

"I am sorry," he said, dashing a hand across his face, though it didn't do much. "I will get cleaned up and—"

Lily laid a hand on his arm to get him to stop talking. "Take some time off. I'll be okay."

"I knew it would happen soon," Edmund said.

Lily pressed her lips together as she tried to find the right words. "Losing someone always hurts." She wanted to offer him more comfort, offer him what he needed. But it struck her then that she barely knew him. Barely knew anyone, or what she could offer. So, she offered him companionship and sat with him in silence.

He could decide to talk if he wanted.

After a few minutes, he shifted, his shoulder brushing hers. She hesitated for a second, then wrapped an arm around his shoulders, holding him. He tucked his head into her shoulder, and Lily could feel fresh tears flowing once again.

Soon after, he pulled away, looking down at the soil. "I am sorry," he repeated.

"Don't be. Don't ever be. Not for this." Lily stood, placing a hand on Edmund's arm as she said, "Take as much time as you need."

CHAPTER 14

A NEW BOSS

Lily kept to her room, unsure of the daily workings of the castle. Even more unsure of her place within them.

As the afternoon approached, she heard conversation in the antechamber—Edmund's office—and opened the door from the inside, laughing to herself at the startled looks of Simeon and a guard, who were looking at the door like they'd been discussing which of them would knock.

Lily smiled, inviting Simeon into her room in Casseterran.

"Baroness." He bowed awkwardly as he shuffled past her.

She nodded to the guard with a smile before letting the door swing closed. Simeon stood just inside the door, looking as out of place as she felt.

Lily cleared the pillows off a chair, then reclined in it. She gestured Simeon toward the couch.

He moved stiffly, uncertain of himself. He, too, wore black, a simple doublet, and breeches with gray detailing. Eventually, he set a pillow aside and perched on the edge of the couch. Based on the complete lack of mourning for the previous master of the castle, he had likely seen tempers flare beyond control. Maybe he'd been the victim once. Or maybe he'd seen her kill D'Lavaud without a second thought. It was hard to pin down where his nerves sprouted from exactly.

"My lady, if I may, where is Edmund?" Simeon asked after a strained moment of silence.

"He is—" Lily paused, racking her brain. She shook her head in frustration. "I do not know the word."

"If I may, my lady?"

Lily nodded for him to proceed, unsure what his hesitance was.

"Mourning?" he suggested in the trade language.

A wave of relief washed over Lily. She barely knew the Casseterran needed to get by. Her relief must have been obvious, as Simeon smiled cautiously.

"Yes!" She added in the trade language, "Mourning. You speak the trade language?"

"Yes, my lady," he said in Casseterran.

"Do you speak it well?" Lily asked, continuing the trade language. Just hearing words in her native tongue was relieving. Albrin had been conquered by a variety of trading groups and thus had developed the pidgin language that was used to facilitate global trade. For the Albrini, it was their native tongue. The energy it took to translate every sentence was draining at best, exhausting at worst. She'd hate for the conversation to have to continue in Casseterran.

Simeon hesitated again. "Yes. I learned it as a child." He was still speaking in Casseterran, and Lily shook her head.

"If you could, I'm much more comfortable if we proceed in the trade language," Lily said. She found herself to be just as hesitant as Simeon, measuring her words.

"Of course." Simeon bowed his head slightly as he responded in the trade language.

Audible relief accompanied her sigh. "What's next?" Lily asked.

"My lady?"

Lily shrugged. "I am guessing you have more experience with"—she gestured vaguely around her—"*this* than I do. What needs to happen?"

"A formal declaration must be sent to the king," Simeon ventured. "Edmund is probably better to help you with that, my lady."

"Declaration?"

"That you claim your title."

Lily frowned, which prompted Simeon to mimic her.

"As Baroness of Avisier," he continued. "D'Lavaud challenged you, and you killed him."

There it was, out in the open. Not only had she killed the man, but she also now had a claim to everything he'd owned. The lives of everyone in the castle were in her hands. If she left, who would her replacement be?

She thought back to Edmund telling her not to let anyone take it. She thought back to the vigil and the funeral. This castle was a community, and they seemed to care for even the lowest of their members. They deserved someone who cared for them. Could she be that person?

Lily nodded, making a mental note.

Simeon pulled out a parchment, his eyes scanning the scribbles. "The first thing I'm concerned with, my lady, is the employment in the castle."

Lily shrugged. She didn't particularly care who worked in the castle and certainly had no desire to cause more suffering than she already had. "Everyone can keep their jobs."

Simeon's shoulders relaxed a moment before he pulled himself back together and cleared his throat. "Thank you, my lady."

Lily smiled. "I'm not in the business of displacing entire castles of people, Simeon."

"Yes, well." He smiled back. "You seem to be the exception there, my lady."

Lily clenched her teeth at the constant repetition of the honorific. She'd have to do away with that later. She forced her voice even as she asked, "What else?"

"There's the gate. Your predecessor insisted it stay closed as much as possible. But, well, my lady, a lot of us have found that makes life more difficult than necessary. We have family in the city—"

"Open it," Lily dismissed the issue casually. While she was there, at least she could do some good.

"My lady, there are security issues."

Lily shrugged. "Plenty of castles around the world keep their gates open from dawn till dusk. There's no reason we should be any different. Simply increase the guard presence."

Simeon nodded.

"I have friends in the city. Tori and Kyraa, they were staying at 'The Black Ladle.' Would you send someone to check on them?"

"Of course, my lady."

They discussed trivial matters for the remainder of an hour. As Head Steward, Simeon was in charge of the day-to-day business of the castle. He distributed payment, decided what needed to be done, and knew all the employees. He seemed to relax through the conversation, though he never entirely dropped his formal air or the titles in every sentence. Lily supposed she would have to get used to it.

Eventually, it seemed all pressing matters were settled.

Lily stood, and Simeon hurried to do the same. "I don't stand by all the little formalities, Simeon." She tried to keep her tone light and easy.

"With all due respect, my lady, I don't think it's a safe habit to break."

Lily nodded, escorting him toward the door. He showed himself out. His movements were less stiff now, his strides less measured and stilted.

Lily sighed at the sight of the empty desk. She supposed she would be going to dinner on her own.

Back in what she was slowly beginning to think of as her room, there was a single long mirror. Looking now, she was far from the beautiful, perfect ladies who populated courts around the world. She'd never minded before. Her small stature meant less to hide. Not wearing makeup saved her time. And she had never particularly cared about her hair beyond a level Jarek deemed acceptable grooming.

In this castle, though, she just looked out of place. The biggest problem was the lack of a hairbrush anywhere in the chambers. That morning, she'd carefully picked as many knots apart as possible using her fingers. It was a temporary solution. She supposed when she met her maids the next day, they would help her solve the problem.

She undid her braid, then put it back in tighter. It was one of the few hairstyles she could manage with her hair in its current poofy state. Smoothing water over the remaining frizz in an attempt to weigh it down helped somewhat, so she moved on to the clothing.

The dress was far from a perfect fit, its waistline sitting awkwardly below her own. She was certain her rushed hem job wasn't even, but there was no use in fussing over it. In time, she could get a better-fitting wardrobe. If she accepted her title, the wardrobe options would be almost limitless.

Eventually, she admitted to herself she had done everything in her power to look more presentable, more like a *lady*. It'd have to do.

She moved over to the window, where the light told her it was nearly time to eat and the smell of food wafted up, causing her stomach to growl. Skipping lunch hadn't been a good idea. After nearly a month of only one meal, she was surprised at how quickly her body had started to crave more.

The hallways were busy, but people gave her a wide berth. The dining hall was nearly empty when she entered, but the few that were present stood.

Castle residents continued to stream in around her as she found the seat she'd inhabited the previous night. Food was laid out soon after by servants that disappeared just as quiet as they had come. Simeon was nowhere to be seen. Lily supposed he was carrying out what they'd discussed. It was a significant number of changes to implement, and it would take a long while for the castle to adapt fully. Edmund was missing too, of course, but she knew of his absence and didn't begrudge him the time.

Tristan Basinger, as he was introduced, sat beside her. They carried on light conversation, setting a time to meet the next afternoon to discuss guard rotations and training procedures.

Simeon appeared later into the meal, apologizing for his tardiness. Lily found it hard to truly believe he was late, as people streamed in and out of the other tables throughout the entire meal.

There was no seating chart, but people tended to cluster with those like them. Knights and men at arms sat at the center table. They were boisterous and loud, and it seemed the least phased by the change in leadership. It made sense then that maids and manservants were the group at the right table. They all seemed to be similarly dressed, though there was no strict uniform. That left the leftmost table for the rest of the castle. Stable hands mingled with cooks, and the odd child refused to stay in their seat.

Over time, Lily would learn most of their names. At present, it was all she could do to keep up with the conversation.

"They were not there when I asked after them," Simeon explained when Lily asked about Tori and Kyraa.

The spike of disappointment that assaulted her couldn't be helped. She would have told them to move on for their own safety, but part of her still hoped they'd have tried to rescue her. She would have rescued her friends if the situation were reversed.

They wouldn't have been able to help her, and she needed to let her grand ideas of them riding to save her go. So, she dismissed herself as the meal wound down, disappointed Edmund had not shown up. She walked out to the battlements, glancing at the spot where the grave was. Edmund was nowhere to be seen.

Her nose led her to the cookhouse. It was a separate building from the central keep, intentionally far enough away to keep a potential fire from spreading. It seemed people were still bustling about inside, though she trusted they were not suffering from a shortage of food in their stomachs. She'd worked in a kitchen long enough to know snacking was a perk of the job.

Barely anyone noticed when she entered—something to be grateful for—and a wave of heat from the oven washed over her. A rack was draped with cloaks, and the bare arms of the cooks revealed that the heat would become uncomfortable if she lingered too long.

Lily found a young woman and asked her for a basket with food from the meal. The woman scampered off as if trying to get her out of the cookhouse as soon as possible. Hands that weren't working weren't welcome in a busy kitchen.

Lily left the crowded building only a minute later, a basket covered with a damp cloth hanging from her arm, then made her way to Edmund's room and lightly cursed the lack of decoration that made her hesitate at the hall of nearly identical doors.

She made her best guess, trusting her gut as she knocked on the door. There was a shuffling, and a flutter in her stomach she hadn't felt since she'd been an apprentice.

A series of footsteps later, the door creaked open a few inches, revealing Edmund's tired face. When he registered that it was Lily, he opened it a little further, leaning against the doorframe. His entire body sagged, a stark contrast to Simeon's rigid formality.

"You were not at dinner," Lily said in Casseterran. "So I brought you something to eat." She held the basket out.

Edmund accepted it, having to open the door further to bring it into his room. He left the door at its new location, setting the basket on his small table. Lily had fully expected him to close it after, but instead, he asked, "Why?"

She shrugged, hands loose at her sides, as Edmund turned back to her. "I never had a mother. I can't imagine what losing one would feel like. And I feel partly responsible, so anything I can do to—"

"It is not your fault."

Lily was a little startled at the interruption. Edmund seemed startled with himself but didn't make any move to apologize. Normally, he had nothing near the rank necessary to interrupt Lily. It seemed that neither of them particularly cared about that technicality. To not be pandered to every moment of the day felt ... nice.

Edmund shifted from one foot to the other in the doorway. "She got to see the sky. That is what she wanted most. She would not have lived much longer. Even if we had not been spotted."

Lily shook her head but couldn't help a small smile at the ridiculous turn those events had taken. The situation it had put her in now. "I mean it, Edmund, take however long you need."

"Thank you."

They looked at each other for a quiet moment before Edmund closed the door, and Lily hurried away, her head down to keep anyone she might run into from spotting the blush on her cheeks.

CHAPTER 15

OLD FRIENDS

I t wasn't as if Lily had no experience in a castle. She had visited Adelaide plenty. It wasn't as if she had never used her rank. She had been sent undercover too many times to pretend she didn't know exactly how she was expected to act.

Lily found the courtly graces coming back to her automatically. Her muscle memory conformed easily to the duties of nobility. She knew by instinct when a slight curtsey was appropriate, so anticipated it from others now. Remembered which goblet was for wine, where the salad fork was placed, and could discuss a range of topics over dinner. Her feet even glided through the steps of traditional dances without much conscious thought. It almost alarmed her at how quickly she could slip back into refined rituals. Though the claustrophobic strings attached had not been missed.

The problem emerged when she thought about the *length*. About time. This wasn't some ruse meant to last a night or two. This wasn't an act. It was suddenly her identity. The steps she knew she had to take felt more like forced jerks that were commanded of her by the invisible marionette strings tied to her limbs.

So, when morning came, and she heard the quiet conversation in the next room, she buried her head under a pillow in an attempt to wake up in Albrin, as if this whole experience was some twisted dream. She'd been entrenched in the harsh reality of her exile for months now, hoping to wake up in Albrin more mornings than she cared to admit.

Hauling herself out from under the plush covers, a few minutes later she was in proper clothes. A simple red dress from the outfits she'd been given. This was the most grateful she'd ever been to Jarek for making her learn how to be a lady, or at least play the part. Of course, she'd been more thankful for all the skills that had saved her life.

She took her time arming herself, delaying the inevitable moment she had to confront whoever was waiting in her living room.

Then she could delay no more and opened the door to what was quickly becoming her life.

A tall woman stood ramrod straight beside the empty fireplace. When she saw Lily, she sunk into a curtsy and dipped her head.

Lily realized she had no clue how to tell her to rise and stop acting as formal as the cavalry during an inspection in Casseterran. She fumbled over her words a moment before finding her train of thought in Casseterran. "Just stand normally. There is no need for the—" She waved a hand as she couldn't find the word.

The woman hesitated a moment before straightening to a still formal standing position.

Lily waved her hand again dismissively as she moved to sit on the couch. "It is going to be a lot quicker if we drop the formalities now." She leaned forward, pulling a particularly uncomfortable throw pillow out from below the crook of her back and tossing it onto a chair.

"Yes, my lady," the woman replied, carefully forming each syllable.

"And you can call me Lily."

The woman wore a simple brown dress with an apron tied around the front. It wasn't the cheapest available option, but it certainly wasn't a material to be considered superfluous. Her coiled hair was pulled back into a professional bun.

She cleared her throat before speaking. "My lady, that's a highly unusual request. Forgive me if this is out of turn, but wouldn't it be better for us to remain as formal as possible? Is it not a safety concern?"

Lily frowned. "Who ever told you that?"

The woman's head tipped a little to the side. "Lord D'Lavaud."

"It's not a safety concern for me. If you would rather keep up the formalities when others are present, by all means, do. But when it's just us, I would feel much more comfortable if you dropped them."

The silence stretched well beyond comfortable. Lily couldn't tell if it was brought on by hesitance or uncertainty. She supposed it wasn't a request the woman got often, so she moved a couple cushions on the couch and gestured to the seats around her. "You may as well sit. There's plenty of room."

Her eyes never left Lily as she sat on the couch beside her, pressing as far away as she could. The offer had been made to make her feel comfortable, but it seemed to have had the opposite reaction from the woman.

"And your name is?"

"Amira."

Lily tilted her head at the name. It was obscure for the continent, but she could've sworn she'd heard it before. "Is that Ifryan?"

"Yes. I lived there until I was ten."

"I spent a summer there once," Lily said.

"Then I'm sorry," Amira replied. "You would have been much more suited to a winter."

Lily smiled at the gentle poke to the obvious fact she came from Albrin and was not accustomed to the intense heat of Ifryan summers. "Well, it is nice to officially meet you. What do you need from me?"

"It's more what you need from me," Amira said, emboldened now that she'd spoken before. "I'm in charge of all the housework pertaining to you."

Lily raised an eyebrow. "Well, what do you normally do?" While she had been in a castle, and a fair amount of housework had been handled by servants, she had no idea how far that service extended to higher ranks, especially in Casseterre.

"Laundry, for one thing," Amira said. "Or, we collect it. Nina and her girls take care of the actual washing, normally." She took a preparatory breath. "Chamber pots, making the bed, tidying, laying out outfits, errands in the town, warm drinks, meals in here if you would prefer, sending messages, in the colder months lighting the fire," Amira rattled off the list so quickly Lily thought it must have been rehearsed. She paused for another breath before continuing, "If you need anything, another maid or I am always just a pull away."

Lily let her confusion show. "What do you mean by that?"

Amira stood, moved over to a tapestry, and pushed it aside slightly to reveal a golden tassel. "If you pull this." She pulled it, and Lily heard the faintest ringing of a bell from beyond the wall. "Someone will be here in under a minute."

Lily stared at it, confused. The bell sounded near, but she doubted that in the middle of the night someone would get through two guards and two doors in under a minute, especially considering Lily's habit of locking everything. Maybe Amira had a key. Maybe Edmund did and had let her in.

"Where does that lead to?"

Amira moved to the other side of the tapestry, pulling it aside and revealing a small area where the lime had chipped away. She pressed on the exposed rock, and after a soft click, a crack appeared. She pulled open a door, revealing a small room. "Someone always spends the night here."

Lily could only manage a surprised, "Oh." It wasn't large, but there was a bed and a stand with water for washing up. A small slit window let natural light into the space. Still, having someone there for her every need felt *wrong*. Jarek had taught Lily to take care of herself. While she appreciated help cleaning occasionally, it felt wrong to have people catering to her day-to-day needs.

Lily looked at the room closer. It seemed a pleasant enough place to spend the night, especially if one was being paid for it. The only drawback was the possibility of being woken at any time.

Lily made a mental note to tackle the finances of the castle. She had no idea what anyone was being paid. To be there for her every need, let alone in such a small space, they would need to be paid a fair amount.

They went on discussing what the day-to-day would look like.

Lily had a feeling Amira would have one of her lightest workloads ever managed.

Eventually, a maid appeared carrying a platter piled high with an assortment of breads, meats, and cheeses.

Amira directed her to set the platter on a table, then dismissed her. The maid practically scurried out of the room. Once she'd disappeared, Amira started to tidy the space around Lily, bustling in and out of the room. When Lily offered for the woman to join her, she merely explained she'd already eaten.

Before she could finish, there was a knock at the door. Lily lazily called for them to enter, not realizing she was speaking in the trade language.

The door opened slightly, and Edmund stuck his head in. "I assume that means come in?" he asked in Casseterran.

Lily's lip twitched in a smile, switching languages. "That is exactly what it means."

There was only a brief pause as Amira looked between them, then slipped around Edmund and out of the room as he entered.

Edmund held the door until she passed and closed it behind him. "I see you met Amira."

"Yes. It seems she was expecting an entirely different person than me."

Edmund shrugged, leaning against the back of a chair. "That is her safest bet, unfortunately."

"You may as well sit down." Lily borrowed one of Jarek's old lines, "That's what it's made for." She moved over to a long settee herself, food momentarily forgotten. She'd never eaten much for breakfast, anyway.

Edmund sat, having to push aside the pile of pillows that had slumped over the cushion at Amira's departure. "I never understood D'Lavaud's obsession with these things."

Lily sighed, tossing a pillow from behind her onto the floor. "They do seem to get in the way." She looked around the wall at the various statues, paintings, and tapestries that filled the space. "There's just too many. Why keep everything in here?"

"Compensating," Edmund mumbled.

Lily bit back a laugh. "And why is the rest of the castle so barren?"

Castles in Albrin tended toward an *entirely* different style. While the royal suites were certainly more decorated than the rest of the castle, the occasional tapestry or vase dotted the hallways. Art was made to be enjoyed. It was bought to show off wealth. Tucked away in a single room, it accomplished neither of those things.

"Selfishness," Edmund responded briskly. "He never wanted anyone else to enjoy anything expensive."

"Can we get this stuff spread around the castle?" Lily asked.

He nodded. "Any particular requests?"

Lily looked around. She didn't particularly care for any of the art. While it was all indeed beautiful, her eye could never settle on one piece long enough to truly admire it. The space was overwhelming, colors and textures and patterns seeming to press in at her. "No. Just get at least half of this stuff out of here." She readjusted herself on the pillows again. "Especially these pillows."

Edmund gave an unconscious half-smile that rested more in his eyes than his lips. "Of course. Do you mind people being in here today to do that?"

"Not at all." The thought crossed Lily's mind about pay. "How do I go about the finances of this place?"

"It is all in your office."

"I have an office?"

Edmund's smile widened like a young boy looking at a new game. "Of course you have an office. I will show you if you like."

Lily stood, brushing off her skirt as if it had gathered dirt.

Edmund held the doors open before leading her down a flight of stairs to a large oak door. It swung open easily compared to what its size would suggest.

The office was an absolute mess. Papers were strewn across a desk that was longer than Lily was tall. A red leather chair sat on the far side, off-center and facing a corner. Blue floral curtains framed an expansive window leading to the inner courtyard. On either side of the room were massive shelves containing an unorganized mess of books, pamphlets, and knick-knacks. Random items were strewn across the floor. A stray shoe stuck out from under the desk, and it smelled like something was rotting.

Edmund seemed just as intimidated as he lingered outside the door.

"How?" Lily's nose wrinkled in disgust.

"He never let anyone in," Edmund said.

Lily took a step into the room, bending to pick up a note that had fallen to the floor. She took a glance at it but stood no chance of reading the Casseterran and tossed it onto the desk amongst the other papers. "This is *weird*, right?"

Edmund nodded. "It looks like he never got rid of anything. But that means the treasury summaries should be in here somewhere."

Lily backed out of the room, slowly shutting the door. "This is a job for more than one person."

"I'll find Amira. She'll know where the others are," Edmund said.

Lily nodded, and he set off down the hall.

Taking a breath of fresh air before she opened the door again, she stepped inside. Each step was made gingerly to avoid whatever was lying there as she braved the cluttered floor. The window opened, at least, and she opened it as wide as possible, desperate to get some clean air in and a breeze flowing.

A gentle knock from behind her drew Lily's attention to Amira. The woman had her arm over her nose in an attempt to block out the smell.

"Leave the door open and come on in," Lily said, stooping to pick up a pile of papers that had fallen off the edge of the desk.

Amira took a cautious step into the chaos. "What is that smell?"

"I wish I knew." Lily shuffled some of the papers on the desk into a neater, less precarious pile. "But, as you can see, I'm going to need some help."

Amira nodded, then rotated and barked something in rapid Casseterran into the hallway. She turned back to the room and began picking letters up off the ground.

Just then, two maids appeared in the door behind her, twin looks of surprised disgust on their faces.

"What happened in here?" one asked, hesitating at the doorway.

"D'Lavaud happened," Amira replied with a sneer. She looked around at the mess. "We're going to need to get this all out."

"It can go to my room," Lily said. "I want a chance to look through everything."

Amira grabbed a pile of papers off the floor. "I'll organize in the room. You two bring things up."

A maid accepted the pile of papers Amira handed her, scurrying off with a nod. The other began pulling books from the shelves, piling five in her arms before they blocked her sight.

Lily approved of their thinking in getting the heavy stuff out first and grabbed a pile of books herself. Amira followed suit, and the three of them worked their way to Lily's rooms. They set the books on an end table, and Amira immediately set to organizing.

After a few of these passes and awkward attempts to open the door without hands, a maid—quite literally—ran into Edmund as they rounded the corner to Lily's room.

They managed to catch the books before the entire pile tumbled to the floor. And Edmund took the top two and opened the doors for the three women.

"How long are you planning to live in a moving zone?" Edmund asked as Lily passed him.

Lily set down the books, then straightened with a shrug. The maids were already moving back down the stairs. "It has to go somewhere. If any of it is sensitive information, it's better here than anywhere else."

Edmund grabbed a stack of books Amira hadn't quite reached yet and used it to prop open the doors. He followed Lily back down the stairs, nodding to the maids as they passed with more stacks of books.

"You know you do not have to do this yourself? They can handle it," Edmund asked as Lily piled books in her arms.

"I know," Lily replied matter of factly. "But it goes faster with more hands."

She and Edmund walked side by side, back up the stairs. With five of them working, the shelves were emptied before the midday meal. Other servants were filing in and out of Lily's room, carefully removing select pillows and eventually a large tapestry.

Lily called the work on the office done for the day once her own legs were aching from the constant trips up the stairs. She had been in extremely good shape before her month of lock up. She couldn't imagine the others were less sore than her.

They found their way down to the main hall together. Platters of food had already been laid out for people to serve themselves.

Lily grabbed a plate, quickly piling on all the materials for a sandwich before anyone could attempt to do it for her.

Her companions took it in stride for their part, filling their own plates, and the maids sat at the table they used for dinner.

Lily glanced at Edmund, who looked set to go to the high table, but she grabbed his sleeve and gently pulled him to sit beside the women.

Once the initial shock was through, a decent conversation flowed. People tended to sit away from them, giving a small bubble of space. And Lily grew hot as she noticed the glances but did her best to ignore them. She didn't want to maintain a separation between her and the people of the castle. She wanted to feel comfortable, and the quickest way to do that was to become familiar.

"I don't care what's allowed. I demand to see the baron!" the shout pierced through the ambient noise of the dining hall.

Heads turned toward the entrance, where a woman was fuming at the guards who had stepped directly in front of her.

After a moment, Lily realized she recognized the voice. It couldn't be...

She stood, moving to where a skirmish was threatening to break out as a woman continued to argue with the guards. Suddenly the woman stopped, eyes locking on Lily and surprise overcoming her face. "Lily?"

The guards looked at Lily, sensing the recognition in Tori's tone.

Lily nodded at them and was quickly buried in a hug from Tori.

"I'm so sorry. I tried to follow you, but—"

Lily pulled back, holding the girl at arm's length. "It's fine. *I'm* fine."

"The things people said, I was so worried..." Tori dashed tears from her eyes before they could fall down her cheeks.

Lily grabbed her friend's hand, gently guiding her out of the crowded hall. She found a nearby empty sitting room, closing the door for some privacy.

Tori couldn't stop looking around, eyes wide at the height of the ceilings and the opulence of the furniture. It must have been one of D'Lavaud's private rooms. Nowhere else had he invested any coin besides the bare minimum.

Still, for a castle, Lily felt the room was pretty normal. Casual enough to explain what had happened. "Have you ever been in a castle before?" Lily asked.

Tori's attention switched to Lily, her previously emotionally strained expression becoming one of plain confusion. She picked up the hem of her cloak, fidgeting with it as she spoke. "Only the outer wall, never inside the keep." Tori looked around briefly. "What? How?"

Lily grabbed the woman's hand again, pulling it off the cloak and leading her to a seat. "Remember how we were avoiding the roads?"

Tori nodded. "Marauders. If we lose, they get everything."

"Well," Lily said, pleased with the ease of a conversation in the trade language. "Apparently, that extends to matters of nobility. I killed the baron in an escape attempt, so this is mine now."

She allowed Tori a minute to process some of the implications she was still processing herself.

"You killed a man?"

"Yes."

"So now you own his castle?"

"Yes."

"How long ago?" Tori asked. She had made an effort to stop fidgeting with her cloak, but now she was twirling the Hawk symbol of a feather that hung on her neck. "I've been worried sick."

Lily smiled. Tori seemed to have come to terms with the scenario much quicker than she herself had. "A couple days," she answered. "Where's Kyraa?"

Tori looked down. "She tried to help. To get into the castle. But someone ratted her out, so she left. She said it was safer." There was an anger in Tori's voice. After all, Tori had stayed despite the dangers.

"It was," Lily's response was short. "You should've gone with her."

Tori looked at Lily sadly. "I couldn't. When I heard the baron was dead, I thought it might be a chance to get you out. I couldn't leave you."

That made sense then. And if Kyraa had fled, it explained why Tori hadn't remained at the tavern. She'd been so close to two criminals; she was lucky to have evaded capture herself. A part of Lily was grateful Tori had stayed for her, was willing to storm into a castle for her. Even if it was dangerous. At least someone believed she was *worth* saving.

"I know," Lily said. "I would have done exactly the same." And, despite knowing it was more dangerous, she felt proud of Tori for making the decision. It would make her a good Hawk.

Tori looked around, dropping the feather. "So, what now? You aren't planning to stay here."

"I don't know what else to do. If I leave, someone else will just take over."

"What if Randson finds us?"

Of course, that was a risk. But they'd been stationary this long, almost a month, and he hadn't caught them. Now Lily had control of a fortified castle—and a small army. That made them a lot less vulnerable. "I think it's worth the risk."

"I hope you're right," Tori murmured.

CHAPTER 16

TRAINING GROUNDS

L ily sighed as she looked over the discarded dresses and slipped into her newly cleaned trousers. This was much more natural and freeing.

Over the week she'd been baroness, she'd begun to settle into a pattern. The mornings were spent coping with the mess that was her office, but at least it no longer smelled. Edmund had arranged her days in such a way that mornings were also spent redistributing art throughout the castle.

Lily would insert herself into random seating groups during the midday meal, attempting to make light conversation and break some of the fear that surrounded her position. If they could only see she was a person like any of them, she fully believed life would proceed smoother for them all.

The knights were the simplest to be around. It likely had something to do with how she had earned her title. They had all been trained to fight, and she fought for her title the same as them, which meant they understood each other. That made her main hurdle her gender, though thankfully they didn't seem particularly bothered, just caught off guard.

Lily walked into her sitting room, staring at the piles of books she had insisted on looking through herself. She'd tried reading the titles over the last few days, but for the most part, they eluded her. Only a few were close enough to words she knew. Half the books didn't have titles at all, just blank spines staring back at her. They were filled with records of what she assumed were transactions based on the numbers, though she could rarely tell what they were for.

Speaking a language was one thing. Reading, it turned out, was an entirely different beast.

Edmund looked up from a paper that it appeared he was editing as she opened the door to his office.

His eyebrows raised in question, and Lily sighed. "Okay, you can't tell anyone this..."

"Okay," Edmund agreed without hesitation.

Lily screwed her face up, hesitant to admit but knowing she needed help. "I can't read Casseterran. Will you teach me?"

"We could find a tutor, if you want," Edmund offered. He ran a hand through his hair.

Lily's stomach knotted at the idea of admitting her problem to a stranger, so she shook her head. "I don't want any more people to know than necessary."

Edmund put a cork in his ink and stood up with a nod. He followed Lily back to her room, sitting beside her as she grabbed one of the books they'd carried up and pointed at the title. "They Were Making Wool," Edmund said for her.

Lily questioned him on the pronunciation of wool, not seeing how that particular series of letters matched the word.

Edmund smiled, explaining how the last letters of words were often left off when spoken. They went through this with the book, Edmund reading aloud as Lily forced her brain to connect the letters with the sounds they were, or weren't, making. She paused Edmund every time they came to a new twist, asking for clarification. He made a capable teacher.

Over the course of the book, he explained the differences between written and spoken words. It wasn't a particularly interesting read. It detailed the best wool harvesting practices throughout history and how it should be taxed. Still, Lily wasn't reading to be entertained. She was reading to learn.

Her brain ached from trying to learn to read, it seemed like, all over again. The words began to blur together. After another hour, she had to call it quits, thanking Edmund for his efforts.

"It will take time," Edmund said. His patient smile offered reassurance and praise. "If we work on it a little each day, you will get there."

Lily smiled back. "That would be fantastic."

⊸◦⊷

The lessons settled into a comforting routine. Each afternoon, the duo would immerse themselves in the pages of a fresh book, polishing her command of the language. And refining Edmund's trade language in turn. It'd become a part of her day that she looked forward to.

Lily reached up on her tiptoes, trying to replace the book on the shelf after her afternoon lesson with Edmund. She struggled to tip it on fully.

"Here, let me." He came over, reaching around her to slide it into place. His warmth met her back. His breath almost fanning against her neck. At the feel of him behind her, his hand around hers, her heart jumped to her throat.

"Thank you." Her voice came out too high-pitched for her liking, and she cleared her throat.

"No problem." Edmund looked down, running a hand through his hair.

Lily couldn't help but notice how close they still stood. She didn't know why it made her stomach feel weightless. Didn't know why she couldn't settle her heart.

Edmund opened his mouth to say something.

"Where are the training grounds?" Lily blurted in a panic. Her heart felt like it would fly out of her chest.

Edmund stepped back, blinking. "Why?"

Lily raised an eyebrow, doing her best to lean against the bookshelf casually. "I have been near sedentary for a month. I need to be able to fight again."

Edmund gave her a confused look. "That display in the courtyard did not seem out of shape."

The compliment warmed something inside Lily, even though she knew it was far from her best work. A part of her imagined what he would think of her in fighting form. She laughed lightly to starve off the blush that wanted to heat her face. "For me, it was."

"I will bring you there." Edmund inclined his head.

She had already changed into her Hawk clothes, so all that was left was for her to grab her bow and a few knives. Edmund waited patiently, then guided her down a series of stairs to a small courtyard between the side of the keep and the outer wall.

It was longer than it was wide, stretching the entire eastern edge of the keep but only spanning five or so yards to the outer wall.

To Lily's right stood a diminutive, shed-like structure. Peering inside revealed a small armory stacked with training weapons and dummies. The ground, where most of the castle yard was thin grass or gravel, was packed with sand. Soft enough if one fell, but hard enough to keep even footing.

A few yards beyond the shed, a pair of guards appeared to be sparring.

Lily noted the similarly dressed woman at the end of the long area. Tori. Her hood hung off her shoulders, letting her growing shaggy black hair flow in the light breeze. As Lily watched, Tori blew a bit of fringe out of her eyes, then released an arrow into the target.

Edmund stopped in the doorway as Lily raised a hand to prevent him from progressing, and they watched for a few shots.

Tori drew.

Lily knew she had a small window, so shouted, "Duck!"

The apprentice flinched, sending the arrow skittering onto the gravel only a few yards ahead of her as she turned to face Lily, not ducking for an instant.

She raised an amused eyebrow.

"What the blazes?" Tori collected herself. Her shoulders were tight, her tone tighter.

Lily shrugged, gathering the fallen arrow and handing it back to Tori. "I wanted to see what you'd do under pressure."

"So you shouted at me?"

"Would you rather I shoot at you?" Lily offered, amused.

"No." Tori groaned to herself, replacing the arrow in her quiver. "I guess not."

Lily stepped next to Tori and aligned herself with the target. "You can't let a startle affect your aim. Either stop or finish the shot," she said as she sighted, drew—

"Boo!"

—and loosed.

Lily didn't flinch. Her arrow soared into the target right where she'd aimed. Then she turned to Tori with a raised eyebrow.

The woman merely rolled her eyes and muttered, "Show off."

"Your turn. Far target, three arrows," Lily recited in retribution.

Tori exhaled, staring down the target. Two arrows flew with no interference. But on the third draw, Lily shot out an arm, jostling Tori's bow arm.

The girl eased her draw and stomped back.

Lily pulled her foot out of the way in the nick of time. "What if I'd had a knife?"

"What am I supposed to do?" She sounded exasperated.

Lily shrugged. "Situational awareness. Get better at assessing threats. It'll take practice—"

"Everything takes practice," Tori grumbled, shot her arrow into the target, then turned to Lily. "Speaking of. You haven't shot in ages. Shouldn't *you* be practicing?"

Edmund had leaned against the wall, watching with an amused smile. His eyes bounced between the weapon and Lily.

She skillfully knocked an arrow to her bowstring, peering at the middle target. In a smooth movement, she drew and narrowed to the target. Her fingers brushed the corner of her lips, and with a breath exhaled, she released the arrow in a minuscule movement of her fingers.

The arrow whistled off.

Then slammed into the innermost circle of the far target.

Lily watched it hit home before she bothered drawing her next arrow. Arms strong but never tense, she repeated the process with composure, now aiming at the nearest target. Her fingers touched the corner of her lips again, and she loosed.

The arrow connected just high of center. Anyone not used to her standards would consider it a perfect shot. Lily considered it a sign of rust.

She hadn't properly adjusted for distance. An amateur mistake that wouldn't be made twice.

Remaining in her square stance, she loosed a third arrow. This time, taking careful steps to compensate for the change in distance.

It landed.

Directly on the crossed lines that marked the center. And it almost made up for the previous error.

A whistle of admiration sounded behind her, and she glanced over her shoulder to see Edmund admiring her work.

"I have never seen anyone shoot like that. Ever."

Lily smiled, turned back to the targets, and shot her next series of arrows. She aimed for various—but always purposeful—points now that her own arrows took up the center. Then gradually increased her speed, getting into the rhythm of the exercise.

Tori resumed shooting beside her, too.

Within a minute, they had so many arrows clustered in the center that they had to switch targets. Filling the space also filled something inside of Lily. The yearning for action was eased by the short session already.

The sounds of the dueling men stopped, and Lily felt at least one set of eyes fall on her.

It was methodical work for her. Nock. Draw. Loose. Nock. Draw. Loose. The entire process only took a few seconds, and the arrows weren't even released at a particularly high speed.

Others might not have been able to keep up with the pace; Tori never faulted. Her arrows thudded into the target an instant after Lily's shot pierced it. Each landed in *nearly* the same place.

They had both been trained to count their arrows as they went. To not know could prove fatal in combat. When the numbers ran out, she withdrew her throwing knife from the scabbard at her side and hurled it at the center of the center target. It was a habit Lily had come to pick up years prior, and she wasn't aware of any other Hawks that shared it. For her, it brought a sense of finality to her set.

She turned to Tori, who had run out of arrows a few shots before her and was now waiting for it to be safe to retrieve. Lily raised an eyebrow. "You were trying to shoot mine out of the air?"

"Trying." Tori's lips twitched in repressed amusement.

Lily smiled as she went to retrieve her arrows. It was possible to shoot an arrow out of the air. She'd seen Jarek do it. Hawks tended to compete, trying to keep each other from hitting the target. It rarely worked. The angles and timing were all wrong to accomplish the feat.

Tucking the last arrow back into her quiver before turning, she noticed three men clustered by the wall. They were chatting lightly, occasionally glancing her way.

Edmund's eyes briefly met hers, and he quickly looked at one of the guards accompanying him.

Lily took a few steps back from where she had been the previous time, then a few to the side, so she wasn't using any of the same angles to practice. She shot another round there, this time pushing her speed up steadily as she had become familiarized with the motions once again.

Tori remained beside her. With each shot, Tori sped up too.

Lily matched her, not caring how long it had been. The competitiveness that drove Hawks to be the best pushed them both. Their arrows were spent much faster this time.

She gathered them again.

The men were now unabashedly watching her and Tori. Some with schooled, icy contemplation, others with commendation.

"How?" Edmund asked.

Lily claimed, "Practice."

"A lot of practice," Tori agreed. *Practice* may as well have been the Hawk motto.

Lily glanced over Edmund's shoulder at the two guards, who were doing their best to avoid being noticed. "Up for some practice dueling?"

They looked at each other, and the taller of the two smoothly shoved the shorter forward.

The smaller man rubbed the back of his neck but didn't retreat. "What type?"

Lily gestured to the wooden sword he had abandoned. "That, and I'll use knives."

She went to the shed, selecting the best wooden approximations of her heavy knife and her throwing dagger.

The man was standing awkwardly. His weight shifted from one foot to the other, and his eyes were darting across the training grounds as he waited. "My lady, what...?"

"Pull blows," Lily said with a smile. "Ready?" She raised both eyebrows.

The man nodded, and Lily lunged forward.

He quickly deflected her knife with his sword, dancing back. Clearly, he hadn't expected her to act so quickly. Now they circled each other and bounced on their toes.

"You can swing," Lily reassured, "I won't be—"

The man cut at her with a backhand.

Lily's knives clanked together in a cross, catching the blow just before it could hit her side. The collision jarred her arms, forcing her only a half step off balance. She had noticed the blow late. Another consequence of missing practice.

Still, she recovered too quickly for him to take advantage of her momentary lapse, stepping forward to close the gap and eliminate his reach advantage.

He brought his sword up, and Lily brought her knives to match it. The move prevented what would normally be a dangerous blade from carving into her skull.

They stood for a minute. Pushed against each other. Tested the other's strength. Then, with one large shove, they burst apart, dancing again just out of reach before moving together in a flurry of blows.

They whirled and clashed. Loud thunks of wood emphasized the conclusion of each collision.

Lily danced away from his slashes and thrusts, trying to work her way within his guard. He, for his part, had abandoned his hesitance. After that first clash, Lily felt the change. His attacks became more determined—with real power behind them—in an attempt to break her guard with brute force.

It was a potential strategy, which was why Lily had switched from the more theatrical catching to dodging his strikes. If he never hit her guard, he couldn't break it.

The man came at her with a particularly quick flurry that she had no choice but to attempt to block.

Her overarching swing caught his blade.

He pulled back, moving for a lunge, knowing she wouldn't be able to catch the move in the crossed blades.

Lily dropped to the ground and darted her leg out to catch the man's forward ankle just as he shifted weight to it.

As a result, his weight was all moving toward an absent support. His lunge lost all power as he tried to catch his balance, but Lily was already ramming her shoulder into his and grabbing his sword arm with one hand, twisting the sword aside as they crashed to the ground.

Her other hand snapped a knife to his throat once his back met the sand with a grunt.

Clearly defeated, he released the sword.

Lily stood, offering a hand to him.

He stared at it for a moment, eyes darting back and forth between the sword and her hand. Then the decision was made. His gloved hand closed around hers, and she helped pull him to his feet, changing the offer of aid into a friendly handshake.

They were both sweating from the exertion. Lily smiled. It was good to be moving again.

The man released her hand quickly, bowing his head to avoid eye contact.

"Good match," Lily said.

He mumbled something incoherent, and she assumed it was meant to be a return of the compliment.

Lily's attention turned to Tori, who was watching intently. After all, it had turned out quite similar to the fighting style Lily had been establishing in their previous training.

The second man was recruited to duel with Tori moments later, and Lily watched, pausing to correct Tori or offer hints. They spent the next hour practicing.

She had even tried to get Edmund to join, but he'd refused in a flustered mess when offered a practice sword.

CHAPTER 17

POLITICAL RIVALRY

In the high-backed chair, Lily sat with a rigid posture, the seat resembling more of a throne. Her eyes surveyed her office, taking in the surroundings with an air of reserved—and insecure—authority. Of course the original baron had such a self-important seat. Even in a room he had clearly never allowed anyone inside of.

Tristan, Simeon, and Edmund filled the remaining chairs, poring over sheaves of notes. Simeon rambled on about the previous year's taxes.

Despite herself, Lily's attention wandered. It wasn't that she didn't care. She was just restless. She was meant for action, not the weeks and weeks of endless meetings and consultations that running a province entailed. A nagging voice infiltrated her head every morning when she woke up. Telling her she was just an imposter. Telling her they'd be better off with someone else.

Every evening when she went to bed, the voice told her this new world would come crashing down around her. She was a thief, not a leader. These decisions should not have been hers to make.

Her office has been newly freshened, and it was finally habitable. All the papers and books had been moved back in and organized.

Some of the books had been moved to the castle's small library, providing shelf space. The rest were organized on the shelves lining one wall. Lily knew where everything was. And most importantly, she knew what they all were.

Her gaze drifted out the window. Smoke curled from the city's chimneys, making artificial clouds in the otherwise blue sky. The days were growing colder, though they were far enough south it would remain temperate by Lily's standards. An unusually cold year, she'd been told.

Edmund nudged Lily's knee, snapping her focus back to the room.

"In just the last week, we've received over two hundred requests for aid," Simeon was saying.

"Two hundred?" Lily asked aghast. It was common to be asked for aid, and she gave it where she could. Tried to make the best of the twist of life that had landed her this position. But two hundred in a week was a lot. "Surely we're nearing the next harvest?" Avisier's climate, she had learned, gave it the blessing of having a year-round growing season. They were constantly replenished with food.

The only time it grew short was right before a harvest.

"Yes, my lady," Simeon said. "It has already started."

Lily frowned. If the harvest had started, there should've been plenty of food to go around. It didn't make sense. "Then why the sudden influx?"

"It isn't as plentiful as anticipated. And with the taxes to the king and the fee to Palliers, we're going to come up short."

"Fee to Palliers?"

Palliers was a coastal settlement on the same river as Aviser. The Marquis, Jeremias, had a reputation. At least, enough of one that Lily had heard of it. He was brutal and coin-hungry. Although that was no different from half the lords in Casseterre. At least she was in good company amongst the morally corrupt.

Tristan nodded. "He guards the mouth of the river, you see. We pay him to prevent Kalturi raiding ships from traveling upriver to us."

"The raiding season is over. Why would we pay him now?"

"He demands it," Tristan said.

Lily leveled her gaze at him. "You know the military capabilities of this city better than anyone else?"

"I would say so, my lady, yes." Tristan puffed his chest out slightly.

"Are they capable of defending a Kalturi raid?"

"At current capacity, yes."

Lily nodded. "Maps of Avisier please, Edmund?"

He stood wordlessly, navigating the rack of scroll cases with ease.

"May I ask what you're intending, my lady?" Simeon asked.

"To stop paying."

Simeon frowned, causing the lines in his face to deepen. "My lady, Kalturi raids aren't something to be trifled with."

"I am aware." Lily's words were harsher than she'd meant them to be. She'd been a victim of the Kalturi, swept off and sold as a slave along with her brother and Princess Adelaide. They'd barely escaped with their lives.

Simeon clamped his mouth shut. A trained response from too many years under an explosive baron.

Lily took a deep breath, forcing the edge out of her voice. "I have personal experience with them. You couldn't have known."

"And Marquis Jeremias is not someone to write off," Tristan added hesitantly.

His name *did* sound familiar. Perhaps he was one of those she should watch out for. But Lily couldn't stand by and let people suffer just because he might cause a problem. Besides, she was a Hawk; she knew how to deal with problematic barons.

"Nor am I." Lily lifted her chin.

Edmund returned to the table, carrying a handful of scroll cases. He plopped them beside his chair and sorted through them, selecting one and handing it to Lily.

She unrolled it, frowned, and said, "This doesn't look like the one you showed me last time."

"Ah," Tristan said. "Right. You aren't Casseterran."

Lily's jaw clenched. "No, I am not."

"The wars have made cartography difficult at best," Tristan explained. "The last accurate maps are from when Casseterre was divided evenly. With the squabbling over territory and numerous border disputes, the divisions became impossible to keep track of."

Lily studied the map. "The entire course of this river is different."

Tristan leaned over the map, searching until his eyes alighted on the signature. "Ah yes. This map was created for taxation purposes. Much of the geography is more representation than fact."

Lily sat back in her chair with a groan. "I need the strategic maps."

Edmund pulled out the cases and examined their labels, reading, "I have farming, trade, but nothing strategic."

Lily rubbed her temples. "And why not?" Her frame slouched back in the chair.

"Makes it harder to attack each other when you do not know the true lay of the land," Tristan explained matter of factly, "No map in Casseterre will risk giving that much away."

Of course not. While Lily had plenty of maps of Albrin memorized, she'd only just started for Casseterre. Discovering she was likely wrong was disheartening. "Fine. Do any of you know the landing depth where the river comes within two miles of any villages?"

Much of Avisier's south was hilly, sometimes rocky slopes. This included large sections of the riverbank. Certainly, there had to be river access, but perhaps they would be lucky, and the land would serve as a barrier against Kalturi raids.

"I will find out," Edmund said.

Lily nodded her thanks, then decided, "We stop the payments to Palliers, at least for the time being. Simeon, what does that do to our situation?"

Simeon picked up a pen and did a few calculations. "No one should starve to death if we continue our aid policies, my lady. But if the next harvest is poor, we *will* run out. And we rely on trade from downriver."

Lily paused to think for a few moments. Cutting them off from trade could potentially be devastating. She didn't need to see all the numbers to know that. But Palliers also benefitted from trade. Would Jeremias be willing to harm himself to get at her?

"I am still new," Lily said slowly. "If he cuts off trade, we can argue that I didn't know of the agreement. It will buy us time, at least."

Simeon and Edmund exchanged glances.

"It's risky," Simeon said.

Edmund nodded his agreement. "These are good people."

"I know." Lily swallowed, looking at those around her. "But we can't make it better without trying *something*."

Her small council looked at each other, silent words seeming to pass between them. Lily was reminded once again that she was the odd one out, the foreigner in a circle they had developed.

Finally, Edmund seemed to nod, and Simeon spoke. "A temporary solution, but we should prepare for if he demands payment."

"So we need to stop drawing from our stores?" Lily gathered.

"In short, yes. But the king's tax—"

"Surely he will understand a poor harvest." After all, that was how it worked in Albrin. In times of plenty, the king and nobility collected. In times of stress, they gave back. The expressions around her indicated Casseterre operated differently. Much differently.

"I'll draft a letter," Lily offered. "The worst he can do is say no."

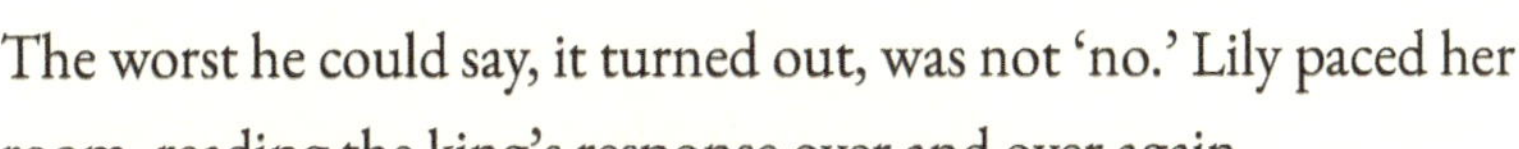

The worst he could say, it turned out, was not 'no.' Lily paced her room, reading the king's response over and over again.

The king had not only refused her request for an extension but had demanded more payment as 'recompense' for the insult.

A subtle crease formed on her forehead as her jaw, now sore from persistent clenching, betrayed the tension she wrestled with. The emotions she worked hard at keeping inside were leaking. She was trying to play by the rules, but she cared more about the people in her province than a king she'd never met. Duty now tethered her to them, and she didn't give in.

There was a knock on her door.

She grunted an acknowledgment to Edmund as he slipped into her room.

"Does this say what I think it does?" she asked.

Edmund took the letter from her and scanned it. "That is bullshit. He can not do that."

"That is what I thought," Lily said, taking the letter back. "I'm not sending any more. If His Majesty," she taunted, drawing out the word as she rolled her eyes, "isn't going to respond when people ask for aid, he *certainly* isn't getting more coin from me."

"Lily—"

"I mean, it is simply ridiculous. Any more is just taking food off people's tables."

"Lily—"

"I might just not respond. What is he going to do, send an army? Apparently, he can't afford it. We have—"

"Lily, someone's here."

Lily stopped her tirade, pivoting to Edmund and taking in his furrowed brows. As her words dissipated into the charged air, she absorbed the sight of his face for the first time. Furrowed brows. Tight lips. The subtle grooves on his forehead. "Who?" she demanded.

"Marquis Jeremias," Edmund emphasized the title, "of Palliers."

Lily took a moment to process the information. She had hoped she and Jeremias would never meet. With what little she knew of him, she didn't see the conversation ending well.

"Where exactly?"

"My office," Edmund replied.

She grabbed his arm, half dragging him to the far side of the room so their voices wouldn't reach the office. "What does he want?"

"A conversation with you, apparently. He would not say what, claimed it is highly sensitive."

Lily narrowed her eyes. "Well, what's protocol?"

Edmund sighed. "You can talk to him now." When her eyes softened with worry, he added, "Or claim you're busy and set a time later."

As if assessing her option for escape, she looked around her. "He outranks me..."

In Albrin, she had operated outside the normal system of ranks. Only the king and her commander were capable of giving her orders. She was still getting used to the intricacies of who outranked who. It wasn't a direct chain of command; she wasn't under Jeremias in that sense, but his title did hold power. And he'd ruled longer, meaning he likely held more sway with the king. The king who already seemed to dislike her.

"Technically," Edmund confirmed.

So ... she would need to maintain control, but she also had to be polite. "Tell him I need to finish something up, but I'll meet with him in a few minutes. We'll meet in my office. And get him out of the antechamber." She cut a glance at the door as she said it, as if she could see the man on the other side.

Edmund nodded, turning to follow through with her orders.

Lily waited a moment before going to the bell. She hadn't pulled it yet. There had never been an urgent reason.

Now there was.

True to her word, within a minute, Amira had slipped through the passage and was standing across from Lily.

"What is it?" Her eyes were wide, her curly black hair a mess. As if she'd come expecting an emergency.

Lily smiled. "The Marquis of Palliers wants to meet in a few minutes, and I am nowhere near ready."

"Right." Amira strode toward Lily's room. "Something nice I assume?"

"Of course," Lily replied, following the girl who was already flicking through clothes faster than Lily could process. "Something I can move in," Lily added when Amira's hand seemed to rest on a rather tight-fitted burgundy dress.

"Planning on a fight?" Amira teased.

Lily's answering, "Always," held nothing of the same light tone.

Muscles in Amira's back tensed as she went back to flicking through the dresses. Her practiced eyes took in more factors than Lily could even think to consider. She passed on dress after dress.

Finally, she settled on a blue gown.

The shoulders finished in a sharp corner, leaving Lily's arms free. The bodice ended in a silver belt around the waist before the skirt billowed out. It was loose enough that Lily's legs would have free motion, but it didn't have so much fabric it would begin to trip her up. The neck cut straight across her body, providing a structure that added an air of authority.

Lily quickly began changing, accepting Amira's help with the gown, and leaving her clothes in a pile—a rare sight. Lily was normally organized to a T. She often had to leave places quickly, and it helped to know where everything was.

Hiking up her skirt, Lily deftly strapped knives to her thighs while Amira sifted through jewelry.

"Simple," the maid muttered to herself.

Given the small size of Lily's collection, she would've expected the process to go much quicker than it did. Then again, Amira paid more attention to fashion in a day than Lily had in her entire life. That was why her job had quickly shifted from maid to modiste.

Amira returned, clasping a simple gold chain around Lily's neck as Lily strapped her neatest-looking dagger to her waist. "Hair?" she asked.

"It looks fine," Amira responded. Lily watched the woman's eyes dance around her face before she nodded again. "Perhaps not the neatest, but that is normal for you."

The slight jab was appreciated. Lily's hair was often a frizzy mess pulled into a functional braid. Without the luxury of an hour to wash and style it, this was the best semblance of order she could hope to achieve.

Lily took a deep breath and briefly touched each of her knives to familiarize herself with what she had—and what she didn't. "We will need drinks and snacks," Lily said, "in my office."

"Right." Amira turned to fulfill the request.

But Lily stopped her with a hand on her arm. "When you bring them, do not leave. Stay outside the door and make sure two guards are there."

"You really are expecting trouble." Amira sounded concerned.

"I always expect trouble," Lily replied. "There's only so many reasons he could be here."

Amira nodded, then left the room.

Lily made sure she was well out of view of the door, in case Edmund hadn't quite gotten Jeremias out with full cooperation. She forced herself to remain still and take measured breaths.

Then, she descended to her office.

CHAPTER 18
BARED TEETH

A guard in the hall opened the door to her office with a bow, and Lily gave him a nod before crossing to a shelf, selecting her chosen book fluidly, and opening it.

Avisier had come with considerably more land than she'd expected. The reason, it seemed, had been D'Lavaud's ambition to expand. He had kept a meticulous list of all nobility and the territory they controlled—updated and edited through the years.

First, the late Baron Rouselle had conquered a few of the neighboring fiefs. That seemed to make him a target, resulting in a long list of duels that ended in D'Lavaud's victory. Then D'Lavaud followed Rouselle's lead, creating an amalgam that consisted of nearly twenty percent of the country. A similar process had taken place across Casseterre, to varying degrees of success. What was once hundreds of equally sized fiefs had been cut down to about fifteen of wildly varying size.

Lily took a seat, flipping through her book until she found the section on Palliers.

Jeremias had won it. There were notes detailing Jeremias's movements across the country. An entire series of them recounting his triumphs and failures. It seemed Jeremias had controlled specks of land, all dotted across the landscape like dripping water. But it was hard to maintain control over noncontiguous territory. For every time he acquired one territory, he lost another.

And by each territory, a single word was noted—conquest. He had killed probably seven barons over the last five years alone. Lily's knives grew heavier, as it seemed more and more likely she'd have to use them.

Edmund poked his head in, forcing her eyes to the door. They made eye contact, and she gave him a small nod that she was ready.

Marquis Jeremias strode in, neglecting even a glance at Edmund. Not even when he quietly shut the door behind him.

Edmund raised his eyebrows in question, closing the door only after Lily nodded once more.

Lily rose to her feet and gave a polite curtsy, no more than rank called for.

Jeremias gave a stiff half-bow in response. He was a fairly large man. Standing, he was heads taller than Lily and outweighed her significantly. His clothes were not sculpted to him, but they were tight enough that Lily could see he carried significant muscle, too.

Despite his graying hair, he looked ready to fight at a moment's notice. In that, he reminded Lily of Jarek. He was dangerous, but there were measures he could take to hide it; measures he was not taking at the moment.

The gloved hand that rested casually on his sword being one.

Lily gestured to the seat across from her as she sat. "I apologize for the wait. We were not aware of any planned visit."

Jeremias perched at the edge of his seat. "No need to apologize. I never sent word." He was speaking in the trade language, which surprised Lily.

"And why is that?" Lily asked, switching to the trade language.

"You speak with an accent. Where are you from?"

Just like that, alarm bells were sounding in Lily's head. She didn't let it show, instead smiling as she replied, "Albrin."

Jeremias chuckled. "You speak well for an Albrini. I'm surprised you bothered to learn Casseterran."

Albrin was one of the few nations that didn't have its own language. Most of the denizens only spoke the trade language, never bothering to learn anything more. Nobility prided themselves on speaking more languages, but it was during her time in Kalturi captivity that she had picked up a bit of most tongues.

There was a short knock, and Lily invited Amira in. The woman entered with coffee and a tray of sliced cake. She met eyes with Lily.

"Thank you," Lily said with a reassuring nod to Amira.

The maid poured them each a cup before curtseying and hurrying out of the room.

Lily poured milk into her mug.

Jeremias raised his eyebrows. "That ruins the coffee." His words were filled with judgment and absent any playful tone.

"I prefer the word *enhance*," Lily replied.

There was a pause as they both sipped and picked at the cake. Lily took the chance to reposition herself, casually moving forward so she could stand more quickly.

"So," Lily began when a polite amount of time had passed. "What brings you to Avisier?"

"Yes." He cleared his throat as he set down his cup. "It's simple, really. I've come to tell you to stop."

"Stop what?" Lily didn't have to fake confusion.

"Don't take me for a fool," Jeremias snapped with an authority that indicated he was accustomed to being obeyed. "First that bastard takes Salaise and kicks me out of the North. Then you kill D'Lavaud? I know the signs of an invasion when I see them."

Lily frowned. "I think you're mistaken. I have no relation to whoever took Salaise."

"De Falchi told me you'll go after Palliers next," Jeremias replied as if Lily hadn't spoken. "Do not set foot in my territory."

"Then I'm afraid your information is incorrect," Lily responded, ensuring her voice remained calm and measured. "I had no intention of doing so."

Jeremias gripped the armrests. "Now, as I'm sure you're aware, I had an agreement with D'Lavaud in exchange for protection from the raids."

Lily took a sip of her coffee before lying. "I was not aware."

"Well," Jeremias replied, "I have not received any payments since you took over."

Lily had a sense she was meant to apologize and promise to right the situation. Instead, she shrugged, a major breach of decorum. "It was a poor harvest. If you don't mind my asking, how was the raiding season?"

"Difficult," Jeremias responded shortly. "That's why high-ranking nobles like me control borders."

Lily smiled. "No, you become a higher-ranking noble by controlling the border."

Jeremias smiled in return as something in his eyes flashed. "You've done your research, so I'll assume you are aware I outrank you."

"I am."

"Well, then, seeing as that's the case," Jeremias began haughtily. "I order you to make the payment I'm due."

Lily laughed. "No."

He set his jaw, saying slowly, "I outrank you. That means you must do what I say."

"You outrank me," Lily conceded. "But you do not control *my* land. I have made no deals with you. We are more than capable of protecting ourselves." It was only partially true, but she doubted the Kalturi would come so far upriver and not attack Palliers first, where they would be weakened enough for Lily to take them.

"I could control your land in an instant." Jeremias growled. "I am merely offering a chance to make the right decision."

Lily set her coffee down, dropping her hands below the table so she could rest one on her knife. "Am I meant to take that as a threat?"

"You can take it however you want."

Lily was now poised for action, though she tried to keep her words polite. "If you have a problem with my decision, you can take it up with the king."

"The king is *worthless*," Jeremias spat. "He wouldn't leave that palace of his if there was all-out war. You really think he cares about raids in the south?"

"How many raids were there?" Lily asked calmly.

"None of your business."

Which either meant none, or entirely too many.

Lily picked up her coffee with her free hand, taking a measured sip before replying, "With the way this conversation seems to be going, it very much is my business."

Jeremias stiffened. "Ten thousand aurus worth of grain, and I will continue to protect you from the Kalturi scum."

Lily leaned back. "If you don't resist Kalturind, they'll just raid Palliers. If it's an easy target there, they will not be motivated to come upriver. Besides"—she shrugged, standing up—"if you actually had any power, you'd prevent passage upriver and cut off trade." It was a gamble, she knew, but she was willing to call his bluff.

Jeremias shot to his feet, too. "Don't insult me."

"I'm merely stating fact."

Because, despite his anger, despite his claims, trade had continued. He had the seat of power, but he did not have control of it. He was nothing but the blustering face of a city that didn't need him.

That's all it took for Jeremias to snap.

He lunged across the desk to grab Lily's throat and ended up with a fistful of her dress as she flinched back.

She was yanked toward him by what he managed to wrap his hands around, and she dropped her feet, becoming dead weight. He clattered onto the table; his momentum meant for the headbutt was pulling him downward.

Lily slashed at the hand holding her collar, and Jeremias hissed in pain, releasing.

He was as fast as a snake, gripping her wrist. Before she could make another move with the knife, he clamped down on her delicate bones, and in a cruel form of retaliation that she herself had practiced, he twisted.

Practically kneeling on the table now, Jeremias's positioning provided the proximity he needed.

Her shoulder screamed as her arm was yanked behind her, her own knife pressed between her shoulder blades. Leaving her with the choice to drop it or stab herself.

So, the dagger clattered to the floor at her feet.

She tried to force her way out of the hold, but he was stronger than her, and it only led to her muscles feeling as if they were tearing. Hot coffee dripped down the back of her dress, and she knew he must be kneeling in it.

An iron grip took the feeling out of Lily's fingers, and his other hand dug painfully into a pressure point in her neck.

But he left one hand free. His mistake. Her advantage.

She reached back, fumbling for only a second as she found the hilt of his sword and yanked forward. *Guards*. Where were the *guards*?

In an instant, the grip released as his focus shifted to keeping his weapon.

Lily turned, delivering a solid punch to his nose.

It landed with a satisfying crunch as Jeremias stumbled back off the table, cursing her and fighting the disorientation. He clutched his nose, which was already gushing blood, and growled, "You're going to regret that."

Lily shook out her hand. "There are guards outside that door. One word from me and you'll have swords at your throat. So, I recommend. You. Sit. Down." She didn't know if she was bluffing or not. They'd created quite a racket. Lily doubted the guards hadn't heard. So where were they?

Jeremias smiled, slowly pulling his hands from his crooked nose. The blood was now dribbling into his mouth, creating a horror scene when paired with the crazed look in his eyes. "You won't get another word."

Lily saw the blow coming and ducked, scrabbling to grasp the dagger she'd dropped. Jeremias lunged across the desk again like a wild animal, sending the already toppled cups scattering to the floor.

Lily dove beneath him through a curtain of dripping coffee to crouch beneath the desk. There was no logic or reason in his eyes. No bargaining. She had witnessed his particular madness before.

This fight would end only in death.

The man ignored his sword, ignored the dagger in Lily's hands, and lunged to tear out her throat. Nails scratched at her skin as rage met its target.

She brought her dagger up to his own throat. But weighty, desperate hands had closed off her airway. It stung. And his reach outmaneuvered her dagger.

Lily tried to cry out, but her voice never reached her mouth. Her pulse pounded in her neck, blocking out the hammering of guards on the door. Her free hand clawed at Jeremias, blood and skin worming beneath her nails.

He made no reaction save to smile wider as her panic grew. Made no sign of pain.

Black began to creep into her vision as her heart throbbed like it would rupture. She tried to take a deep breath to calm herself, only to have a wave of panic when no air reached her lungs.

She kicked, leaning back, but there was no force behind it as even her hand began to tremble.

The madman became a speck amongst blackness, and Lily knew she had no choice.

She flicked her wrist, cutting the artery that supplied blood to his brain.

The pressure on her throat released, allowing her to gasp for air. Allowing her starving lungs to expand.

Shoving her way over the man's thrashing body, she stumbled to her feet, then slipped down again as her legs were incapable of holding her weight.

Jeremias lay in front of her. His desperate kicking made enough noise to wake the dead.

The door finally burst open with a splinter of woodchips, two guards entering with swords drawn and assessing the situation. Their faces held hesitation—and wonder.

Edmund appeared behind them, abject horror painted across his face. "Help her!" he demanded, pulling them out of their pause.

They rushed to Lily, ignoring the body, whose twitches were becoming less and less pronounced. They'd all seen combat. Nobody recovered from that much blood loss.

Edmund reached her first, moving into her slowly expanding field of vision.

She dimly heard him questioning her over the thunder of blood returning to her ears and took a deep breath, tasting iron. Still, she could take a deep breath.

"I'm fine," Lily croaked as she tried to use the bookcase to push herself to her feet.

Edmund grabbed her arm, supporting her as she shakily stood. "You're not fine," he argued. "You need to be seen by a medic." He helped her walk to the door.

She gained strength with each step. With each breath. Her legs felt sturdy enough to support her weight. But she saw the fear in Edmund's face, the helplessness. So, she put some weight on him.

Edmund made to turn for the infirmary.

Lily shook her head, then immediately regretted the decision as it felt like her throat was compressed again. "No. My—room," she rasped.

So, they made their way up the stairs. It seemed to take longer than ever before to reach her chambers.

Edmund held the door open.

Lily made her way through, collapsing onto her couch.

"Don't say anything. Not until we get a chance to talk," Edmund warned in a low tone.

Lily smiled to let him know she'd heard. She didn't want to speak, anyway. Not when she could feel where one side of her throat had touched the other.

Edmund sat next to her, clutching her hand. It was more for his comfort than hers.

Lily swallowed, then swallowed again, trying to swallow the pain away but only succeeding in making it worse.

There was a knock at the door, and Edmund took the liberty to invite them in.

Amira entered, soon overtaken by a familiar man Lily knew as Tedic. He had been the one tending to Cecilia through that long night. He had never given her a surname, though she must have seen it somewhere.

Tedic crouched, setting his bag on her coffee table as he scanned over her, taking in the damage. "What happened?"

Edmund cut a warning glare at her, but she had to at least explain her injuries.

"He tried to strangle me," Lily whispered, hoping it would help the hoarseness.

Behind Tedic's back, Edmund gave a slight approving nod.

Tedic turned to Amira. "Get us cold water." The maid scurried out of the room as Tedic returned his attention to Lily and added, "Don't whisper, just speak softly."

She nodded, then winced as it sent pain through her throat. How she stopped the whimpers from worming their way up her swelling throat, she didn't know.

Lines of concern appeared on the bridge of Tedic's nose. "Do you mind if I touch it?"

"No," Lily replied as softly as she could.

Tedic gently pressed his fingers against her throat, but Lily couldn't tell what he was feeling for. After a moment of silence, he nodded to himself. "No serious damage. Not much I can do besides give you something for the pain."

Amira returned with the water, quietly setting it on the table before retreating to stand at the ready.

Lily smiled at the worry she could see growing around her. "I'm fine."

"Let me see here." Tedic rummaged through his bag before pulling out a few leaves Lily recognized as cirin. "These will help the pain. I do have to warn you they're incredibly bitter."

Lily took the herbs in her outstretched palm. "I know." She tossed the leaves into her mouth, chewing enough to release juices before rinsing down the unpleasant taste. Her throat burned at the action.

Tedic noticed and reassured, "I'll tell Ryia to get you soft foods for the next few days."

"Thank you," Lily said lightly.

"Does anything else hurt?"

Lily's shoulder was sore, but she knew there was no damage. The cirin leaves would handle it just fine. "No."

"Right"—Tedic began to repack his bag—"I'll check again tomorrow. Stay hydrated. No exertion until you are completely healed." He leveled a serious gaze at Lily, which she chose to ignore.

"Thank you," she repeated.

Tedic took that as his cue to leave. He gathered his supplies and made a hasty exit.

Edmund held out the water to Lily.

She smiled at him. "I don't need to drink it all now."

Edmund set the water down. "I'm sorry. I'm just trying to help."

"I know," Lily replied. She grabbed his hand, waiting until he looked at her. "I've been through worse, Edmund. I'll be fine."

"You shouldn't be talking."

And though Lily had been through worse, the genuine concern in his voice made her heart grow warm. If he wanted to take care of her, maybe she could let herself be taken care of. She guided him to sit next to her, then released his hand and grabbed her glass.

"I killed him," she said plainly, then took a sip to ease the soreness.

He nodded, running a hand through his black curls. Blowing out a breath, Edmund said, "He challenged you."

Lily frowned. They certainly had never been on friendly terms, but it wasn't as if he had actually challenged her to anything.

Just attacked. She could argue self-defense in front of the king if needed. It was true, after all. But she hoped it wouldn't come to that.

"No, he—"

"He challenged you," Edmund snapped, cutting her off. "He challenged you," he repeated, softer. "And you won. Which makes all his land yours."

Lily fell silent, drinking in the words. Maybe he hadn't challenged her, but she was the only witness. She had killed one baron already. Was it hard to believe she'd take more land?

What did that make her? Any better than the man whose body lay on her office floor? It was just more proof she'd never be more than a *thief*.

She'd faced no retaliation for taking Avisier. If she said it was a challenge, that could free her from any charges for Jeremiah's death. She could avoid an entire trial, avoid it growing far beyond their provinces.

"I am a Marquess," Lily said when the sound of her own scratchy voice became preferable to the silence.

"You are a Marquess," Edmund agreed, his voice little more than a whisper.

And with that, he helped her steal Palliers. Whether she wanted it or not, there was no going back now.

Edmund leaned in, tenderly tucking a stray strand of her disheveled hair behind her ear. Once the wayward lock was secure, he lingered there, his arm falling around her. Its weight brought comfort, and she found herself closing her eyes as she took in the feeling of his warmth.

Lily leaned forward to set her glass on the table, and when she sat back up, she leaned closer, almost pressed against his warm chest.

His breathing rustled her hair, tickling her scalp.

She looked up at him, looked into his compassionate eyes, and smiled.

The initiation was uncertain—she couldn't discern who moved first, or if it was a harmonized response—but suddenly, their lips met. And they were kissing.

She could feel the concern in the gentle way his lips pressed against hers. In the way his body hovered close but didn't suffocate her.

His hand brushed her waist, sending starlight flooding through her core.

She gasped and moved to deepen the kiss.

Edmund pulled back quickly. Before she could kiss him back.

"I—I am sorry. I should not." He ran a hand through his hair, looking down. "My lady, I stepped out of line." Yet he remained seated beside her.

Lily smiled at him. It had just been an instant, but her heart had already skipped a beat. Her body already felt off-kilter. Every inch of her was electric. Her muscles were shouting at her to act, a familiar feeling of being poised on an edge, ready for anything.

She moved forward tentatively, a hand going to Edmund's blushed face. "It's about time." And she leaned in, bringing her lips just a bit closer to his.

If he moved away again, she'd stop.

But he didn't. His eyes darted between her eyes and her lips.

She took the leap, seized her heart, and pressed her lips to his.

Then, his restraint *broke*.

His hands trailed up her spine before finding themselves entangled in her hair, pulling her body closer to him.

Her heart seemed to fly out of her chest as she pressed herself into him. She'd felt alive before, felt the energy pulsing through her. Never once had it been caused by this. By joy.

Fear, anticipation, and determination could all set her on fire. But for the first time, this *fire* was *joy*.

CHAPTER 19

BEHIND CLOSED DOORS

Lily and Edmund sat on opposite sides of the couch as Tori gave a report. No one knew of their kiss, and they'd agreed to keep it that way for a while.

In the month since claiming her title as Marquess, Lily had been swamped with paperwork. It turned out that a major port city took more to run than Avisier. Edmund took on most of the more mundane day-to-day tasks around Avisier to lighten her load. Tori stepped up to travel the nearby provinces as Lily's eyes and ears, too, so they'd know if there was another threat like Jeremias before it came to blows.

"The further north I get, the worse the rumors are," Tori explained. She stood by the fireplace to present and was doing a remarkable job of keeping her hands still at her sides. Lily had insisted she practice some of these formalities as a means of finishing her training. "You planned to take Palliers. You murdered Jeremias. King Aldrich sent you to conquer Casseterre."

"*What*?" Lily felt her face wrinkle in confusion. "Did you track down the source?"

"As much as you can with any rumor," Tori beamed. "They seem to be coming from Salaise. It recently switched hands to a man called De Falchi."

"Do people believe them?" Edmund ran a hand through his hair, and Lily grinned at the boyishness of the action.

Tori shrugged, using her hands to emphasize her point. "It's gossip."

"But no signs that anyone plans to act on it?" Lily prompted.

Tori shook her head.

"You need more allies," Edmund prompted. "I think you should consider the Carpentras's invite."

Tori looked between them, and Lily gestured for her to sit.

She plopped into an armchair.

"Baron Tibost of Carpentras has invited us for a diplomatic visit," Lily explained. "Have you heard anything about him?"

Tori shook her head and twisted the hem of her cloak in her hands. "No, sorry. I haven't had a chance to head east yet."

"He is a good man," Edmund insisted. "He hasn't given us problems in as long as I've been here."

Lily pursed her lips. The rumors were concerning. Already they'd sent one would-be-murderer her way. If she'd learned anything as a Hawk, it was that words had power. She needed to get ahead of them before they swamped her. Prove she wasn't power-hungry and slaying her way through the country.

She nodded. Then nodded again. "Accept the invitation."

⚬

The roads to Carpentras were clear, but that didn't stop the muscles in Lily's back from stiffening. The trees had been cut back a good five yards from either side of the road. That significantly lowered the chance of bandits or an ambush. Or it at least deterred them. They would choose somewhere easier to target. Still, there was something about being on the road again that felt dangerous. Especially when her positions, titles, and property made her a worthy challenge for bandits. She had come to like the security of Avisier.

Lily took a deep breath and released it at the first signs they were nearing Carpentras. The white lime wash of the city was in stark contrast to the green fields around it. They'd ridden a few hours the night they left and all of the previous day.

Now, as the sun was nearing the horizon, they were nearing the outskirts of the city.

"You'll be fine," Edmund said.

Lily glanced at him. "You severely overestimate my experience." He knew, of course, she'd spent time in castles before. Otherwise, Avisier would've been in chaos.

"Just remember to keep your chin up, and let others serve you," Edmund said. "We're here to support you. Trust me."

"I do." The words slipped out before Lily could really think them through. As she mulled them over, she realized they were true. There was something easy about being with Edmund.

Lily tugged on the sleeve of her red blouse, trying to remember Jarek's training. People see what they expect to see. People would be expecting to see a noble lady, so that was what she would give them. It wasn't her first time playing the part.

With a start, she realized she was no longer playing. The letter from the king demanding more taxes also contained a signet ring. A stylized lily. Not very original, but it was hers. She really was a noble lady now. She just wished it hadn't come with demands for coins.

"You look worried," Edmund stated.

"I am worried. I feel unarmed and unprepared. Are you sure my Casseterran is good enough?"

Edmund tilted his head. "Plenty, certainly better than my trade." Over the last few months, while he had been teaching her to read Casseterran, she had begun teaching him trade. He was a quick learner but was still nowhere near able to hold a conversation.

"And I'm fully armed," Tori said.

Lily had forgone the bow, deciding it looked too hostile. She still wore her knives at her side and one strapped to her ribs beneath her shirt, but she had also had to abandon the spares that normally dotted her limbs. Tori, on the other hand, was in standard Hawk attire and fully armed, traveling under the guise of Lily's personal guard.

It did make her feel better to have Tori at her side, even though she suspected the woman was just as nervous.

They crossed the bridge into the city without issue. Lily supposed, due to the relative proximity of the cities, her group had never traveled far enough from a castle for anyone besides its owner to torment travelers. Carpentras was a small province, about half the size of Avisier. Size meant nothing to authority, but with Jeremias dead, Lily technically had the higher title. Baron Tibost was much more established within the country. By her estimates, that put them on about equal footing.

Edmund and Tori fell behind Lily, riding in formal positions and leaving Lily to pick through the city on her own as she headed their party. The crowds there parted quicker than they had in Avisier, or the obvious authority of their ensembles told people it was wise to get out of the way.

The white castle at the top of a hill was hard to miss, and she followed the route to it easy enough.

The gates to the castle were open, but guards were surveying the few people who dared to venture through the guardhouse. Lily stopped as a guard approached her, asking for identification.

She nodded to Edmund, who produced the paper inviting them to the castle.

"Marquess Lily—of Avisier," he announced, smoothly covering for the fact she'd never told him a last name.

The guard glanced at the seal affixed to the bottom of the parchment, recognized it, and allowed them through. He called up to his counterparts on the wall, announcing her arrival too.

They were ushered under the raised spikes of the portcullis and into a narrow bailey, where they were greeted by many pages offering to take their horses.

Lily took that as their official invitation to dismount but still waited for Edmund to dismount first, hand his horse to a page, and come over to hers. His presence was merely for appearance as he steadied her beneath her shoulders while she dismounted. He quickly and politely stepped back. A shield for Lily while she straightened her tunic after it had been pulled up by the saddle.

Another page stepped forward, bowing, and offering to show them to their rooms.

Edmund waited for Lily's nod before accepting.

The castle was moderately decorated. Curtains framed every window, and the hallways were dotted with the occasional vase or tapestry. Nothing was overly luxurious, but care was taken to make the place look good.

The little group was separated, each led by a page to their individual rooms. Lily was guided inwards and upwards. After all, the statelier quarters would hardly be on the ground floor. She stifled her questions as they continued past the main floors of the keep. The page led her further and further up, till Lily realized they were in a turret clinging to the side of the central tower.

Two guards stood outside a large oaken door, barely blinking as they appeared. The page ignored them, opening the door for Lily. She followed him in, clenching her jaw as she passed the guards. In a tower with only one exit, the idea of guards that weren't hers at the door set her on edge. It was too much like being in the dungeon again.

"Your luggage will be brought up in a few minutes. Is there anything else you require before dinner, my lady?"

"No," Lily said before looking around the room. "You may take your leave."

The page bowed, backing out the door, and Lily listened, waiting for the sound of a lock, but none came.

It was a simple guest suite. There was no separation between the sitting area and the sleeping area, but there was an attached room for necessities. Small windows were spaced every few feet, and Lily peered out to discover she was nearly six stories up. The furniture was decent, a padded green sofa and matching chairs that mercifully lacked throw pillows.

Lily waited while her luggage was brought up, instructing the servants that she would unpack herself. Instead, she left a few moments after them, darting past the guards before they had a chance to say anything. They didn't give chase as she wound her way down the tower to the main levels.

A passing servant mindlessly told her where Edmund and Tori would be staying.

There was a distinct lack of guards outside Edmund's room when she knocked. He opened the door only a moment later, stepping aside so she could slip in before anyone noticed.

He smiled. "I expected at least another half hour before you showed up."

"Tower room," Lily said, taking a seat in a hard wooden chair to look around. Edmund's room was furnished with only two chairs, a table, and a bed. The bed at least looked comfortable, but it clearly wasn't one of the prime guest rooms. "With two guards."

"So?" Edmund asked, clearly not seeing her point.

"It feels like a trap. It would be easy to lock me in."

"Or," Edmund suggested with an amused tone, "they're guarding you from harm."

Lily doubted it. In Casseterre's political climate, holding someone prisoner could lead to a lot of gain. Or being held prisoner, as Lily was living proof of.

"Regardless, I feel safer with you."

Edmund looked startled at the admission. And words didn't form.

Lily smiled gently and added, "We make a good team. I can trust you."

Edmund bowed his head at the compliment. "We do."

"Tell me how dinner works again?" she asked, leaning her elbow on the table.

Edmund took the chair across from her. "Well, someone will probably come to your room to escort you down. It will probably be a small meal, just us and the most important in the castle. You will be announced and escorted to your seat, likely beside Baron Tibost. Let him lead the conversation. And avoid any talk of business."

"And at the end?" Lily asked.

"You'll be invited for coffee in another room. This will last twenty or so minutes. Then we move to the ballroom for dancing."

Lily wasn't sure why she was asking so many questions. She'd attended formal dinners and dances in Albrin with Princess Adelaide. Still, her head spun at the idea of a night of activities in Casseterre. Avisier had been a whirlwind as she got her feet under her. They'd had no time for balls or fancy dinners.

Some small part of her worried Randson would be there, though she doubted he would find her there if he hadn't in Avisier. Things were going too well for her.

Eventually, the other shoe was going to drop.

Edmund reached across and squeezed her shoulder reassuringly. "You'll be fine."

"I hope so."

Lily sat quietly as Edmund began to unpack his bags and hang clothes in the wardrobe. She lit a lamp as the light coming through the window dimmed, an excuse to linger in the space just a minute longer. "I suppose I should get ready," Lily said when there was nothing else to do. She stood and made her way to the door.

"See you in a bit," Edmund said, throwing a smile over his shoulder.

Lily returned the smile, crossing the threshold and closing the door behind her. She went uninterrupted as she made her way to her rooms. It seemed most of the castle was getting ready for dinner themselves. No one had noticed a Marquess wandering the unfamiliar halls.

Lily unpacked a single bag, pulling out an elaborately folded blue dress.

She slipped the dress over her head, shimmying into the stiff bodice. It settled nicely on her hips; the skirt flowed out to brush just above the floor. It was a dress made for the steadily approaching winter, with bishop sleeves ballooning at the shoulders and cinching at her wrists. The fabric had a lovely, subtle floral pattern woven into it. The shoulders covered her back nicely, a feature Lily had never requested. She suspected one of the maids had caught a glimpse of her scars and taken them into consideration.

Lily took her hair down, letting it flow past her shoulders. It was in nice shape, which she owed to the fact it had been in a braid since she last washed it. Still, there were a few frizzy bits from riding. She smoothed them down with water, not daring to brush them for risk of the mess doubling.

A small necklace finished the look just as there was a knock on her door. Her hands fiddled with the clasp for a few moments before addressing the noise.

Lily opened it to find a maid waiting.

The lady curtseyed. "I have been sent to escort you to dinner, my lady."

Lily followed her wordlessly. She was led to the first floor and past the grand entrance to a minor dining room.

This wasn't the great hall, where Lily knew the majority of the castle would be eating. This room was much smaller, dominated by a large dining table. The roof was lined with wooden beams, which trailed down the walls and to the floor, making it seem like they were within the ribcage of a giant tree. An elaborate dining spread was laid out, with perhaps the most silverware Lily had ever seen outside of Princess Adelaide's wedding to Brennus, who had been Lily's childhood friend.

Edmund and Tori stood as soon as Lily entered, prompting the table to follow.

Lily was escorted to the final empty chair, and the maid pulled it out for her.

She sat with a nod to the man to her left. He would be Baron Tibost, the woman on his other side, his wife, Baroness Marina Tibost. Edmund sat to her right, and so it went around the table, alternating male and female.

Tori had forgone the normal Hawk's cloak, seated on Edmund's other side, opting instead for their formal uniform. The primary difference was the lack of a cloak and a white shirt, maybe a change of shoes.

There were, of course, no bows in the room. The men wore formal swords at their hips. Tori had managed to argue in a heavy knife and a dagger it appeared, and Lily herself was visibly unarmed, though there were blades strapped to her thighs and one under her bodice. A habit time had taught her to always keep. They were accessible through slits cleverly hidden as pockets in the folds of her skirts.

"Lady Lily," Baron Tibost said with a smile. "It is a pleasure to make your acquaintance."

"The pleasure is all mine," Lily replied. "Let me take this chance to thank you for the invitation to your beautiful castle."

Baron Tibost was not a thinly built man. Though he wasn't particularly tall, Lily had no doubt he was near twice her weight. He wasn't fat either, mostly muscled and filled out with a healthy diet. The type of man built for a fight—and trained for one.

He held a title in Casseterre. Lily was reminded that very few nobles there were the cushy, undisciplined type that could be encountered in so many places. The majority had either fought for their position or fought to keep it.

His smile didn't falter for a second as he gestured to his wife. "Allow me to introduce Baroness Marina Tibost, my lovely wife."

Marina smiled at Lily as the first course appeared before them. The first streaks of gray were beginning to show in her hair, but her smile was friendly as they exchanged pleasantries.

Marina then moved to converse with Edmund, as was considered polite. Baron Tibost fixed his attention on Lily. "They say you come from Albrin. Is this true?"

"Yes," Lily said. "I was born and raised there."

"Whatever brought you to Avisier?" Tibost asked, surprised.

Lily took a sip of her wine before answering, deciding to chance a joke. "A horse."

Tibost seemed to be caught off guard, but he recovered quickly and gave a polite laugh. "I suppose it would be a long way to walk. Of course, there is a boat somewhere in there."

Lily maintained a polite smile. She enjoyed the lighthearted jests. "Yes, that did seem the best way to cross the channel."

"If you do not mind my asking, what did you do in Albrin?"

Stole. And then hunted thieves like herself. Neither of those was a good answer. Lily shrugged, allowing herself a minute to swallow food. "What everyone else did, I suppose. Find a way to eat."

"I have always wanted to visit."

"You should. It's lovely in the summer."

"Unfortunately, if you leave a castle here for too long, it tends to not be friendly when you return."

For a brief moment, Lily considered the invitation may be a trap once again. But if she were truly only there for a few days, it would be nowhere near long enough to siege a castle.

"Of course."

CHAPTER 20

FAMILY MATTERS

The meal passed without incident. Everyone was on their best straight-backed, immaculately polished behavior. Edmund had been right; business had been set aside for later discussion. Conversation centered around the weather, fashion, and food preferences. All harmless subjects and, luckily, ones she had a decent vocabulary of.

Tibost stood after servants whisked away the last of the dessert dishes.

The hall fell into a polite quiet as he smiled and said, "I'd like to invite everyone to join us for coffee and dancing in the great hall." He gestured to a pair of oak doors and those dining took it as a signal the meal was complete.

They rose around her, some chatting with people they hadn't sat near and others filing into the new location.

Lily stood, setting her napkin down and looking for Edmund. He and Tibost were conversing near the wall as people filed past them. She decided not to interrupt and made to follow the crowd to the second room.

As she stepped through the doors, the room opened up, soaring in height. The wooden beams were continued in there, now dotted with chandeliers that looked to be made from antler. Much more of the castle's population was present, gathering in small clusters throughout the space.

To one side of the room was a series of tables draped in a green cloth. People swarmed the coffee pots atop them. The familiar scent wafted to Lily, calling her in that direction.

There was a gentle touch on her elbow, and she turned to see Marina. The woman pulled Lily aside with a smile. "Is your room acceptable? Is there anything you need changed before the night ends?" Marina's voice was laced with honey.

Lily bit back a retort that it felt like a trap. "It is lovely."

Marina breathed, her shoulders dipping slightly. "I am so glad. We had a few extra decorations brought up. We do not usually have guests there but..." she trailed off, waving a hand. "It no longer matters, I am simply glad it is to your tastes."

Lily frowned. "Why do you not normally have guests there?"

"It just normally is not decorated for them. We only use it if very low on space, but my husband insisted, so I had to try and spruce it up. You know how men are." Marina's voice took on a conspiratorial tone. Then she paused, seeming to consider. "Did you really kill Baron D'Lavaud?"

Lily was shocked at the woman's bluntness. Throughout the meal, she had been laced with court charm. Easy enough for Lily to navigate, though she knew the woman wasn't the sweet crooning wife she made herself out to be. Lily had been to enough balls to know that demeanor was always fake, anyway. Everything was a game, careful maneuvering to get what you wanted.

So why was Marina letting her see past her mask?

"I did," Lily replied cautiously. "It was self-defense."

"Then you might stand a chance," Marina mused, her eyes darting to where her Tibost and Edmund were still talking.

"A chance of what?"

Marina took a deep breath. "Everyone in this country is ambitious. Rumor has it D'Lavaud's death was an accident and, well, Avisier is a sizable chunk of land." Marina took Lily's hand in her own. "You seem a nice girl. This country—what type of men do you think come to power?" she asked.

"I assure you, I have been around worse." And she had been. Though the scars on her back were the worst, her body was covered in them. Each one well and thoroughly earned. Each a mark of her survival when others had not.

Marina frowned, but it was gone in an instant. "You certainly are brave." Suddenly, something in her face shifted as her eyes landed on something behind Lily's shoulder. "Ah, here come our men."

Lily turned, making eye contact with Edmund as he and Tibost stood at the door, scanning the room. Edmund made his way over to her, laying a gentle hand on the small of her back.

The touch was so simple, yet so unexpected that Lily flinched.

"What were you ladies talking about?"

"Politics. Edmund, how has this country not been taken over? Uleta is ambitious, and quite frankly this government is a mess."

Uleta was a country that bordered Casseterre to the south. They'd once had a great empire, and now spent their efforts trying to recreate it. One desperate act after another.

"Uleta ruled this part of Casseterre once," Edmund explained to Lily. "It's protected by international treaty."

"That doesn't stop the occasional skirmish," Tibost said as he draped an arm around Marina's shoulders. "They grow more frequent every year. Though the mountains are impassable in the winter, so I wouldn't worry at the moment."

"That's enough of politics!" Marina's bubbly voice interrupted. "You can babble about that tomorrow. Tonight is for catching up. Edmund, dear, how is your mother?"

Edmund's hand tensed on Lily's back. "She's dead." His voice came out lower than she'd ever heard it, with an edge to it she was unfamiliar with.

"A pity." Marina frowned and confessed, "The Rouselles were much better neighbors than D'Lavaud. We visited each other often. Your mother and I were close friends, you know."

"Funny," Edmund said, pinning Marina with a glare, "she never mentioned you."

"We lost touch after she moved to Uleta," Marina replied dryly. "That does not mean we weren't friends once. I am sorry to hear of her passing."

Lily studied Edmund's face. Hard lines had set in it, a darkness passing over his features. Then it was gone in a moment, his brow softening. "I appreciate it, but perhaps we should move on to happier matters?"

Something wasn't adding up. Edmund's mother had lived in Avisier. That's why Edmund knew everyone so well. Why he seemed capable of running the place. He'd grown up there and managed to keep his job as a secretary when his mother was imprisoned for insulting D'Lavaud. But why would they have visited the Tibosts?

"Certainly," Tibost obliged. "One of our mares has just given birth to a beautiful foal. Perhaps tomorrow we can pay them a visit."

"I'm sorry." Lily shook her head to clear it. "You must be mistaken. Edmund's mother was not a Rouselle."

"Oh, but she was," Marina said with a frown. "Did he not tell you?" Her gaze flicked to Edmund. "I am sure there was a good reason."

There better have been. Baron Rouselle had ruled Avisier for years before being killed in a duel. If Edmund was Rouselle's grandson, that made him the heir to Avisier. It made him her alternative.

"Yes, I am sure there is," Lily replied dryly. She turned to Edmund. "And that reason would be?"

Edmund bit his lower lip. He looked between the two women. "Honestly, I thought she had told you."

Lily bit off a retort, suddenly aware of all the eyes in the room. She took a breath, looking at Tibost. "If you will excuse me for a moment, that coffee is calling my name."

Tibost chuckled tightly. "Of course."

Lily left without another glance at Edmund. She couldn't bear to look at him. Her cheeks were on fire. She had thought Edmund trusted her. To hide this? Maybe he really didn't.

Tori hustled over from where she had been frozen beside the coffee station. "What just happened?"

"I don't know," Lily replied. She grabbed the woman's arm, moving them into a corner to break the gazes that were stabbing into her back. They were easily brushed off when she held her composure, but now that it was slipping...

"You look like you fell asleep in the sun." Tori kept her voice low.

Lily sighed, glancing around the room at the small groups that had formed. Edmund seemed to have vanished. Tibost was having a heated discussion with Lady Marina in one of the other corners.

"Did Edmund ever tell you his mother was Cecilia Rouselle?"

"No?" Tori beckoned to a passing servant, snatched a glass of water from their tray, and handed it to Lily. "Why?"

The glass was cool in Lily's hand. She pressed it to her overheating face. "Baron Rouselle was D'Lavaud's predecessor." And unless it was just a coincidence, that meant Cecilia had been the rightful heir to Avisier before D'Lavaud. And now, Edmund was. Lily was ruling what should have been Edmund's province. And he'd *let* her.

Or had he? He'd taken care of most of the tasks. She'd thought it helpful that he filtered out the unimportant ones, but how could she really know what he'd stopped before it reached her? Maybe he'd just been manipulating her. Using her as a shield against threats like Jeremias as he ran things behind the scenes.

"Take a deep breath." Tori laid a hand on Lily's arm. "I'm sure it's a simple misunderstanding."

"How is that a misunderstanding?" Lily said, louder than she intended. She shut herself up by taking a sip of cool water. It did help, some.

Tori gave her a pitying tilt of her head. "I see the way he looks at you, Lily."

"What? Like I'm some game he's been winning for the last three months?"

"Like he *cares* about you."

Lily froze.

The weight of Tori's words pushed her shoulders down, pushed her head down. She wanted to curl up into a ball.

She'd grown to like Edmund. His goofy smile, the way he was patient with her when she learned. The way he never tried to stop her from doing anything. Now she just wished she could wrap herself in her cloak and disappear.

Tori looked toward the center of the floor. "I think the dancing will start soon. Pull yourself together."

Lily nodded. She took a few deep breaths, letting years of professionalism wash over her. In her line of work, there was no room for fear or doubt. No room to ruminate for hours over what someone had or hadn't told you. She pushed the feelings of betrayal aside and focused on the matter at hand.

The people of Avisier trusted her to work with their best interests at heart.

Baron Tibost approached her, bowing formally.

She curtseyed in response, taking the Baron's offered arm as he led her to the center of the dance floor. They both waited a moment, taking in the pace of the melody. Baron Tibost moved first, and Lily followed his lead.

It was a fairly standard four-step tempo, one Lily had danced plenty of times before. She was stiff, and the turmoil that had roiled through her only minutes before still worked its way out of her system.

"I am sorry," Baron Tibost said quietly once the others had begun to join in the dance. "We thought you were aware." He must have been able to feel her stiffness.

She willed her muscles to relax and take in the flow of the music. A well-timed spin allowed her a moment of respite before she answered, "I was not."

They made their way around the floor, turning slightly with each set of steps. He stood a polite distance away, his hand more hovering over her waist than gripping her there. For that, she was grateful. She'd danced with too many men who pulled her into their chest as if they had a right to do so.

"If you wanted to turn in early, I wouldn't blame you," Tibost replied.

Lily was grateful for the understanding. Everything she had seen from this man had been nothing but polite. She let her focus wander from the steps to analyze his features. His eyes were soft, and his jaw had a concern set to it.

The distraction made her stumble slightly, but he gripped her hand tighter to help her regain balance. Her eyes caught on Edmund, who was watching them intently.

"The last thing I want is to be alone," Lily admitted. She pressed her lips together, trying to appear nervous. Maybe he would take pity on her. "I would appreciate some answers, if you have them."

"Admittedly, I do not have many. Marina was always better friends with Cecilia than I. While her father and I spoke of business, they would walk the gardens together."

"How long have you been the baron?" Lily asked. D'Lavaud had been in charge for years. And if Cecilia had a whole life in Uleta—that was another conversation entirely.

"Since my father died when I was young." Tibost caught Lily's glance. "Natural causes, luckily. Fifty years ago now." He spun Lily to a trill in the music. "Baron Rouselle reached out to me, hoping to continue the friendly relations our fiefs enjoyed. I tried to return the favor with D'Lavaud, but he turned me down."

"And that's why you reached out to me?"

Tibost nodded. "I had no idea Edmund was there. We knew they returned after the breakup, but then D'Lavaud took over and that was the last we heard. I assumed that man had ended their line."

Lily lapsed into silence. There really wasn't anything to say. Over Tibost's shoulder, she saw Edmund had returned to the gathering.

She jerked her head away from him quickly, and Tibost looked poised to question her.

"Sorry, I am ... a little distracted."

"I understand. I know the song is not yet over, but we can stop if you wish."

"No," Lily blurted. Because she knew Edmund would want to talk to her. He'd offer her some petty excuses she didn't want to hear. At least he couldn't approach her while she was locked in the dances.

CHAPTER 21

A DANCE OF DECEPTION

Lily was swept into dance after dance. She maintained polite conversation but couldn't stop her mind wandering. Edmund had always been so kind. And he'd been the first to kneel the day D'Lavaud died. Maybe he had been okay with her in charge. Maybe he'd decided he didn't want authority, didn't want the danger that came with it. Princess Adelaide had expressed that sentiment to Lily when they were younger. Or maybe he was using her as a human shield. As he openly admitted, he was no good in a fight.

Edmund approached where she and one of the knights danced. "May I cut in?"

The man stepped back, clearly having seen the earlier confrontation and not about to get in the way. Before Lily could protest, Edmund took her hand and wrapped an arm around her waist, sliding into the space the previous man had just evacuated. "I've been trying to talk to you all night."

"And I've been trying to avoid you all night," Lily quipped back. Edmund swept into the music, dragging Lily behind. Everywhere his skin touched hers, tingles followed, like butterfly wings beating against her skin. Her back was tense under his hand. Her movements less graceful as every muscle in her body yelled at her to do anything beyond letting him lead her in the dance.

"How could you?" Lily swallowed at the way her voice cracked. She looked up to hold back the tears that were threatening to fall.

"You haven't exactly been honest with me either." His grip tightened on her hand.

Her eyes shot to his as her jaw set. "What do you mean?"

The music sent them into a complicated series of steps that had them both more focused on not making a fool of themselves than on their discussion. Edmund's hand was light on Lily's back, patiently guiding her. Not that she needed it.

"I thought you weren't raised noble?" Edmund asked as the music settled into a slower rhythm once again.

"I wasn't," Lily replied, smoothly flowing into a spin. "I had to learn for work."

Edmund smiled as she twirled back into him, pulling her a little closer than they'd been dancing before. "Whoever taught you did a good job."

Lily grinned despite herself. "I could say the same for you." Her frown found its way back. "Stop trying to distract me. The very least you owe me is an explanation." If this dance was to continue without her storming off, that was what she would get.

"Yes, I do." Edmund sighed. "My mother was Cecilia Rouselle, daughter of Baron Archibald Rouselle."

"The Baron D'Lavaud killed?"

Edmund nodded tightly. "Yes. When my mother was old enough, she married a wealthy man in Uleta. It was a business match. My brother and I were born there, grew up there."

"You have a brother?" Another potential wrinkle in this whole thing.

"I don't speak of him because we don't get along. When Uleta's political climate ... shifted, my mother and father were on opposite sides of the issue. As were my brother and I."

Lily couldn't imagine what political issue could divide a family like that. She couldn't imagine not getting along with her brother, Nick. But if the parents had never truly been close, maybe it didn't take all that much.

Edmund placed both hands on her waist, lifting her from one side of his body to the other in time with the music. Lily did her best to remain calm and graceful despite her lack of familiarity with the move. Soon they were back to graceful, sweeping steps.

"Is that an Uletan move?" Lily teased.

"Yes, actually," Edmund replied, a tinge of pink coming to his face. "I learned there when I was a teenager."

"So that's before you decided to run Avisier behind my back."

"What?" Edmund nearly dropped her hand. "Lily, I'd never betray you. I swear."

"Then what have these last few months been?" Lily hissed. "Do you have any idea how embarrassing it is to not know that about your—"

About her what? Their relationship was stronger than just coworkers, but they'd never defined it. She knew Edmund liked her. He'd certainly taken the time out of his day to help her when he could've found a million excuses. And she was certain she would have run Avisier into the ground without him. But what did that make them?

Edmund squeezed her hand. "I was waiting for the right time to tell you. I did not know the words in your language. And you did not know them in mine."

He guided her around the dance floor with expert grace. Part of her wanted to stomp on his toes as revenge for how calmly he seemed to be taking the whole situation. "When I was fifteen, it became too much. My mother returned to Avisier, and I went with her. It was a good few years. My grandfather employed me as his secretary. My mother tended to the garden."

Lily gave him a confused look.

"She didn't have to," he hurried to say. "We were well provided for. But it was her hobby."

Edmund twirled her again, and on the return kept spinning so she ended with her back to his chest. His arms were wrapped around her, and they swayed for a couple beats.

Lily cursed her body for how it wanted to melt into his embrace. Then she twirled out again, and they returned to their starting positions.

"When D'Lavaud came, my mother tried to stop him. She was injured. She never fully recovered, as you saw. But the people liked her. There would have been an uprising if he had her executed. So, she quietly disappeared. Very few people were told she was in the dungeon. I don't think he ever realized we were related."

"I'm sorry." The words spilled out of Lily's mouth before she could stop them. And they were true. What Edmund had been through, what he'd hidden to survive. That wasn't something you just told anyone.

And he was right about her keeping secrets. She knew he saw how cautious she was when they were in town. She knew he refrained from asking why she was in Casseterre in the first place. He'd told her now. Was that because his hand was forced, or because he trusted her?

The music ended, and Edmund released her waist. He bent down, kissing the back of the hand that remained in his. Butterflies darted from where his lips touched up her arm and then into her chest, leaving her feeling lighter. "I could not live with myself if you thought I was using you, Lily. I hope you forgive me."

◆

Lily slipped away from the dance not long after that. Grabbing the bag of fancy clothes she'd been given, she stole to her room.

A pillow and one of her bags were easily thrust under the covers, and together a rough approximation of herself was assembled. Under the dim light coming through the windows and weak inspection, it would pass. The Tibosts had been nothing but kind, but it wasn't worth the risk of it being a trap. Jarek had always told her to assume the worst to avoid being surprised by it.

She changed into night clothes and threw a cloak on top, peeking only her head out to the guards. "Would you two go check on my horse? I thought I heard her outside. I just need someone to check that she is safe."

"Of course, my lady," one of the guards said, giving a slight bow.

"You really ought to both go. She can be a bit stubborn with strangers," Lily said.

The second guard looked annoyed, but he bowed briefly before following the first down the stairs. Maybe, if they left so easily, it wasn't a trap after all.

Lily waited a minute, giving them plenty of time to get out of her path before she darted out her door. With her head down and in the flickering torchlight, she doubted anyone would look her way twice. Luckily, she didn't run into anyone on the brief journey to Tori's room.

Lily paced in the dark, not daring to light the small lantern on the table. She looked to the door at the sound of footsteps in the hall, freezing in her tracks.

The door eased open on well-oiled hinges, and Tori jumped back when she saw Lily. The woman put a hand over her heart, stepping in as she took a couple of calming deep breaths.

Her eyes darted around the room, taking in the lack of light and Lily's bag. "What are you doing in my room? Are we running?"

"No," Lily replied. "I'm just worried about staying in the tower."

"Right." Tori took a moment to compose herself. Then she sat on her bed, pulling off her shoes. "So, you danced with Edmund?"

"Ye-es," Lily drew out the word, not entirely sure what Tori was aiming at.

"After you found out he's been hiding things from us?"

"Yes..." Lily grew suspicious of the mischievous glint in Tori's eye.

The girl leaned back, supporting herself on her elbows. "Do you like him?"

Lily was glad for the darkness hiding the heat in her cheeks. "People dance with each other at these things all the time. It doesn't mean anything."

"It does when you leave immediately after."

Lily smiled. Tori had been more observant than she anticipated. That was a good skill in a Hawk. It was unfortunate Tori had left so close to earning her golden feather.

Tori took Lily's silence as agreement. "You do like him!"

Lily ducked under the pillow that was suddenly hurtling toward her head. "Do not!"

Even in the dark, Lily could tell Tori rolled her eyes. Tori dug through a bag, pulling out her nightclothes.

Lily realized her silence had lasted too long, and replied, "He lied."

"He ... didn't tell you everything," Tori said slowly, "But you haven't told him everything either."

The bed squeaked as Lily sat. When the girl had changed, she sat beside Lily. "Randson may be an ass, but living with him taught me that when you want information, you have to volunteer some in return."

Lily raised her eyebrows. "That's generally for witnesses or interrogations."

"I still think it applies here," Tori insisted, "It's time to open up."

Lily grumbled, "We are being *hunted*. I don't want to put him in danger. If Randson goes after him—"

"He's only a target if you like him," Tori teased.

And there it was. Edmund meant nothing to Randson if he meant nothing to Lily. Lily knew it was true. Not only that ... she also worried Edmund would be scared away by reality. This way, they could ignore the problem, at least for a while.

"He's told you his secrets," Tori continued and climbed into bed, tucking herself in. "And it can't hurt to have him on our side."

Lily began to lay out her bedroll on the floor. "It could hurt a lot. If he decides it's too dangerous to stay." To stay for her.

CHAPTER 22

NEGOTIATIONS

Lily snuck back to her room in the early hours of the morning when the sky was light, but the sun wasn't visible. The guards had rotated, and she lied and told them she'd just gone for a walk. Their belief was comforting. It meant they never intended to lock her in.

It was easy for her to rise early. Troubled thoughts had kept her awake most of the night. She couldn't imagine functioning without Edmund at her side. Then again, if anyone else had committed that sort of deception, she'd never trust them again.

Then there was what Tori said. Lily couldn't deny the heat that rose to her cheeks whenever she thought of herself and Edmund together.

It was all too complicated to deal with on top of the day's politics. So, she asked to eat breakfast in her room. The maids obliged, delivering toast, jam, and two eggs, as well as a pot of hot coffee. When Lily asked for milk, they were confused but obliged her.

Perched within a window box, she witnessed dawn unfurling its golden tendrils over the formidable mountains that formed a natural boundary between Casseterre and Uleta. The peaks, at the early hour, seemed to cradle the first light of day, and Lily dreamed of the fresh mountain air as she waited to be called to the meeting with Tibost.

A knock on the door startled her out of her thoughts.

She rose, straightening her skirts before opening the door a crack. When she saw Tori's familiar face, she opened it wider.

"He's waiting for you in his office. Edmund was supposed to tell you, but I thought you might prefer it if I came."

"Thank you."

Tori extended her arm in a mocking imitation of how Casseterran men escorted women around.

Lily laughed, interlocking her arm with the woman's.

She was led down a series of hallways, where Tori didn't even bother knocking before opening a heavy oak door. They were in an antechamber, with a desk placed on one wall and a long bench placed on the other. Across from them, a door stood open, and Baron Tibost was just visible through it.

He approached upon spotting them and promptly bowed. "Lady Lily, thank you for agreeing to meet with me."

Lily curtseyed in response, remembering all her lessons in formalities. "The pleasure is mine, Lord Tibost."

"Your escort may wait in the antechamber," he stated as he rose.

Lily gave Tori a slight nod. The woman plopped onto the bench, seeming more at ease than Lily felt.

Lily walked into the office. It was large, with wide windows providing an alternative view of mountains that rose from the ground like teeth. Their tops were blanketed with clouds now, which flowed down their sides and into valleys.

In the corner, a fireplace smoldered, heating the room.

Tibost stood behind a desk placed near it. He gestured to a chair across from him, and Lily sat, adjusting her skirt so she could access her knives if need be.

"Would you be more comfortable proceeding in the trade language?" Tibost offered.

"Yes," Lily almost burst out with relief. True, she had practiced her Casseterran for the occasion, but her pride wasn't worth risking a miscommunication.

He returned to his seat, shuffling a few papers. "I thought these might be of interest to you, but they're in Casseterran."

Lily thought of how Edmund was so patiently teaching her to read. When she came to a word she couldn't figure out, he'd help her understand the letters needed to be pronounced, and those that didn't. Normally, she'd have him help with formal documents. That wasn't a weakness she was prepared to admit.

"I can read it," she said, holding her hand out.

Tibost passed her the papers.

Her eyes frantically scanned the page for words she knew. Instead, she found mostly numbers. Trade records between the two fiefs. And, at the bottom, a signature that read Rouselle.

The types of goods were a little harder to make out, but Tibost saved her the embarrassment of asking. "It's a record of trade between Carpentras and Avisier. We used to be close allies before D'Lavaud took over. It's an alliance Carpentras has missed dearly. The border between us is long, and it was comforting not having to guard it." He cast his gaze out the window at the mountains. "There have been more crossings recently. No large parties, but enough to make you wonder." His attention turned back to Lily as he said, "I would like to be able to move forces from our shared border to my border with Uleta, but I can't do that unless I have an ally on the other side."

Lily raised her eyebrows. "Would that not make our border vulnerable?"

"Did you face any problems on the journey here?" Tibost looked offended.

Lily shook her head.

Tibost nodded once, seeming satisfied. "That road is at the heart of both our territories. The only forces to threaten it are us."

That made sense enough. Of course, bandits could always be an issue, but they took far fewer resources to control than the threat of a rival territory.

"Do I have an ally on that border?"

"What does Avisier stand to gain?"

"You'd also be able to lessen your presence, reallocate troops to Palliers now that you control it."

It sounded tempting. Or like a trick. Edmund would know if the man could be trusted, but Lily couldn't ask him. "Or you want me to lessen my presence there to move your own troops in."

Baron Tibost nodded as if expecting the objection. "You're learning how things are here quickly. That is not my intent."

"I need some guarantee."

Tibost tapped on the table as he looked around the office.

Lily's eyes caught on the glimmering metal of his signet ring. It bore the symbol of a dog. Tibost must have noticed her gaze because he plucked the ring from his pinky and examined it.

"Strange how something so small can mean so much."

"That much gold would change the life of most people," Lily countered. It's what had caught her gaze. There was a time when she would have contemplated if she could take it without him noticing.

Baron Tibost nodded. "So it would." He slid the ring back on and sighed. "I've heard that there was a time it would've changed yours," he said.

Lily shrugged, her words coming out brisker than intended, "I wasn't born noble."

"There's no problem with that, not in this country," the baron replied. "Though I understand you faced problems with it in Albrin."

"What?" slipped out before Lily could stop it.

"I've heard the rumors," Baron Tibost said with a smile. "And I know there's a kernel of truth at the heart of every rumor. So, I dug."

Lily's chest tightened as the man continued.

"I do not think you are here to conquer Casseterre, as De Falchi claims. But I do think you were chased out of your home for reaching too high. You robbed the Albrini king."

Lily nodded, not trusting her voice wouldn't shake if she spoke. The details were muddy, but that was what had happened. Someone who knew the truth had started the rumors.

Her face heated as the baron studied her. She felt pinned to her chair like a hunting trophy to the wall. She swallowed the frog in her throat. "Then why would you trust me?"

"Survival is not a crime, Lily." The smile had never faded from his face, but it softened a little. "To me, that means you have what it takes when things get rough. And with De Falchi's recent expansions, that's someone I want on my side." He finished, "You want certainty. I can offer you this. I will keep my title as baron, but I would sign on under you as duchess."

Lily took a moment, letting the words tumble through her mind.

Albrin did not have dukes and duchesses, but she was familiar with the concept. He would maintain administrative control over his land, his title would still pass to any heirs, but it would place her between him and the king in the chain of command. More importantly, his territory would become more of a subset of hers than something separate.

"I don't know much about the laws surrounding things like this," Lily admitted.

Baron Tibost gave her a pitying look. "How are you after last night?"

Lily shook her head. "I'd rather stay focused on business."

Tibost chewed on his bottom lip, looking around the room. "How about this, I'll draft a written proposal. It's been an informal agreement in the past, but with times as they are"—he shrugged—"you can bring it back with you to Avisier. Consult your advisors and your records. Get word back to me within the month."

Lily raised an eyebrow, folding her arms. "You'd allow me to leave without making a decision?"

"Your reputation proceeds you, Lady Lily. I doubt I would be able to *allow* you to do anything." Tibost chuckled.

Lily was a little taken aback by that. While she supposed it was meant as a compliment, she wondered what exactly he'd heard. She wasn't about to ask, but she hoped her reputation hadn't spread any further. Perhaps it was time for Tori to have a lesson in managing rumors. It certainly wasn't something Lily could do from Avisier.

"Why would you make an offer like that?"

Tibost chewed on his lower lip once again, as if he was testing out the words before he spoke them. "Unlike many in this country, I inherited my position. While I have done what I must to maintain it"—a graceful way to avoid saying he'd killed people—"I do not have that drive others do. We have enough strife with the raids as it is. I do not have the resources to halt De Falchi's expansion."

He spoke as if she should know about De Falchi, so she pretended she did. Lily met his eyes, searching for some sign of a lie. He held her gaze steadily. There wasn't a twitch, nothing to indicate what he said gave him any discomfort. He had wrinkles around his eyes; a sign of a man who spent plenty of time smiling. The lines in his brow were not deep. They were there, as was every other age-related line, but they didn't give the appearance of a man accustomed to scheming.

"You want to shift his target to me," Lily stated.

"His target is already on you. I want you as a shield."

Boots crunched against gravel as she walked through the garden. At this time of year in Albrin, the trees would be barren. Her feet would've been marching through snow instead of gravel. Here, the trees still held proud coats of green leaves. There weren't flowers, but the garden was still gorgeous.

Tori must have sensed Lily's tumultuous mind because she gracefully ignored her as she walked by. Tibost had given her directions to the garden and the promise of a written proposal. Now Lily wandered amongst hedges, mulling over the events of the last few days.

She found a fountain in what she presumed was the middle of the garden. The water was off for the season, pooling only in the fountain's base.

The voice in the back of her head told her to run. It was getting too dangerous. De Falchi knew things he shouldn't. Someone had told him, had convinced him she was a threat.

She hoped Princess Adelaide had convinced her father that Lily's banishment was enough. Lily and Nick had saved the princess's life enough. Surely, they were owed some respite?

It broke her heart to know the princess probably thought of her as little more than a common thief now.

The reflection of a thief stared back at her.

Her eyes were narrowed with suspicion. As she watched, her cheeks grew hollow, her face filthy. Her hair tangled itself until she was looking at the panicked little girl who had made one dumb mistake. She'd have to leave. *Again.*

She missed morning rides with her brother and Jarek. She missed the peace of living in their small cabin. She'd missed it since she'd been assigned to Evesbury. Part of her wondered if she'd enjoyed being a Hawk because of the job, or just the camaraderie. The way it had given her a family. A purpose.

It wasn't fair. She dashed her hand through the water, and her reflection returned to normal, tears streaming down her red cheeks.

Lily turned, looking back at the keep.

Shutters were opened as the sun reached its zenith, providing the occupants with much-needed light. A figure moved in one of the windows, drawing Lily's gaze. The curly black hair was familiar as Lily swore she locked eyes with Edmund. Then he stood, walking away from the window.

Her heart ached at the thought of saying goodbye to him. At the thought of leaving.

No, she wouldn't say goodbye. She couldn't lose another person.

CHAPTER 23
REVELATIONS

E dmund nodded as Lily explained Tibost's proposal.

She'd launched into her retelling to both of her companions as soon as they were out of the city to avoid a chance to talk about what had happened the night before. They had left that afternoon, so they would be able to travel for nearly half a day before making camp.

"I feel like I remember something like that. We'll have to look through the records to be sure."

"Lily," Tori said slowly, "Are you sure you've thought this through?"

Lily eyed the apprentice, sensing where this particular line of thought was going. "I know it seems too good to be true. But I don't want to just keep fighting my way through this country. We need allies."

"Allies for what?" Tori insisted. "What is your goal here, Lily? This would be three whole provinces!" Both women were startled at the outburst. Tori looked down, twisting the reins around her fingers.

Lily bit her lip. It was different. It was dangerous.

"It's better than being on the run." Lily tried to force her voice to remain calm. "You're the one who wanted to go to Avisier in the first place," she said. That wasn't strictly true. Kyraa had suggested it.

"On the run?" Edmund asked.

Lily's heart froze in her chest. In the heat of the moment, she'd all but forgotten Edmund was there.

She shot a glare at Tori, whose gaze rose to meet Lily's. "We're in too deep, Lily. You need to tell him."

"Tell me what?" Edmund asked in strained trade language. He was following their conversation, but some part of Lily was guilty of hoping he wasn't.

Lily sighed, feeling the muscles around her spine tighten. "It's a bit of a long story, and really better told in a castle."

"Don't do this," Edmund said, "Please."

Something tugged at Lily's chest. The way those blue eyes were looking at her, she couldn't disappoint him. "Fine," Lily said. "When we camp tonight, then."

Edmund looked away, gazing past her to Tori.

Lily found something to keep her busy the rest of the day, pretending to examine tracks or listen for something. Anything to keep from having to address the fear that was now squeezing her chest.

Even as the sun touched the horizon, she made to forge on. She knew she was running. Some part of her feared wrecking all the good she'd found.

"Lily, it's time to stop."

Lily hadn't expected Edmund to say that. Maybe it would come from Tori. But the voice had been undeniably Edmund's.

She turned, knowing he was right. They were at as good a camp as any. Any delay now was just her *running* from a new problem. And she was done running.

"You're right." Even as she said it her throat tightened, as if trying to prevent her from saying the words that would continue the trudge toward losing someone who had become crucial in her life. They worked their way off the road, so they were sheltered from view by a small cluster of trees.

Edmund hitched his horse to a tree, ignoring Lily as he began to unload the animal.

Lily and Tori just let their reins drop, knowing their horses wouldn't wander far, and they didn't turn to each other until the animals were cared for.

"I'll go get some fresh water," Tori said, holding out her hand for their canteens.

Lily handed hers over, grateful the woman would at least pretend to give them some privacy. When she was out of earshot, Lily took a deep breath, idly rubbing Rista's side.

"Do you know what a Hawk is?"

"No," Edmund replied. He stood behind her, where he had set his supplies for the night, and waited for Lily to begin.

"In Albrin, we're a sort of law enforcement. The basics—bandits and tax evasion—but also protecting the throne and whatever comes with it."

"So what are you doing in Casseterre?"

"My brother and I—" Lily swallowed against the tears that were building up. The memories of her life before Jarek had found them weren't pleasant. "We weren't always on the same side as the Hawks."

Edmund nodded, processing what that meant.

She had been a criminal. She supposed she still was. She'd stolen Avisier from him. She was refusing to comply with the Casseterran king's taxes.

"Anyway," Lily continued. "Somehow, the king found out. Randson, another Hawk, was sent to kill me. I don't know if Nick was implicated, too. I didn't stick around to find out. I just ran."

"Are all Hawks as dangerous as you?"

Lily now rotated to look at Edmund, even though her eyes couldn't focus on his face through the tears. "Yes. And I know I should've stayed and fought back, so you don't need to say it."

A silence stretched between them as Lily squeezed her eyes shut against the burning. The shame gnawed at her as she waited for Edmund to yell, to tell her he should've left her in that dungeon. Even worse, he could tell the King of Casseterre.

"I don't blame you," he finally whispered.

For the second time that day, Lily froze at Edmund's words. When he took a few slow steps toward her, she was still as stone.

He reached out, gently taking her hands in his. "I wasn't going to say that. I don't care that you ran. I don't care if you were a thief. We'll get through it, alright?"

Lily's mouth was dry.

Suddenly, Tori couldn't get back with the water fast enough.

"Am a thief," Lily corrected, her voice hoarse. She looked at the dirt beneath her feet. Unable to make eye contact with him. "I am a thief. Avisier should be yours."

Edmund squeezed her hand. "You haven't taken anything from me. Or anyone since you've gotten here, for that matter. You may have once been a thief or a Hawk, but to me, you're just Lily. You aren't a job title."

"I don't want you to get hurt," Lily choked out, holding back a sob through sheer force of will.

"That's a risk I'm willing to take," Edmund responded, much more certain than Lily felt. "You shouldn't have to do this alone. I don't want you to do this alone."

There was that kindness. The kindness that had helped her through everything. The kindness that was going to get him killed. The kindness that made her next words so much harder.

"You don't have to stay. I won't make you."

"You don't have to. Lily, I'm staying. Not because you're the Marquess. Not because I think you need me. You're clearly capable on your own." He laughed a little, and Lily couldn't help grinning at the odd series of events that had led them there. "I'm staying because I love you, Lily."

And with those words, whatever tenuous hold she had on her emotions snapped. Her mask slipped. The importance of always shutting down her feelings evaporated.

Lily pulled her hands free from his grip, throwing her arms around his neck and pulling him in. *Needing* him close.

"I love you, too," Lily sobbed.

Edmund gripped her tight, one hand on her back, the other holding her head against his chest. "I'm not leaving. Not if you're a wanted criminal. Not if you tried to kill the King of Albrin. Not if someone tries to pry us apart."

A cold tear rolled down Lily's cheek, and before she knew it, she was bawling. Months of tension, of having to stay strong, came pouring out of her.

Edmund's grip tightened as she leaned into him, desperate for something solid. He stood still, rocking her back and forth slightly as she cried into his shoulder.

They stood like that until Lily lost track of time. Until she ran out of tears. And Edmund held her until she let go, taking a step back and wiping her face with a weak smile.

"There's a lot more I should tell you."

"There is," Edmund admitted. "And there's a lot I should tell you. That I should have told you sooner. But we have time, and we have each other."

"We should start getting camp ready."

Edmund turned, grabbing his bedroll and laying it out. "Do you want a fire tonight?"

Lily shook her head, wiping her face with her sleeves. "I'm a little paranoid right now."

"Alright"—Edmund grabbed her bedroll and rolled it out—"camp's ready."

"We might want a tent." Lily smiled, laughing. "It's already getting cold."

"I, for one, definitely want a tent," Tori declared, striding back into the clearing and handing out full canteens.

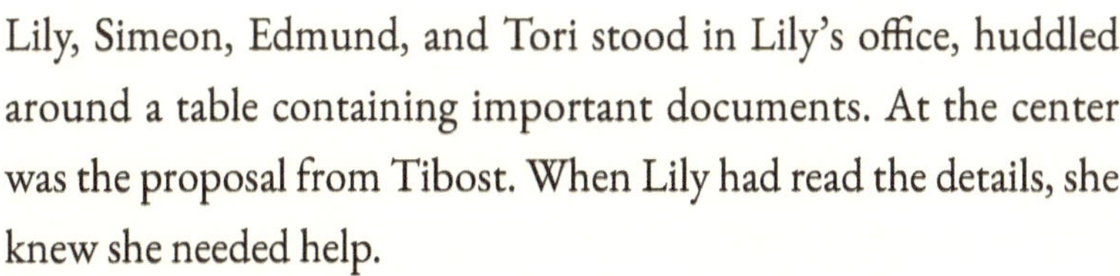

Lily, Simeon, Edmund, and Tori stood in Lily's office, huddled around a table containing important documents. At the center was the proposal from Tibost. When Lily had read the details, she knew she needed help.

"It's a good deal," Simeon said. "We have had the agreement with Carpentras in the past, but the way this is formalized is beautiful. I want to meet his steward."

"But to give me formal control? It just seems too good to be true," Lily protested.

Edmund ran his hand through his hair. "My family has known his for a long time, even if I haven't. I want to trust him."

Simeon nodded. "It isn't entirely unprecedented. And he did put a clause in that he'd retain control of Carpentras if you—"

"Died," Tori filled in for him. "And with that much land, people will come after her."

All eyes turned to Lily as she thought. She had to admit it sounded like something her old self would advise against. But it also sounded tempting. In a way, Avisier had become her new Evesbury. She'd grown to care for the people. This deal would keep them better fed, even if it put her in more danger. She trusted Edmund to work out the logistics.

"So then, what does that make me?"

"You'd be a duchess," Edmund said. "To keep the territory separate and Tibost in charge of it, you'd have to outrank him."

"Is the king going to approve that?"

"It doesn't matter." Edmund passed a slip of parchment to her. "With the territory in Palliers and Carpentras, you'd have more men under your control than he does."

"He can call the entire army."

"He can call them," Edmund replied. "But they're far more loyal to their local lords than the king."

"Jeremias called him worthless."

Edmund scoffed. "That's one way to say it. Would any competent king have turned a blind eye when you won Palliers?"

No, definitely not. Even with Rule of Conquest, merging the two provinces was powerful *politically*.

"People are going to notice, Lily. They already are. You're becoming a target," Tori argued.

Jeremias had made that clear. It seemed, when she'd stopped running, something else had caught up with her. "We aren't alone now," Lily said. "We're behind castle walls with men at my command." And even Randson couldn't single-handedly take a castle. *Unless he brought the Albrin army with him.*

Lily took the pen in her hand and scrawled her signature at the bottom before she could second guess herself.

Tori reached out as if to stop her, but it was too late.

It may as well have been written in stone.

CHAPTER 24

THE VISITOR

Lily rode alongside Tori in the late afternoon light. Tori's return from a patrol of the provinces had been the perfect excuse Lily needed to get out of the castle. She had met Tori in Carpentras, partly to speak to Tibost and partly so they could ride back to Avisier together. The castle had become a different type of prison.

As much as she envied Tori's freedom to go where she wanted whenever she pleased, Tibost's words echoed in her head, 'Unfortunately, if you leave a castle here for too long, it tends to not be friendly when you return.'

It was official. She was a duchess.

Over the few months following, Tori had spent nearly every other week on the road. She always returned with a story and a smile. Lily was glad for her, but still felt a pang of jealousy each time.

"It's a good thing you agreed to Tibost's deal," Tori said.

"Why is that?"

Tori shifted in her saddle, fidgeting with her reins. "Well, I may have gone a bit beyond your borders." The way she said it sounded like a confession.

Lily chose to ignore the tone of voice. "And?"

Tori looked over at her, settling her hands. "The baron to your north, his name is Jaubert, has given his support to De Falchi. Apparently he's a duke now, and a powerful one at that."

Lily's jaw clenched. "How powerful?"

"At least as much as you." It was a statement, but Tori's voice rose as a question.

Lily looked at her and raised an eyebrow.

"Fine," Tori said. "He's pretty much surrounded Lucetia at this point."

That *was* powerful. Nobody but the king held control of the capital, but neighboring provinces tended to be favored. Proximity to power begot more power.

They continued in silence as Lily pondered the news. She was glad for the alliance with Tibost. There may soon be a day when the troops freed up would come in handy. Her control of Palliers was also to her advantage. Though she was cut off from trade with Albrin, she had access to most of the southern coast of the continent, potentially down to Ifrya if she could secure large enough ships.

As she thought, the hairs on the back of her neck stood up. Instinct stirred in her gut, but she didn't let on that she knew someone was hiding in the trees, stalking them.

She glanced over at Tori, who nodded. The apprentice had come a long way in the year since they'd left Albrin. She'd been pulled out of the life of learning and thrown straight into doing but had adjusted well.

Tori turned to look at Lily, either sensing the attention or sensing their pursuer.

Lily gestured with her eyes to a branch.

Tori pointed to herself in question, and Lily nodded. It was a trap they'd used before. Life in Casseterre had been good to them, but not always easy.

Tori kept riding, showing no signs that something was wrong.

Lily squeezed Rista to keep going.

She swung a leg over the saddle-horn, timing her jump with a rock near the trail. Then landed like a cat. Her legs absorbed the impact before concealing herself in the bushes.

Ahead of her, Tori reached up, caught a low-hanging branch, and pulled herself out of the saddle. After a moment of hanging, she was able to muscle herself up and blend into the canopy. When their pursuer entered the space between them, they'd be surrounded. It was an ambush Lily had been taught years before, when a particularly nasty bandit had decided to double back and tail Jarek.

Lily heard the lone rider as they approached.

A shaggy brown horse rode into sight, its master cloaked and hooded. The man rode with a bow ready. The little horse whinnied, and Lily tensed.

In a flash of clarity, the horse and rider became *familiar*.

The leaves rustled as Tori moved.

The rider's head snapped in the same direction.

"Stop!" Lily shouted, springing from her concealment and into the middle of the trail.

The rider leapt off the horse as an arrow flew from the trees. They rolled to cushion their landing and brought up a longbow, which was aiming at the same tree line.

For a moment, the world was frozen.

Then the rider rose to their feet as it became apparent no further attacks were incoming.

Lily clenched and unclenched her hands by her side, feeling the sweat on her palms. Could it really be?

Slowly, the rider turned, revealing a familiar face with a scruffy beard.

"Lily?" the man asked, not believing what he saw.

"Jarek," Lily stated.

Jarek took a few tentative steps forward. A million emotions flashed across his face faster than Lily could name them.

Then, before Lily could recognize it, Jarek had drawn back a fist. He connected with her upper arm, nowhere near a full-strength punch. No, he would never actually hurt her. It was one of the light blows they would exchange when sparring during her training. Still, it conveyed the anger apparent in his voice when he shouted, "I thought you were dead!"

Lily rubbed her arm. Maybe it would leave a light bruise. "I suppose I deserved that."

She was folded in a bear hug, unable to move.

"I thought you were dead," Jarek repeated softly.

"I'm so, so sorry," she replied, hugging him back.

Jarek let her go and held her at arm's length. Lily could see tears brimming in his eyes, matching her own at the reunion she never expected. He turned away growling into the trees, "Now, who tried to shoot me?"

Lily sighed. "Come down, Tori. It's just Jarek."

Tori swung down from her place in the tree with a flurry of leaves. She looked down, shuffling her feet in the dirt. "Sorry, Jarek. I couldn't see your face."

"Make sure you know who you're targeting before you do something you can't take back." Jarek's voice was that of a mentor, low and even.

Tori nodded, accepting the criticism in stride.

"You're Randson's apprentice, aren't you?" Jarek's eyes narrowed as he observed her. "Well, not anymore, I suppose."

"No." Tori said with a conviction that made Lily swell with pride, "I'm much more than that."

Jarek appraised the woman briefly before turning to Lily. "Why'd you bring her?"

"That's not mine to tell," Lily replied. Then she whistled for the horses. "As much as I want to catch up," she said to Jarek, "I'd like to get to Avisier before dusk. Coming with?"

Jarek nodded, mounting his horse.

Tori and Lily's horses came trotting back from where they had waited just out of sight. Lily mounted Rista and waited for Tori to follow suit before leading the way along the winding trail.

"What happened in Albrin?" Lily asked, trying to keep from sounding desperate.

Jarek glared at her. "Three Hawks vanished. You vanished. You abandoned your post, and we didn't know until your reports stopped coming in." His voice was sharp with anger. He seemed to gaze off into nowhere. "Everyone thinks you're dead. Adelaide didn't leave her room for a week."

"Three Hawks?" Tori asked.

Jarek looked at her a moment longer than was comfortable and nodded. "You two and Randson. After talking to the villagers, we realized he attacked you. We tracked him south but lost him in Fallhafen. And, well, he was a Hawk. The trail was cold."

So, he had followed them to the continent at least. The hair rose on the back of Lily's neck, and she shared a nervous glance with Tori.

"Why would he run?" Lily asked.

Jarek's gaze was harsh. "He rallied a village against a fellow Hawk. That's treason." He paused before adding with a glare, "And instead of stopping him, you gallivanted off here."

Lily flinched at the bitter truth behind those words. She had known her past would catch up to her, and while she'd assumed Randson had the king's support in his actions, she should have stayed to face the consequences. She should have made sure the people were safe.

"And you didn't send a letter to anyone. Not the king, not me, not your brother. You left us to piece it all together."

"I thought you knew," Lily said quietly. "Randson found out about when I was a thief. King Aldrich sent him to deal with me."

Jarek looked at her like she'd grown two heads. "The royal family knew. They let me give you a second chance."

Lily grew silent. They knew. She had spent months hiding it from Princess Adelaide, and she'd known the whole time. She had run, thinking she'd be banished or killed, when she'd been *forgiven* long ago. And her mentor, the one who had helped her hide it from the other Hawks, had known the entire time.

Her chest ached.

It was hard to look at him.

They broke clear of the trees to see the bridge arching over the river Lily had learned was the Maussonne. Avisier's walls towered above the other side as Lily's and Tori's horses took the now famil-iar route to the castle proper.

Jarek didn't question as they rode through the gate. Which was good, because Lily didn't want to explain.

They dismounted, handing their horses to stable hands, who had come out to greet them. It was routine now. Delegating tasks to those who worked for her felt normal, and it allowed her to focus on other things.

Jarek remained awkwardly atop his horse, taking in the bustling courtyard.

Lily stopped a servant and instructed them in Casseterran to take care of Jarek and make sure he had everything he needed. Turning to Jarek, she gestured at the woman. "This is Karina. She'll get you somewhere to stay for the night."

"Lily!"

She turned to see Edmund half running out the door of the keep, a smile beaming across his face. She met him halfway, pulling him into a tight hug.

"Good to have you back," he whispered into her hair.

"Good to be back," she replied.

Edmund broke the hug. "So there are a few things you need to see to. A note from Lucetia..."

Lily glanced over her shoulder to see Jarek arguing that he could take care of his own horse and Karina waiting patiently to show him to a set of rooms. Tori was already nowhere to be seen. Part of her wanted to check with Tori to make sure she was okay. But more of her needed to get away from them both to process.

She grabbed Edmund's hand and planted a kiss on his cheek. "Let's get some coffee and go over it."

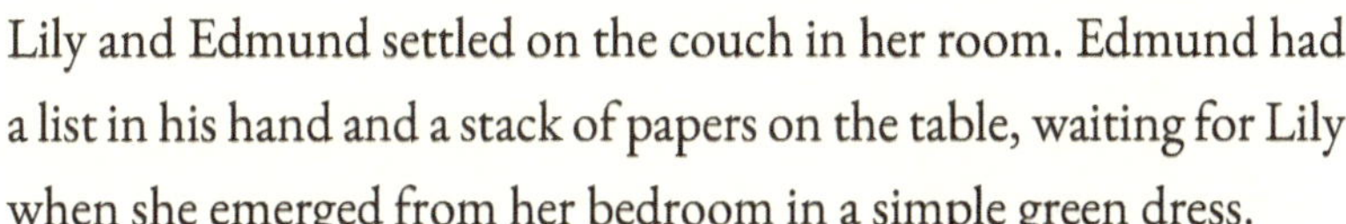

Lily and Edmund settled on the couch in her room. Edmund had a list in his hand and a stack of papers on the table, waiting for Lily when she emerged from her bedroom in a simple green dress.

"Who was that?" Edmund asked, pouring Lily a steaming cup of coffee from the pot Amira had made the second Lily rode through the gate.

Lily accepted the cup and took a seat, leaning forward to spoon in honey. "Jarek."

"Jarek?" Edmund asked, "Your old mentor Jarek?"

"Yeah." Lily leaned back, setting her feet on the table. She tried to switch the topic, "What did I miss?"

Edmund leveled an annoyed gaze at her. "What was *Jarek* doing in *Casseterre*?"

Lily paused. Hawks didn't just wander foreign countries, he had to be there with a goal. And Lily had distracted him from his mission. Now that he knew she was alive, would she be expected to go back? Did she *want* to?

"I don't know," Lily admitted. "I told him we'd talk when we got here." She looked at Edmund to continue with his job.

He took a moment, then nodded, sorting through some papers. "Well, there's word from Lucetia."

"Oh?" Lily raised an eyebrow, her interest piqued at the mention of the capital.

Edmund smiled. "But we can get to that later," he teased.

Lily bolted upright, nearly spilling her coffee in the process. "Nope, that one first."

Watching Edmund's smile widen told Lily that it had been a joke. Still, to prevent spilling, she set the coffee on the table. "So?"

"The king has sent word that his health is perfectly stable. He's also requesting fifty knights be sent to Lucetia."

Lily frowned. "Fifty? That's a full garrison."

"It certainly doesn't indicate that his health is stable," Edmund agreed.

Lily leaned back, resting her head on Edmund's shoulder. "Don't send them."

"That's what I thought. There's also been a Kalturi raid in Palliers."

"It's a bit early for that, isn't it?"

"A bit," Edmund agreed. "But who knows with them? Palliers lost ten men. They're asking for reinforcements until the end of the raiding season."

"Send them," Lily said. "Carpentras got the planting done early. They should be able to spare half a garrison."

Edmund took her through a handful of matters that required her signature. Then he stood, turned, and offered his hand.

She took it, allowing him to escort her down to dinner.

The meal was already in full swing. Lily spotted Tori and Jarek seated a little away from the others. Tori was doing most of the talking while Jarek nurtured what Lily assumed was coffee.

"Should he be at the head table?" Edmund asked as he and Lily made their way around the room to their seats.

Lily shook her head. "He'd prefer not to be."

Of course, that meant instead of spending the meal catching up, she had to spend it making polite conversation with Tristan and Simeon.

As the meal wound down, Lily glanced at Jarek once again. He was staring at her, and she recognized the million questions in his eyes. She couldn't put this off much longer. She jerked her head aside to indicate they should talk elsewhere, then excused herself.

Just outside the dining hall doors was a better place than any to stop, knowing Jarek would wait a moment so anyone paying attention wouldn't know they were leaving together.

When he appeared, she led him into a small side room, and she shut the door behind them. "Sorry about that. There was a Kalturi raid I had to deal with."

"You're the lady of the castle?" Jarek asked in an accusatory tone.

"Duchess." She sighed. "I suppose it's time I start explaining."

He gestured for her to start, so Lily recapped the story of her travels.

Jarek's face remained unreadable. Every now and then he chimed in with a question, and Lily would clarify. When she was done, there was a long moment where neither of them spoke.

"The people seem to like you," Jarek commented flatly to break the silence.

Lily nodded. "Casseterre is ... a rough country. Lords like D'Lavaud aren't exactly uncommon here. All I have to do is not kill people for a mistake and it makes me better than the last guy. I couldn't just leave them to someone else like that, and I was—am—a criminal. I couldn't go home."

Jarek frowned. "We would have welcomed you."

"For all I knew, there was a bounty for my head." Lily laughed.

"So you started building an empire?"

Lily found the accusation unfair. "Why are you here anyway, Jarek?"

"Word reached Albrin that King Oland is close to death, and I was sent to make sure whoever takes over is favorable."

In her years of training under Jarek, Albrin had never cared about foreign thrones. Princess Adelaide had spoken of it, sure, but that was her job as a princess. The way Jarek's eyes darted away from hers was all too telling. He wasn't necessarily lying, but he wasn't being forthright, either.

Just like he hadn't told her that her crimes had been forgiven...

Lily felt the distance between them. What had once been a few feet was now a gaping chasm.

She leaned back against the door with a hurt sigh. "If you don't want to tell me, just say so. I know I can't make you, but the least you could do is not lie about it."

"You can't make me?" Jarek asked skeptically.

The accusation stung. Of course, when she'd been his apprentice, she'd never dreamed of becoming nobility. He had no idea how much she'd changed. He'd seen power go to people's heads in less time than she'd been gone.

"No." Her voice was pained but calm. "You aren't a prisoner here. You're free to come and go whenever you please."

Jarek turned away from her, examining the room. It was the same sitting room she'd re-united with Tori in. Knowing Jarek, he would find it gaudy. Certainly, the tapestry of women dancing around a fruit tree could be seen as excessive.

"Do you plan to stay here?" Jarek asked as he completed his circle and returned to her.

"As you said, King Oland is ailing. If the impending power vacuum is concerning to Albrin, imagine how concerning it is to the people here. I can't leave them."

"You want the throne?"

Lily felt her eyebrows raise in shock. "No. Not at all. I can't do that."

"Then come with me."

Lily shook her head, looking down. "I can't." She could *feel* the disappointment radiating off Jarek.

"You're still a Hawk."

"No," the word shot violently. Harsher than Lily intended. And she took a breath before adding, "This country is volatile. King Oland is gathering soldiers. I can feel it. Something big is coming. Whatever is about to happen, I can't just abandon them to it."

A muscle in Jarek's jaw tensed, the only outward sign of his anger. More than he normally showed.

"He wanted fifty men from me. I didn't send them," Lily admitted. Jarek was there to help Oland, and she was hindering him.

"That's treason," Jarek pointed out casually.

Lily swallowed once as the realization set in. How many counts of treason was that against her now? Still, she wasn't exactly afraid. She had already taken a barony with no repercussions. He didn't have the men to prosecute her. "So was attempting to steal from the royal family."

A tense silence followed as if one wrong word might set the room ablaze. Her jaw began to ache, and she realized she was clenching it. Even after all this time, she couldn't help who she was. She was a criminal at her core, and no amount of food or coin had changed that about her.

"You travel between castles with no escort?"

Lily blinked. Of course that was his question. She knew he'd thought it through. It seemed innocuous enough, but so did most of his questions.

"I don't need one. I can take care of myself. No reason to risk someone else."

Jarek watched her, and she met his gaze unflinchingly. After what seemed like an eternity, he nodded once. "They're lucky to have you."

CHAPTER 25

ELECTIONS

In the days that followed, Lily found ways to keep herself busy. It wasn't that she didn't want to talk to Jarek. She spent the evenings asking for updates about Nick and Princess Adelaide, and Jarek was happy to provide. But they danced around what had happened in Evesbury, just as they had danced around what would happen next.

But as the days went on, the weight of Jarek's revelation pressed on her. It didn't change anything, but it changed *everything*.

She needed out of the castle. She needed space to just think without someone asking her what she was thinking. She needed to decide what was most important to her.

Jeremias's son was a baron now, and Lily had traveled with the reinforcements to Palliers without wanting to alert her newest appointed noble. A baron is what he would remain unless his competency was called into question. So far, he'd been unremarkable. He was too worried about figuring out what he was doing in the moment to make plans about what to do next.

On that visit, the townsfolk seemed contented. They'd hardly noticed the change in leadership. They just cared about putting food on the table for their families.

When Lily had ridden on to the castle to enquire about the baron, she found out he wasn't present. It had taken more asking than she wanted, but she finally discovered he'd been called to Lucetia, the capital city. The king had fallen bedridden, and he had no heir.

The hard riding that resulted meant she'd returned nearly a day before expected.

Now, she handed Rista off to a stable boy, something she was certain Jarek would disapprove of. A year ago, she would have too. Nowadays, she'd grown to trust the stable hands. It helped that the little horse seemed to like them. Perhaps they snuck her extra apples.

She charged down halls and up the stairs to her office. No doubt word would spread quickly that she'd arrived. She unlocked the door to her office and opened it, stooping to pick up the letters that had been slid under the door.

Edmund handled most of her necessary correspondence, but there were some things he simply didn't have the rank to open, even with her permission. One of these things was the letter in her hands bearing the ostentatious seal of a dragon that King Oland insisted on using.

She tore the letter open, her eyes quickly scanning through all the formalities to the meat of it.

It wasn't the king writing, but someone else on his behalf.

Lily's brow furrowed as she read further. The king had fallen ill and was requesting the presence of the nobles to 'swear fealty to the new ruler of the land.'

She tossed the letter aside, as it contained nothing she didn't already know, and shuffled through the papers to find an identical envelope. Once in her hands, she read the contents just as quickly as the first. The king's illness had progressed rapidly, resulting in his death.

The final paragraph summoned her to Lucetia. The date indicated it had likely arrived soon after she left for Palliers. She'd have to leave the next morning to have any hope of being on time for the funeral, and whatever bickering over the country followed.

She clutched the letter and set out to find Edmund and have him tell her exactly what that meant.

The normal guards weren't in the hall outside Edmund's office, which made her pause. He could dismiss them, but she couldn't fathom why he would. As he would gladly admit, he was useless in a fight. Voices filtered under the door, and as her steps fell into a trained silence, she got close enough to make out the words as she strained to decipher them.

"I'm supposed to stop her," Jarek's voice filtered out from under the door. "I didn't know it was Lily." If it weren't for that second sentence, Lily wouldn't have hesitated before going in. At least, that's what she told herself.

Edmund's voice replied, "Why does the King of Albrin care what's happening in Casseterre?" His voice was calm and steady, the same voice that she'd rely on to council her decisions.

She could visualize Jarek's shrug in the pause. "It's a new power rising. The rumors that reach Albrin are of someone conquering vast tracks of countryside. You know nothing comes out of the rumor mill the same as it went in."

Conquering. Lily hadn't seen herself as a conqueror. She'd merely dealt with each situation as it appeared. Now, she thought of how it must look from the outside. She'd seized a vast amount of land in a startling matter of months.

"Aldrich and Oland are friends. So when Oland asked for help, Aldrich sent me."

Lily's gut tried to climb up her throat. 'Stop' was practically code for kill. Hawks weren't assassins, but often, dealing with a threat meant eliminating it. She couldn't believe Jarek had any will to harm her. But she'd been gone nearly a year now. Things had likely changed in Albrin, and maybe not in her favor.

And he'd never told her she'd been forgiven. Kept it to use against her. What else could he be hiding?

"She speaks of you like a father."

"I know." That was pain she heard in Jarek's voice. Jarek, who was normally stoic. The last time she'd heard that she'd been bleeding out on the floor of a cell, a hairsbreadth away from dying.

Tears welled up in her eyes at the memory.

She'd been so close to death then. If that's what it took to get any emotion from him...

Lily brought her hands up to dash away the tears. The shift of her weight made a floorboard creak, and she froze, cursing the old castle—and her emotions.

"*Quiet*," Jarek hissed, barely audible.

Her breath was unbearably loud in the ensuing silence.

Footsteps approached the door, and she schooled her expression as neutral as she could. Maybe she could come up with some excuse...

The door opened to reveal an angry Jarek. His glare held danger; it was the type of glare she'd never seen turned on her before.

She blinked, and it was gone. Angry, still, but the same anger she'd known as an apprentice. The type that it had taken her years to not want to cower from. So she straightened her shoulders and tipped her chin up slightly, hoping the posture would grant her more confidence.

"You were listening at the door."

Lily remained silent. There was no point denying it. Not to him. Jarek could always spot her lies, even when he hadn't caught her in the act. But she couldn't withstand his accusatory glance for long. She shifted her weight with another creak, crossing her arms and chewing her lip for a moment before admitting, "I was about to walk in, and I heard you talking about me. So yes, I stopped to listen."

"I heard the board creak."

Lily ignored the obvious attempt to change the subject, to fall back into that familiar mentor and apprentice verbal sparring. "It's not a coincidence I ran into you in those woods, is it?" And, despite her best intentions, Lily couldn't help but shift under his gaze. Her next words were articulated weakly, as if speaking them granted them truth. "You were sent to kill me."

If it wasn't Jarek, she would have sworn she saw a flash of hurt in his eyes. "We aren't assassins, Lily. You know that." His voice was almost a growl at the accusation.

It sent a shudder down Lily's spine.

"We both know what 'stop someone' usually means," she countered and met Jarek's gaze evenly. One of them would be the first to back down. Usually, it was Lily. It was always Lily.

She searched his face for some indication of his thoughts, but he was as unreadable as ever. She couldn't bring herself to fight him and hoped that meant he couldn't bring himself to fight her. After all the times he'd saved her life, it would feel a waste.

Or maybe that hurt in his voice was at the possibility of Lily dying. Maybe, once again, he would save her life. This time from himself.

Jarek looked away, and Lily sucked in a breath.

He met her eyes again, gaze softer. "I'm not going to kill you, Lily. Once I tell Aldrich what you've accomplished here, he'll agree."

Because her life had always been at Aldrich's mercy, never Jarek's. He hadn't saved her, not like she thought. He'd let her spend years trying to pay back a debt never owed. Guilt that she should never have had to carry for so long.

Lily pushed past him into Edmund's office.

He let her, though he was easily strong enough to stop her.

"The king died," she announced to neither of them in particular and tossed the letter on the desk in front of a nervous-looking Edmund.

The color drained from his face as he read it.

"Should I go?" she asked, her back to Jarek.

"You have to," Edmund muttered.

Lily was tired of being told what she *had* to do. It had the potential to be a bloodbath, one she'd rather stay far away from. She was content with her corner of the kingdom.

"Oland didn't have an heir. What's the process for deciding the new king?"

Edmund swallowed. "Someone will be presented as the presumptive heir. It takes two-thirds of the holdings to approve the new king." His brow furrowed in thought. He shook his head as if to clear it, focusing on Lily's face. "We need to go to your office."

He was already up, grabbed Lily's hand, and practically dragged her down the halls until they were outside her office. Jarek could do as he pleased for all she cared.

Lily produced the key from her pocket, fidgeting with it in the door while Edmund tapped his foot anxiously. He shoved his way through the door the second they heard it unlock.

Lily lit the lantern as Edmund barreled to the shelves, madly scanning the spines of books. He grabbed two and set them on the desk. Then he snatched the lantern from Lily as he began pouring through them.

Jarek stepped into the room behind Lily. "What's happening?"

"Don't know," Lily responded and moved to stand behind Edmund, reading the books over his shoulder. One was a list of territories and land areas. The other was one of the many law books she'd seen Edmund pore through on occasion. She still didn't understand half the legal jargon they used.

As she watched, Edmund took out a piece of parchment and began rapidly scribbling out numbers. He glanced back and forth between the books before circling a number and sliding the sheet to Lily.

"Is that right?" he asked.

Lily scanned the numbers. It was a long series of additions that, at her quick glance, looked like it was done correctly. Then there was a number divided by three. The answer was a few less than the answer to the addition.

"Looks right. Why?"

Edmund glanced at his book, then back to Lily. The color drained from his face as if the blood was being sucked out of him. His eyes darted to Jarek, who had moved to peer curiously at the books. "You control just over a third of the land."

"So?" Lily asked with a shrug.

"You decide who the next king is."

"They're going to try to kill you," Edmund said. "If anyone does, they'll crown themselves. You were right. You shouldn't go."

He paced in front of the fire that was heating Lily's room as she perched by the window, looking out at the stars. Lily had already decided she would go to Lucetia. She'd seen how people suffered under a king who didn't care. The least she could do was try to help before she dealt with whatever fallout would come from Albrin.

Edmund's mind had changed the instant he realized how much weight she held. His arguments had ranged from fleeing the country to holing up and gathering forces in Avisier, all of which Lily had waved aside. Thus, this argument had dragged on into the night.

Jarek, no doubt, was preparing for them to travel the next day. He would encourage Lily to go. The interests of his king depended on it, too.

Her anger at him had been forgotten at the crisis in front of them. He was still her mentor, still the closest thing she had to a father. She felt better with his advice, even if she might disagree.

"Perhaps they'll be more distracted by whatever is happening in the North. Tori was up there, and, apparently, provinces are falling every month. They'll be too distracted with infighting to notice me," Lily hoped.

Edmund's face scrunched up, "I suppose the northern lords are probably busier with that. But you shouldn't mind it too much, your duty is to Avisier."

Lily's heart ached at the puppy-like expression on his face. Edmund had a deep care for Avisier and its people. If he could solve every problem in the fief, he would. She stood, squeezing his shoulder. "You can take care of it. You practically do already."

Edmund laid his hand on hers. "And what if something happens to you?"

"I'll be back. I promise." Lily smiled.

"I know you will. I'm just ... I'm worried." He ran his other hand through his hair in a way that made Lily's heart sing.

Her eyes darted to his lips and lingered there.

He hadn't made a move toward her since their return from Carpentras. Hadn't even sat close to her when they talked. In that month, she realized just how important his closeness had become.

"Not mad?"

"Not mad," Edmund confirmed.

Lily put her hands on his chest, looking up at him.

His expression softened to a smile as his hands circled her waist. "I love you, Lily."

Pushing herself up on her toes in return, she lightly brushed her lips against his and pulled back just enough to speak. "I was worried I ruined it."

"Never," Edmund said before his hands moved up to cradle the back of her head. He held her in place as he lowered his lips to hers.

The kiss was firm and passionate as if he was trying to drink in her very soul.

Lily gripped at his back, pulling herself into him and pressing their bodies together. Edmund broke the kiss for just a moment before they were together again.

They moved together, stumbling around the table until Edmund lowered her onto the couch, their lips never breaking contact. Once there, he straddled her, one hand holding himself up, the other holding her cheek as he pressed kiss after kiss into her lips, her jaw, her neck.

Small gasps left her lips.

She twined her fingers in his hair and pulled him back to her lips. Wanting more of him, she arched up into the kiss, giving back every inch of passion he had poured into her. Every missed contact of the last month was made up for as she pushed with her hips. Then her body was flipping them, and she laid on top of him.

He made a pleased sound into her mouth. Against her lips.

She pulled back, and they were both breathing heavily. Their faces were inches from each other. "I *need* to know I'll be able to come back. I need to make sure Avisier is stable, and I need somewhere safe."

"Okay," Edmund replied. His arms moved around her shoulders, pulling her into his chest. "Do what you need to do. I'll be here. *Always*."

CHAPTER 26

DEADLY MEETINGS

The ringing from each baleful toll of the funeral bell bled into the next and echoed through Lily's head. There would be thirty-six, for each year of King Oland's reign. Lily had lost count of which were real and which just bounced around in her skull.

Nobility stood around the open casket like a flock of crows waiting for their chance to feed. They may as well have been crows, for all Lily could make out of them. Even the men wore black veils that obscured whatever emotion they felt. There was no way to tell who she was expected to swear fealty to. No way to tell who felt joy or sorrow at King Oland's death.

They stood in the open courtyard of Lucetia's palace, and the bright colors of spring flowers and occasional bumbling bee were at odds with the statuesque crowd.

The final crack of the bell sounded, and it was like a sigh passed through the crowd. Humanity finally revealing itself.

Lily resisted the urge to rub her ears and free her head from the ringing.

Draped in garments that had surrendered their original darkness to the wear of time, fading black to gray, a man stood before the closed casket, delivering a lengthy speech. The oration, adorned with phrases Lily presumed were poignant metaphors in Casseter-ran, gradually became an indistinct hum in her ears as she allowed her focus to drift away. How was anyone expected to focus after that bell?

Soldiers picked up the casket, lifting it into a black carriage to be paraded through the streets. The carriage lurched into motion, pulled by four large black horses. Even from her spot in the back, Lily could see the sweat beading on their coats as the spring sun beat down.

The nobles fell into a two-by-two line like ants, following the carriage onto the crowded streets of Lucetia. Lily fell into step beside another woman, their long black skirts trailing just above the dirt.

They were met with eerie silence and downturned faces from the assembled crowd, who were dressed less in black and more in close approximations to it. Faded gray and dull dark blues. There was no singing, and Lily was convinced the glimmers on faces were more sweat than tears.

Beside her, a woman staggered, and Lily hurriedly reached out, steadying her with a supportive grasp, helping her to her feet. The cobblestones were rough, and Lily knew the route through the city would not be kind to a twisted ankle.

"Thank you," the woman whispered, her voice full and sharp. A slight rasp spoke to her age.

"You're welcome."

The woman's head cocked to the side at Lily's response, indicated more by the shifting brim of her hat than her veil. How the woman didn't feel like she herself was dying under that hat was beyond Lily.

"You're Lily, aren't you?"

She looked around, but everyone remained too caught up in their own scheming to pay heed to the two women in the back of the procession. "Yes, and you?"

"Collette Costex. Baroness of Koire." There was a splash of pride in the woman's voice, and Lily smiled. Then the woman continued, "Keep your head low, Lily of Avisier. There are men here who'd like to take it from you."

Lily's jaw clenched, and she reached for the spot where her knives should have been. But no one in the procession was permitted to be armed. "Who?"

"I believe you'll find out tomorrow."

Lily eyed the heads that bobbed with each step. She supposed it was much more likely one of the men had been chosen. Perhaps the De Falchi she'd been hearing about.

For the entire journey to Lucetia, her mind had been filled with consideration and was still no closer to an answer. She didn't want to swear fealty to a complete stranger. Even in Albrin, she'd bristled at the idea, only doing it because she was friends with the princess. But unless she did, Casseterre would have no ruler. She could only imagine the fighting that would ensue—and the people who'd be hurt in the crossfire.

They reached a park, and the crowds thinned. They were led to a large tomb and stood like statues while the king was moved inside the white marble walls.

Lily felt her eyes wandering over the nobles, the only ones who had managed to dress in true black. Again, the overwhelming feeling they were not mourners came, but scavengers waiting to strike at what remained of his power.

She searched for any sign of De Falchi, but she knew he wouldn't show his face. None of them would until the next day, when they would meet, approve the next king, and leave without another word. At least, that's what was supposed to happen.

These matters were never that simple.

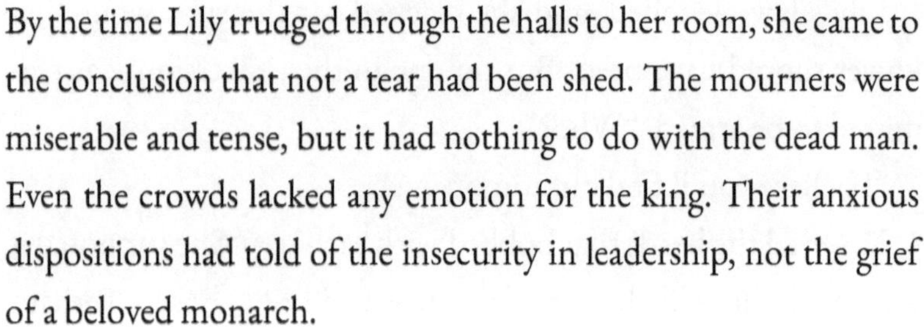

By the time Lily trudged through the halls to her room, she came to the conclusion that not a tear had been shed. The mourners were miserable and tense, but it had nothing to do with the dead man. Even the crowds lacked any emotion for the king. Their anxious dispositions had told of the insecurity in leadership, not the grief of a beloved monarch.

"How was it?" Tori asked.

Lily collapsed into a chair, removing her veil and tossing it across the room so her face could finally cool down. "Uncomfortable. Barely anyone there had met the man." Her feet ached from the slow procession down the cobblestones.

They'd arrived in Lucetia for the funeral only the night prior. They were hustled into a suite of rooms, each bedroom connecting to a central living space. That was where they sat now, Jarek lounging in the armchair across from Lily, Tori on the couch.

"Did anyone stand out to you?" Jarek handed Lily a mug of coffee. Only nobility had been invited to the funeral itself, leaving her two companions to sit in the suite.

"Everyone was veiled," Lily responded, taking a sip of her coffee. "We'll see at the vote tomorrow."

"There was no discussion, no one mentioned who was being ratified?" Jarek asked.

"None."

Lily had spent the entire time listening for those whispers. She didn't know how the successor was chosen, but she'd been reassured they had been. It had all played out before she arrived.

"It's not something people here like to discuss," Tori said. "When you took Avisier, all I knew was the baron died. I couldn't get a word about the succession out of the town." That explained how she hadn't known Lily captured Avisier until they'd spoken.

Lily leaned her head back. "It was sort of sad. No one was there because of the dead man. It was just to see who gets the crown next."

"You shouldn't go," Tori said.

Lily bolted upright. "What?"

"I spoke with some of the servants while you were gone." She shifted in her seat, turning to better face her. "They confirmed a suspicion of mine."

Lily leaned forward, making a go-on gesture. From the corner of her eye, she could also see Tori had gained Jarek's full attention.

The woman looked between them both before continuing, "They think it's going to be De Falchi."

Dread curled itself like a snake in Lily's stomach. "De Falchi?"

Tori nodded. "I've been hearing his name more and more, and it's usually connected to something about you. Rumors, mostly, but some of it is scarily close to the truth." Randson. He had to be working with Randson. One look in Tori's eyes proved she knew it, too.

"Have you ever tried to get close to him?" Lily asked. In Tori's position, she'd be unable to resist the curiosity.

"I have," Tori enunciated. "But I can never find out anything about him. Nobody ever knows where he is, just where he's been."

"That's ominous," Edmund commented.

Tori bobbed in agreement. "I know you don't want to swear fealty to De Falchi, Lily. Either you make a very powerful enemy. Or lots of smaller ones who would prefer you support them. You can't win."

"I've survived plenty of enemies in the past."

"And had just as many close calls," Jarek snapped. "You're not invulnerable."

"So what? You want to decide instead, right? Whoever's best for Albrin? That's why you said you were here in the first place. Isn't this what you want?" Only when her final words echoed back to her did she realize the venom in her voice. She expected Jarek to retaliate, to say something about how he'd saved her, on how she owed him or Albrin.

Instead, Jarek leaned forward and set down his mug. When he spoke, his voice was level and measured. "You have over a third of the land. Nothing will pass without your vote. Don't you think everyone in that room would kill for your power?"

A silence fell over the room. Of course, with that system of government, murder was the quickest way to get power. And right now, Lily's head could be worth the crown.

"So ... what should I do?" Lily asked. She was back to sitting in that little cabin in the woods, asking her mentor for advice. Her posture sagged, and a sense of helplessness spread over her shoulders like a blanket. "I have a big enough target on my back as it is."

Jarek shrugged. "I think you should be queen."

"I can't be queen."

"Why not?" Jarek asked. "You haven't mentioned coming back to Albrin since I got here. Do you even care about the oaths you took?"

It was like a knife to Lily's gut. She had sworn fealty to the King of Albrin. And she hadn't thought of it since leaving his shores.

He continued, "No matter what you choose, someone will be out for you. As soon as they realize you have the deciding vote. At least this way you'd have an army to protect you."

"I'm not a queen," Lily said lowly. "I wasn't born for this."

"No," Jarek snapped. "You were born a farmer. And then your parents died, and you were a thief, lucky to see the next day. And then you became the first female Hawk. And now you're a duchess. Queen doesn't seem to be much of a jump anymore."

It wasn't, not from what she was doing now. But it would mean severing any remaining hope of returning to her life in Albrin. To the people she yearned to reunite with and the simplicity of that cabin.

Lily set her coffee down with more force than she intended as she stood up.

She turned to push through the door that led to the room she and Tori were sharing. The door slam reverberated through the room, sounding harsher in the silence. Sinking into the bed, she buried her face in a pillow as her body was wracked with sobs.

The truth was, these were the options she had been mulling over the entire journey to the capital. If she took the throne, she'd be giving up any hope of returning to her life as a Hawk. If she didn't, someone would try to kill her for it. And she was no closer to safety than the day she left Albrin.

Time had turned its back on Lily, and she knew it was time to choose.

CHAPTER 27

THE PAST CATCHES UP

When Lily emerged from her chambers in the morning, the others were gone. They were likely readying the horses, waiting just outside the castle walls to make for an easy escape if something went wrong. That, at least, they had all agreed on during the journey.

She denied the assistance offered by the castle servants, dressing herself instead. The blue dress was of the looser style she'd grown to prefer. It allowed her more freedom of movement.

What would come of the meeting remained out of reach. But if there was conflict, she would be prepared. So, she pulled her hair back into a bun atop her head and added a few decorative pins to dress up the protective style more.

With little fanfare, armed guards came to her door to escort her to the throne room.

Lily was forced to add her bow to a table piled high with weapons. It seemed she wasn't the only one aware of the potential violence that could ensue. She'd hidden a few daggers under her dress, and no one bothered to search her, so she was able to keep them. One on each thigh, accessible through slits in the gown. And two under her corset, which weren't much use in a fight, but if she was arrested or captured, they'd be invaluable to have with her.

The throne room stretched out like an endless corridor, its grandeur revealed in its two-story expanse. Above, the second level boasted a series of arched stained-glass windows, set slightly inward, casting vibrant hues into the space. Sturdy columns stood sentinel, supporting the arches and forming a narrow walkway that encircled the chamber. A guard stood at each of these columns, each holding a sword. They were the only weapons in sight.

Fifteen lords and ladies, each in their own colorful outfits and stripped of weapons, were escorted to the middle of the room and stood in a line before a raised dais. There was no indication anyone had done the math and realized the power Lily held, but they were only just being introduced.

Upon this elevated dais rested an intricately carved wooden chair, adorned with sumptuous red velvet upholstery.

The *empty* throne.

A squire with a hat twice the size of his head entered through a side door.

He stepped in front of the dais, and Lily heard stifled laughter at the absurdity of the sight. Then he cleared his throat and began boasting about a new king who had fought in wars and against political corruption. A king who was a warrior. The squire wasted no time in detailing the new *king's* exploits.

At first, the bristling nobles around Lily seemed excited. Then, as the squire droned on, adding lists of accomplishments, the energy became annoyed. After all, Casseterre was a kingdom built on war and conquest. That's how most of those in the room had come to power. And they all knew the ongoing list had transformed into flowery ways of saying simple things. It had lost all meaning.

After what seemed like an eternity, the squire moved to open the door with a deep bow.

A tall man strode to the dais from the doorway.

The elaborate gold and red doublet he wore clung to his toned abdomen. Atop his brow sat a thick band of gold. At his belt, he wore a sword, but he also wore two jewel-encrusted daggers that made Lily twinge in jealousy.

Then she realized.

Panic spiked in her heart. Very few people carried a set of daggers like that, even fewer nobles.

Her eyes found their way to his face. They took in his self-satisfied smirk as he scanned the assembled nobility.

Lily's gut churned, even as the nobles on each side of her dropped into deep bows. She glanced around her, hoping someone else could see what was wrong with the situation, but found she was the only person still upright.

Her attention snapped back to the man. "You," she snarled.

Randson's smirk transformed into a smile. "Lily, I didn't expect to see you here." He spoke the trade language, his words laced with vinegar. "I believe," he said as if pondering some great question, "you are supposed to be bowing."

Lily reeled in her anger and disbelief to present a false smile. "You're not supposed to be here. What happened to Lord De Falchi?"

Randson let out a short bark of laughter. "Some Hawk you were if you never figured that out." He tilted his head for a moment, eyes piercing her, but Lily gave no sign of how deep the insult had landed. "Hawk, in Casseterran, is Falchi. Lord De Falchi is?" He waved a hand for her to finish as if prompting a toddler.

"Lord of the Hawks," Lily breathed.

"That's right." Randson sneered, advancing on her. "And you're the pathetic little thief who can't seem to stay down. You're the reason they banished me, you know? I managed to track you to Casseterre before I lost your trail. No matter, I became something here. Something better. And now it seems fate has rewarded me again," he boasted. "So, kneel. Swear fealty to me, or face the consequences."

Lily's mind raced.

Around her, unease grew. What had been a rehearsed, easy bow was turning strenuous as they had received no signal to rise.

The guards stirred, but they stayed by the walls. After all, they did not yet have a king to take orders from.

Lily's feet remained planted to the ground, though she longed to dart out the door. Now wasn't the time for doubt. Her people relied on her.

"Actually"—she prayed her voice didn't sound as shaky as it felt—"you need a two-thirds majority." There were a few mutters from behind her, but Lily continued, "A two-thirds majority that you do not have."

"You'd better recount," Randson snapped. "Fourteen out of fifteen is well above two-thirds."

Lily smiled, injecting mock pity into her tone. "You never learned to read Casseterran, did you?"

Randon's eyes narrowed.

"Two-thirds is defined by *land holdings*. I happen to hold just over one-third of Casseterre. Which means that, without my approval, you can never truly rule Casseterre." Pride swelled in her chest as she spoke her next words. "Without me, you are *nothing*."

"Kill her," Randson said casually as if he was ordering a dog to 'come' instead of murder.

The guards stepped forward, and many of the nobles hurried to retreat from the bloody scene they anticipated.

"He is not yet king," Lily's Casseterran cut through the air like a sword.

The room froze.

Swallowing her rising fear, Lily turned to face the assembled nobility. She knew she had to phrase her next words carefully to avoid a challenge in this land of technicality. "I will not fault you wherever you stand, but I invite you to stand with me. I know this man, and he is no king."

Lily stalked toward the door, parting the flustered crowd.

She heard Randson draw a blade and darted through, closing the door to the solid thud of a knife embedding itself where her back had been an instant before. It was shortly followed by an angry roar.

Snatching her bow and quiver off the table, she burst into a sprint before the dumbfounded guards could catch her. There was little resistance as she tore through the halls and out the gate.

She outran the orders to stop. Outran the chaos unfurling at her back.

A whistle had Rista galloping toward her, closely followed by her companions.

Jarek and Tori had arrows notched at their bows and were scanning the castle walls. They didn't ask to be updated, their training impeccable.

Lily vaulted onto Rista's back, guiding her loyal mount toward the welcoming cover of the foliage. The duo vanished with her companions trailing, leaving only echoes of distant shouts reverberating from the castle walls behind them.

It had been an hour of riding before Jarek brought his horse beside her and grabbed the reins. His firm grip forced her to slow down, eventually guiding them to a stop.

"We have to keep going," Lily argued. She tried to yank her reins back.

Jarek's grip tightened. "We are a safe distance away. You need to tell us what happened in there."

Lily pushed against the mounting panic in her chest. "I think I just started a war."

"You what?" Tori asked, aghast.

The words began to pour from Lily's mouth against her bidding. "I don't know. I saw him and I just, I couldn't let him be king. And I couldn't do nothing." Lily shook her head, trying to clear it. "We need to keep moving," she argued. "If he's coming with an army—"

"No one can raise an army that fast," Jarek replied. "Take a deep breath."

Lily took a breath that wasn't near deep enough before trying again to yank her reins free.

"Deeper," Jarek ordered, his iron grip refusing to loosen around the reins.

She tried to calm her heartbeat at his instruction and tried to find her advantage in the mess she'd caused. Two Hawks were with her. Randson couldn't raise an army that fast. Her land outnumbered his.

After a moment, Jarek asked again in a calm voice. "What happened?"

"De Falchi isn't working with Randson. De Falchi *is* Randson."

Tori turned into a statue.

Jarek cursed. Then cursed again.

Lily found herself mentally echoing the sentiment. Still, the panic was starting to calm, her heartbeat slowing again. She eventually shook her head. "It's my fault. I should have dealt with him in Albrin, but I ran. This is my mess to clean up. You should both leave."

"And do what?" Jarek asked. "Is it your fault he's here? Yes. But you can't change that now. So stop thinking of only yourself, stop running, and face the problem like the Hawk you worked so hard to be."

Lily took another deep, shaky breath. She pressed the heels of her hands into her eyes, dropping the reins.

Her heart was pounding in her throat as she focused on the feelings of the world around her. The breeze tugged at her hair. Rista shifted below her, then exhaled loudly. Her mouth tasted of blood, and she washed the taste out with the leathery water from her canteen.

Only when the thunder of her heart quieted enough to hear birdsong did she open her eyes to see Tori watching her.

"You don't have to stay," Lily said quietly.

Tori shook her head, her eyes seeming to grow more focused. "He can't be king. He doesn't get to hurt anyone else. I'm staying."

CHAPTER 28

PICK YOUR BATTLES

As Lily approached Ducortros Castle, a steady stream of supplies rumbled in on carts. Situated to the north of Avisier, Ducortros was under the governance of Baron Dupuis. The castle, a solitary structure, occupied the heart of an expansive open field, a sentinel overseeing the ebb and flow of resources.

This part of the country consisted of large flat plains, which made it hard to take advantage of geographically. There was no hill or river to provide a natural defense. Instead, the tree line had been cleared some two hundred yards from the walls. The castle's primary advantage was it stood watch over the only road connecting the north and south of Casseterre. The ideal road if one needed to transport the carts and supplies for an entire army.

Lily and Jarek fell into the line of carts approaching the castle gates. "They don't look ready for a siege," she worried aloud.

"They will be," Jarek reassured her.

If Randson had any plans to attack Avisier, he'd have to bring his army through Ducortros. They had decided to concentrate their forces on the bottleneck, instead of spreading them out across allied territories.

They were greeted warmly at first.

The warmth was quickly replaced with near panic at the news they brought.

With the movements of both armies, it looked as if Ducortros would be the place they finally met in truth. It would be the sight of a large-scale battle, instead of small border skirmishes.

Jarek offered to camp outside the walls, knowing rooms would be in short supply. He was told in no uncertain terms how ridiculous that was. He would take a night or two to help Lily plan and coordinate before riding out to track Randson's army. His role would be to keep her updated on movements and if any groups splintered off. It was the same job he would do in Albrin, only now he was doing it for her. Lily would be eternally grateful for how quickly he'd offered his expertise.

What was once a suite of rooms now held a staging area for the commanding officers. A central strategic command center to prepare for what was to come. The coffee table had been raised by stacking it on storage crates so that they could stand around it comfortably. A crude map was sketched on large sheets of parchment until a proper war table could be moved in.

Baron Dupuis was the last of the men to arrive in the crowded room. Ducortros was his holding. When Lily found her land growing, he had been one of the few to reach out peacefully, establishing a good trade between the two regions. She'd never met him in person, but they'd exchanged plenty of letters.

"Did I miss anything?" he asked, closing the door behind him.

"Not at all," Lily replied, looking up from where her group of Hawks was standing around the table. The map was scattered with little figurines to show where units of men were located. A small cluster of blue in Ducortros was the last to be laid out.

Dupuis moved to stand beside the table with a slight bow to Lily.

Lily instinctively looked to Jarek, who ignored her long enough for her to realize this was her meeting to run. "Right, so, for Randson to proceed further south, he will need to use the road, which means he'll likely try to take Ducortros. We estimate two weeks until they have enough troops gathered to mount an attack."

"How many?" Dupuis asked.

Lily looked to Jarek, trusting his memory of the numbers more than hers.

"Five thousand," he said.

"We estimate we can get three thousand here in time to cut him off," Lily said.

Dupuis frowned. "That's not as good of odds as I'd hope."

Lily shrugged. "If we go into siege, we can only expect five hundred in reinforcement."

"Actually"—Jarek frowned at the map—"that might not be the worst idea. If we can get Randson to target Ducortros, we won't need as many men in the city. The rest can attack once Randson's force is worn down and break us out of the siege." He shifted a few figures out to a spot in the woods. "That could be enough to crush Randson's force. It may not win the war, but it would be a step."

Tori nodded, twirling a pen in her hand. "If we bring in a relief force while they're attacking the castle, there'd be nowhere for them to retreat."

Lily looked at the map thoughtfully. In a siege, it traditionally took three times the men inside to take the castle. It could be a quick way to turn the numbers in their favor. "Except then we'd be trapped. There's no way to communicate between us."

Edmund looked between the Hawks. "Don't you have some secret code or something?"

Lily nodded acquiescence. "We do, but Randson also knows it."

"That doesn't mean you can't get a message out," Baron Dupuis said, drawing confused glances. "I've lived here my whole life. Follow me." He smiled.

Jarek and Lily exchanged glances, then decided he was worth trusting. They followed him up a tower as he explained, "This tower is the most fortified part of the castle. And that includes an emergency exit. How are you with heights?"

"Fine," Lily replied. She thought she could see where this was going.

Her suspicions were confirmed as they passed through door after door and across removable sections of floor. This tower was meant to be defensible, with multiple positions to hold and different places to fall back to. It was smart, but only with a way out. Otherwise, it was just an even smaller place to be trapped.

Dupuis didn't stop moving until they reached the top of the tower. The room was simple. Wood barrels lined the walls, and a single window let light in. Lily imagined the barrels were stocked with enough food and water to last weeks.

He unceremoniously shoved a barrel out of the way, and it seemed lighter than Lily would have expected had it been full. Dupuis knelt, then turned to Lily. "Can I use a knife?"

Wordlessly, she reversed her knife and handed it to him hilt first.

He dug the blade between boards of the floor, prying one up enough to get his hands under it, then pulled up the board with a creak, setting it aside before pulling up two more. The gap was just wide enough for a person to fit through. "It's nothing fancy, but ... it's a way out."

Lily approached cautiously, peering over the edge of the hole to see a ladder disappear into the darkness. "A secret passage. Where's it come out?"

"I don't know," Dupuis replied. "My father never let me go. But he made sure I knew where it was, just in case."

"That's rather convenient," Tori said, approaching to stand beside Lily.

"They aren't uncommon here," Edmund added and peered over Lily's shoulder. "Most of the castles Uleta built probably have them. But killing the owner..." He shrugged. "A lot of them probably took the secret to their graves."

Jarek looked to Lily. "Is there one in Avisier?"

"I've never looked," Lily replied.

"There was," Edmund answered. "They flooded when my grandfather was a child and were walled up."

Lily inwardly sighed with relief. She'd have felt like an idiot if there had been another potential escape route, and Cecilia could have lived. "We'll have to find the other end."

"Easiest way is to go through," Jarek grunted.

"Right," Lily replied, straightening from her crouch. "Of course, that means going through a probably very tight passage in the dark."

"But someone needs to check if there's a blockage," Jarek directed his comment to Lily.

Dupuis looked at the two of them. "Why don't we just go now?"

"Lily's claustrophobic."

"Am not."

"Then why don't you go?" Jarek asked. There was a little twinkle in his eye. A dare.

"Because"—Lily folded her arms—"I have a lot of things to coordinate right now. I don't have hours to disappear to who knows where."

"You're claustrophobic?" Tori asked, a grin spreading across her face. "Is that why you didn't want to go into Avisier?"

"No," Lily grumbled.

"Why don't I go?" Tori suggested. "I'm not contributing much here."

Lily looked at her, considering. She *had* handled herself well enough when Lily was in the dungeons under Avisier. While she valued the girl's ideas, this was exactly the type of job Hawks were meant for. They weren't meant to be standing around discussing war strategies.

"Fine. But we'll have someone here in case something goes wrong." She looked around, turning a question to Dupuis. "What type of supplies do you have?"

"A little of everything."

They found two long coils of rope and tied the end of one to an empty metal cup. The other end Tori held. If she was in trouble she could yank, sending the cup tumbling and alerting whoever waited on this end. Tori traded out her bow and quiver, which would be useless in the tight confines, and slung the second coil over her shoulder in case the first ran out. Then she fastened two lamps to her belt but didn't light them.

"I want to save the fuel for when I need it," she reasoned. "I'll still have the light from above for a while."

"Don't try to clear any obstacles," Lily warned. "We don't want a cave-in. Come back and we'll gather supplies to stabilize it first."

"I'll be fine," Tori said as she lowered herself into the hole. She glanced up, her face a pale circle against the darkness. Even the image of another descending into the tight confines made Lily's stomach clench.

Jarek rolled his eyes. "Don't mind Lily, she's never had to send an apprentice off on their own before."

Lily fondly remembered all the warnings Jarek had given her and Nick the first time they'd separated. They'd been fine, but he hadn't been himself with worry.

Tori grinned. "See you in a few hours." With that, her form retreated into the darkness.

They continued the discussion at the top of the tower. Lily's eyes kept returning to the cup and the rope trailing off of it, but it didn't budge. After a few hours, they were interrupted by a metal clank as Tori tossed a burned-up lamp through the hole.

A second followed, then two coils of rope before Tori finally peeked above the floorboards.

"It's clear," she said with a confident smile. "It comes out in a bush in the woods. The tunnel is pretty dark, but a lantern will last long enough to get out."

"Then we have our way out," Jarek said. "We don't want the entrance to become obvious, so we should use it minimally, but we will be able to get messages to a group of reinforcements."

"We?" Lily asked. A nervous anticipation gripped Lily. She was excited something could work out, but being trapped would always make her nervous. Still, she would rather be bait herself than have someone else be.

"Randson has one Hawk, we have three"—he cut a sharp glance at Tori, who was poised to interrupt—"and *you* need to learn to stop discounting yourself. You're a Hawk."

Tori closed her mouth and nodded, allowing Jarek to continue.

"A Hawk's skills are not in being a general, they're in scouting and espionage. You need to stay here, but we don't. We need to be out there"—Jarek pointed out the window to emphasize his point—"making sure Randson isn't pulling anything funny."

Lily glanced at Tori, who nodded and mused, "And there needs to be someone outside who can get you a message if things change in the siege."

Lily looked between the two set faces. They weren't asking; they were telling her. She debated arguing. They were her family. She wanted to keep them close to her and far away from Randson. But they were Hawks. They also needed their freedom.

"Stage from the relief force. And one of you should always be in that camp."

Jarek leveled an annoyed gaze at her. "I have been doing this longer than you, Lily."

Lily turned her gaze to Tori. Of course, Jarek knew what he was doing. Tori did, too, but Lily couldn't help feeling protective. "Listen to him."

"I will."

"And you're only to scout the army. Stay far away from Randson."

"I'll be okay, Lily." Tori edged closer to her.

She almost reached out to grasp her arm, then stopped herself. "Of course you will," Lily said but couldn't help looking to Jarek even as she said the words.

I'll watch out for her, he mouthed.

CHAPTER 29

FRIEND OR FOE

A few days later, Lily gazed out from the ramparts to the growing cloud of smoke. It looked to be coming from just beyond the borders of Ducortros.

The entire horizon was swathed in the thick gray stuff. It made the morning air taste acrid as if it had somehow rotted. One of Randson's favorite strategies had been burning land Lily controlled—or was close to controlling. She shouldn't have been surprised, but seeing the column of destruction fill the sky hit Lily like a hammer.

This was the first time she had seen it, not just the consequences or aftermath.

In the courtyard below, they were preparing for that destruction to reach them. Barrels clattered as they were rolled across the cobblestones and men shouted orders at each other.

A small force would hole up inside of the castle and hold it against the attacking army.

Then, when the focus was on the castle, the force hiding in the woods would strike. Randson didn't have Hawks with him, and he'd be pinned down at the center of his army much like she was.

If all went according to plan, Randson would be trapped between the two armies, left with no choice but to surrender.

Only, that was if they could hold the siege until a large enough relief force gathered. And if Randson didn't find out.

The problem was, Randson was thinking as many steps ahead as they were. They had to assume he knew of the relief force gathering and would try to take the castle before they arrived—or target the two groups separately.

There was a shout from one of the towers, followed by the sound of a horn. In the courtyard below, all movement stopped, then resumed tenfold as men rushed to man the walls.

Lily's hand went to her knives, though she knew they would be useless. It was too soon; they weren't ready. That was the signal for 'enemy approaching.' She wasn't ready.

Darting into the keep, pounding up the stairs against the tide of people flooding down, she made her way through the masses. The tower stood on the corner of the castle, and there was always a watchman atop. Lily found the watchman now, who was peering at the horizon with his hand, shielding his eyes from the sun.

"Where?" Lily asked, coming to stand beside him.

She shielded her eyes as she followed his extended finger.

Emerging from the cloud of smoke was a group of mounted men. Lily watched as they continued to emerge, approaching at a gallop. After a minute, it seemed the group would grow no larger. There were about a hundred of them, far from enough to siege a castle.

Some sort of trick, then.

"Ready on all sides," Lily said, then darted down the stairs.

A horn blared behind her, the four notes indicating readiness on four sides. She caught a soldier and told him to relay her orders to each watchtower to maintain their posts.

He bowed, but Lily was already sprinting her way out to the walkway on top of the walls.

Soldiers were gathered on one wall, opposite Lily, muttering over the approaching group.

Lily rushed over to them, shouting, but was unheard because their noise. She looked around, not wanting to waste time going around the wall. Eventually, she hoisted herself up on the inner crenelations, took a deep breath, and bellowed as loud as she could, "Hey!"

A few men turned, then nudged the men around them. The noise died as attention, aside from a few furtive glances at the approaching men, turned to her. Without the soldier's noise to compete with, Lily only had to raise her voice, not shout.

"Man every wall! Do not leave your posts!"

Lily had discussed posts with the men's commanding officers. They knew where they were supposed to be during an attack. In the excitement, it seemed they had momentarily forgotten. Still, once she stepped down, they resumed movement, now spreading out from where they had gathered.

Lily looked out from her wall, eyeing the tree line. There was no sign of anyone, but she knew at this distance she stood no chance of spotting a competent Hawk waiting to order an attack on an undefended side of a castle.

She would feel comfortable once there were more eyes. So, she waited, watching that side until she judged the approaching men were close.

They swung wide, advancing toward the front gates instead of the castle wall.

Baron Dupuis was already atop the gatehouse when Lily approached. He nodded to acknowledge her, but his eyes never left the fifty men facing them. He called for the men to halt, his voice easily cutting across the open ground.

They stopped, save one man who brought his horse a few feet ahead.

Lily nocked an arrow to her bow.

"Parlay!" the man called, waving a small white banner.

Dupuis glanced at Lily.

Now that she was looking at these men up close, they didn't seem like a fighting force. They were armed and armored, yes. But the armor was smeared with blood. A handful of the men were without helmets; their faces were smeared with a dark liquid Lily hoped was blood. Chest pieces were dented, and more than a few men held themselves awkwardly in the saddle.

"Tell him to dismount and approach the gate."

Dupuis repeated her request.

The man waving the white banner hesitated. Then he rolled up the banner and tucked it into his belt. He swung his leg over the horse without the trained grace of a knight. When his feet hit the ground, one did before the other, and he almost toppled over. Untrained or a trick waiting to bite her, Lily didn't yet know.

The man grabbed the reins and walked his horse back to one of his men before approaching the gate, sword sheathed and hands in the air. His gate was stilted, clearly favoring one leg.

Lily waited until he was clear of his men before returning her arrow to its quiver and climbing down the ladder that had been put up to quicken an ascent of the walls.

She could see the man through the two grates separating them.

He was large, a knight by build, and fully armored. She could also just see the dark skin of his face as he pushed his visor up. Closer now, his armor appeared to have been torn off of one leg. His pants, which had at first appeared brown, were actually white, their new color courtesy of the dried and crusted blood. That explained the limp. Despite his raised hands and furtive glances at the guards posted on the walls, he held himself confidently.

He made eye contact with Lily and took the last few steps to stand outside the portcullis before he carefully dropped his hands to his sides.

"I take it you're Duchess Lily?" he called across the six-foot gap separating them.

"Why are you here?" Lily called back.

"I come in peace. My name is Baron Gaspard."

The name sounded familiar. Had one of Tori's reports about the North mentioned him?

Lily remained silent, and Gaspard nodded in the direction of the smoke. "I'm from Lidon." Definitely northern. It was the closest province to Albrin.

"So?" Lily asked, not quite seeing his point. Most of the northerners had sided with Randson.

"Lidon has fallen. We barely made it out with our lives." His tone was low and angry. If what he said was true, they'd have ridden weeks to get there. For what purpose?

Lily folded her arms, not quite believing what she heard.

"I come bearing gifts," he said upon seeing her hesitation. "If I may?"

She gestured for him to go ahead.

Gaspard reached inside his pocket, pulling out a small parchment. "It's the title to Lidon. Yours, if you accept us."

She took a step back to see the men manning the gates and called an order up to open the outer portcullis. She didn't need the land, but if he was willing to offer it, she had to at least entertain the idea.

If the man tried anything, he would be easily trapped between the two iron grates.

Gaspard hesitated only a moment, perfectly reasonable considering the space beneath the gatehouse was informally called the murder cage. Still, he stopped in the middle, waiting for further action from Lily.

"What of the rest of your province?" Lily asked. "Have you abandoned them?"

"No!" Gaspard blurted. "No. Never."

"Then how did you get here?"

"We were separated from the rest of the garrison during the attack. There was nothing we could do. Nothing ... save join the side fighting him."

"The enemy of my enemy is my friend."

Gaspard nodded acknowledgment, then held out the parchment once again. "My men are willing to fight if you'll have them."

Lily wanted to take it as a blessing. But they were injured. They may not be much use in a battle. And every mouth to feed mattered in a siege. She wished Jarek was still in the castle so she could ask his opinion. He and Tori had left the day after their conversation under the hopes they'd get out before Randson set a scout onto the castle. If he didn't know they were watching him, he wouldn't hide things as well.

Lily had to remind herself she wasn't an apprentice anymore. She was a duchess; she had to be confident enough to make these decisions alone. "We are short on space. Your men will be sleeping in the courtyard."

Gaspard smiled. "That's how sieges tend to work, isn't it?"

Lily smiled at the familiarity, at the way he assumed she had the same experiences as he did. "It seems so."

Gaspard bowed, tucking the title away as he turned and limped to the cluster of mounted men.

Lily waited until he was a decent distance away before turning to go back up. Dupuis was waiting for her and offered a hand up the last section of the ladder. "Do you know him?" Lily asked as she straightened and looked over the wall.

Dupuis nodded. "We've met once or twice. Not enough to really form an opinion on him."

Lily looked back at the keep. "Do we have any spare rooms?" She was fairly sure she already knew the answer.

"No," Dupuis responded. "We could put him in with one of the lieutenants. And the men in the courtyard."

Lily nodded, her gaze turning back to where the man now approached a second time, bringing his horse as his men began to retreat to the edge of the woods. Dupuis gave the orders to one of his men, who went to see that they were followed through.

Lily began pacing around the walls, eyes scanning the forest, and Dupuis walked beside her. "Why is the forest closer on this side?" Lily asked.

On the other sides of the castle, the trees had been trimmed back five hundred yards, a necessary measure considering it wasn't raised above the surrounding countryside. On the south side, trees crept within a couple hundred yards of the base of the wall.

"The clearing is natural," Dupuis explained. "Instead of clearing that constantly, we decided to leave it."

Lily supposed it was plenty far away to serve its purpose. No soldier would be able to get within attacking distance unnoticed. Still, if she had noticed it, Randson would as well. "Post an extra watch on this wall, just in case."

CHAPTER 30

CLAUSTROPHOBIA

Randson's army moved like ghosts in the night. One day, Lily's men had been hauling in firewood and rocks for the siege. The next, they were staring out from the ramparts at a line of enemy faces.

The strange part was the campfires. They were still miles back. It forced them to close the portcullis and gate days ahead of schedule.

Lily waited for days, hoping Jarek or Tori would come through the passage with some news of why they'd moved. Randson's men never attacked. It seemed they were more there to cut off supplies. But supplies were just as important as men in a siege.

Every day, the tension in the air grew more palpable. It was torture for the men to know an attack was imminent, but not when. The biggest risk was that, over time, they'd get too used to the other army. Once that happened, they wouldn't be as ready to repel an attack.

Lily needed to force Randson to show his hand first.

She clutched the lanterns in her hands, wishing for a way to get Rista outside without anyone noticing. Unfortunately, if Randson was with his men, an exit out the front gate could mean death for Lily.

Dupuis moved the barrel, and Lily began prying up the floorboards. Tori had gone through the passage twice, once to make sure it was clear and the other time to make sure no one was suspicious of her sudden disappearance.

At least she knew there was no collapse.

She took a deep, calming breath as she hooked the lanterns to her belt for the descent. Both hands were needed on the ladder.

Lowering lowered herself into the hole in the floor, she trusted her feet to find the rungs. It was a narrow passage, large enough only for one person. Even before Dupuis replaced the floorboards, the walls started pressing in around her.

"Let me get going a little," she called up as his face appeared.

"Alright."

Lily climbed down. The darkness enveloped her, pushing the air out of her lungs. Stealing from her with shadowy hands.

She closed her eyes. That way, the darkness didn't seem so bad. Taking a few deep breaths to assure herself that yes, she could still breathe, her progression paused.

For a moment, she tricked herself into believing she was in a tree.

Then she began to move and felt the wall brush her back. Her eyes flashed open, and she was reminded just how narrow of a passage she was in.

Without any conscious intention, her hands and feet started moving. Down. Down. If she got to the bottom, the walls wouldn't crush her. If she got to the bottom. Down. Down. Down. The walls were tight enough to force her heart into her throat.

Her stomach joined it as a foot slipped.

The momentum stopped one hand from grasping at the next rung, and in an instant, she was hanging by just her fingertips. She closed her eyes and swallowed in an attempt to return her stomach to its proper location. Her heart thundered in her ears, and she could've sworn it was echoing in the surrounding chamber. As she glanced down, she was thankful for the darkness hiding the extent of the fall that pulled at her.

Her foot struck the wall behind her, and after a moment of fumbling, was back on the rung. She clung to the ladder, wrapping her arms around the rungs as she willed her heart rate to settle. After a few deep and desperate breaths, she resumed her climb.

Tears of relief rushed to her eyes when her feet touched the ground and the tunnel opened up. It wasn't much wider, but it was enough that she couldn't feel the walls. It was enough.

She knelt to the ground, fumbling in the dark to light her lantern. Eventually, a spark caught. Light illuminated rough stone walls and an uneven dirt floor. There were sporadic wooden beams as additional supports too.

Lily shuddered at the thought of how long ago they had been put in.

She dimmed the light to conserve the oil and set off into the darkness. At a brisk pace, she would be out of the tunnel in an hour. She intended to not spend a second more in the close confines.

After entirely too long, light that wasn't produced by her lantern began to peek in. The ceiling had become dirt. Though the walls were still lined with stone, wooden braces became much more common.

Lily put out her lantern, now desperately moving toward the light of day.

The tunnel narrowed, and Lily was forced into a crouch, then a crawl. Her heartbeat skyrocketed again as the opening grew narrower and narrower, but she could see daylight, so focused on that to repel the fear.

Eventually, the dirt became stone once more, and Lily pulled herself through the small opening and had to shove away branches of a bush as she wormed out, now practically dragging her legs behind her.

She rolled free of the bush, facing the sky and panting. Then she launched herself up, realizing that she would have been in danger if anyone stumbled across her. A quick scan of the area around the tunnel revealed that it was still well hidden. Then she was off to find the rest of her army.

⸻◆⸻

The sound of hammers on metal reached her first. Then the smell of wood smoke. Then male voices shouting obscenities at each other as the pickets around the war camp came into view.

Two men were arguing over whose town had the better bread. Based on their language, suggesting either wasn't the best was a major insult to their honor.

"As long as it's fresh, does it really matter?" Lily asked.

Both men jumped, hands going to the hilts of their swords as they found Lily amongst the shadows of the trees. She stepped forward, pulling back her hood. "You really should take sentry duty more seriously. If I'd wanted to get past you, you never would have noticed."

The men glanced at each other, then one of them stepped forward, clearing his throat. "This is a war camp, lady. I don't think you want to be here."

"I'm exactly where I need to be." Lily shifted, holding her hand out to present her signet ring.

The man leaned down to inspect it, and she watched his eyes widen. "Yes, of course, my lady. Can we help you find anything?" His tone shifted from polite disinterest to a nervous formality Lily still wasn't comfortable with.

"I should be just fine," Lily replied as she took her hand back and pulled her hood up once again. "Don't let it happen again." She strode off into the camp, keeping to the shadows out of reflex.

An hour later, she wished she'd taken up the offer. She had seen the traditional military layout of Albrin war camps, but this was chaos. Tents were clustered in groups instead of neat rows. Wagons moved down narrow walkways. Even finding the center amongst the maze of carts, fires, and tarps was proving to be a challenge. At least everyone was too caught up in their own business to pay her any attention as she slipped between them, searching for even one familiar face.

"Lily?"

Lily whirled, peering back through the crowd. She caught a glimpse of a green cloak and started moving toward it.

As she got closer, the crowd parted, revealing a tired-looking Tori with a grin on her face. "What are you doing here?"

"Looking for you, actually."

Tori beckoned Lily to follow, leading a well-known path through the tangle of people toward an inconspicuous, if slightly larger, tent. "This is the staging tent," she explained as she ducked in. "Jarek just went out again this morning."

Lily closed the flap of the tent behind her, straightening. It was barely tall enough for Tori to stand in, which explained the chairs set in a loose circle. A flap in the ceiling was opened to let in natural light, illuminating the specks of dust held aloft in the air.

Tori shrugged her quiver off and plopped into a chair.

Lily sat across from her, scooting the seat in the dirt a little. "It took me an hour to find you," Lily said. "This place is chaos."

A war camp was normally organized. Everything would be in a pattern, with easy paths between locations. No matter if a country organized in rings or a grid, there would be some consistency to it.

Tori shrugged. "These men aren't united. They all have their own little groups with their own leaders. I spoke with the generals, and they say this is the best we can expect until they get to know each other better."

Lily knew camaraderie was important, and she grated at the blatant lack of it. If she'd had her way, this army would have been training together for years. But she supposed with a country so divided, people were only loyal to those they knew.

"What is happening with Randson's army? They've been staring at us for days."

"It's a fake-out," Tori said confidently. "He sent a few hundred men ahead. We think it was to lure out our relief force. The bulk of the army is still a few days back, where I imagine you're seeing some campfires."

"Do they know about this camp?"

"Jarek doesn't think so," Tori replied. "I'm ... less certain." She shifted, reaching for the cord on her neck, then stopped herself. "They seem to have a contingent moving extra slow. We're worried they're meant to come in after we join the battle and try to pin us."

Lily nodded, glad to know they had the situation in hand. "That's good. Keep an eye on them, and if a group splinters off, deal with them."

Tori looked up sharply. "Deal with them?"

"As far as I'm concerned, you're a Hawk. I trust your judgment."

Tori straightened a little in the chair, a subtle glow of pride sneaking into her eyes. "Of course. Is there anything else?"

"When they do attack, start moving the instant you know what the back contingent of the army is doing. We can't risk them taking this castle."

"I'll pass your orders on."

Lily stiffened at the idea. She supposed she was in charge, and they were orders, but it felt wrong to be directing an entire army. Hawks worked alone or in small groups, not as generals. Yet it seemed that was her role now. If she somehow survived this war, people would continue looking to her as a leader.

As she slunk back to the castle, she considered the implications of the war. If she won, she wouldn't be able to fade into obscurity. She would have to make decisions that would affect the entire country. She'd need advisors—and a council. And would have to do something to prevent those people from putting a knife in her back the first chance they got.

Lily could've sworn she was in prison again. She was practically chained to her desk, cursing the sheer amount of paperwork that came with a war. Each document added to the growing sense of dread in her stomach and the tightness in her shoulders.

All the reports she had skimmed contained news of someone dying for her cause. Fifty in total now. It was at these moments, when news of another death reached her, that she missed Nick the most. She missed his positivity yanking her out of the dark pit she was rapidly falling into.

She'd written to him at the start of the war, letting him know she was alive. That was a month ago now, and she'd received no response.

A month and fifty men dead. She'd met most of them at one time or another, though she could only remember a few faces. Was this what war was like for royalty? This feeling of helplessness as soldiers died following orders? Were they dying to protect her or something else?

Edmund was beside her every second. Without him, she was certain she would have drowned under the sea of papers. She'd scrawled her signature more in the last few days than she thought she would in her life. At night, or after a particularly grim description, he held her and dried her tears.

The one break was the castle singing. It was the same song they had sung when Edmund's mother died, a haunting melody that rose and fell like sobs. Lily knew the words now. She knew the loss expressed in the low parts; it reverberated through her bones. More importantly, she knew the high parts which promised to continue on and offered a spark of hope.

It was a song for the dead and for the hopeless.

They sang it for those who were long gone and for those who would leave soon, but they also sang it for those who continued to fight. They sang it to bolster their resolve after another day staring down a larger army. Seeing the castle gather in the courtyard to light candles and sing brought tears to Lily's eyes more often than not.

There was no order; no one called for it to happen. But like clockwork, everyone who could put down their work was singing.

Just as the sun went down, someone would begin to hum. Someone else would pick it up, and before long, the whole castle was rising in chorus. Candles were raised in the courtyard, one for each death they'd heard the news of thus far.

"Are you okay?" Edmund's voice came from the door.

"Fine," Lily replied without looking up from her notes. They hadn't been able to get as many supplies in before the siege as they'd have preferred, and she was doing new calculations to figure out how much they needed to ration. It was a gamble. If they were too cautious, the men wouldn't have enough energy to repel an attack. If they were too well-fed, and Tori and Jarek's division failed, they'd be starved out.

"You don't look fine."

She felt the couch cushion sink as Edmund sat next to her. His hand pressed firmly down on her knee, stopping the shaking Lily hadn't noticed.

"We're at war. I'm stressed."

He picked his hand up and glanced pointedly at her leg as it began shaking again. "This isn't your normal stress."

She kicked out her leg, resettling it somewhere more comfortable, and the shaking mercifully stopped.

"It was going through the tunnel, wasn't it?"

"No." Lily curled her legs up under her.

Edmund gave her a kind smile. "It's okay. It was brave of you to go in, and I admire that about you."

"It's not about the tunnel," Lily snapped, watching Edmund's face fall. "I'm sorry." She grabbed his hand. "You're just trying to help, I shouldn't have snapped."

"Thank you." They lapsed into silence for a few moments before Edmund ran a hand through his hair and asked, "So, what is it?"

"The siege," Lily admitted. She finally set the notes down, turning to face Edmund. Their knees brushed as he curled up on the couch beside her.

"The siege was your idea," Edmund said, confusion lacing his voice.

Lily nodded, eyes darting around the room as she thought. "It was. But ... I've never actually been in a siege before. I didn't think it would be this ... suffocating."

"I think we all feel that."

"You aren't shaking."

Edmund laughed, hand running through his hair again, "I'm terrified, Lily! You've turned my life completely upside-down!"

Lily's jaw set. She stood, moving to look out the thin window of the keep. It was enough to let light in during the day but narrow so that nobody could climb in through it. As such she had to almost press her face to it to make out the details of the candles being lit in the courtyard as the first notes of the song flit to her ears.

"I'm saying it's okay to be scared."

"I'm not scared," Lily grit out.

Edmund's footsteps were gentle as he approached her. "Talk to me. Is it the claustrophobia? Maybe you should go for a walk on the walls?"

"It's not the claustrophobia!" Lily snapped. She whirled on him, and he took a frightened step back, his eyes widening. "I can't be trapped again! Last time, your mother died! The time before that..." She choked on a sob, and before she knew it, her legs gave out on her.

Face in her hands, surrendering to the weight, she sank to the ground.

Edmund was soon there, an arm wrapped around her shoulders. "Hey, hey. It's okay. I don't blame you for that."

Lily's shoulders shook, and he squeezed tighter. His free hand gently pried her hands away from her face, and he shifted so he was kneeling in front of her.

Then his hands cupped her cheeks, tilting her face up to meet his gaze.

She grabbed his wrists, feeling ashamed of how her arms were shaking.

Their eyes met, and together, they took a deep, slow breath. She mimicked him, filling her lungs against the panic that was washing over her. Only to panic more, as it felt like a rope was tied around her chest, keeping her from breathing.

"I can't breathe." She wheezed.

"You can, and you will." His voice was calm and gentle and the opposite of everything she felt. His hands moved down to her shoulders, and strangely, the weight eased some of the tightness in her chest. "Look at me."

She did.

He took an exaggerated deep breath, and Lily did her best to follow him. He stopped short of a full breath, just as Lily's lungs were begging to protest, and started blowing it out.

The breeze moved some of Lily's hair, tickling her neck as she copied him. In this way, he helped her through three more breaths. She nodded on a final puff, and he smiled.

This was not a smiling situation. Lily glared at him. "What?"

"Your eyes are beautiful when you cry."

She let out a short howl of laughter. "That's really what you're thinking about right now?"

"It worked," he pointed out. "You aren't crying anymore." His thumbs ran beneath her eyes, wiping away her tears.

"I still feel like I got kicked by a horse."

"You aren't shaking, either," Edmund added. "You needed to get that out of your system."

Lily sank into his arms as the emotions ran through her. She cried some more, but they were gentle tears, not the outburst that had overtaken her earlier. It was like her bucket, which had overflowed, was being slowly emptied on a field of flowers.

By the time she was done, her body ached like she'd been in a fight.

Edmund stood her up and moved her back over to the couch. Once there, he held her, as the last notes of the song faded in the air, and long into the night after that.

CHAPTER 31

THE SIEGE BEGINS

After five days of no movement from the men in the trees, Lily had called another meeting.

"What if he tries to use the small force to keep us here, and go attack the other army in the meantime?"

"He could get men through for it, but not a supply chain. He needs to take this castle at some point, or his soldiers won't be able to eat," Edmund said.

Gaspard made a contemplative sound, stroking his chin. "Randson may be brash, but he's not an idiot. He knows he needs this road, and he can't have it without taking the castle."

"Or, he could attack them then turn to us so we don't have a relief force, we'd be forced to give up—eventually." Lily kicked herself for the mistake. She never should have allowed her force to split, she never should have allowed them to be trapped.

Edmund laid a hand on Lily's shoulder and squeezed.

"He really hates you." Gaspard nodded at Lily. "Convince him you're here, and he won't be anywhere else."

"If I reveal myself, I'll end up with an arrow through the heart," Lily snapped.

Gaspard held his hands up defensively. "That's probably true. Why does he hate you so much?"

Lily wanted to ignore the question, but all eyes in the room were on her. She shifted in her seat. "He, umm..." her mind scrambled to find a way to explain without mentioning that she was a criminal.

"I may have a solution," Edmund said. They looked at him, and he looked to Lily. "I'd like to show you."

Lily's shoulders sagged with relief at the well-timed interruption. She took his offer, allowing him to lead her out of the room and up the tower.

He stopped just before the final door. "Close your eyes."

"What?"

Edmund rolled his eyes. "It's a surprise, so close your eyes."

Lily sighed, closing her eyes as Edmund guided her with a hand on her elbow up the last steps. He opened the door and led her through, turning her and positioning her somewhere near the center of the room.

"Alright," he said. "You can open your eyes."

A blue rectangle, longer than she was tall, filled the wall. It featured a golden, stylized lily in the center.

Lily took a step forward, feeling the fabric. It had solid weight to it. Looking to one side, she could see it had loops attached.

It clicked in her head.

She turned to Edmund. "A flag."

"*Your* flag."

Lily's head whipped back to the flag. A stylized lily. Well, it was quite a literal interpretation, but that was good for a banner that had to be seen at a distance. She enjoyed the simplicity of it. The corners of her lips turned up as Edmund wrapped his arms around her waist.

"The lily is because ... well, your name and your seal. The blue symbolizes peace and calm. I thought it was about time we get some of the formalities drawn up."

Lily pressed a kiss to his cheek. All members of nobility had a symbol. Even though she'd been given a seal, she still didn't think of herself as one of them, not really. It felt more like she was playing dress-up. The ring felt borrowed, like it had belonged to someone else.

Paired with this flag, a weight settled into her stomach. These were *her* people she was fighting to protect, not someone else's.

If the castle flew her flag, Randson would take it as a challenge. He would focus his attempt on them.

"There's something else, too."

As she watched, Edmund lowered himself to one knee.

Her eyes widened as he pulled out a ring with a green jewel set in it.

"I know right now things seem bleak. I know they were bleak when we met. But I made a promise to stay by your side. And, if you'd let me, I'd like to make that promise official. Lily, will you marry me?"

That electric feeling was back. She had never been more certain of her heart, as it was now soaring. In that moment, Randson could have shot her, and she'd be happy.

"Edmund, I..."

The tears came to her eyes as a hundred horrible possibilities flashed in her mind. Them having a child, and her having to bury both. Edmund jumping on a sword meant for her. One of them holding the other as they died of some horrible sickness. A knife at Edmund's throat, and the decision, the people she stood to protect, or the love of her life.

Edmund frowned at Lily's hesitation, but he didn't speak. The understanding that filled his eyes crushed Lily's heart.

The sky was collapsing around her and crushing the air from her lungs. Finally, through the tears that were falling, Lily managed to choke out, "We're at war. I could be dead tomorrow. You could be killed."

Edmund took her hand in his, passing a comforting squeeze. "All the more reason. Lily, outside Carpentras, I made the decision to stick with you. I knew the risks then, and I know them now. If we die, I want to do it married to you."

Lily knelt and pulled him into her, sobbing into his shoulder once again. "Never leave me."

"I won't," Edmund promised, stroking her back as he held her tightly. "If the siege ends tomorrow or if it drags on for months. If we win or if we lose, we'll do it together."

"We can do some good in this world. *You* can do good in this world. And I want to be by your side while you do."

Lily's heart squeezed tight. She pulled back with a smile, though her face was drenched. "I want that too."

Edmund smiled, gently caressing her face as he wiped the tears off her cheeks. "Is that a yes?"

Lily laughed, grabbing his face. "Yes. Yes, I'll marry you."

She pressed her lips to his, feeling their now familiar softness as he smiled, pulling him closer. Lily laughed as he tangled his hands in her hair.

He stole her laughter with another kiss and pressed into her. The love and tenderness and heart-wrenching reality of their union wrapped them in a moment of stillness. Edmund pulled back with a smile and confessed, "I could die now and be happy."

Lily wiggled away slightly, smiling as he echoed her thoughts. She propped her head on one hand. "You still haven't given me the ring."

Edmund laughed, grabbing her hand, and gently sliding the ring on.

A perfect fit.

CHAPTER 32
DESTRUCTION

S houts rang across the courtyard later that day. Lily looked up to see a soldier turn, leaning down over the railing to shout, "They're here!"

She shot to her feet, scaling a ladder in an instant. People were already bustling back and forth on the western side of the castle. Men crouched with loaded crossbows, aiming through arrow slits.

"Awaiting your orders."

"Hold," Lily said without a glance. She approached one of the arrow slits, not wanting to expose herself above the wall.

The man shuffled aside, letting her peer through.

An army was mounting at the edge of the trees. Lily could spot maybe two thousand men making their way onto the field and forming a wall of metal. She had no doubt more were still concealed.

There were a hundred men on her wall. A hundred men seeing a force twenty times their size mounting. A hundred men bristling. Waiting for the order to shoot. Waiting for the chance to make sure as much of that force would not reach the walls as possible.

As a unit, the wall of men began to advance. Randson had been smart about choosing to attack from the west. The evening sun was at their backs, making it hard to pick out any individuals as targets.

Against an Albrin army, it would have made no difference. Archers would send a volley flying. They didn't need individuals to aim at. The crossbows favored by the continent were different. The long reload and mechanical release meant targets had to be specially selected.

But up close, the power could puncture most armor.

The opposing army was clear of the trees now; three thousand men marched shoulder to shoulder. There was no sign of cavalry, though Lily knew horses had to be somewhere. Being mounted only made storming a castle harder, but she had a hard time believing no one had ridden across the country.

"Wait until one hundred yards," Lily instructed. "Then individual shots until they reach the wall."

In a hundred yards, they would maybe get off forty shots in total. But most of them would hit at that distance. It wasn't enough to stop a single attack, but it would take a toll over time. Hopefully, it would be enough to make them think.

Three thousand men.

They had been expecting five thousand. Gaspard had brought a hundred inside the walls. That still left a nearly two thousand armed soldiers unaccounted for.

"Where are they?" she muttered to herself, standing as the wall's commander replaced her behind the crenellation.

She scampered to the northern wall, crouching to peer through an arrow slot. Seeing nothing, she darted around again. Confused glances were thrown as she made her way further and further from the obvious threat.

She had to know where the remaining men were.

Even on the south side, where the trees were closer, sneaking an army across the grass would be impossible. Unless, of course, all eyes were on the force storming the opposite wall. Unless cries of alarm went unnoticed, as men attempted to scale the wall.

She found the wall's commanding man. "Keep your men here. If something comes up, find me immed—"

She was cut off by the sound of ladders crashing against the top of the western wall. There was a chorus of wooden thunks as spears were deployed, stabbing down at the men attempting to scamper up the dangers of the ladder.

Lily turned her back to the open field. This would be the telltale moment. Whether the situation became a siege, or the castle was overrun that night.

Crossbows would be useless to help. Not with the movement. The chance was too high of hitting an ally. Lily put an arrow on her string and crouched down. The men knew their orders. Her shouting would just add to the confusion.

From below, her army stormed up the courtyard ladders, joining their comrades now that the point of attack was clear. They seized rocks from the prepared stacks, leaning between the crenellations to hurl them at the bottom of the ladders.

Cries of pain reached Lily. Someone called out, and three men rushed to a single ladder. They crouched together, heaving it out until gravity carried it away from the wall.

Another ladder fell into place beside the newly evacuated space. It was pushed away just as quickly. With a start, Lily realized her men were winning the battle.

She'd never been on the defending side of a siege before, but she could now realize why attacking was so difficult. The attackers were forced into easily defensible bottlenecks. The defenders needed far fewer men to knock down one ladder than to fight the five men putting it up. Of course, with proper siege machinery, that would all change. But Lily had no intention of letting the siege last that long.

Lily ripped her gaze back to the tree line. If this had truly been meant as a distraction, it had been a good one. There was no sign of life. No sign of movement. She kept her eyes moving, trusting her peripheral to pick up on anything. Staring at one spot tended to blur her vision, making her miss things to the side.

Still, there was nothing. No sign of the missing men. No threatening approach. Just the darkening sky and the grass and the trees.

Lily made her way back to the tower that joined the southern and western walls. She peeked through an arrow slit to survey the field. The grass was trampled down toward the center, where it looked like the men had concentrated their large numbers to hide behind the shields that now protected their heads from crossbow fire. Though that didn't stop the crossbowmen from trying.

Just behind the bulk of those soldiers, some fifty yards away, was an overturned cart. Likely it had been used to help transport the ladders, but it looked like a broken axle had stopped it just short of providing cover against the wall. Still, a few men huddled around it to take advantage of the shelter.

It wasn't worth using her arrows to fire at the masses, so Lily turned to the doorway to pick off anyone who made it to the top of the ladder.

A horn sounded, some signal to Randson's army, as she sent an arrow deflecting off a man's helmet. The resulting unconsciousness led to a domino effect down the ladder.

Then a thunderous boom broke the air.

The wall shook beneath her feet as she pressed her back against the wall of the tower. Around her, men were doing the same, a look of sheer panic in their eyes.

Lily dared a glance through the arrow loop. There was no siege weaponry. No towers or trebuchets. There hadn't been time to build any. But there was black smoke seeping out of the cart.

The men shrank back from the wall.

"Stay engaged!" Lily shouted.

The wall beneath her shook again, and as she watched, a man toppled over.

"Goodness sake!"

Lily's head snapped to a man who was rapidly limping toward the wall.

"Screw your heads back on men! I didn't hear an order to surrender!" Gaspard's words were louder than the shouting and louder than the resounding cracks that shook the wall as he seized the ladder and began hauling himself up.

Lily watched, dumbfounded. She expected his leg to give out at any second. Instead, he heaved himself onto the battlements, instantly charging forward to shove at the top of a ladder. His presence energized the few of his men still on the wall. Their change, standing more upright, shoulders further back, revitalized those next to them.

A ripple of movement had the wall looking like it had the first attack. Anticipatory, anxious, and, most importantly determined.

They were on their toes, weapons drawn to face the onslaught that made its way up the ladders.

Then they stopped, at least in the center.

A berserker of a man encrusted in rage hopped onto the walkway after making his way up the ladder. He swung his sword wildly, with no discernible purpose besides keeping people away until the man behind him was on the wall.

The two men then stood back-to-back, effectively putting a wedge in the defenses that held the wall.

In an instant, her decision was made.

Lily nocked, drew, and shot in one deadly, fluid thought.

The berserker man didn't go down, even as an arrow tore through his throat. His face was bright red as he slashed and tore, making it impossible to step near him.

Lily sent three more arrows into his center of mass.

He stumbled back a step, then two, before falling. But he and his friend had bought more than enough time to replace him, and the wall was still shaking.

She made another snap decision, retreating to the adjacent wall and ordering men to replace her. Her only hope now was to flood that wall with soldiers before Randson could, shaking or not.

The faces she passed were a blur as she shouted orders, straining to bellow over the ongoing thunder. She stopped in the middle of the wall and looked back at what she could see.

At this distance, the keep blocked Lily's view. What she could see was so swarming with men she was surprised none had fallen off. It was impossible to get a good shot. No matter how good her aim was, she couldn't help the constant shifting that all but guaranteed someone would replace her target by the time the arrow impacted. There was no way to tell if the replacement would be friend or foe.

Lily looked at the men around her.

An energy radiated off them. They were hounds straining against a leash. They could see their comrades fighting. They wanted to help. But they knew they couldn't abandon their posts without orders.

It was hard to tell who was winning in the chaos. She caught flashes of the crude blue armbands she'd had fashioned for her men, but she saw just as many black neck scarves.

Lily's head whipped around at the sound of a series of thuds.

Along the south wall, a set of five ladders fell into place. They hadn't been watching the field. At least she knew where the rest of Randson's men were.

Her patience had won. Lily's soldiers sprang into action, pushing against the ladders as men tried to climb them. She waited, an arrow already on the string to shoot the first enemy who appeared.

The first unlucky man popped above the crenellations, only to fall away as her arrow found its way into his shoulder. Lily shot each time a man appeared, but there were too many. She was forced to duck as a spear jabbed at her from atop the nearest ladder.

The attacker surged ahead, knocking into one of her soldiers and forcing him back, back, until he was pressed against the wooden railing of the walkway.

Lily drew a knife, abandoning the bow at close range.

The second man on the ladder now stood steadfast in front of it, guarding his companions as they ascended. Her initial blow caught his thigh in a deep cut, and she ducked under the sweep of his spear.

Stay inside the range. That was how she dealt with most weapons.

The spear was good for keeping people away but not a helpful defense if they were already within a foot.

Slashing across his chest, she left behind a gash as he bellowed with rage.

"The ladder!" Lily shouted at the man she'd saved. Out of the corner of her eye, she saw him dart around, parrying a sword on his own blade.

She just managed to slip aside of a knee to the gut, only to barrel into a shield. Caught off guard, she tumbled back.

The man swept with his spear again, hitting the leg that bore most of her weight and causing her to crash onto her back.

Her head was spared the pain of slamming into stone by meeting only air. The edge of the walkway cut a harsh line into her shoulders. The man above her smiled, revealing he was missing half his teeth.

Lily lurched upwards, her head barely clearing beneath the railing as she swiped at his legs.

She made contact. A sickening thump spilled into the air as her blade connected midway down his shin.

With a scream of pain, he kicked, his boot smashing into Lily's face.

The blow forced her to fall back as fire erupted from her nose. Her grip remained tight, but her vision blurred. No other choice. She attempted to roll away but found herself stopped by a knee pressing on her chest so hard she was surprised her ribs hadn't snapped.

There was no air in her lungs as she fumbled for a breath through the blood pouring into her throat.

Then the pressure eased as the man collapsed in a limp heap on her legs.

Lily bolted upright, shoving the newly made corpse off. An arrow stuck out of his shoulder. She turned, looking to see who had fired.

A cloaked figure stood on the opposite end of the wall, bow still raised. She had saved her.

Tori took a step forward.

Just as an arrow slammed into her chest.

And the sounds of the battle went silent as Tori's scream pierced the air. The woman crumpled to her knees, clutching at the gray shaft that extended from just beneath her collarbone.

She curled forward, her cries of pain louder than even the cacophony of blades and screams and that unceasing boom on the walls. Casseterrans rarely used bows. How...

"Get down!" Lily shouted, yanking the nearest man to the ground.

Of course, that order only confused the men who were doing everything in their power to hold back the swarm of enemies scaling the ladders.

Lily wiped the blood from her nose and scanned the wall. One of her men fell. A blade was pulled out of him with a sickening slurp. He joined a steadily growing number of bodies clogging up the walkway. She slid down the ladder into the now abandoned courtyard, sprinting the length of the wall to where Tori's screams had become whimpers of pain.

She scrambled up the inner ladder, coming to a kneeling position beside the woman. "It's okay. You're going to be okay."

Tori took a few ragged breaths. She was hunched over as if she could prevent herself from further damage. Blood trickled from the corner of her mouth. "Get off. The walls." Each word took monumental effort, sending another cascade of blood with it.

A warning.

Lily grabbed the woman by the shoulders, ignoring her cries of pain as she dragged her away from the immediate conflict. No vital organs had been pierced—or she would have been dead already.

"Jarek," Tori spluttered as blood dribbled out the side of her mouth. "Coming."

A deafening crash split the air, freezing everyone where they stood.

Lily looked over to see a cloud of dust rapidly expanding from the far wall. Except there wasn't a wall. There was a pile of rubble, and as the dust began to settle there were mangled bodies and far too large pools of scarlet.

As she watched, a large dark sphere rolled to the center of the courtyard, leaving a deep red trail of blood in its path before it came to a rest. Looking through the hole that had once been the western wall revealed the cause of the destruction.

In the middle of the field, where the broken cart had once been, was a stout metal tube with smoke trailing from a circular opening in the front.

Lily's eyes fell back to Tori, who was looking up at the sky. Her breathing was slow and shallow. Too little to sustain life. The wound gushed with each weak heartbeat.

A cruel shot.

Wet hands gripped Lily's own. "Ow," the woman said weakly.

Lily held Tori's hand close to her chest. "You'll be alright," she lied. "We have medics."

"Go help," Tori wheezed. "Jarek is close."

But not close enough to end it in time to save Tori. How many more lives would be lost while she kept waiting for help? She should have fought Randson in Evesbury, and now the people she cared for were paying the price.

Tori's grip loosened, and her hand dropped. Her eyes were erratic, darting between the clouds as the last of her life bled onto the stone of the wall. "Go," she gasped.

Lily tore her gaze away, and her soul shattered. One shard stayed behind with the dying girl, and Lily picked up the rest to use as weapons. This had to stop.

She sprinted to the keep, her movement breaking the stillness that had fallen over even Randson's soldiers. Lily thundered up a series of steps to the tower. If Tori had come, it meant Edmund had let her in.

They ran into each other on the steps, both moving with such determination they failed to notice the other approaching. "Your nose—" Edmund said, steadying her in his arms.

"We need to parlay. Now." Lily pulled away from his grip, searching him for any injury.

"We can't—"

Lily yanked him to the arrow slot, where he could see the space a wall used to exist in. Now it was only rubble.

"But Jarek—"

"They broke down a wall," Lily said. "We need to parlay. Now."

Something in Lily's voice broke into whatever thoughts Edmund was having. He drew himself up, a mask of professionalism sliding in over the panic. "Right."

Edmund led her up the stairs to the top of the tower. A man stood by a horn and a long list Lily didn't bother to try to read. "Parlay. Now."

She rushed to the window, peering out.

Sure enough, Jarek's forces had appeared. They were clearing the woods, charging at the back of Randson's army. But Randson's men were swarming over the rubble they'd created. It wasn't the pincer that was needed.

On the other side, they were likely faring even better.

Lily sighted and shot, a desperate attempt to help someone, anyone, in the time it took for the trumpeter to sound three ascending notes.

Men hesitated, but none of the clashing stopped. Stopping without acknowledgment would be suicide.

So, the fight continued on. An attacking ladder was pushed back. Someone plummeted to the ground, neck bent at an unnatural angle.

Then, mercifully, three notes split through the air.

Parlay.

CHAPTER 33

THE DUEL

Lily turned on her heels, dashing down the steps, and Edmund followed after her. "Lily, what are you doing?"

"What I need to," she replied without stopping. The face of the man with a broken neck flashed in her mind. She could have sworn she heard the crunch, despite knowing she was too far away at the time.

The repetitive thump of their shoes on stone bounced off the walls, making the walls seem closer and closer with each passing second. Lily picked up her pace, hearing Edmund curse as he stumbled.

"Lily, wait!"

Edmund caught her sleeve as Lily reached the ground floor.

Lily had seen Tori fall to Randson's arrow. She knew the girl was dead. She'd left her alone to choke on her own blood. But it was to save however many people she could.

"What?" She turned to Edmund, feeling the tears falling down her face as she saw the body of the enemy soldier, saw the way his companions tried to protect him even in death.

Edmund released her sleeve and placed his hand on her shoulder. "What are you doing?"

Lily didn't see Edmund. Instead, she saw Gaspard collapse, never crossing the country to find her. "Ending it."

"How?"

With a shake of her head, she watched Jeremias twitching on the ground and then stilling and shutting her eyes. Tried to force the images away.

It only made them more vivid.

"I can't do it. I can't keep making people die for me."

"You aren't making anyone do anything," Edmund pleaded. But Lily had watched Cecilia lay there, her breathing labored and weaker every second as she continued on the slow trudge toward death.

"For, because of. There's no difference. I'm done. This war ends here."

Lily turned again, storming through the halls as she wiped the tears from her eyes. They were replaced before her vision could fully clear. She saw Tori, eyes wild with rage, prepared to kill the man she had expected to walk through the cabin door.

She was on fire. Her back screamed in pain as she shut her eyes against the memory. Hands were slick with blood. Some of it hers, some of it not.

"You were fighting for a reason!"

She whirled at Edmund's shout.

He caught up to her, grabbing her shoulders. "You were fighting for a reason." His voice cracked before he continued, "If you surrender now, it all means nothing."

"We couldn't even last a day, Edmund. This was meant to be a siege..." Lily's voice cracked. "We couldn't last a single day." Some general she'd turned out to be.

"Don't leave me." Edmund's face was slick with tears. His lips were trembling as he squished his eyes shut against the pain within.

She rose to her tiptoes and kissed him. Their lips pressed together, desperate and hot and wet as they realized it could be the last time.

Edmund reached up, wiping a single tear from Lily's face. The trail behind his thumb was cool. He was cool. She was fire and pain and strength and weakness. Her knees shook, but she pressed herself up and into him.

He entwined his hands in her hair, gentle and smooth. And cool. He pulled away, locking eyes with Lily.

"If I die—"

"No." Edmund's arms tightened around her, pulling her into his chest as if he could absorb her, keep her from leaving by making them one. His heart was beating nearly as fast as hers.

She could melt there, safe in his arms. He'd keep her from overheating forever. Save her from that desert.

Or she'd die in the next hour.

A sob wracked her body. "If I die, do not let him be king. I don't care about the Rule of Conquest, he can't have control of a country. Promise me."

"I will." His voice was only a whisper. It was only a breeze on her hair, gone the second it was muttered. But it had happened. She was sure of it. He had happened to her, and she would forever be grateful.

Lily sniffed, then took a deep breath, pulling away enough to take in his face and the love she saw there. "Walk with me?"

He took her hand and squeezed. "Always."

As she walked, the tears dried. Her heart still raced, but the heat pulled away from her face and her chest as cool air flooded in. She had fallen apart in Edmund's arms, and now she put herself back together piece by piece. Each step allowed the puzzle that was her become more whole.

Her determination grew. Step by step. Whatever came next, she would face it head-on. She would go down swinging for the people who couldn't.

Her knees took her weight better as she pushed her shoulders back. By the time they crossed through the doors, Lily's face had returned to its normal color. She fixed her eyes ahead, steadfastly ignoring those moving the dead and injured. They stepped over a pile of rubble as they made their way to the front gate.

"Is he there?"

"Not yet."

Lily turned to look at Edmund.

"I'm with you." He squeezed her hand again as the portcullis rose, the metallic clanks grating against the eerie quiet.

Lily let go, stepping under as she put an arrow on her bowstring. Some of her men flanked her to prevent any foul play. Behind her, she heard Edmund scale the ladder to stand atop the gatehouse, as close as he would be able to get.

The crowd parted as Lily and her escort stepped free. Anyone coming too close could be deemed an act of aggression and end the ceasefire. She recognized some of the faces, didn't recognize others. They were mixed. Randson's men and the men Jarek had brought.

The portcullis closed behind her, sealing her off from what was meant to be a stronghold. What had very nearly been a stronghold.

There was a flash of green. Then Jarek was at her side. "What are you doing?"

"Ending it," Lily replied, refusing to look at his face. Instead, she scanned, searching for Randson.

"We could have done it," Jarek hissed. "We have the numbers. You don't have to do this."

"I do," Lily replied. "If not to win, I have to do it to remain whole."

"I can help." Somehow, Jarek's voice remained calm. Lily wasn't entirely sure how he achieved it.

"No. This is my fight. I'm done—" she choked at the memory of the first time she'd heard those words from Tori. "I'm done running. I'm done hoping it will just get better."

"This isn't the answer!" Jarek cried.

Lily's eyes found his face then. She saw the pain, saw the panic as he tried to undo what had been done. "Tori's dead."

Jarek's face shifted, the harsh lines softening. He opened his mouth to say something, then shut it again. His jaw set, and the skin around his eyes drew tighter. Understanding settled. Randson would pay.

He gave her one grim nod. "Make him angry. People make mistakes when they're angry." One last bit of advice from a mentor.

Lily *knew*. That's what Lily was worried about. She was filled with so much fire held back by a thin, wooden wall that grew weaker by the moment. "I'll try."

Jarek stepped away, fading into the crowd before it parted.

Lily was used to seeing Randson in the same uniform as Jarek. He now looked nothing like that. Gone was the green cloak. It had been replaced by a red cape hanging lopsided from his shoulders.

The simple tunic had been replaced with an ornate embroidered doublet. At least, Lily thought, he wasn't wearing armor. A metal breastplate completely changed fighting style, and it wasn't something that could be swapped and added like a shirt. That's why she continued to wear no armor herself.

Randson's hair was meticulously slicked back, his countenance contorted into a smile that failed to reach his eyes. A fleeting touch of surprise momentarily flickered across his face. "I thought I'd shot you."

Lily saw the arrow buried in Tori's chest. The arrow had been meant for her.

"Ah!" Randson continued, "The apprentice. Pity, I bet you brought her here to protect her."

Lily bristled. That *was* why she'd brought Tori. But Randson had followed, and Lily had only brought Tori to her death.

"She was your apprentice." Lily's voice broke. "You were supposed to protect her."

Randson's smile grew. It must have been obvious he'd struck a nerve. "Ready to surrender, sweetheart?" he sneered.

"Don't call me sweetheart," Lily snapped.

They had lapsed into the trade language. Around them were murmurs of translation, spreading everything they said outward.

Randson seemed unbothered by the venom Lily tried to lace in her tone. "You've lost. Surrender now, and maybe I'll spare the rest of your men. I can't say I'll do the same for you."

"When has that ever been my solution?" Lily asked. "No, this is going to be—"

"Are you betrothed?"

Her hand itched to hide behind her back, but she resisted. She wouldn't show him weakness.

"Too bad you won't live to see your wedding day."

Lily struggled to come up with a retort, but he'd caught her off guard.

Randson's eyes scanned the wall. "Where's the traitor?"

Lily's heart jumped to her throat.

"Standing in front of me," Lily responded.

His eyes snapped back to her. "I'm the rightful King of Casseterre, and it's time you admit it."

"You're the rightful king of *nothing*," Lily retorted. "You can't possibly expect me to just stand down."

His eyes rolled. A posture of lazy contempt. "We can go back and forth all day, but I've been on the road for quite a while, and I could use a good night's sleep. So, either you get out of the way, or I make you."

"I challenge you." Her words were crisp, settling her decision in her bones.

"What?" Randson looked at the men surrounding as if expecting them to laugh. No laugh came. If anything, even the wind stopped whistling as the realization settled over the battlefield.

"You heard me."

Randson laughed. Then laughed, then laughed. Until Lily was sure everyone around them was uncomfortable. "You called this parley. I have more men, more land, and a pair of balls. Why would I ever agree to that?"

"You want to be the Casseterre's king. That's how things are settled here."

There were a few murmurs of agreement, quickly silenced by Randson's glares.

"You think you can beat me?"

"I *know* I can."

Randson scoffed. "You fled Albrin the second you saw me."

"You followed me across a continent, and now you're too scared to face me?" she taunted.

Anger flashed over Randson's face, twisting his features into a grotesque mask. "No bows," Randson growled. "I want to see the fear in your eyes when I kill you."

"Agreed." Lily unslung her quiver, watching Randson as he did the same. "First blood."

They dropped the quivers at the same time. She felt footsteps behind her as someone came to take the discarded equipment off the field. Behind Randson, one of his soldiers did the same.

"No." Randson's eyes bore into her own. "To the death."

A cold hand gripped her spine, causing her to stand straighter. Lily had known he would want her dead. But she had to try, at least once. "Fine."

The two armies formed a rough circle, searching for a balance between too close and too far.

Lily drew her blades. She twirled them once, twice, getting used to the weight in her hands. Randson's knives and stance matched her own. The same training showed in their bent knees, weight on their toes, and ever so slight bounce as they circled each other.

Lily lunged forward in a feint. He knew her reach was shorter than his. Missing him by a good few inches wouldn't draw any suspicion.

He danced back half a step, not even bothering to react with the deadly blades in his hands. "That all you got?"

Lily shrugged. "You haven't done better."

Something in his eyes shifted. He moved into an attack, setting his arms for a complicated series of blows. Lily saw the set-up and sidestepped, only to be caught on his outstretched foot. Rather than stumble around, sacrificing all control to balance, Lily dropped.

The crowd gasped as Randson moved, slamming his knee down in an attempt to pin her arm.

She yanked it free just in time and spun to one knee, slashing out into the space he'd occupied. Only, he wasn't there.

"Behind you!" Edmund shouted from the ramparts.

She spun and threw up her arm to protect her face.

Randson's dagger bit into her forearm. Lightning shot up Lily's arm, causing her whole body to shudder, and a mangled cry of pain escaped her.

She looked up, meeting Randson's eyes. A sick smile spread across his face as she took in the hunter that she'd run from for so long.

"Long."

He pushed on the dagger, sending another bolt of pain jolting through Lily's body.

The dagger clattered out of her hand as the muscles protested, cramping up her entire arm.

"Live."

Lily tried to push back, but it was as if her arm belonged to someone else. Numbness began to seep from the wound and toward her hand.

"The king."

Something in Lily snapped.

The fire that was pressing against her skin, burning her from the inside out, the fire Edmund had controlled back down to a candle flame. It tipped, exploded, and spread through her until she was certain the watching armies would see her glowing. If she were to fall, he would fall with her.

And for the first time, Lily looked at the dagger buried in her arm. The glint of metal was replaced with the sickly drip of her blood. Her hand tightened around her remaining dagger as her gaze rose to eyes full of hatred.

Randson had never cared about anyone but himself. His attempt to kill her in Albrin was for his own ego, not because the king had ordered it. Now he just wanted the satisfaction of seeing her dead so he could take everything she'd built and corrupt it.

She would *never* let him.

Lily yanked her arm down and off the blade, diving to the side out of its path. The maneuver brought a roar from Randson, and he lunged toward her as she scrambled to her feet. She wasn't too proud to backpedal, ducking under Randson's angry, erratic swing.

She hurled her knife toward him, and he jumped to the side, watching it sail by into the dirt. Lily snatched a knife off her thigh while he wasn't looking.

At first, it was a chuckle, then a sickly sweet, "Poor, dumb little girl. Loses both her knives." He turned to her, fake pity taking over his face.

With a flick of her wrist, she released the knife from her thigh.

It buried itself hilt deep in Randson's gut.

Lily backpedaled out of his reach, knowing it would be far from instant death. Still, it was better than he deserved.

Randson looked down at the knife in his gut and back up at Lily. He dropped his knives, hands going to the hilt. There was defiance still marking his face.

Then he fell to his knees. With a grunt of pain, he yanked the blood-soaked knife out. The wound began to gush, and soon he fell into a puddle as red as his cape.

The silence was deafening.

Then, metal scraped against gravel. Boots shuffled as the man behind Randson looked at the body, then looked at her.

He dropped to one knee, head bowed.

Then his neighbor, then the person behind them. The movement spread like a ripple in a pond, going up the wall and across the battlefield. The only sound was movement as two armies wordlessly knelt.

CHAPTER 34
REUNION

Lily sat with her head in her hands, staring at the urn that held all that was left of Tori. It was supposed to be a joyous day, but all she could think of was the people who didn't live to see it.

Most of the soldiers were buried in mass graves near where they had fallen. There was no way to identify all the bodies or return them to their homes. It had been a long, solemn week, as graves were dug and the song was sung for the fallen on both sides.

She couldn't bear resigning Tori to the same fate. She deserved to rest at home. Her family deserved a proper chance to mourn. To stop the decomposition, Tori had been cremated. She'd traveled with Lily ever since. And would continue to until Lily found someone to take the other Hawk home.

There was a knock on the door, and Lily looked up to see Edmund poking his head in. Despite being in a new castle, he still had an office outside her room. "She's here," he said.

"Right," Lily stood, smoothing down her skirt. "Let her in."

Edmund held the door open, revealing a blond woman in a long green dress. The woman smiled, waiting as the door closed behind her. "I'm so glad to see you."

Lily abandoned all formalities, embracing Adelaide in a tight hug.

Adelaide hugged back, resting her head on Lily's shoulder as she muttered, "You scared me. You were presumed dead."

"I didn't think I'd see you again." Lily pulled back, taking Adelaide's hands and guiding her to a seat.

"So, we have some things to work out," Adelaide said solemnly. She sat like a queen, poised and perfect.

Lily did her best to copy her posture and nodded. She realized they were entering an intricate world of technicalities.

"First," Adelaide said with a tilt of her head, "you will always be welcome in Albrin. You have done more for my country than I could ever possibly repay you for."

"I sense a 'but' coming."

Adelaide nodded slowly. "Yes." She smiled, but the smile didn't reach her eyes. It was a diplomatic, comforting smile. "It would be a conflict of interest for you to remain a Hawk," Adelaide said and pulled out a scroll. "We need you to retire."

Lily's heart froze in her chest. She'd dedicated nearly a decade to being a Hawk.

Edmund's words echoed in her head: 'To me, you're just Lily. You aren't a job title.'

Adelaide's gaze was gentle as Lily accepted the document. Her injured arm shook with the effort to grab it. Adelaide laid a hand on her shoulder. "Let me help."

"I'm fine," Lily bit out.

Adelaide recoiled back but said nothing as Lily reached across herself with her good arm to grab a pen and inkwell. She scanned the document. It was a standard statement of retirement. The same one all Hawks who lived to old age signed.

"Do you need me to sign first?" Adelaide asked.

Lily nodded, swallowing the frog that had crawled up her throat and handing Adelaide the pen. The princess signed with a practiced flourish. Her signature was full of loops and swirls. Her signature *belonged* to royalty.

When Lily's signature joined hers, it was short and blunt. Lily looked minuscule next to Adelaide's full name. And her lines were shaky and uncertain.

But it was done.

Adelaide waved the paper so it could dry. When she leaned back, her eyes landed on the urn. "The apprentice."

"Tori," Lily interjected. "And she was as good as any full Hawk."

Adelaide reached into her pocket and pulled out a gold feather strung on a leather cord. "And she'll return to Albrin as one." Adelaide stood and tied the cord around the neck of the urn. "I'm so sorry for your loss," she said as she returned to her seat.

There was another knock on the door. Lily called for Edmund to enter, and he came in.

"Do you want dinner here? I can tell Jarek and your brother—"

"My brother?" Lily's head jerked to Adelaide. "He's here?"

Adelaide beamed. "It was last minute. We couldn't get word to you. I'm surprised he hasn't found his way here yet."

"He's actually right outside."

Lily shot up, pushing past Edmund and into the hallway.

Nick was pacing back and forth, running his hand through his messy brown hair. Jarek leaned against the wall beside him, an amused look on his face.

"Nick?"

Nick froze. His back to Lily. She saw his breathing quicken. Then he turned, his eyes wide as he saw her. "Lily?"

Lily smiled, tears coming to her face. He was fine. He was safe and unharmed. She'd been told by Jarek, of course, but seeing it made it so much more real.

"I thought you were dead!" He stormed toward Lily and shoved her.

She slammed back against the wall, but she didn't care.

Nick buried his head in his hands, and his shoulders heaved as he tried to hold back tears. Lily wrapped her arms around him, and the next thing she knew she was being squeezed so tight she couldn't breathe.

"I thought you were dead." Nick was sobbing now.

Lily closed her eyes, holding him tight until he straightened. Her own emotions were barely kept at bay.

He wiped the tears off his face, taking a deep breath. "Sorry."

"You're here. And that's all that matters. Let's get some dinner," Lily said, leading him and Jarek through Edmund's office and into her rooms.

Edmund closed the door after them. Soon, a hearty chicken pot pie was brought in. They sat around the low center table, joking and catching up.

Then Adelaide saw the ring on Lily's finger as she was reaching for a refill of coffee. "Wait, you're betrothed?"

"Yes," Lily drew out the word as Adelaide grabbed her hand, turning it back and forth to examine the ring.

"Who is he?"

Lily raised an amused eyebrow as Edmund put his arm around her shoulders. "You've actually met him." Lily planted a kiss on Edmund's cheek, only to feel a slimy chunk of chicken hit her face.

"Gross. You're my sister."

Lily scowled, grabbed a carrot, and tossed it at Nick. Unfortunately, carrots flew nothing like knives, and she ended up hitting Jarek, welcoming a chorus of laughter from the room as she tried to hide behind Edmund.

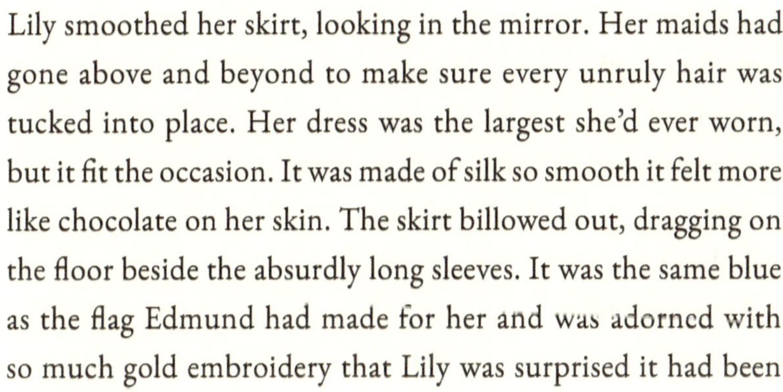

Lily smoothed her skirt, looking in the mirror. Her maids had gone above and beyond to make sure every unruly hair was tucked into place. Her dress was the largest she'd ever worn, but it fit the occasion. It was made of silk so smooth it felt more like chocolate on her skin. The skirt billowed out, dragging on the floor beside the absurdly long sleeves. It was the same blue as the flag Edmund had made for her and was adorned with so much gold embroidery that Lily was surprised it had been completed on time.

The door opened behind her, and Edmund entered the reflection of the mirror. He was dressed in a sharp suit and looked much more comfortable than Lily felt. "Ready?"

"As I'll ever be," she responded, turning as he put his arms around her and planted a sweet kiss on her lips.

He pulled back and offered her his arm.

She took it, allowing herself to be led down the deserted halls of Lucetia.

Everyone would be in the throne room, aside from the few guards who stepped out of her way with a bow—and the cooks, who were probably panicking in an attempt to have food ready for the ball.

They reached a small antechamber by the throne room. Edmund left her with another kiss on her cheek, going to take his spot in the front row and ensure everything was ready.

Amira had somehow beaten her down the stairs. She now helped haul a cape that was twice the size of the coronation dress over Lily's shoulders. It had been used in ten Casseterran coronation ceremonies, each and every time on a man much larger than her. She was nearly dwarfed by the size, but Amira tucked and pinned a few places, and it seemed as if it had been made for her.

"You're amazing at that."

Amira smiled. "Thank you, Your Majesty."

The robe still held a length impractical to walk in. That was why they had stored it just outside the throne room.

Amira helped carry the train, arranging it behind her as she stood in front of the tall walnut doors. She set it down and stepped back with a curtsey.

Lily was grateful for the small bit of familiarity she'd brought to Lucetia and took a deep breath, then another, forcing her hands to lay at her sides instead of bunching up the skirt. Once she felt ready, she signaled at the guards standing beside the massive doors.

They grabbed the elaborate gold doorknobs and hauled them open.

The throne room was packed with people. Most of the castle staff were present, as well as every noble in the country. Outside the castle, Lily knew the entire city of Lucetia was waiting to see their new queen. Her stomach tightened at the thought.

Light shone in through towering windows. The ceiling was painted with elaborate designs that spiraled down the arches supporting it. An aisle had been formed between rows of benches, leading up to a golden throne on a raised dais.

The last time she'd entered this room, no one had been paying attention to her. Now a thousand heads swiveled to watch her enter.

Lily stepped onto the long blue carpet, then stepped again. She had to fight back the urge to pick up her skirt to make it easier. The robe dragged behind her, pulling on her shoulders. She looked at the throne, not trusting herself to keep a straight face if she looked anywhere else.

Six people clad in formal, pristine black stepped out from the walls, coming together to meet her at the dais. It was her council, which had been voted on by the people of Casseterre. They stood between her and the throne, each dressed in their finest garments.

Milo D'Aboville stepped forward. He wore a black suit contrasted with a slicked-back head of red hair. His face held an agreeable smile that didn't quite reach his eyes. Milo stepped forward again, presenting her with an ornate golden sword. "Lily Valores, do you swear to protect Casseterre against all who may wish her harm?"

Her new name sung in her ears. Rather, the addition of a last name. She didn't have a family legacy to carry, but she was starting one.

"I do." That line had always been in the coronation oath. They'd re-examined it a million times. Some lines had been cut, but this one had survived.

Lily took the sword in her right hand, surprised at the weight. She supposed the gold had taken away all practicality.

Milo stepped back and was replaced by Alex Jaubert. He was about forty and well-established in the country. The type of man

Lily knew would cause problems. But today, he seemed to have toned down his personality that normally dominated a room. He held a thick silk scarf, a new edition to the coronation meant to represent a blindfold.

"Do you swear to rule Casseterre and her people justly and without bias?"

"I do."

There were light murmurs from the crowd behind her. Having Alex say that line, when he was rumored to have allied with Randson, was a pointed statement. She had made a promise. No one who had sided with Randson would be blamed for their actions. It was something she intended to stand by.

Lily shifted the sword to lean in her left hand. She hadn't regained dexterity and could hardly elevate her hand without it shaking. She draped the scarf around the hilt of the sword before transferring it back to her right hand.

Then Alex stepped back to allow Collette Costex to replace him. Her gray hair was pulled into a neat bun. She wore a simple black gown that made her look five years younger than she was.

Her election had filled Lily with relief that she would not be alone in a room full of men. She felt a companionship with the woman. While their backgrounds were almost entirely different, they shared one key similarity. Both had come to power in worlds dominated by men and had to fight for every drop of power they held.

It seemed that was working out fairly well for both of them.

Collette stepped forward with an orb Lily had been told was solid gold, and she assumed that statement didn't encompass the jewels that coated it. "Do you swear to maintain the laws of Casseterre?"

"I do."

Lily held out her left hand, palm up, begging that Collette would place the orb in her hand before it started shaking. When the woman did, it sent tingles shooting up to Lily's neck.

She grit her teeth against the feeling. At least the weight was enough to dampen the involuntary trembling. She could deal with the tingles for the remainder of the ceremony.

Dylan Adnet stepped forward. He was average in all aspects of the word. A farmer, chosen to represent the people who sustained the country but had been left out of its governance for far too long. He had been given black formal attire that was just a smidge small for him, but he was beaming with pride anyway. Dylan held a goblet half filled with wine.

"Do you swear to treat all citizens of Casseterre with respect, regardless of race, gender, creed, or rank?"

"I do."

It was an altered line from the original oath. A change for a new Casseterre. Dylan brought the goblet to her lips, and she took a sip of the sourest wine she had ever tasted. She hadn't managed to talk her way into having it switched to something sweeter. Though she'd tried.

Dylan withdrew the goblet and stepped back into line.

Aaron Chopin moved next. He was a wealthy merchant, and the size of his gut looked the part. He held up a large medallion.

Having examined it before, Lily knew it had an intricate design of cracks spread across it. The significance of it lay in its representation of unity, as it was worn by the inaugural king to unite Casseterre during his coronation.

"Do you swear to serve Casseterre as one country, with one government?"

"I do."

She ducked her head as he slipped the ribbon around her neck. Then, he stepped back.

Baron Tibost held a crown. It consisted of a thick golden band inset with precious gems. More gold bands arched to form a sort of dome, connecting in the center to support her fleur-de-lis. A plush red velvet material covered the interior, further elevating the regal atmosphere of it.

"Do you swear to use your powers to further the interests of the great nation of Casseterre and all that inhabit her?"

"I do."

The crown descended on her head, and she was shocked at the weight. She rose to her feet as the council parted, revealing a small podium with a single document, ink well, and pen.

Lily stepped forward, setting the sword down to take up the pen.

She signed her name on the new Casseterran constitution. She'd practiced the signature a million times after taking her new last name. It fit well on the line. The first signature. A new constitution for a new Casseterre.

The council filed to the constitution one at a time, placing their signatures beside her own. Each loop of a letter and end of a name was another piece of optimism forming in her country's future.

She took up the sword and stepped to the throne. Then she turned, looking at the assembled crowd for the first time. It was a mix of people. Knights, farmers, seamstresses. Children and adults. Someone from every province. No group had been left out, though a few people had grumbled at her insistence they reserve invites for the poor. She breathed in the hope that filled the room and sat.

"Long live the queen!"

Edmund shouted it half a second before the crowd rose up in the cheer.

It repeated over and over.

Lily couldn't stop the smile from reaching her face. They were cheering for her. For prosperity and peace.

Their voices ignited something, and that fire burned in Lily again. Their future would burn bright.

CHAPTER 35

EPILOGUE

Lily's eyes blinked open at the light coming in through the curtains. She rolled over, and her gaze fell on Edmund.

He looked so peaceful in his sleep, not that he ever looked particularly stressed.

As her hand delicately moved, she brushed aside one of his curls, resulting in his eyes opening. The way the light hit them made the blue in them glow before he shifted into the shade. "You need new curtains."

Lily laughed. Edmund's ever-growing list of renovations would get tackled at some point. For now, the castle had to wait. They had a country to rebuild.

The wedding yesterday had been a good start.

After a few months of letting some tensions from the war settle, people were much more cordial with each other. The formal affair had been stuffier than Lily would have preferred. Between Edmund's instance that the country needed a celebration and Adelaide's instance that a royal wedding was for the people, not the couple, Lily had caved.

At least her friends in Albrin ranked high enough to not seem out of place amongst the rest of the nobility. They'd come a few days early to try and spend time together. Lily knew the wedding wouldn't provide much respite from the constant work of rebuilding what had been wrecked.

With Edmund beside her, officially now, it seemed a little less daunting. His support meant the world to her.

"What are you thinking about?" Edmund asked in Casseterran.

"Nothing," Lily replied in the language she was finally starting to feel truly comfortable in.

Edmund raised his eyebrows in doubt, and Lily laughed. "Yesterday was a good break, but there's a lot of work ahead of us."

Edmund caressed her cheek and asked, "Are you worried?"

Her eyes closed at the touch, enjoying the closeness of him. "Yes."

She felt him shift on the bed beside her and gently press down on her shoulder, so she obliged, lying face down on the plush pillows.

He straddled her back, hands finding her shoulders as he began to knead at the muscles there. "We can do it."

"Everyone looks at me like I know all the right answers."

Edmund brushed a kiss to the back of her neck, just above her scars. "I don't think there are any right answers. This country needs someone to shape it."

Lily moaned as Edmund found a knot and spent the next minute working it out. When he finished, he rolled off her, lying in bed as she turned to look at him once again.

He pressed a gentle kiss to her lips. "I'm sure you'll make something beautiful."

ACKNOWLEDGMENTS

I want to begin by thanking my partner. Aidan, thank you for making me write on the days I didn't want to. Thank you for cooking, so I could take that time to focus on my book. Thank you for reading the entire book every time I finished a major edit. This truly would not have been possible without your support.

Mom, Dad, thank you for inspiring a love of reading in me. Thank you for buying me books on road trips. Thank you for all the library visits. Mom, thank you for tricking me into reading by mispronouncing my favorite character's name.

I also want to thank the Grand County Community of Writers. Thank you for believing in and supporting a young writer. You welcomed me at a really difficult time in my life, and your encouragement helped me find some light in the dark.

ABOUT THE AUTHOR

Stories have always been Lela Myers's escape from the world. From a young age, she's been obsessed with all things royal, medieval, and adventure. Her books are a way to share the things she loves with people who also wish they were born a princess. When she's not writing, she can most often be found curled up with a good book or unable to stop scrolling on her phone.

For more from the author, visit: https://www.lelamyers.com